Rosina,
Enjoy!
Your Cousin (JK)
A.J. Questenberg

SNOWBOUND

A novel of suspense

by: A.J. Questenberg

D1565769

This is a work of fiction. It in no way depicts real people or events, and any resemblance to real people or events is purely coincidental. The location is real; however it has been fictionally depicted as well.

ISBN; 978-1442107458

Acknowledgements:

To God who made a way when there was no way, and for making a path in the wilderness then leading me through it. I am forever grateful.

To Rich, Angela, Holly and Regan

Chapter One

Samantha Egar tossed and turned finding sleep elusive. Even after a hot bath, dressing in warm flannel pajamas and slipping between clean sheets, she laid awake in bed waiting, but for what? The wolves, she wondered? Some noise? Finally, after two hours, she slipped off into fitful REM sleep dreaming her father was calling to her, a man she had never met.

She awoke early the next morning to a jarring ring.

"Hello," she said into her cell phone, once locating it amid the tousled blankets as she rubbed sleep from her eyes.

"Sam, is that you?" A husky female voice asked.

"Yes?" Who on earth was calling her at, she reached for the digital alarm clock, 7 a.m.?

"Sam! How are you? This is Angie!"

Now fully awake, Sam said, "Angie? Angie Eckenridge!" How long has is been?"

"Way, way too long! I know you hate this kind of stuff, but, I've been dreaming about you, dreams you would not believe!"

"What? Dreaming? About me?"

"Jeez, how quickly we forget! Don't play innocent! I've been having this feeling that something's wrong with you. Am I right?'

"You are amazing. Out of the blue you call me to tell me you've been dreaming about me? That something's wrong here! I'll give you this; you are remarkable. And you're right! I do hate this kind of stuff!"

"So, something is wrong! I was really hoping I was off this time, that you'd be okay."

Sam climbed down the stairs of her old farmhouse to the kitchen to make coffee as Angie talked, hiking up her flannel pajama bottoms and woolen socks as she went. The house was drafty and cold in the winter. She didn't care, Angie's voice heated her from the inside bringing back so many memories of the fun they shared in college she basked in their warmth, and realized just how much she missed her. But her mind wasn't moving as fast as Angie talked, her mental brakes locked skidding out of control in another direction along an icy road, just like her life at the moment.

"I get the feeling you're in some kind of danger. Is something going on that you can't explain?" Angie asked.

"Yes." Sam sighed in resignation as she reached for the coffee grounds in the cupboard and slipped a filter into the coffeepot. It was futile to try and hide anything from Angie.

"Have you heard I bought a house?" She didn't wait for an answer. "Well, I did and it sits way out here in the toolies. Up north? You know—the Iron Range? It's nice out here, I really like it, but I'm having trouble with trappers, they've been setting wolf traps illegally and I've been springing them, and someone . . . I suspect a trapper . . . has been leaving nasty love letters in my mailbox almost everyday." She felt better talking about her concerns.

"Oh yeah, and the guy I bought the house from? He's sort of stocking me—I think. But those things are not why I'm so unnerved. And I am unnerved . . . It's this house. Something's wrong with this house."

"What do you mean, something's wrong with the house?" Angie smelled an adventure in her near future.

"There are noises, strange noises I can't explain away, inside the house and believe me; I've tried to rationalize them out of here! Even the dog and cat are terrified. Things move of their own volition—things that aren't supposed to move at all! I can't explain any of it. It's scaring the you-know-what out of me."

"So why haven't you called your old college bud for help? I mean, really, you know that's what I do in my spare time. Never mind. I can take some time off work. I'd like to visit. See your new house?" Angie asked point blank.

"I would love that. When can you be here?"

"I'm on my way."

Sam hung up the phone slowly, not wishing to let Angie go. Retrieving a cup from the cupboard, she fixed a cup of fresh brewed coffee for herself, picked up Kitty and stroked the cat's head after seating herself at the kitchen table. The cat rubbed itself contentedly against her flannel-covered arm.

As a wildlife biologist, Samantha still had work to do in the field even if Angie Eckenridge her best friend from college were coming for a visit and it was January. Work during the winter months fluctuated according to the weather and normally she didn't get out as much because January was usually bitter cold. It is not uncommon for temperatures to fall to thirty below. With wind chill factored in temperatures often plummet to fifty, even sixty below zero. But thanks to an El Nino, January, 2001 was balmy compared to the norm. Sam traipsed through the woods as much as she could to take advantage of it.

Even so, Angie wouldn't care. She was as devoted to her work as Sam was to hers, so while Sam was in the field, Angie would be studying the house, looking for the psychokinetic source to the things terrifying Sam.

Sam stared out at the snow-covered shrubbery surrounding her back yard already comforted knowing Angie would be there the next day. Maybe it wasn't smart to be easily consoled, especially with the crying, she thought as she sipped the hot brew still staring out the window. In spite of everything, she loved the farm, the yard, everything about her new home.

She also found comforting the fact that she had made new friends—most of them neighbors—since moving in. Even so, Angie's company would be a welcome relief. They were so close Sam could tell her anything. "That's what makes her such a good psychologist," she said to Kitty still stroking her fur. The cat purred in contentment. Aside from Angie, Sam trusted Bernice Jennings, one of her new neighbors and friends, implicitly.

Hypnotized by the large, wet, falling, flakes, she took her mental time machine back to the day she first met Bernice. They both stood in a grocery store check out lane at an Eveleth supermarket one sunny spring day shortly after Sam moved to the farm.

Bernice Jennings stood in line behind Sam pretending to read an article in a newsstand periodical. She peaked around the paper's edges at Sam as she lounged her robust figure against a grocery cart full of groceries, and absent-mindedly tended two teenage children, Sam assumed were hers. Both children pestered Bernice about a dance in the neighboring city of Virginia that night, and a slumber party at a friend's house, pestering Sam couldn't help but overhear.

Sam felt someone watching her, so she turned around to come face to face with Bernice's smiling countenance. Since that was the first welcoming gesture made to her by any of the locals, Sam returned the smile. This stranger looked content and happy, had rosy red, plump cheeks and a broad smile that sparkled from her eyes as well as her mouth. Sam liked her immediately. The teenagers shuffled their feet in apparent embarrassment at their mother's boldness in speaking up to a total stranger. Bernice introduced herself and her children confiding that she thought Sam might be her new neighbor, and appearing delighted when Sam confirmed she was.

As Bernice spoke, Vicki, the thirteen year old daughter, standing behind Bernice, eyed Sam with open curiosity. Mike, the fifteen year old son, pinched Vicki in the arm attracting Bernice's attention immediately as Vicki protested, loudly. Bernice chastised them both then hugged the pair kissing their cheeks, much to their chagrin.

That was a pivotal day for Sam. Meeting Bernice was the first in a series of new neighbor introductions. Later, many more occurred in Bernice's kitchen, a place of warmth and love the likes of which Sam had never before experienced.

At Bernice's house Sam met the Spencer sisters, two more neighbors. The elderly women, Bernice told her before they met, were once prostitutes. The meeting took place during brunch one Sunday morning after Bernice and her family returned home from church.

Bright spring sunshine beamed into Bernice's kitchen through big south-facing bay windows. Everyone sat at an antique oak, round, claw-footed table in front of the windows. Lilac bushes just outside the patio doors were in bloom sending their fragrance gently wafting throughout the kitchen. Birds chirped. Somewhere someone mowed a lawn and its distant din lent soothing background noises to the lively room.

As Sam arrived, she stepped over the threshold into a room alive in red checked gingham. Fragrant odors tickled her nostrils as animated conversation assaulted her ears. Her mouth salivated at the smell of homemade banana bread fresh from the oven.

"So you're the one out there in the woods," Gladys Spencer said.

"That has all these wonderful woodsmen in an uproar," her sister Inez finished. The Spencer sisters even smiled in unison.

"Samantha here is a scientist," Bernice said introducing Sam to the Spencer sisters who were seated beneath a Lord's Prayer plaque.

Ignoring Sam, in unison the sisters said, "Prove the existence of God," to Bernice.

"Now you know that can't be done scientifically; it's a matter of faith," Bernice answered.

"You'll have to excuse us," Bernice said turning to Sam. "Every time these two come over here, they want to argue about the existence of God. Personally, I think they're hoping I'll give them some insight that will help them to believe."

"Oh, you do, do you?" Inez pretended shock. They all laughed.

"Well, it's good, I think, that everyone can discuss the reality of God without fighting. That doesn't happen often. Never discuss politics or religion, you understand, if you don't wish to argue," Sam offered clumsily.

The women stared at her for a moment saying nothing. Bernice broke the impasse by moving over to the counter and pouring Sam a cup of fresh brewed coffee, then slicing hot banana bread and offering it to her company.

As she moved about the kitchen, Bernice kept the conversation flying while, along with her guests, her family came and went from the room. The atmosphere was electric, as Bernice stopped in the middle of one conversation with her friends to pick up in the middle of some unrelated conversation with a family member, and then returned to the original conversation without missing a beat. She seemed to be the center of everyone's attention as she showered them all with warmth and love.

And since the Spencer sisters liked to debate the existence of God with Bernice, they naturally turned to Sam to get her take on the subject.

Sam told them she had been raised in a Catholic orphanage, and was well versed in religion but that she had left it behind as she grew up. She didn't like their rituals, she told them, or the scorn the clergy had for women. Even the church's doctrine excluding everyone except Catholics as heathens turned her stomach. So, no, she told them; she didn't go to church. About God, she said, yes, she believed He existed. When she finished speaking, everyone was quiet.

Bernice patted Sam's hand when Sam finished speaking, and said, "well, you've come to the right place, dear. We'll all gladly be your family. And just like you can't pick blood family members, you might have to take some of us just as we are," she put her hand up to cover her eyes, winked and pointed at the Spencer sisters.

The Spencer sisters merely raised their eyebrows and pointed at Bernice. Sam laughed. It was a good group; she wished they hadn't asked her about God though, because then her mind flew back to the days she spent growing up in the orphanage. She hadn't told them the whole reason why she had left the church. Secretly she felt that God didn't love or want her, that she wasn't good enough. She felt abandoned by Him as she had been by her parents. When she was seven years old, all she had wanted to do was serve God. By the time she was eighteen, she thought God was dead. Now at the age of forty, she felt herself being drawn back to the spiritual but knew that organized religion held little for her. She saw God's hand in nature. She had even started reading the Bible again, but she was searching for a new way to communicate with Him, thought she could communicate with Him.

"I see God in nature. That's how I know He exists. Nature is too perfect not to have been created by the divine," she smiled at the group as she picked the conversation back up.

"'Look under a rock, I'll be there,' the book of Thomas," Bernice said smiling at Sam and patting her hand.

"Well . . . we've never seen Him anywhere," the sisters said in unison, just an octave above a whisper. Sam and Bernice both heard.

"Well," Sam said, "maybe I can take you two out in the woods sometime. I'll introduce you to some of the things He's made. Maybe you will see Him where I see Him. Besides, if we're all family now, we'll have to get into agreement about some of this." Sam chuckled and winked at Bernice.

"Oh, we see how it's going to be. You and Bernice are going to gang up on two old ladies aren't you?" Gladys feigned disapproval.

"Okay then, but we have a question for you. Why the hell did you buy a haunted house?"

"What are you talking about?"

"Oh, don't play innocent with us. We've been out here a damn sight longer than you have and everybody out here knows your house is haunted. The only one that won't admit it is Bernice, here," Gladys pointed at Bernice as Bernice got up and moved over to the stove.

"Haunted house!" Bernice spat with her back to her guests. "How can you believe in such nonsense?"

"How can you not?" Inez said. "I mean isn't God the great supernatural being? Aren't there supposed to be angels?"

"Yes, He is;" Bernice swung around to face her guests, her face livid with anger. "But it isn't Him that's involved in haunted houses. If there is such a thing, then it's his nemesis that created it, and why would you want to play around with something like that?" She held a wooden spoon in her hand and shook it at her friends, she was so angry.

"Don't get your knickers in a twist here, Bernice," Gladys was not fazed by this display of temper. "We're right and you know it. Maybe it has nothing whatsoever to do with your God, but you know it like we know it—Samantha's house is haunted and has been since that professor disappeared; you've heard those stories Bernice, don't deny it."

"Okay, okay, I've head those stories, but hearing stories doesn't mean any of it is true. That's what the word "story" implies, that it is fiction, fake, false, a lie!"

"Hey, folks, remember me?" Sam was taken aback by this argument which she could tell had been going on long before she had entered the room. "And what do you mean, my house is haunted?"

"Ain't you noticed anything weird over there honey?" Inez grew serious. "We've seen lights on in that place when no one was living there. We've heard noises too, sounds like crying. You can hear it all the way up to the road, for Christ sake!"

"Don't you use his name in vain in my house, Inez! I'm not going to tell you again!" Bernice bounced back to the table, gripped the edge, still with the wooden spoon in her hand as she stared Inez in the eye.

"Well, what about you Bernice? Have you seen anything funny over there?" Sam tried to get Bernice to settle down.

"The kids said they have. If I've told them once, I've told them a million times not to go over there, but you know how hard-headed teenagers can be, especially that son of mine. He takes after his father, you know," she said this to the Spencers as if sharing a private joke. "Well, he and his friends decided to investigate the house for themselves one night and he came home telling me all kinds of stories. You'll have to ask him about them. I've forgotten most of it."

As she finished speaking, Bernice plopped herself down on one of the chairs at the table fanning herself with a potholder she held in her opposite hand.

"Look, Bernice, I'm sorry I rattled your cage there girl— you okay?" Inez was stricken by Bernice's appearance. Her face was flushed and she was wheezing as she tried to catch her breath.

"Apology accepted, Inez . . . I think I'm starting the change of life or something. Seems I'm flying off the handle real easy lately. Get flushed and have to fight for breath too. But I'm not kidding when I tell you to watch you're mouth in my house." She laid the potholder down and looked Inez in the eye.

"You're right dear, this is your house. I shouldn't have needled you just cause I don't agree with you."

"And how is that better half of yours? I see he's got some friends down there at the barn looking at that old bull," Gladys said as she looked out the window at trucks with cattle trailers attached rolling into the yard and parking down near the barn.

"Oh! That better half of mine is playing cowboy again with his cowboy friends from Wyoming and Montana!" She turned to Sam, and said, "The only point of contention my husband John and I have ever had in almost twenty five years of marriage was when he bought that Brahma bull from a passing rodeo. The thing is meaner than a snake and a damn sight bigger! If I had my way, we'd be serving him for supper!"

Inez burst out laughing. She couldn't believe Bernice said "damn."

The rest of the afternoon went smoothly and Sam learned that legends surrounding her house were many and were so deeply imbedded into local lore that teenagers used the house as a place to scare their dates. She wondered if she had made a mistake by buying it, but the neighbors were so nice that she thought she had to have been on the right track.

At Bernice's kitchen table, Sam also learned that Bernice had married John right out of high school, and had wanted nothing more than to be a farmer's wife for as long as she could remember. She wanted a big family with lots of kids running in and out the house, to work for the Lord, and "to be of assistance to others" which was exactly how she was living.

Too, Bernice refused to accept the scorn her church sisters had for the Spencer sisters because of their pasts and for Samantha because she was a scientist, something Sam had not known until that day. Bernice made sure everyone who visited her, including her church sisters, felt right at home in her house, and her husband John supported her completely.

Sam met John and a few of his cowboy friends when they came in for lunch, and she found John to be a quiet, unassuming farmer who loved his family dearly judging by the way he looked at them. He raised both beef cattle and crops, and the Brahma bull he had named Steamroller.

The women spent the rest if the afternoon in light hearted banter. Though Sam had been a stranger earlier that day, she wasn't one by the time she left. As the sun painted the sky scarlet in the early evening twilight, and she walked down the sidewalk strolling over to her pick-up getting ready to leave, she found Gladys, Inez and Bernice right in step behind her.

"Now, dear, you go on and take some of this left over casserole. Just heat it up when you're hungry. It tastes even better after it's been sitting awhile. You'll love it," Bernice purred as she handed Samantha a glass covered casserole dish while she climbed into her truck.

"You take some of this, too," Gladys winked and pulled a Kerr canning jar from her jacket pocket. It was filled with a clear liquid. "You try some of this at night when it gets cold. It'll do you good."

"Now don't you hesitate to call on us," Inez said pointing to herself and Gladys as Sam put everything on the front seat beside her. "And take no note of those stories we've been telling. There's nothing for you to be scared of." Inez had her fingers crossed behind her back.

"You can call me anytime, too," Bernice said. All the women walked with Sam as she backed the truck up and turned it toward the road. As the three women called out more invitations to their homes, Sam managed to drive out the driveway waving out the window at the others who waved back and who remained in the yard still waving as she turned onto River Drive and headed east for home.

Driving, a feeling of warmth washed over Sam like a gently flowing waterfall. The neighbors were so nice. She had been lonely but felt that was all about to change. Besides that, others thought her house was haunted too! If only they knew the half of it, she thought remembering the first night she heard something in her house. She was thankful for her pets; they saw and heard it, too, so she knew she wasn't loosing her mind.

Chapter Two

As Sam visited with Bernice for the first time, Arthur
Noone, who lived across River Drive just east of Bernice's house,
was in his basement scrubbing his arms with Lava soap. He
scrubbed until his skin was mottled red and pruned.

"You know this is all your fault, don't you mother?" he
said while observing his blood spattered face in the cracked mirror
hanging on the dirty brick wall over the concrete wash tubs.

"You were right about one thing, though. Someone has to
deal with it. And let's just say I'm up to the task." He chuckled at
the sight of himself scrubbing the gore from his flesh. How he
loved his work. But even with that job done, there was still more to
do, so he went to the broom closet and took out the mop and
bucket, filling it with warm water and adding bleach to it. He'd
probably go through a couple gallons, as messy as it was. Clean up
had to be perfect, but that was okay with him. He loved the menial
labor feeling great satisfaction with his work once it was
completed to his meticulous standards. Still, the room was getting
a bit overcrowded. He had almost fifty years worth of work stored
under his modest ranch style house.

His work had not been difficult to accomplish. Keeping
nosy neighbors at bay had been the real challenge, especially the

two whores living next door. Noone shook his head in disgust at
the thought of the Gladys and Inez Spencer who he detested with
all his heart.

Whores! Living right next door to him! There ought to be
a law! Of course, he'd met worse and had kept company with some
of them, but they had all been men. There was a difference.

After cleaning for an hour, he sat aside his mop and pail,
walked over to the brick chimney, and pulled out a cigar box,
which he kept hidden behind two loose bricks there. Carefully
opening it, he looked inside staring down at photos, reflections of
his handiwork over the years. Excitement tickled his every nerve
ending as he eyed his creations which he carefully documented
photographically, each memory a joy.

But the first, that was his favorite, although certainly not
his best work. "What was his name?" Noone tried to recall, but
there had been so many since, it simply wouldn't come to him. He
put the photos away, and made sure they were hidden again safely
before returning to his cleaning.

When he finished he went upstairs and got under a hot
shower letting the scalding water spray his still lithe body as he
covered himself in lather from a bar of soap. He loved the feel of
the hot water, the smell of the soap cleansing him, but the real
cleansing, he knew, came with each creation he stored downstairs.

He dressed in a silk smoking jacket and sat down on the
couch to light his pipe. It was a quiet Sunday. Tomorrow would be
different. He'd dress in a pin-stripped suit and coat, climb into his
shinny red, brand new Dodge Ram pick-up and head for the city of
Duluth, the St. Louis County seat where a county board meeting
was scheduled. He never missed them.

Noone liked to talk with county commissioners at length,
men of his era, men who knew how men behaved together,
especially after the official meeting concluded. That's when

commissioners liked to handle a lot of the county business. By law they knew they were not supposed to have their little irregular visits when all board members were present, but no matter, no one ever called them on it and that's how things got done.

And Noone, being a regular at those meetings and so accommodating to the commissioner's needs, was someone they respected, trusted. Commissioners listened to his ideas on how the county should be run and enjoyed the lavish attention, time and money he showered on them. In his pin-stripped suit, with his impeccable grooming and gray hair, Arthur Noone was the picture of success, wealth, intelligence, and health, and did not look his sixty seven years. All impressive to commissioners, who in turn looked their ages, were not too bright, and had enjoyed only modest success over the years, most enjoyed failing health, as well. Not one commissioner ever asked Arthur Noone what he did for a living.

That Monday was no different.

Sheriff Skip Gilbert was another matter all together. He didn't like Noone and made no attempt to hide it, which didn't help him in dealing with commissioners. It didn't matter to Gilbert. Something was wrong with Noone, and one way or another, he'd find out what it was just like his father had tried to do when he was sheriff before him.

"Look fellas, that guy is bad news; and if you're smart, you'll watch your ass around him." He confided to commissioners often enough, but they never listened.

Gilbert was not a man to pay commissioners undue compliments, either, or court their favor or seek their guidance, not like Noone did. Gilbert didn't believe commissioners were doing a good job and he didn't approve of their little indiscrete meetings. They were illegal! Not only that, but commissioners liked to give state contracts to relatives over other bidders, which was also illegal. State contracts are supposed to go the lowest bidder, which was not usually the relative.

Commissioners also vaguely sensed Gilbert's views about them viewing him, in turn, as a mild threat, all though none really believed he would ever turn them in, and, after all, Gilbert was an elected official too. The voters liked him, so they would never push him too far for fear he might actually make his complaints about them public.

For all their playing of politics, Gilbert knew that none of the commissioners were very sophisticated. They consisted of two retired farmers, one retired teacher, one retired social worker and two retired small-town business owners. They were no match for Arthur Noone; Gilbert felt it his duty to at least try and protect them from themselves. He lectured them often enough about the inappropriateness of their informal get-togethers, but they continued to have them with Noone's blessings.

Gilbert knew that, too. He hoped that someday some smart reporter would get in there and watch dog them, maybe get some dirt on Noone, and he couldn't wait for it to happen. If the only way they could learn, was the hard way . . . well, then, let 'em learn the hard way, he thought.

In the meantime, Gilbert was required to report to all county board meetings once a month with every detail of his office's business. If they had no other chance to communicate, they did then and Arthur Noone was always there when they did, listening. It made Gilbert's skin crawl to know that Noone was privy to the Sheriff's Department business. It was none of his concern. Gilbert quietly seethed each time he had to handle the department's private affairs in front of Noone.

As he sat in at the May, 2000 county board meeting, Arthur Noone pondered just what it was that had turned the sheriff so against him; he didn't really care, he was just curious.

As far as his own interests were concerned, he'd have his way in the end, he always did. If he didn't get it that day, he'd get it the next. Gilbert couldn't stop him. He had his own contacts in the sheriff's office, so he knew what was going on at all times; that's how he managed to stay one step ahead of everyone.

In May, Noone wanted the county to find a way to get rid of the Spencer sisters, telling commissioners that their property was an eyesore. Without investigating, commissioners would go home hoping to find some long unused statute in state law to get rid of the women.

They, too, knew the Spencer sisters. Everyone on the Iron Range knew of the whores living on River Drive, and though they never told Arthur Noone that they personally knew the sisters, more than one had been their client. Commissioners feared discovery, so they were happy to oblige the kind gentleman who always made them feel so good about themselves. He was a fine, upstanding citizen, morally indignant with the two old hens, and who wouldn't be? Of course they would try and find a way to help him. And of course Noone knew all along about the commissioner's dalliances with the Spencers and banked on that to get his way.

So every other month or so, Noone looked for new ways to get the county to harass the Spencers. He wanted them gone and he would elicit the commissioner's help every chance he could to accomplish his goals.

On more than one occasion Sheriff Gilbert had to point out that what commissioners were proposing against the sisters was illegal. As property owners, and taxpayers, the sisters, too, had rights; the county attorney confirmed that often enough.

Still, Noone tried. He never worried about any of it though; if his harassment didn't get rid of them, he would run them off some other way, the harlots. He also knew the sisters were afraid of him and he enjoyed that.

As he stared at Gilbert sitting at the table with commissioners, a foreboding rushed over him, a feeling that had been washing over him more and more of late.

It started just after he met Samantha Egar. She looked so much like the professor he was drawn to her like a magnet. He followed her through the woods while she worked knowing he shouldn't, but he couldn't seem to stop himself. He wanted to be near her, smell her perfume. His body ached at the thought of her; he hadn't felt that way about a woman in more years than he cared to remember.

She didn't like him though. Every time he came upon her either on the road or in the woods she told him she didn't want his help. He loved it when she got sarcastic, or tried to threaten him away. He went along with her when she tried to shoo him out of the woods— imagine—shooing him away like a pesky pup! He smiled at the thought. That, too, didn't really matter. She would love him one day, he would see to it; whether she liked it or not, just like he did with the professor's wife Janice.

But the shadows, where did they come from? Nothing like that ever appeared before the Egar woman arrived—so why now? He wondered. Was she the cause? Some sort of witch? Bitches usually are, he thought. Lately, the shadows were everywhere; he couldn't seem to escape them. They buzzed through his head, too, like bees buzzing over a honeycomb, droning on and on and on, telling him how to do things. Sometimes they sounded like his mother.

Every once in a while he saw them, fleetingly, out of the corner of his eye, no matter where he was. No definitive shape, just dark, billowy wisps next to him one moment and somewhere else the next. He could feel finger like tickles across his flesh when he was home alone with them, and sometimes when he was in the woods looking for Samantha, they would sneak up on him. He grew more and more convinced that she was the cause and he wanted her to make them stop!

Staring at Skip Gilbert's back as Gilbert talked with commissioners, Noone wondered why he was seeing shadows. He worried about it. Didn't want anyone else to know, see how tense he had become, see his anxiety or see him watching flitting shapes from the corner of his eyes. No one else seemed to see them, so he dared not tell anyone about them. As he sat with commissioners in their conference room, he fought to keep his face calm, placid, unrevealing. He was good at concealing his true emotions. He'd been doing it for a lifetime.

He had asked his mother to help him get rid of them, but she had only laughed at him, said he had a job to do; that he had better get to it and forget about "shadows," all the while acting as if she didn't believe a word he said. She called him a baby, of all things. Good Lord! Look at all the work I've done for her over the years! More than any of her other sons, that's for damn sure, he thought as commissioners droned on about county business, and still she treats me like a child!

While Noone was lost in thoughts of his mother, Gilbert picked his file folder up off the big conference table, excused himself from the county board meeting, turned and found himself face to face with Arthur Noone. Their eyes met and held. Noone was so preoccupied with thoughts of his mother's mistreatment it took him a split second to realize the sheriff was directly in front of him staring him in the eyes.

Every police instinct Gilbert had went on red alert as he and Noone held their gaze. Noone's stare sent a chill up his spine. The creepier Gilbert felt, the harder he stared, so much so, Noone was forced to look away first. Good, Gilbert thought and walked out of the room.

Commissioners broke for mid-morning coffee and rolls inviting Noone to join them after Gilbert left. Noone smugly listened as commissioners attempted to impress him with their skillful management of the county.

They weren't half the man he was and he knew it, remembering how he had managed to put himself through college by working odd jobs when he was a kid all alone in the world with no one to help him. Only a select few went to college in those days. All the while he was in school he worked at getting excellent grades and managed to save enough money to buy the little farm where he still lived, all that was more than fifty years before, at a time when it wasn't easy for poor kids to go to college. Since then he had purchased many other properties and managed to make an excellent living without every having to work for anyone other than himself, excepting those few years he was in college.

He was as good at money managing today as he was then seeing good returns on most of his investments. Of course, it hadn't hurt him any when he used his brother Joseph to steal things that he sold on the black market. By the time Joseph died, Arthur, older by fourteen months, had accumulated a small fortune. It never hurt that he had inherited Joseph's little nest egg, either. He often wondered how his ignorant brother had managed to put so much money away. He also wondered how any brother of his could be so dumb. That had to have come from their mother's side of the family.

But that nest egg of Joseph's? That wasn't dumb. How did he sock so much money away, without my knowing about it? Arthur often wondered over the years. Joseph just should have never told me about it; that thought brought a smirk to his face.

Remembering Joseph's surprise that day down in the mineshafts gave him another reason to smile.

Commissioners didn't notice.

Chapter Three

On a beautiful, balmy June late afternoon Sam worked in the forests not far from the Spencer's house. Since she was often unsuccessful in spotting the wolves because their hunting territories covered approximately one hundred square miles, she and fellow biologists from Duluth collared the alpha pair with GPS tracking systems when Sam first discovered the pack earlier that year. The GPS system allowed Sam to track them better and to use her time more productively. Whenever the pack was out of range, she studied other signs of their behavior, or took care of paperwork. This particular day she decided to get to know her neighbors better.

Sam walked up behind the Spencer house from out of the west side forests surrounding it. She fought her way through willow brush thicket, which scratched at her bare arms and tore at her brown, medium length hair that was loosely held back in a ponytail. When she broke through the last tangle of bramble, the large Spencer log cabin greeted her all aglow in early evening twilight.

She walked up the well cared for lawn enjoying the smell of freshly mowed grass and the willow tree branches that were lazily blowing in the breeze. She crossed over to the front porch running her fingers through her tangled mess of hair to comb it and redo her ponytail, where she saw the Spencer sisters sitting on the front porch enjoying the early evening twilight.

"Hey!" She called loudly apparently startling the sisters as they jumped up gasping and grabbing at their chests.

"What the hell are you doing? Trying to scare us half to death?" The women said in unison.

"I am so sorry," Sam said truly regretting startling them so, "I thought you would have heard me coming up from behind the house. I made a lot of noise."

"Heard you? Honey, we're old ladies! Between the two of us, we have about one half of a good ear! Next time you come up behind us, for God's sake shout or something! Crimminy sakes girl!"

It was then that Sam noticed the double barrel shotgun resting against the front porch railing in front of Inez's rocker. It felt like her heart down shifted into fourth gear to pull a wheelie and burn rubber on asphalt inside her chest.

"I apologize. I had no idea. Please, forgive me. The last thing I wanted to do was to frighten either one of you. I would have called first, but I was out back working and decided on impulse to drop by." After spinning out, her heart settled down to idle in first gear. She sighed with relief.

"Oh, that's okay, honey. Just gave us a start is all. You come on up here and have a sit down. We'll get you some tea." The two women regained their composure quickly.

Sam walked up onto the porch as Gladys went inside to get iced tea for everyone. Inez found another rocking chair just inside the door and hauled it out onto the porch for Sam. The threesome sat rocking in silence sipping cold tea, each one recovering from a severe fright.

After a few minutes of quiet and out of the blue Inez burst out laughing and said, "What the women around here are worried about is that maybe we've slept with their husbands . . . and maybe we have! But," Inez paused to look hard at Sam, "if they weren't so afraid of sex, we would have been out of business! Besides, we're seventy two and seventy three years old now! We don't do that anymore."

Taken aback, Sam laughed nervously at her outburst. When she recovered enough to consider it, she wondered why the women were so jumpy, and why did they have a shotgun with them? Did it have something to do with their pasts? She looked out toward the access road that ran along the north side of the house and noticed that the bramble and willow brush was so thick she couldn't see the road except for the driveway next door.

Inez was about to speak, when Gladys said, "You ought to watch out for Noone."

"Watch out for Noone? Why?"

"Something about the old buzzard; he ain't right," Gladys continued. "We've lived next door to him for forty years now, and he's tried to run us out of here every year since. There's just something wrong with him. Never have been able to put my finger on it, exactly."

"He's tried to run you out of here?" Sam asked.

"Yep. Every year he tries something. Doesn't like women," Gladys continued as if speaking to herself. She almost whispered. "I tell you, I'm not scared of much, but sometimes, if he's looking at me, it's as if something dead passed through me. It's unpleasant as hell."

"Tell her Gladys. Tell her about that time he ran up on you when you were with that client. Go on, tell her!" Inez said.

Gladys looked uncomfortable. She knew what her life was like as a hooker. She also knew that Sam hadn't a clue. She didn't want to be the one to tell the story. Inez poked Gladys in the ribs. "You go on and tell that child. She knows what we did once. If her ears are so virgin they can't take the truth of the thing, she's got the problem, but you need to tell her what happened!"

Gladys nodded at Inez. "I was with Johnson, Clem Johnson one night about twenty five years ago. You do know who Clem is, don't you? Your nearest neighbor?" Sam shook her head no. She hadn't met him yet. She leaned forward in her chair with her elbows on her knees listening.

Gladys continued. "Noone must have seen me going over there. He knew why I would visit an old bachelor farmer. Maybe that's why he followed me."

"He gave us, Johnson and me, just enough time to be taking care of business when he walked straight in Johnson's front door like he had an invitation.

'Whore!' he said to me in a voice that boomed across the room. 'Whore monger' he said to Clem. He started damning us right there. You should have heard him. He was quoting scriptures I ain't never heard before, but that's what he sounded like—a preacher. I was terrified of the evil I heard come out of his mouth about women. Now I am a whore. I know what I am, but he was talking about all women. He hates 'em! I ain't never heard anything like it." Gladys paused taking a long draw from her ice tea glass, setting it back down carefully, her hand, trembling.

"Noone was so wrapped up in what he was saying that he didn't notice Clem go for his shotgun. Clem brought it up on him and fired at Noone's feet. Let me tell you, my ears still ring from that blast going off next to us in that little living room of Clem's. Yeah, that's where he caught us . . .

That shot brought Noone back to his senses though, and out of his preaching mode let me tell you! He looked like he was somewhere else that whole time he was preaching, on some pulpit in hell, I reckon. Clem, he said to Noone, 'You best get off my property. If I catch you on it again, I'll use this here gun on you and bury you in my manure pile.'

Noone takes off without another word, in complete silence, couldn't even hear his feet as he walked across the floor. It was creepy, the way he came in and out of that house like that. Clem ain't never seen Noone on his property since, neither.

We see him though." Gladys indicated herself and Inez. "We can't help but see him, he always smiles and waves at us. It makes my skin crawl."

Gladys stopped rocking and sat unmoving in her chair. She stared at the lush willow brush blocking the view of the public access road between their property and Noone's, a road all three had to use to retrieve their mail from mailboxes on River Drive.

The Eveleth postmaster wouldn't allow the mailman to drive up each driveway when delivering rural mail, so the three were forced to share a space on River Drive. Gladys and Inez were careful to always walk together to the mailboxes, all the time hoping they wouldn't run into Noone. They didn't, often. He was the reason they encouraged the willow brush to grow so thick between their house and the road. They didn't want to see him, ever.

Gladys sat quietly after she finished speaking looking like she had traveled back in time to that night at Johnson's.

"She's remembering," Inez said. "Leave her be. I tell her to just forget it, it's past, but them memories; they come on her all of a sudden, sometimes . . . It's an ugly life, whoring." Inez joined Gladys in her silence and rocked quietly next to her.

The sisters never said another word about their lives as prostitutes to Sam.

Gladys brought her tea glass to her lips and sipped. She grimaced as the cold liquid touched her tongue.

"You best ask some of the other neighbors about the local trappers, too. Try the sheriff—Sheriff Skip Gilbert, from Virginia? You look him up, talk to him about both Noone and a trapper nicknamed Shorty," Gladys said. As quickly as she had slipped into the past, she slipped back to the present without missing a beat. "You might be interested to know something about that house of yours, too."

Sam left when she finished her iced tea never mentioning the crying inside her house or her pets' strange behavior. As she walked home, she thought about a passage from the Bible, Deut. 18:11-12 (NKJV) which says: "or one who conjures spells, or a medium, or a spiritist, or one who calls up the dead. For all who do these things are an abomination to the Lord, and because these abominations the Lord your God drives them out before you."

"Lord," she prayed, "I understand what you're saying. The problem is I don't wish to traffic in ghosts and spirits but they are trafficking in my house. What am I to do?" She let her prayer go at that and hoped for an answer.

The two and a half mile walk home was uneventful and Sam was glad to finally walk up her own driveway where willow trees whispered in the breeze and the twilight lit up the evening sky. Crickets and frogs trilled melodies from the creek and warm breezes wafted up from the south licking Sam's hair as she gingerly stepped up to her back door surveying the back yard and the transformation it had gone through already. All manner of plants in clay pots of varying sizes thrived and the stone pavers she used to build the back yard patio looked wonderful, their orange color glistening in the setting sun. She opened the glass patio doors and stepped into the kitchen spending the rest of the evening going over her log books then retiring at 10 p.m. She spent an uneventful night sleeping, something for which she was extremely grateful, it happened so rarely anymore.

She got up early the next day and went back out into the woods. As she worked, she trampled over and through downed brush. She walked over water filled moss bedding the forest floor. She crossed fallen logs and watched as squirrels collected nuts, as a doe and her fawn took off in fright at her approach, their white tail flags blasting a warning, and as blue jays made a nest in the trees.

She had just walked into a clearing when she heard engine noises sounding as if they were coming from the west down what looked like an old logging road. The engine noise grew louder as an old green John Deere tractor came chugging into view. Sam could see who she believed was Clem Johnson sitting behind the tractor wheel, and could tell by the look on his face that he was none too happy to see her there. She must have crossed over onto his property.

He stopped the tractor as he came alongside her, and stepped down speaking as he did. "You that woman that's studying them wolves, ain't ya'," he said as he landed onto the ground in front of her, smells of manure lingering about his black and red checked jacket and blue jean coveralls.

"Yes, yes I am. My name's Samantha Egar." She extended her hand to shake his but he ignored the gesture.

"Them damn critters been killing my cattle! I'll shoot 'em if I have to." He spat a wad of chewing tobacco out the left side of his mouth, some of which splattered onto the whiskers he hadn't bothered to shave off that morning.

"Mr. Johnson. You know that's illegal. And I know you have never done anything to hurt any one of them." She stood with her hands on her hips tapping her foot impatiently against the moss-covered ground.

He laughed. "They was right. You have got some spunk,

don't ya! I'll tell you something, though. If the government didn't pay me something for my losses, I'd be shooting those thieving sons-a-bitches everyday. You betcha! It's lucky for them thatthey's kinda pretty. I'll give something that's kinda pretty a little leeway." He winked. With that he got back up onto the tractor.

"Mr. Johnson. You've lived out here a long time. Is there anything you can tell me about my place? I recently bought the old Noone farm, you know."

"Yeah, I know. There's plenty I could tell you about that place, but not out here in the woods. You come over fer supper tonight and I'll tell you a few tales."

"That sounds fine. Is there anything I can bring?"

"Just yerself. I'll see ya' at seven," he said starting the engine and bringing the lumbering, noisy old tractor to life. No conversation was possible with that engine running, so Sam just watched as Johnson drove back the way he had come. The squat old man, about eighty years old, sat ramrod straight behind the wheel.

When she arrived for dinner, Sam found Johnson's old farmhouse amazingly well kept. Not a speck of dust lay anywhere. Bookshelves spilled over onto other furniture inside his otherwise neat house. Framed photos lined the walls of the hallway, many snapshots of Johnson posing with Minnesota State dignitaries. Sam recognized a few of Johnson's companions though not all. The photos were old. He didn't comment on them, and she didn't ask, but from the looks of things, Clem Johnson had been heavily involved in Minnesota politics at one time.

He brought her tea while he had coffee and they sat at the dinning room table. He no longer smelled like the barn as Sam half expected he would. Instead, he had bathed, dressed in slacks, put on a clean white shirt with a bow tie, polished his penny loafers, and splashed on some Old Spice. He looked dapper pushing out his chest and preening a bit for her. She tried not to notice.

Dinner was served precisely at 7:30 p.m. The two strangers enjoyed a simple meal of baked chicken with a brown rice side dish, baked acorn squash, a mixed fresh salad with onions, lettuce, tomatoes, cucumbers and croutons and a pumpkin pie for desert made out of tofu and honey. It was delicious. Johnson had even baked a loaf of fresh brown bread to have with dinner. After dinner they went into the living room to enjoy an after dinner drink. Johnson grabbed a sweater before seating himself in what Samantha could tell was his favorite chair. It was well worn and there was an ashtray on an end table next to it, with a number of books and the local newspaper within easy reach on the ottoman in front of it.

"Fer' the life of me, I can't understand why ya' bought that place? Someone should have told ya' what you'd be in fer' with that Noone fella." Johnson spoke without preamble, lighting a pipe filled with cherry blend tobacco. The scent wafted throughout the room.

"How long have you been out there now?" Johnson asked her.

"A couple of months, just about," Sam answered. The meal, the company, and the atmosphere of Johnson's home, were so normal, so warm and homey, she wanted to drink it in, savor it. She wasn't sure she wanted to talk about her house anymore.

"How many cows do you milk Mr. Johnson?"

"You didn't come here to find out about my farming practices. You came here to find out about your house. And I'm gonna tell you a few things whether you want to hear 'em or not." He laid his pipe down and looked her in the eye. He sat forward in his chair to get eyeball to eyeball with her. She could smell his cologne. The flirty glint in his eyes was gone.

"There was a couple owned that house a few years back. It must have been in '62 or so. They was nice. They had little girls, twins . . . I think. They didn't look alike, though. The girls was babies when they moved in. That couple got chummy with Noone right off. Bought the place from him, too, just like you did," Johnson looked at her out the corner of his eye appearing to gauge her reaction. "He tells folks now that he was rentn' it to 'em, but he wasn't. He sold it, just like he did you.

Anywho, I'd see him going over there all the time. I wondered how they could stand 'em; he's so polite, and all. Something is wrong with a person when his manners is always perfect. Can't trust 'em, I say."

Johnson didn't mention anything about his run-in with Noone in his own house. Sam blushed at the thought of it. If Johnson noticed, he didn't let on.

"That couple's name was Browne—I think—Browne with an 'e'. I heard gossip about 'em, though I found most of it hard to believe. Some around here said she was having an affair with Noone. I ain't so sure. I saw the professor and his wife together. They looked like they loved each other. It was plain."

Sam listened intently as Johnson continued his story.

"He was an English professor. He liked books. Him and me had some nice talks in the woods. I met him out there at the same place I met you, today. He'd walk out there all the time. He was a city boy, you could tell, but he weren't scared of notin' when he was out in them woods, not like a lot of city folk. He liked 'em, the woods, I mean. They seemed to like him too. It was odd. Wildlife would come real close to him. I would never have believed it if I hadn't seen it with my own eyes.

He worked at the community college in Virginia, teaching. He sometimes worked odd hours. He was also writing a

book, he told me once, a fiction novel. We had a number of
conversations in the very same spot you and me met up in today.

It was strange. If I hadn't known you was a girl, I'd
thought I was seeing him all over again out there today. You look a
lot like him, as a matter of fact," Johnson scrutinized Sam's face so
intently, she started to grow uncomfortable. When he realized what
he was doing, he sat back and said, "Oh, sorry. I didn't mean to
stare at you like that. It's just kinda' odd, you know, you lookin' so
much like him and all.

Well, anywho, when the professor was at work Noone
would go over there—to your house. No telling what those two
were doing, Noone and the professor's wife, I mean, cause not too
long into it, they both took off to Canada. But that Noone fella', he
don't like women."

Johnson let that last sentence lie, pausing, and taking a
long draw off his pipe. He waited a full minute before speaking
again, "No one ever saw her again. He came back from Canada
about five years after they disappeared . . . alone.

One other thing odd about it—the professor, he was never
seen again, neither. One night he's home, the next, nobody knows
where he is, no one ever sees them girls again, neither.
I called the sheriff about that. They did some kind of investigation,
they said, but they didn't turn up anything on the professor or the
two little girls. No one knows what happened to any of 'em, not
even the wife. I got my suspicions though."

"Please—tell me." Sam was completely wrapped up in
the tale.

"I suspect Noone and the wife of killing both the
professor and the kids—that's what I suspect. They're buried
someplace on that property. When Noone came back from Canada
alone, my guess is he killed her, too, up there. Left her up there,

probably buried out in the woods someplace. Who knows? I'll doubt if I'll ever know.

Other things happen over there now. Sometimes I go by the house on my way to the river at night to net some fish. Don't tell anyone, but that's illegal," he leaned forward in his chair and winked at her as if daring her to say something about it. She ignored the challenge. "Anywho, I'll see a light moving through that house. It looks like it starts in the basement and climbs all the way to the attic. Four floors!

I even snuck over there once—when I thought no one was around? I was going to get a good look inside. Maybe a transient was staying there. They do that sometimes. Them and drunks find their way back here and sort of camp out.

Well, when I went in through the kitchen door—it was unlocked—I thought I heard a noise downstairs . . . crying. Then I heard footsteps climbing those basement steps. One by one they kept climbing up, getting closer. I held my breath. Finally, the noise reached the top step. I could see that pretty glass doorknob turning. I snapped out of it then and got the hell outta there, but by the time I moved the basement door had opened and the sobs were booming off the walls. It sounded like that noise came from everywhere at once. It reached a pitch I can't even begin to describe. Damn near wet myself it was so bad! Me! A Korean War veteran! Wet'n myself!

The gist of the story is . . . I think the professor and his little girls haunt that place. I think he's still crying for his wife. At her betrayal—I mean."

When he finished his story, Clem Johnson apologized if he'd frightened her. After a short time, she made her excuses and left, not telling him she had already been terrified, all he had done was confirm her worst fears. She felt both relieved and dismayed. She was glad to get the background on her house, to know she wasn't alone in what she had seen and heard herself, but at the same time, she hadn't wanted her worst fears confirmed.

When she got home, she stepped into the house dreading the thought of staying there alone. She didn't want to hear the crying anymore. She didn't want to know the house's tragic past. It was as if the house grieved for a family that no longer lived there.

In the intervening months, psychokinetic activity still flourished inside the house, but the severity had lessened and Sam was no longer afraid of it as she had been in the beginning. What she wanted most was to find a way to ease the grief that permeated her surroundings, perhaps dispel it forever, so she could make the place into a warm, welcoming home.

As she sipped her coffee that morning after Angie's call, reflecting on her time at the farm, she hoped with all her heart that Angie would be able to help. She couldn't wait for her to get there.

Chapter Four

Sam discovered immediately that wolf traps were being set in the woods south of Eveleth once she began her research in the area. Each time she found one she pulled and destroyed it because wolf trapping is illegal; they are on the endangered species list. She hated the sight of the steel toothed traps; more often than not they maimed the animals so severely, if they weren't killed by the trap, they had to be put down. She considered the traps a means to torture the animals and nothing more.

When a number of the local trappers discovered she was pulling traps, they came to resent her for meddling in affairs they felt were none of her business.

She had not gone head to head with any one individual over the issue in the two years since she started work in the field, but that all changed one July, 2000 day.

Sweat poured down her face as she stepped into her old truck after working in the woods all day. Humidity at almost one hundred percent with a temperature in the high nineties, it was sweltering work and thoughts of a sweating glass of ice-cold beer seduced her into stopping in at Tony's on her way home.

Tony's, the most infamous hot spot on the Iron Range was located at the west end of River Drive, just off of Highway 53 and only ten miles from Sam's house.

It was early evening as Sam stepped inside the dimly lit cavernous like room, and moved over to sit at the end of the horseshoe bar ordering a beer from bartender Jack. The 350 seat capacity club was nearly empty except for four men sitting at the other end of the bar.

Dressed in work clothes, jeans, T-shirt and hiking boots, that were filled with grass stains, dirt, and sweat stains, Sam's hair was also unkempt, her face smudged with dirt, and she couldn't seem to stop scratching her badly chewed neckline where sand flies had gnawed ceaselessly on her flesh. Her deeply tanned skin was mosquito bitten and blotchy.

She looked forward to a hot bath and having the following day off. Weather forecasters predicted that the weather would be the same. It was too much. The humidity drove her and every bug in the woods, wild. Deer flies, wood ticks, ants, hornets and a million others seemed to attack any warm bloodied mammal that had the gall to stay inside the deep thickets where no breezes could blow them away, which is where Sam had been all that afternoon. No, a day away from the incessant buzzing of flies and mosquitoes, inside her air-conditioned home, was just what she needed.

And at that moment, she gave no thought to her appearance as she sipped the ice cold Miller Lite relishing the cool comfort of the air-conditioned bar and the cold liquid pouring down her parched throat. Even so, her itchy neckline drove her to distraction as she scratched her flesh raw, wishing she had thought ahead to bring the Calamine lotion with her. As she scratched, she noticed that the men at the other end of the bar were watching her with intense interest.

Immediately she wished she had cleaned up before stopping in. Did she look that bad? Even after forty years, her insecurity popped its ugly head up to taunt her with doubt and fear at the most inopportune times. She always assumed she looked her worst, even when she didn't. And as hard as she tried to dispel the momentary lapse into negativity, thoughts of how her parents had discarded her like an old rag immediately challenged her self-esteem, which inevitably flowed over into other areas of her life.

It took a few minutes before she entertained the idea that perhaps the men at the other end of the bar were trappers. Maybe one of them was responsible for the love notes being left in her mailbox, love notes that threatened her life. Perhaps one of them was Shorty Kivimaki, the trapper the Spencer sisters warned her about. Considering the possibilities, she went into red alert. No longer was the happy feeling of contentment with a difficult job well done lulling her into a false sense of security. She looked closer at the men, realizing that one of them had to be Shorty Kivimaki, considering the description the Spencers gave her. She wished then that she had taken their advice and gone to see the sheriff, but she had put it off.

She had talked to the sheriff's department about the notes, but apparently, they weren't taking them seriously. When she first moved to the Range, she knew local trappers didn't like her. She learned that from reading negative letters to the editor in the local newspaper about herself and on occasion, finding a nasty note on her truck's windshield, but when she started receiving daily love notes left anonymously in her mailbox, she knew a serious shift in attitude had taken place. The nasty letters to the editor, even the notes on the windshield, bore no thinly veiled deaths threats, not like the letters did, letters she started receiving no sooner than she had moved into her farmhouse.

Her old sense of insecurity rose up to keep her from insisting on seeing the sheriff in person about them. After all, who was she to complain?

Now the strange men were watching her and whispering amongst themselves. One of them, a six-foot-seven-inch giant, got off his barstool and strolled over to her as the bartender said, "Shorty, you better not start noth'n," confirming Sam's suspicions.

She studied the man as he approached her. He wore a black and red checkered shirt with tight fitting blue jeans. His blond, wavy, shoulder-length hair glistened in what little sunlight there was dappling through the commercially challenged barroom windows, so splayed with advertisements, they let in little light. He held his hair off his face with a red bandanna. Shorty towered over Sam grinning down at her.

She looked him dead in the eye refusing to be intimidated. He stood so close she could smell the Ivory soap he washed with. She sat bolt upright and held his gaze refusing to say a word.

"Me and my buddies over there, we think it's you that's been out in the woods messing with our traps. We think it's you that's been studying them wolves. We right?"

"Yeah—you . . . and your buddies over there . . ." she flipped her head to the side to include the other three at the bar, "you're right," She didn't let go of Shorty's eyes, but eased off her barstool to stand toe-to-toe with him.

"We don't take too kindly to women messing in our business. This is just a friendly warning, you understand—we wouldn't want to see a pretty lady such as yourself getting hurt, now would we?" He flashed a perfect set of teeth in a big toothy grin, but with eyes as cold as the Antarctic.

"Cut the crap buster." Sam's voice wasn't loud, and it wasn't friendly. "I'll remove every one of those wolf traps every time I find one, and I'll tell you something else," one hand on her hip, her index finger waving in Shorty's face, Sam glowered up at him. "I'm going to start collecting wolf traps and taking them to the DNR, so you just better back off before you find yourself in a pile of shit so deep, you'll never climb out." At five-feet-seven-inches Sam had to crane her neck back to look up at Shorty, but she didn't care—she refused to let go of his stare as she pushed her way in closer to him.

"We got ways of dealing with uppity women."

"Ohhhhh! I'm scared!" She stepped in even closer, eyes blazing. She was fed up with people trying to intimidate her, one letter too many had been left in her mailbox. She wasn't about to take any crap from him or anyone else, ever. One thing instilled in her at the orphanage she grew up in was that she had to fight to survive and she would do whatever she had to.

It was then that bar owners Anthony Franco and Tony Botticelli walked through the door. They stepped between Sam and Shorty immediately recognizing brewing trouble when they saw it.

Shorty backed off as the two men stepped in. Sam held her ground regardless of the new turn of events, which angered Franco, so he grabbed her wrist intending to throw her out of the bar. To his great surprise, Sam used the hold he had on her, grabbed him, threw the five-foot ten-inch Franco against the wall, and twisted his arm severely behind his back. All the while, she never said a word.

Silence roared in Sam's ears as an unnatural quiet enveloped the room.

She heard Botticelli first when the roar died down, "We own the place woman! Let him go!" He managed to get her to release her hold on Franco.

"Get that bitch outta' here!" Franco screamed at Jack in such a rage, Jack stepped back away from him inching down the bar closer to Shorty and his cronies. Franco, the cool headed one of the two bar-owners rarely displayed a temper.

Botticelli grabbed Franco by the arm and pushed him toward a door that led to a room no one could see into from the bar. Franco fought Botticelli's grasp, trying to get away so he could throw Sam out himself, but Botticelli fought back even harder pushing Franco back as Franco screamed at Jack to throw her out, his face ablaze in anger. After backing up as far as he could, Jack froze down near the outdoorsmen. They looked like a gaggle of geese gathered on the other side of bar standing statuesque. None were in a hurry to offend Franco fearing he'd 86' them forever. He'd done it before. Even Shorty wouldn't move.

The only one not intimidated by Franco's show of temper was Sam. She stood her ground, relaxed her body, got centered and was ready to do battle with every one of them if need be.

"Throw her outta' here! Do it now!" Franco screamed at Jack even as Botticelli half pushed, half drug him finally forcing Franco into the back room, and slamming the door behind them.

Sam calmed down a tiny bit once Franco left the room, but she was very wary of all the other men still in the room with her. She could see that none of them, not even Shorty Kivimaki, was making any attempt to move in on her. Each stood as if welded to the floor.

Moments later the back door re-opened. "You come back here," Botticelli ordered Sam, while she eyed him with suspicion. She didn't want to go anywhere near Franco, but Jack, who had thawed enough to come back up the bar, whispered telling her it would be okay; they owned the place.

Still wary, Sam followed Botticelli, but stood on the threshold of the back room before entering letting her eyes adjust to the dimly lit space in front of her. She could see Franco sitting at a table underneath an enormous mounted moose head. The blond Italian had a look on his face that said a lot of things, none of which meant "come here you sweet thing."

"You shouldn't have grabbed me," she stated simply and to the point looking Franco in the eye as she remained where she was and as Franco glared at her. She guessed that perhaps his silence might be more deadly than his rage.

"Yeah—I gathered that." Franco growled from inside what looked like a bear's den. He had an, "I smoke too many cigarettes" voice, deep and raspy.

Sam remained where she was determined not to show fear in front of him. She sensed Franco was real trouble. He wouldn't be backing down.

Botticelli grabbed three beers from the bar and stopped at the threshold next to Sam as he re-entered the back room. He gently took her arm after giving her one of the beers, and led her over to the table where Franco sat. On the way over, he said, "Now what was going on out there? How does such a lovely woman incite so many male insurrections?"

Oh brother! Sam thought as he oozed on the charm. It didn't take her long to see why Tony's was known on the Range as the place to be. But silly compliments had never been popular with her, all though she knew most people sucked them up.

"Here, sit beside us and tell us who you are." He took her elbow, lightly guided her to the seat next to Franco seating himself on her other side effectively boxing her in. They sat on a bench covered in leather behind a utilitarian table, the kind found in restaurants everywhere. Sam counted seven such tables running the length of the bench, about twenty five feet, most with extra chairs on the opposite side. Each table held a fresh pack of cards and an ashtray. Three pool tables vertically lined the middle of the room. On the north wall next to the door leading into the bar was a counter with a cash register on top of it.

"We sell off sale, too," Botticelli said after noticing her taking in the room.

"We've never seen you in here before," he stated as a question that he didn't need an answer to. "Why don't you tell us what happened out there?"

She kept her gaze on Botticelli and told them what happened, still unsure about Franco. As she spoke, Botticelli sent silent signals to Franco over Sam's head confirming what she was saying. He had already got the low down from Jack.

"Those men can be dangerous." Botticelli warned when she finished speaking.

"Not as bad as she is—where did you learn a move like that?" Franco asked, smiling at her for the first time and radiating such sexual magnetism, and danger, Sam flushed.

"The martial arts. I use it to stay in shape. It also comes in handy when you work alone. You need to know how to take care of yourself," she stammered. She wasn't sure she was making sense. What she didn't tell Franco was that she had never used any of the moves before, except in class, and was amazed they came to her with such ease when she needed them.

She looked hard at Franco and gulped, "I'm sorry about what happened out there. I thought you were one of his friends. I reacted."

"Forgiven," he said looking her in the eye and smiling as he leaned in close whispering in her ear. His baritone, husky voice brought another, deeper flush to her face.

"Hey Franco," Bottecelli interrupted, "what the guys gonna say when they learn you got beat up by a dame?"

Franco laughed leaning away from Sam. She immediately longed for him to move in close again. "They can find out whether or not I'll beat them up." The edginess in Franco's voice made her shiver.

"You better watch out for Shorty, though," Botticelli said turning his attentions back to Sam. "He is real interested in you. Jack said he's planning something."

"Sheriff Skip Gilbert is on his way here. We've already told him what happened. He's going to see you home," Botticelli added with an air of authority that effectively gave Sam no room for argument.

But that had never stopped her in the past. "I really don't need an escort," she told him.

"Yes, you do—trust me. You need an escort." His authoritarian air set her teeth on edge. She didn't like it, but never lacking in common sense she took their advice about accepting an escort and letting the bar-owners think they were doing her a favor. Besides, she had wanted to meet this sheriff and give him a piece of her mind. She might even get a chance to ask him a few questions.

She had started the late afternoon by just wanting a cold beer after a long, hard, hot day of work. She hadn't had time to enjoy much of one before Shorty tried to start something. She ended up getting a whole lot more than she had bargained for. Maybe an escort home wasn't such a bad idea, she thought as she waited for him to get there enjoying the beer Botticelli bought her.

Franco insisted she stay in the back room with him and Botticelli while she waited for the sheriff to arrive. And even though the late afternoon had started out badly, she ended up making two new friends by the time the sheriff arrived shortly after 9 p.m.

As Franco introduced the sheriff to Sam, he hid his surprise that the sheriff himself showed up and not one of his deputies. He preferred Gilbert to any of his deputies anyway, so he was confident the dame would get home safely, although he couldn't figure out why he gave a damn if she did or not.

Sheriff Skip Gilbert found himself right where he wanted to be that night. He had heard of Samantha Egar, many times. Local trappers kept complaining about her to him, saying she was removing their traps pretty regular. He suspected that if enough complaints were filled, many hoped she'd be driven to move away and they'd be rid of her. He often wondered if she'd crack under the pressure. When the call came in from Tony's, on an impulse he had answered it in person; something he rarely did.

As he drove to the bar, Skip Gilbert decided to follow Samantha Egar all the way to her house just to make sure she got there, then inside, safely. After all, she had a lot of enemies. He also hoped to gauge her character by talking to her in person. Was she what everyone said she was—a meddling bitch? He doubted it. All he knew for sure was that she was getting threatening notes left in her mailbox, but that she hadn't made any.

She had called his office often enough about the notes. Everyone there knew about them. She had been calling for months complaining. Each time she did, she talked to a different officer about the downright nasty, handwritten, threatening notes that were being stuffed inside her mailbox almost daily. None of these notes had postmarks, so she reasoned that whoever was leaving them had been hand delivering them. Gilbert thought that her guess was as good as any he or his officers had made, but he also knew that few of his men would ever acknowledge that, especially Gene Trelavonti.

When Trelavonti took a call from her, as soon as he hung up he derided her all around the office. The other officers loved it, apparently as they laughed at most every vile thing that came out of Trelavonti's mouth about her. Gilbert wasn't happy with the situation. She had a right to protection even if she wasn't born on the Range. She also had a right to protection even if she was a woman working in a man's world.

To make matters worse, she lived so far out in the country the mail carrier wasn't allowed to drive all the way back on River Drive to her driveway to deposit her mail. She had to post a mailbox over a mile west of her house at the last turnaround. The mile drive on the dirt road into her house usually wasn't drive-able in the spring; it got rutted up real bad with frost boils breaking through the roadway threatening to swallow any wheel bold enough to cross them. To top all that off, most folks living that far out had to fight tooth and nail just to get the county to plow the road in the winter. Consequently, no one lived near enough to her mailbox to keep an eye on it for her.

Gilbert knew she figured the threatening notes were from a local trapper. He also knew that because her farm was so isolated, she worried about the seriousness of the threats, which told him she had some common sense. A damn site more than Trelavonti, he thought.

He suspected that the angry trappers calling about their traps were telling the truth, too; their traps were being pulled; but he didn't believe Egar was the one doing it. She had to be smart, he reasoned; she was a wildlife biologist after all. Wouldn't she know the difference between a legal and illegal trap?

As he escorted her home, Gilbert kept his eyes on the taillights of her truck while they drove out to River Drive. He checked his rear view mirror watching for anything unusual once they were away from city lights. When the only lights twinkling were those of the stars, he turned his attention back to the Ranger 4X4 in front of him. A taillight was out. It didn't look like much of a truck to him. "You'd think a scientist would make enough money to buy a decent truck," he said to the empty seat beside him. "Jeez, that thing looks like it's about ready to fall apart!"

He watched the road, took in the surroundings as he drove, ever the policeman scanning his environment for signs of danger. The road was in pretty good shape. He knew it well enough to watch for the bad spots prone to potholes.

The police radio crackled and groaned as Harriet Hornblower's voice called out: "Sheriff, you out there? Your dad's been trying to call you!" She said in a tone designed to riddle him with guilt.

Harriet wasn't happy about working for Skip Gilbert; she preferred the former sheriff, Skip's father, Stan. Most of his deputies did, too. It was an uphill battle for Skip to gain their respect and he kept telling himself that they just had to get used to him. It had only been three months since his dad retired. He was both irritated and proud of the fact that the deputies liked his father so much. Still, it made his job tough.

He joined the sheriff's department just out of college, but had worked in central Minnesota for most of his career. Until his father's retirement, no job openings in St. Louis County had come available. He would have loved to work with his father. It would have made his transition to sheriff in the county easier, too, but what could he do? Things were the way they were.

The radio crackled as he picked up the receiver and told Harriet he got her message. He turned off River Drive and onto Samantha's driveway.

There it was. The house he had heard so much about. He was real interested in Sam's house for a number of reasons, but mainly because it was a thing of legend. He'd heard lots of rumors about it. Haunted, most folks thought. He wondered if she knew that. He admitted to himself, as he drove up the driveway that he was just as curious about her haunted house as he was about her. He pulled up behind Sam, shut the squad car off, turned out the lights, and stepped out of his vehicle.

Sam was already at the front door. "You don't have to follow me in, sheriff; it looks like everything's OK."

"If you don't mind, I'll just check things out before you go in," Gilbert wasn't asking permission. He edged in front of her stepping into the small foyer knowing there was a good possibility that something might be wrong and it was his duty to make sure she'd be alright before he left.

That wasn't such a good idea as far as Fuzz was concerned. Sam's little mongrel dog expected to see her walk through the front door and when she didn't, and a stranger did, he bared his teeth and went for the sheriff's pant leg. Amid the dog's yelps and howls, and the sheriff's screams for help as he tried to dislodge the feisty little mutt from his trouser leg; Sam stumbled into the foyer doubled over with laughter.

"Call your dog off lady!" Gilbert shouted. "Call him off or I'll hit him!" He was already going for the Billy club in his service belt.

"Fuzz, get out of there!" The dog let go of the sheriff's leg and ran behind Sam's legs still growling, barking, and snapping his teeth in the sheriff's direction. Occasionally he ran out from behind her, yipping at Gilbert, then retreating back as fast as he could move.

"Really, sheriff, you're going to hit a tiny little dog with that? Don't you think you're big enough to handle him on your own?" Sam was no longer laughing.

Exasperated, Gilbert had already put in a long day. He didn't need anymore headaches. It was only 9:30 p.m., but to him it felt like a week had passed since he slept last. He had been working straight the past 24 hours on what he suspected was child abduction, this time a young girl, and his investigation efforts weren't getting him anywhere. There had been a number of child abductions in St. Louis County over the last 30 years, young girls and boys, and this one "felt" like it was connected. He didn't like it.

After all that, he sure as hell wasn't going to let this particular single woman, someone who had already irritated a lot of folks, go into her house alone after an altercation with Shorty Kivimaki. It wasn't wise, even if she did own a sorry assed mutt who bit him.

"I'm sorry Ma'am. The dog gave me a fright. Got bit once, bad, as a kid, had this thing about dogs ever since. I didn't mean to overreact."

He looked truly chagrined to Sam. He also looked tired. "Well, I'll forgive you. Fuzz must have caught you by surprise."

"He did Ma'am. I didn't know you had a dog. But since I'm here anyway, maybe I should have a look around before I leave. It can't hurt, and by the way, he may be fierce," Gilbert pointed at Fuzz who still growled at him, "but I doubt if he'd scare away too many intruders—once they got a good look at him, that is."

Sam smiled. She pointed to the steps leading upstairs and those to the basement, told Gilbert to go ahead and look over the house as she went into the kitchen to make coffee, picking up Fuzz and taking him with her as she went.

When he finished, Gilbert found his way into the kitchen by following the scent of fresh brewed coffee. He removed his hat, and slowly walked into the room, hoping beyond hope that she would offer him a cup. He needed it "Your house checks out fine Ma'am. No-one else is inside."

"Why don't you call me Sam, Sheriff? Everyone else does"

"Skip Gilbert, Ma'am, ah, I mean Sam—Skip."

"Would you like some coffee, Mr . . . .? err, Sheriff." When he nodded his head yes, Sam poured him a cup and sat it down on the table opposite her. Gilbert remained standing until she motioned to him to sit down and join her.

"Them trappers, the local guys? Well, they really aren't to be taken too lightly Ma'am . . . err, Sam," he said as he stirred milk into the cup. "You know Shorty can be downright dangerous sometimes. I personally have busted him for assault. And most trappers don't take too kindly to you removing their beaver traps, either."

"Beaver traps? Who is removing beaver traps? I've only pulled wolf traps. You mean to tell me those idiots don't know the difference?"

"They aren't 'idiots' Ma'am," Gilbert snapped, surprised by his own outburst. "You may be a scientist and spend all your time out there in the woods, but so do they. They may not have your college degree, but they know just as much about the outdoors as you do, and a little more, I'd wager." Gilbert said scathingly.

"I'm sorry. You're right; I go off half cocked sometimes. And it's getting so tense out there in the woods that I want to lash out at someone. Forgive me, and don't tell them I called them 'idiots.' I really don't think they are, you know. But you might want to note that the only traps I'm pulling are wolf traps. I don't know anything about any beaver traps."

"Enough said, and I'll look into it." Gilbert fussed internally about asking her deciding to go ahead and come right out with it. "Err, Sam, you know, there are a lot of rumors about this place, your house I mean, I've heard all kinds of stories about it being haunted and all, ever since I was a kid. You find those stories true?"

"Sheriff! I have a hard time believing that you would entertain ideas of haunted houses!" Sam feigned great surprise to mask the fact that she really was surprised to have him ask such a question. She had learned from the Spencers that many believed her house was haunted, but to have the sheriff asking about it—

somehow that made it seem worse. She hadn't known there were haunted house rumors about her farm before she bought it. The real estate agent's funny attitude toward the place popped into her mind and she realized for the first time why he had acted so oddly about the place.

"It's not so much that I believe, Sam, it's just that, well, I've heard stories."

Gilbert was fishing, hoping to land a whopper, Sam could tell. "Well you know," she looked around the room to make sure no-one else was listening, "I've seen things . . . lots of things . . . things that can't be explained?"

Dealing with as many people as Gilbert dealt with over the years, he knew a whopper when he was about to hear one. He didn't interrupt.

Sam continued: "It starts at midnight, the clock, the grandfather clock in the hall? It gets louder and louder as the seconds tick off towards half past midnight. That's when I hear chains rattling and groaning noises coming from all over the house. That's when the windows start opening and shutting. And once, a friend and I were playing with the Ouija board and it told us that the entity haunting this place was the devil himself? Can you believe that?"

"Yeah, and I think that right now the devil is sitting right across from me."

Sam laughed. At least he's not dumb, she thought. "Yes, sheriff, the truth is that there is something strange about this place," she said in all seriousness, "and I wouldn't be surprised to find it is haunted, whatever that means."

Gilbert just looked at her. "Are you all right here by yourself?"

"Yes, I'm fine. I have a lot of friends to go to if I need to get out of here."

"Maybe we can find some help for you and this house," he said as he picked up his hat and walked to the kitchen door. He had no clue as to what kind of help she would need. He stepped onto the back steps and descended into the back yard.

"Thank you sheriff, I don't know what kind of help a haunted house can get, but it was real nice of you to offer—it was also nice meeting you, too." Sam closed the door behind him and shut out the lights. She sat back down at the kitchen table and watched through the kitchen window as Gilbert walked over the backyard checking out the hedges. She smiled then went upstairs to bed.

The sheriff's questions about her house had unnerved her, though.

Chapter Five

Still sipping her morning coffee, Sam spent a lot of time thinking about Angie, knowing she wouldn't arrive until sometime the next afternoon as she was coming all the way from Fargo, North Dakota.

Slow to start the day, she finally got dressed and donned a pair of cross-country skies for her travels into the neighboring woods. She would work behind the Spencer sister's house once again, so she planned to stop in for a visit.

Gladys and Inez sat on their all season front porch rocking away in wicker rockers in comfortable silence. Neither one chose to break it with conversation until Sam opened the porch door behind them and said, "Hello. I was working out back there and thought I'd drop in and see how you were doing.

"Hello dear! Please come on up here and sit." Gladys got up and went inside the house. "I'll bring out some tea," she said as she opened the screen door and went into the kitchen.

"Aren't you two a little cold sitting out here in January?" Sam worried they might catch pneumonia.

"What's going on over there?" Inez asked as she stood up wiping her hands on a hand towel she had stuck in the waistband of her apron, irritated by Sam's show of concern. It always irritated her when younger people assumed she was so feeble minded she didn't know how to take care of herself in cold weather.

"What are you talking about?" Sam asked, surprised. Inez looked so angry.

"I'm talking about your house, dear, your house. What's going on over there? And please, don't play innocent with me. It'll never work."

Sam blurted, "I've been hearing noises . . . I think. But really, it's just my imagination. I thought I saw something, too." Her voice trailed off as she finished speaking.

"Humph! That must have really been something! I saw you. I saw you cowering beneath the covers with Mutt and Jeff on the bed with you. Who do you think you're fooling?'

"What do you mean, 'you saw me?' How could you have seen me?"

At that moment, Gladys stepped back out onto the porch with hot tea for everyone. "Here, Samantha, you take the big mug. Have a bar, too. You must be famished, working out in the cold all afternoon."

Gladys heard what Inez had told Sam, adding, "You mustn't be too afraid of Inez here; she sees things in her dreams. It's the damnedest thing, but she's kept the two of us out of some serious trouble over the years with them dreams of hers. I tell you, if she has something to say you really ought to listen."

Sam sipped her tea staring at her companions, who stared right back at her.

"It's that house," Inez said without preamble. "It wants you there. Something is going on inside it that has a direct correlation to you and another woman. She's coming. She's a dreamer too. When she gets here, I want to meet her. She's a powerful dreamer—like me."

Sam shivered, but not from the cold. The Spencer sisters had no way of knowing about Angie or the fact that she was coming for a visit. Sam had never mentioned Angie to them.

"She is powerful," she confessed to Inez, "and when she gets here, I'll make sure the two of you meet. Her name is Angie Eckenridge and she's an old friend of mine from college. You and she were meant to meet," she said staring at Inez.

Inez reminded Sam of Angie's way of "knowing" things. It was unnerving in college when Angie, out of the blue, would say what Sam had been thinking or feeling. To find that her new friends, too, "knew" things, was also unnerving.

The sisters offered Sam a ride home that afternoon, which she accepted. She was tired. It was beginning to snow and she anxiously awaited Angie's arrival. Visiting the Spencers was an excuse not to go home when she knew she couldn't concentrate on paperwork, or much of anything else. She didn't want to be home alone for too long even though not much happened lately. Still, she never knew when plates would start flying out of the cupboards or knifes from across the room.

"Don't worry too much about Inez, dear," Gladys confided in Sam when Inez went into the house to retrieve their coats. "She sees things, but like I said, she's kept us from serious harm over the years. I know she wants to do the same for you."

On the drive home Gladys, who always rode along with Inez wherever she went, told Sam the story of her house reiterating much of what Clem Johnson had already told her. But the story had mythologized over the years, so Gladys wasn't too sure what exactly did happen and what was myth, but the house had gained notoriety for certain.

As the three women rode in Inez's black, 1965 Pontiac Tempest, Sam told them of how she came across the farm, smiling as they turned onto River Drive and the glass packs on Inez's Tempest rumbled. She was more than a little surprised. She never pictured them owning a car much less a muscle car in mint condition that looked and sounded like it belonged in the garage of a sixteen-year-old during the 1960's. Inez confided, "Nice, isn't it? It is in original condition. I know because I bought it brand new and have had it ever since," she winked at Sam in the rear view mirror.

When asked as they rode, Sam told the women that when she found her house she had been out scouting for a likely place to continue her research; she hadn't been looking for a house. The pack of wolves she had been studying died; a truck hit one as it was trying to cross Highway 53, while the other fell into a mine pit one thousand feet deep and broke its legs dying slowly of starvation and infection. Sam accidentally found that cub in the spring while hiking in the mine pits just outside of Virginia, four miles north of Eveleth. The cub's body had decomposed, so she sent it to the University of Minnesota to have it analyzed. She had to know if an irate hunter had killed it, but the autopsy showed the animal had died from the after effects of the fall. Even the alpha male had disappeared that year.

With the loss of the two cubs from the previous season, the alpha female had to have been alone when she denned up that spring. Because the alpha female stays with her litter for three weeks after giving birth, without the rest of the pack to feed her, Sam guessed she and the litter had died, too. Sam never found her; she never found the male, either. She hadn't seen any of the pack by mid-summer and had almost given up hope of ever seeing them again, although she continued to search for them off and on over the fall and winter.

That was why she was out looking for a new research site that beautiful spring day. She had driven south of Eveleth about twenty miles finding the area surrounding River Drive had retained its pristine wilderness, and thought it a likely place to find wolves. Warm breezes wafted pine and fresh grass scents through her open window as she drove along the old dirt road that day. Her old Ford Ranger 4x4 quietly took her back through willow brush covered lumber roads next to the St. Louis River, and on back up onto River Drive where she continued traveling east. That's when she came upon the farm that felt so much like home from the first moment she laid eyes on it.

The house, as they knew, stands back from the road a quarter -mile, but is clearly visible from River Drive. Two old northern pines stand sentry at the driveway entrance. They appear to hold court over the graceful willows that line the rest of the drive. Willow Creek runs south to north through the property emptying into the St. Louis River just north of the farm boarders a half-mile. The house stands amid apple, Northern pine, blue spruce, willow trees and lilac bushes, and for the life of her, Sam couldn't understand why no one else had ever been as smitten with the farm's beauty as she was. But of course, at the time, she knew nothing of the strange goings on.

She fell in love with the rolling hills, creek, fields, timber lined property boarders, and buildings immediately. When she walked up the drive that first afternoon, it was as though she had walked it many times before, as though she were meant to be there.

The long, unattended lawn was brown with dead vegetation and still frozen over with winter's frost when Sam first saw it. But she didn't see that or the debris that had accumulated outside next to the out buildings, or that some of the trees in the pine grove to the north were dead and falling down. She saw green expanses, lilacs in bloom, and a vegetable garden. She saw fresh paint on everything, and a back yard fit for a queen with cobblestones and plants, lots and lots of plants.

Since the door to the house was unlocked and no one was around, she went inside seeing it, too, as it could be not as it was. With color on the walls, a new tile floor throughout the kitchen, patio doors leading to the back yard and a good scrubbing she had completely redesigned the interior the minute she stepped over the threshold. She proceeded to look throughout the house. It was eerily familiar.

And even though she was imagining how it could be, she forced herself to look at it as it was, finding no room for complaint. With a little elbow grease, it would be lovely.

There was no for sale sign posted on the property that day. But when she drove past the farm only one week later there was one at the end of the driveway, so Sam immediately called the realtor who placed it. The box style, four-story farmhouse with one hundred twenty acres of land and outbuildings in good shape, was selling for a fraction of what it was worth, she learned.

Amazed at the asking price, she was not about to question her good luck, she told the sisters. Luck was how she saw it; finding the house the way she did and having it cost next to nothing. She'd been saving for a house for years.

When she talked to the realtor, Sam Snide, about the farm, he had acted peculiar, she recalled to the sisters. Snide was pleasant and welcoming when she told him she was interested in a property he represented, up until she told him which property.

Of course, Snide knew about the rumors, knew who owned the place and had nothing but praise for Arthur Noone. Yet as he spoke, he avoided looking Sam in the eyes. He acted as if he were lying, or misleading her about something. But when it came to the farm, Snide was animated. He confided to her that Noone had just placed it up for sale with him that week and that he had counseled Noone that he could get much more for it than he was asking.

She kept her excitement in check. She didn't want Snide thinking she was too eager, but she did tell him she was very interested writing out a check for earnest money. She took two days to mull over what she was considering, and found no argument with any merit against buying the place. The farm was empty, she paid cash, and though the legal proceedings had not concluded, she was moved in by March 1.

Sam learned at the close of the sale that Arthur Noone lived just down the road from her new farm, two-and-one half miles. She didn't think anything of it at the time, although she wondered why Snide hadn't mentioned that fact until the deal was done. She forgot about Noone as soon as she got into the house.

In less than a month she felt like she had always lived there and all during that time, nothing really eerie had happened, she said to the sisters, although at times her pets acted strangely.

As she talked, Inez drove so slowly Sam was pretty sure she could walk home faster than they were moving, but she didn't really mind. She was in no hurry to get home. The slow speed gave her ample time to fill the sisters in on those first moments in her new house.

The sisters sat silently as Sam continued to tell them that her favorite time of day inside the house was at night. She chose the upstairs, east facing bedroom for herself from which she often sat looking up at the stars in the night sky. She felt as good in her bedroom staring out the large windows as she did when she was camped out under the skies in a tent.

During the day she wandered the fields, learned the lay of the land, and looked for traces of wolf scat or kill. She started at the creek with its borders of heavy willow brush. She traveled the hills, wandered the bordering forests, all the while watching for wolf sign. She was overjoyed when she first discovered some on her own property. It was up in the Cedar swamp at the far-eastern border and looked like an old dening site.

She also saw sign of deer, bear, brush wolves (coyotes), and what she thought might be a mountain lion. She saw where a moose had used the trees to brush at its antlers, and sign of rabbit, fox, and many kinds of birds, including an eagle. She listened to the sounds of the birds, the quiet of nature and drank in the smells of the earth, the fresh air.

The Spencer sisters listened quietly as Sam described the property. It was as if they were walking its expanses right along with her.

Sam told the sisters about the fish in the creek, that the soil was good for planting, and that the fields would be good for hay stumpage in years to come. She noticed that no noises from the outside world penetrated the farm's recesses except for an occasional over-flying airplane. It felt as if she were alone in the world. She loved it.

Sam also told the ladies about some of the challenges she faced since moving to the Iron Range. One of which being the threatening notes left in her mailbox.

"You're kidding!" Gladys said turning in her seat to look Sam in the eye. Sam was leaning on the back of the front seat as she talked, so when Gladys turned, they were nose to nose. "Why didn't you tell us about that?"

"What good would that have done?" I thought it might frighten you."

"Frighten us! Hmmppphh!" Inez said with disgust. "You heard what we did for a living in our youth? You honestly think something like that is gonna scare us? I don't know who to be mad at, the one leaving the notes, or you for thinking we are such big chicken shits!"

"Sorry," Sam said feeling chagrined.

"Look here, kid. We know more about how bad it can get around here for women than anybody does," Inez went on. "It didn't take us long to learn that Iron Range men, in general, have few qualms about using violence to control women. Beatings are so common most men see it as their right. Them good old boy Range men ain't too keen on women butting into affairs they think reserved for them, none neither, like hunting and trapping, if you get my drift. Heard some of their opinions about wolves too, and they ain't looking at conservation none.

Rangers ain't too keen on strangers, neither. They'll call you a "pack sacker" in a minute if you weren't born and raised here."

"Personally, I blame the iron ore mining industry for most of that," Gladys said. "And most men up here work at the mines. Take that one in Eveleth for instance. Don't that look like an erect penis to you?" They all laughed at the image. "Yeah, and it spews orange soot like seed out over everything, even the graveyard down below it, let me tell you! What it is, is a steel fisted bully that seems determined to control all it surveys. Seems to me, those companies want the men's lives from birth to death; then they work at tearing them apart, one shovel full at a time, until any man working there becomes a steel like automaton, cast in iron and steel." Gladys was on a roll; she got angry just thinking about it. Many miners had been her customers over the years and she knew intimately what effect the mines had on them.

"Brother Structures are planted all over the Range, all of which ensnare young men into their bellies with the lure of good income and benefits. Once in, most rarely escape, becoming dedicated to the Company who, in turn, incites fear with threats of job loss and layoffs while wailing about small profit margins and imported steel." Gladys took a long deep breath. She wasn't finished.

"Most mines wouldn't hire women up until sometime in the 1970s when women gained some equal rights, forcing the mines to open their doors. Even so, a lot of guys worked to make women regret coming there. They harassed them with sexual innuendo and veiled threats of violence, including rape. Men didn't want women working where they worked or earning the same wages they earned, and the mining companies encouraged their bad behavior because they didn't want the women there, either." Gladys seemed to be finished.

She didn't say it but Sam guessed that she and Inez had been victims of some of that violence. Gladys also didn't mention, nor did Inez, that they bankrolled a lawsuit against the mines supporting the women who had gone through many of the terrors they just told her about. She learned that later from Bernice.

"So, the next time you got troubles; you talk to us. We have more clout than you might think. Now, go on with your story." Inez never took her eyes off the road although she still wasn't driving any faster than 10 mph.

Sam told them then of the crying noises, how they frightened her, how the house felt like it was under a cloud of sorrow. She told them of her pets and how they acted real strange whenever anything occurred.

The sisters just shook their heads. By the time they reached Sam's driveway, no one in the car was speaking. It dawned on Sam as they drove up her driveway, that she had made friends with most of her new neighbors, yet none of them had ever called on her, or dropped by her house for a cup of coffee and a visit. She decided that should change, so as they pulled up in the circular part of the driveway next to the house, Sam asked the women in.

"No, dear, we don't have time today. Maybe after your friend gets her," Inez said.

"Are you sure you aren't afraid of my house?" Sam asked as she pulled the door handle and the back door opened.

"Now, you needn't think anything like that," Inez said, "but I will tell you this. I do pick up on things, more than just dreaming . . . you know?" Sam had spent so much time with Angie, she did know, and nodded her head yes. Inez continued, "Well, I ain't ready to go in there. Gladys here has been pestering me about it for years, because of the rumors, you know. But I know this. There are spirits in this world and some of them shouldn't be messed with. Demons? You understand? I know we give Bernice some flack about God and all, but it's Him that needs to be working in this house. I don't know enough about demons to try and drive them out. Hell, I don't even know if it's demons you got! Maybe you got some tormented soul in there that needs some relief, but I ain't equipped to handle that, neither. My sister," Inez patted Gladys' arm, "and I have gone through so much in our lives, I can't bring nothing sinister to us now. We actually live in peace most of the time. I intend to keep it that way."

Inez paused then turned around in the seat to look at Sam. "But you got that friend coming and something tells me if she's here, too, I can come in. Sounds strange, don't it?"

Gladys patted Inez's arm and said, "In the meantime, you be careful in there and you call us if anything goes wrong. We'll get over here as fast as we can and take you outta here; we can do that. We got some powerful friends, too, so if you need help with any of them trappers, or old Noone himself, you just let us know. We'll sick the hounds on them." Gladys looked like she'd love to pick a fight with Noone.

Disappointed, Sam stepped out of the car, and stood for a long time in her driveway watching as the Spencer sisters turned their car slowly around and headed back toward home. When they were out of sight, Sam turned and looked at her house. She thought she saw a face in the kitchen window. She rubbed her eyes and looked again. Nothing.

Chapter Six

Biting cold hung in the air the afternoon of Angie's arrival. It was colder than it had been all season, and even though the sun beamed in through the all-season porch windows where Angie and Sam sat eating dinner, Sam knew it was all an illusion. Sure the sun beamed and the heated porch was warm, but the sun this time of year was deceitful.

The windows offered views of the east fields more pristine than Angie had ever seen as the two women ate and enjoyed quiet conversation. Weathercasters had predicted a warm up late that afternoon and possibly some snow showers. Toward the end of their meal, the women watched as clouds covered the horizon and the first flakes of the predicted snowfall fell gently across the land.

A white-tailed deer appeared on the hill by the creek pawing at the snow-covered ground and nibbling grasses that lay buried beneath. The women sipped wine within the warm confines of the porch watching in silence. While eating, the animal edged closer up the hill toward the house. The doe, colored the dirty brown of winter, had a spotted fawn at her side, small, and fragile looking. It had been born late in the season.

As the women watched the doe put her ears flat against the sides of her head. Sam told Angie she was agitated, but she couldn't see why. She sat forward on her white wicker chair gazing hard out the window, setting her wineglass on the floor in front of her, peering out trying to locate the source of the doe's agitation.

Then she saw it, a form she was intimately familiar with. A lone timber wolf skulked over the hard packed, drifted snow, slowly toward the pair of deer. The doe lowered her head pounding her front hoofs into the ground as a warning. The wolf paid no attention. He came in closer. She struck out at him as he approached from the left, but missed her mark. The wolf lured her out further into deeper snow as she attempted to strike him twice more, each time missing because of his lightning quick agility.

As the wolf and doe tangoed across the deeply drifted hillside, the fawn fought to stay close to its mother, straying further and further away floundering in the deep snow. When the doe was far enough away from her fawn for the wolf to reach it safely, the wolf moved swiftly over the top of the snowdrifts to grab the bleating baby into its steel trap like jaws. With jaw strength capable of crushing fifteen hundred pounds, the wolf made short, easy work of the fawn.

The doe, now winded and exhausted from her struggle, couldn't navigate the deep snow quick enough to reach her fawn. Too tired to move, she stood staring, her tongue lolling from her mouth, panting, as the wolf gracefully scampered off, hastily scurrying out of danger with its meal, the fawn's bleating silenced.

Angie jumped up, exclaiming, "Why don't you do something to stop that? Shot that thing!"

"In the first place, the wolf didn't do anything other than survive!" Sam stood up with hands on hips, spitting words out with such ferocity Angie sat back down. It was an old argument; one Sam was tired of having. "He's feeding himself. Period. In the second place, that fawn had little chance of surviving a Minnesota winter, anyway."

"It was so cute. We should have done something!"

"When man interferes with nature there is always a problem. Leave it alone. The wolf is doing nothing other that what it has been created to do. Weed out the herd."

"I don't see why they can't be stopped from killing innocent little babies!"

"That baby would have died anyway. It was born way too late in the season to have ever survived the winter."

"I know you have guns. Why didn't you shoot it?"

"Are you listening? Why should I kill it? Just because it kills?"

"We should protect the deer!"

"We do. There are more deer in Minnesota right now than there were in the entire country at the time it was settled. People should quit taking care of them."

"Quit? What kind of person are you?"

"A good one! Man keeps interfering with nature, disrupting the balance. They think they know more than nature knows. They're wrong! It's got to stop."

"Mankind does the humane thing. You didn't."

"Don't you accuse me of anything. How do you know what I've done? You've been here all of an hour and already you're judging me? I study wildlife; maybe I know a little bit about what I'm talking about here. And since when does man do the humane thing? They haven't done the humane thing since the beginning of time!"

"I still think you should have done something to stop that wolf. It was cruel."

"Nature is not cruel; it just is. Man is cruel."

"Yes, I agree."

Angie had hit a nerve. Sam couldn't remember a time when she didn't love nature and all forms of wildlife. She knew from the time she was a little girl that working with animals would be her life's work. She had studied animal behavior diligently for more than twenty years. People always got upset after seeing a predator take its prey. Sam wondered if it was just human nature. Humans always seemed to attribute "evil" motives to predators. Predators did only what they were programmed to do, feed themselves. She was also no fool; knowing that once in a great while animals behaved unnaturally, went on a killing rampages, bears and wolves in particular, killing much more than they could consume, but it was rare. But didn't humans do the same? The only difference was that humans no longer had to kill to survive. They had to invent reasons to kill. Something they are very good at.

"Alright—I'm sorry I brought it up." Angie reconsidered her argument. She gave Sam a sidelong look. "The wolves really mean a lot to you, don't they?"

"All animals do. Deer included. I get upset when we, as humans, upset the balance of nature. Denying the predator the right to be what it is is wrong. That's the bottom line," Sam said picking up her water glass and taking a long draw from it. She chided herself for her outburst and flash of anger trying to bring her passion under control. "But wolves aren't why you're here. They are my area of expertise. You're here to help me with your area of expertise—haunting." She fought to keep her tongue under control, but failed.

Angie answered coolly, saying, "Yes, I am."

These types of fights were not uncommon between the two. Neither one had had such an argument in so long they had forgotten how badly they could irritate one another.

They finished out the remainder of the evening in silence. They were cordial when they went to bed, but barely. Sam tried in vain to smooth over the altercation, but her efforts were half-hearted and stifled. It was not an easy evening.

The next day, Sam went into the woods early planning to stay overnight. Angie was still asleep when she left and she was glad of it. Maybe a few hours apart were what they needed. She remembered how that had always worked in college. She couldn't believe how easily they had slipped into their old pattern of behavior. How long had it been since they had visited for any length of time? She couldn't even remember.

As she hiked through the woods, across fields, and through gulleys, a feeling of unease settled inside her chest. For some reason the fields, woods, and landscape felt eerie. She felt like she was being watched, and it wasn't the first time. As she trekked on, she saw smoke tendrils rising up over by a grove of pine trees she was approaching. When she reached the grove, she found a discarded cigarette butt still smoldering. Whoever had smoked it had to be out there with her. Was it an irate trapper? She made a one hundred eighty-degree turn slowly taking in everything that surrounded her. That wasn't the first time she had found signs indicating she wasn't alone in the woods like she thought she had been. Uneasiness settled over her, and she got jumpy being startled at the tiniest of noises. She walked on, quickly turning to check and see if anything was behind her; she did this often.

Sam forced herself to think of Angie. She had completely forgotten how they used to argue in college. How could she have dismissed that from her mind so completely? Did Angie remember? Was she still angry? She doubted it. They used to forgive one another pretty quickly without ever apologizing.

By late afternoon, she was comfortable enough to take a break to listen to a weather report, which was calling for severe cold. She was still uneasy in her surroundings, so she packed up and headed for home thankful to use the weather as an excuse to get out of the woods. But as a seasoned camper, she knew how to care for herself out of doors even in severe winter weather. She always backpacked a tent, small stove, extra warm clothes, a radio, and other supplies to keep her warm a few days in case of an unexpected blizzard. Though she had those things with her, she wanted to go home, get out of the woods, and make sure Angie wasn't still angry with her.

The snow was deep and the going tough. Periodically she took off her snowshoes to scramble over brambles full of fallen branches and other forest floor debris, slowing her down considerably. When she cleared the deep forest, she snow shoed over snow filled depressions at the bottom of step hills and up over wind-blown, snow-barren hilltops.

She worked up a sweat and looked forward to a hot shower and sleep in her own bed when she got home. She was happy knowing that Angie was there and that she wouldn't be alone even if they did have an argument the day before. She shook her head at the thought and smiled thinking about how things hadn't changed much between them even with the extended separation.

Sam wondered what Angie had been up to in her absence. Angie's clinical, objective approach to everything she found comforting under the circumstances. She didn't know how one applied clinical research methods to paranormal investigation, but she was sure if anyone could do it, it was Angie.

Angie always did love a good mystery, she remembered as she made her way up a steep hillock. Angie told her once that she couldn't remember a time when she wasn't reading about ghosts and haunted houses. She was only twelve when she stopped reading fiction and began reading true case histories. It was about that time, too, that she started to dream.

She told Sam, that once as she sat at her family's kitchen table eating dinner with her mother, father and six siblings, she had a vision. While looking at her mother, her mother's appearance changed. In an instant, Angie knew that the woman sitting across from her at the kitchen table wasn't her biological mother, but she never worked up the courage to ask her mother about it. She told Sam she was afraid of the answer.

Angie couldn't hold Sam's thoughts forever, however. She was weary, but she also knew she was close to home, which kept her going. She crossed the last hill before reaching her house walking up through the grove of pine trees where the snow wasn't as deep. When she reached the porch, she plopped down on the snow filled steps to take off her snowshoes. She pulled herself up climbing the stairs while her leg muscles screamed in agony from beneath her heavy clothing. She took off her heavy backpack dropping it next to the back door on the porch. Her outer garments came off slowly with each aching muscle in her body protesting any and all movement. She slowly hung her jacket and pants on hooks inside the back door, right off the porch. Already the heat of the house warmed her. She was glad to be home.

"Hey girl! It's good to have you back!" Angie said warmly as Sam crossed the threshold into the kitchen, the argument of yesterday already forgotten. They hugged. "Damn, it's good to have you here!" Sam said. She smelled fresh coffee and eyed the cups of steaming brew sitting on the table. "You must have seen me coming! Is that a latte?"

"I did and it is. Boy, have we got a lot to talk about," Angie winked and pointed around the room. There was camera equipment everywhere. By the time Angie showed Sam all she had done, it is 6 p.m.

The fresh air, exertion and early Minnesota middle winter darkness combined to make Sam want to crawl into bed and fall blissfully to sleep, but the latte was not only delicious, it kept her alert.

"I know you're tired, Sam, but we should get started. Why wait any longer? The first thing I'd like to know about is your dreams." Sam clutched her coffee cup so tightly her knuckles were white as Angie sat down across the table from her anticipating her every word.

Angie noted that Sam seemed tense guessing she probably didn't want to talk about her dreams. She had seen that often at the office. Most people don't take dreaming seriously. But dreams often reveal things the dreamer can't face while awake, or things their conscious mind has buried, but their unconscious mind works hard to reveal hidden truths to them. People tend to block out fears they don't understand, as well. Their dreams, then, become an avenue whereby they can learn how to deal with their dilemmas. All they have to do is relax and recall the dream then let the solution reveal itself.

Angie held to the theory that people's déjà vu experiences first manifest to them in dreams. Though the dreamer rarely recalls their dream upon awakening, in the future they find themselves in the midst of a scene that had been shown them in a dream. That's why when in the grasp of a déjà vu experience, they usually can't recall exactly where they had experienced the same thing once before. Angie hoped to use Sam's dreams as a tool to clear up the mystery surrounding her house. She felt sure Sam was repressing something important . . . if she could only get her to open up.

Sam relaxed saying, "The dream I have most often is about a man," she said. "He beckons me to come with him then shows me things." She told Angie: He calls out to me—holding out his hands as he climbs the basement stairs. I watch as he comes all the way into my bedroom. His mouth is moving, but I can't hear what he is saying. He taps on the walls in a room familiar to me, but foreign just the same. I don't know which room it is but I know it is inside this house. He shows me a picture of his family. A woman, little girls and the man himself (all of whom have blurred faces) stand on the front lawn. The house is behind them. The trees are much smaller, but it is my house. The man's personal history takes on a living dimension. I don't understand, yet I feel part of it in the dream, like I am one of the family. Then the man takes my hand and leads me to the barn. He goes behind a hidden door motioning to me to come with him.

When Sam finished, it was late. She and Angie went upstairs to their separate bedrooms.

Angie contemplated what Sam had told her rehashing it in her mind, searching for clues to help solve the puzzle of the house.

Sam fell fast asleep and into dreaming almost immediately. Just as the man took her hand leading her into the barn once again, she felt herself being shaken.

Angie stood alongside her bed and said, "Did you hear that?"

"Huh—What?" Sam rubbed her eyes trying to focus. She saw Angie standing there in flannel pajamas. What was she doing in her bedroom? Sam finally remembered that Angie was visiting.

"Wake up Samantha! Wake up! You're dreaming; come on, get up!"

Sam sat up in bed looking about the room. The dream had already started to slip away from her. Angie remained quiet—as if she knew Sam was trying to hold onto something. Then little by little the dream crept back into Sam's consciousness.

"What time is it?" She asked.

"One a.m."

"I have to get out to the barn."

Angie didn't argue; she simply asked where Sam kept the flashlights. The moon was full and the night cold.

Outside they were greeted by strong winds tossing the pine tree grove about, which, in turn, cast eerie shadows along the halogen lit brick walkway between the barn and the house. Snow banks towered on either side drifting the walkway in as the wind howled through the trees. Anticipating such events in winter, Sam made sure all roads and pathways were kept clear once winter weather set in, so they found easy passage down to the barn.

"Watch your step here, Angie. The brick is treacherous when covered with snow. It's as slick as all-get-out." The women walked into the wind with their heads bent to protect their faces from the stinging snow. They didn't have to go far to reach the barn.

The days when animals occupied the wooden box stalls inside the barn had long since died away, but the smell of fresh hay lingered inside as the two opened the barn doors. Spiders had taken up residence with a vengeance; their cobwebs clung to everything, harness, doorways, stable walls, and ancient junk that lie strewn about.

Sam planned on turning the barn into an office, a project she decided to start in the following spring. The barn was much the way it had been when she purchased the farm. Because of that, she easily located the area she had seen in her dream.

Immediately she began to clear away debris from in front of what she dreamt would be a library. Junk, consisting of old tires and wood stacked against one wall, they hauled over and placed in front of one of the box stalls. The pair moved the remnants of an old horse drawn buggy to another part of the barn.

Angie followed Sam's lead without question. When finished, the women looked at each other as they gathered their strength to heave a large piece of plywood away from what Sam suspected hid the doorway into the library. They groaned from the weight of the wood and choked on dust and cobwebs sticking to their hair as they inched the wood away from the wall. It had been in the same spot so long, it had attached itself to the dirt and grime that littered the barn floor. After they dislodged it from its grounding moors, the wood moved easily, so much so Angie almost lost her footing as Sam heaved the wood forward. They started laughing. Their laughter stuck in their throats once they saw the doorway.

Sure she had dreamt of a doorway, but dreaming about it and finding it in the natural were two different things. Sam was struck dumb. Never before had a dream of hers come true. Tentatively, she tried the doorknob. With groaning and grumbling, the door gave way opening into a room that was too dark to see into. Each woman stood at the threshold looking in, and calling up her courage to cross and enter.

As she stepped inside, Sam remembered her flashlight, turning it on and running light from the left to the right, quickly, taking it all in. Angie turned hers on, too, and the two got a good look at what had been boarded up for a long, long time.

Before them stood a library full of books, cobwebs and dust, bookcases lined the walls from floor to ceiling, at least ten feet tall, and full of volumes that hadn't been opened in decades. The meager light beams from the flashlights illuminated two big leather chairs in the middle of the room with end tables on either side of each. Lamps stood from behind each chair. Footstools rested in front. Sam moved over to a chair pushing on the seat cushion, testing it for strength and stirring up waves of dust bringing on a bout of coughing. Angie stood alongside her slapping her on the back, trying to help her.

As Sam's coughing subsided, they noted a chest sitting on the floor between them. The same chest Sam had seen in her dream rested slightly left of the chair she stood in front of. When she saw it, she pulled it over in front of the chair sitting down, and trying to open the lid.

"Will you help me?" She asked Angie when the lid wouldn't budge. Angie joined Sam, and together they pushed and pulled until the chest lid creaked open. Sam's hands trembled when the lid finally gave way. Dust spewed up from the chest, choking her again until she had to drop the lid for coughing. Angie pulled a footstool up and sat besides her patting her on the back once again, then opening the chest to look inside after Sam's coughing fit subsided.

Both women, now sitting on the ottomans with their backs to the doorway, were so intent on what they were doing they paid no attention to anything else.

Inside the trunk were all the papers Sam dreamt would be there. Everything was exactly as her dream showed her it would be.

"Hello ladies."

Chapter Seven

Arthur Noone stood silhouetted in the doorway. The shadows were getting worse. He wondered why as he fought for control.

Sam and Angie screamed at the sound of his voice, jumped to their feet, stood side by side, and joined hands as they turned to face the voice that came from behind them. Instinctively Sam let the trunk lid down quietly as she turned while hers and Angie's bodies blocked it from view.

He hoped his gasp was not audible and said, "What are two lovely young women doing out of their house at one a.m. on a night such as this, shifting through an old, dusty barn?" He quickly assessed everything about the women and the room.

"If you want to move heavy items, you really should give me a call Miss Egar—or is it Ms.?"

It took awhile, but Sam regained her composure enough to realize Arthur Noone was on her property in the middle of the night.

"Just what are you doing here?" She didn't bother to disguise the anger in her voice. Angie squeezed her hand hoping Sam would shut up. Her nails cut into Sam's flesh. Sam tore her hand away and stared at Noone.

"You know—I had the strangest feeling something was wrong here. I thought I'd better check—and look what I find."

"Where's your car?"

"Oh, I don't usually drive. I like to keep in shape, you see. You would be amazed at what I can still do. Sixty-one years old in the spring and I can keep up with men more than half my age. I walk everywhere. It keeps me healthy."

The man before Sam belied that fact. He looked good. He looked healthy. He was even handsome for an old man. His tawny brown skin and his once black hair made Sam think he might be Italian, or Spanish, especially when she considered his brown eyes, with gold highlights, which were unreadable spheres that, on anyone else would project warmth and friendliness, but on him reflected nothing.

"I used to come out to this room with the English professor when he lived here. We did a lot of reading together. That must have been about thirty eight years ago. Imagine. The place sure looks like it could use a cleaning. Maybe you ladies would let this old man use the library?"

"I do thank you, Mr. Noone, for your concern with my welfare. But I don't believe there is anything for you to be concerned with. As for the use of the library, we'll see. I hate to make promises I might not be able keep." Sam smiled sweetly as she took Noone's arm and led him to the doorway of the library then out of the barn.

"I'll even see to it that you get home safely." She said sweetly, but firmly as she walked Noone to the garage opening her truck door and unplugging the tank heater motioning to him to get in. He did. She jumped behind the wheel, started the engine and drove Arthur Noone back over the two miles he had traversed to get to her house.

"You know . . . you look a great deal like the man that used to live here. Did you know that? The professor." A delicate smile lightly touched the corners of Noone's lips as he tried to elicit a conversation out of Sam as they rode to his house.

He was telling her something, she knew, but she didn't know what he was really saying so she listened intently.

"Who is that lovely woman I saw with you in the barn?"

Seething, Sam said nothing until they reached his driveway, where she pulled her pick-up over after shifting down into first so the truck would idle smoothly. She said, "That's none of your business, and if I find you anywhere near me or my farm again, without an invitation, I'll put you in jail. Do you understand me?" She said nothing more but stared him in the eye.

He got out of the truck without saying another word. He shut the door and walked off up the access road between his and the Spencer house. As he walked, he contemplated the resemblance between Samantha Egar and the professor. That resemblance was the reason he sold her the place for such a pittance in the first place.

Imagine, he thought, I let her have that place for nothing and she kicks me off of it! She's got a lot of nerve. Then, most women do. She needs a man in her life to teach her right from wrong. The way I hear it she has never been married. It would be interesting . . . teaching her, his thoughts drifted off.

He remembered the day she went into the house that first time. He saw her then. He was in the kitchen pantry behind a closed door. Her resemblance to the professor was so striking he almost gasped when he saw her face that first time. That's what held him back, kept him from opening that pantry door, kept him from touching her, then.

The same thing happened in the woods when he first saw her there. She was pulling his wolf traps and hanging them in the trees. He watched her as she worked keeping himself hidden in alder brush. He couldn't see her face. When she turned around, he did gasp, but she didn't hear him. It was as if an apparition stared back at him, knew he was there, and accused him. Of course, she did not see him. He regained his composure enough to realize that it wasn't the professor that he saw. It was just someone who looked like him; that's all, and that someone was destroying his traps. He'd put a stop to that.

He knew exactly how to teach her a lesson about meddling in his business. That would be easy. That same day he started pulling Shorty Kivimaki's legally set beaver traps. He knew Shorty, although they weren't good friends. He was familiar enough, however, to know Shorty would blame the "pack sacker" for pulling his traps. The newcomer no one knew anything about, the woman who had the temerity to meddle in a man's affairs would be an easy target for him. All he had to do was pit her against the locals and they'd take care of his dirty work for him.

Whenever he could after that day, he managed to get to Shorty, talk to him. He played on Shorty's ego, sympathizing with his loss of income, and talking about the meddling woman out there in the woods. Shorty put it together the way Noone wanted him too, blaming her for his beaver traps.

Noone decided as he walked up to his house that night that he would deal with Samantha Egar in a much more intimate manner. He gently massaged the front of his pants slowly, methodically. When he finished, he cast his eyes toward the Spencer sisters' cabin . . . and smiled.

Back home, Angie was in the kitchen drinking gourmet coffee and reading a journal while smoking a cigarette.

"I didn't know you smoked," Sam said as she walked through the kitchen door. She had never seen Angie light a cigarette in all the time she had known her. It was surprising.

"Don't do it often, only when I'm onto something big." That was all Angie said. In front of her on the kitchen table sat an armload of material from the trunk; a fire burned in the fireplace making the room warm and cozy.

Sam was grateful. For the first time in a long time she felt peaceful inside her own home. Her heart warmed as she looked at her old friend sitting there at her kitchen table petting a dotting dog. Angie was a real comfort. Angie broke that peaceful reverie with, "He's dangerous."

"Noone? Yeah, I think so too, but I don't know why." Sam said sitting down at the table opening a manila envelope as she moved, remembering what Inez and Gladys had already told her about Noone. She tried to read but couldn't concentrate. The room was unnaturally quiet.

A piece of wood fell in the fireplace-grate. Flames swooshed up the chimney in a flash then were gone, startling both Sam and Angie. The kitchen lights flickered, then went out. Neither woman spoke but both looked this way and that as they waited instinctively for something more to happen.

A draft wafted into the kitchen lightly tickling their faces. The breeze grew in intensity until it blew with gale like force, while the overhead lights flashed as if bolts of lightening. Soon, a tiny tornado whirled in front of the women grabbing up papers and careening them about in such a fury they flapped in the women's faces for a moment then flew helter skelter about the room. The funnel shaped phenomenon turned counter clock-wise whipping papers left and right. Amid the chaos, some of the papers flapped angrily into a pile in front of Sam. More papers fell into a pile in front of Angie. Then, as quickly as it started, the wind died, but the lights stayed on. Both women were so dumbfounded neither one moved or spoke. The room was stiflingly quiet. The two had paper cuts across their cheeks.

Afraid to move, they clung to one-another's hands but remained seated. They listened intently for any sign of commotion, waiting in anticipation for something else to occur. Tension hung in the air. Fuzz lay under the table growling. Kitty was in Sam's lap, her claws digging into Sam's leg. She stood up without uttering a sound and flung the cat from her lap.

That was when they heard it, an almost imperceptible creak. Slowly, as they watched, the basement door began to open. Just a crack, then inch by inch by inch it gaped a little further, a little further, and a little further into the kitchen until it hung completely ajar. The empty maw stared at the women, a testament to absurdity, but they couldn't move for being frozen with fear.

This was a new emotion for Angie when dealing with the paranormal. She had seen almost every supernatural event that there was to see, but none had ever had the emotional intensity this event was producing. She could feel it in the air. She had enough wits about her to know that it had yet to run its course.

Bang! The basement door slammed shut, shaking the kitchen cupboards, vibrating over the floor, rattling windows. Again and again, it opened, shut, opened, shut, slamming into the door jam with such force, it cracked the moldings. As if that weren't enough, kitchen cupboards started opening, shutting, and slamming back and forth in their moors. Utensils went flying. Knifes and forks imbedded themselves in the furniture, walls. Pots, pans, plates, glasses, food; everything in the kitchen left its place of origin only to come to rest someplace else throughout the kitchen. The phenomenon lasted five minutes in such a cacophony of noise Angie and Sam covered their ears in terror, as they ducked a flying knife here, a can of string beans there and breaking glass everywhere. They attempted to hide from the commotion underneath the table. Then, all of a sudden, the chaos stopped.

When Sam worked up enough courage to peek out over the tabletop, she saw Angie peeking back at her from the opposite side of the table. She wore a look of elation.

"I've read about it. Talked to a few patients who claimed to have seen it, but never have I witnessed such a blatant demonstration of psychokinesis! This is wonderful! I'll check the camera equipment; make sure it was video taped. I knew this was going to be a big one!" Angie spoke more to herself than to Sam even though she was almost shouting with joy.

"What do you mean, 'you knew?'"

Angie calmed down enough to hear Sam and said, "I've been dreaming about you lately. I told you that. The first time I dreamt of you, you were in grave danger. The second dream showed me that something was going on inside this house. I've seen your house, the barn, everything, even the wolves. I've seen it all. I've been dreaming it."

"Yes . . . I know it sounds absurd. But I think my dreams directed me here. That's why I called." Angie paused, thinking. It was as if she had forgotten someone else was in the room with her she was so engrossed in thoughts about documenting future events. She had no idea how her words might be impacting Sam.

"What?" "What?" is all Sam could think to say. Her mouth closed only long enough to form the word and utter it twice before dropping open again.

"Yes—you're in danger. I know it! But you're supposed to be here. Someone called you here. I'm not sure whom yet, but I sense it. I bet I grabbed the wrong papers from that chest. That's why they scattered so. But we can wait until morning before we search for more." Angie, still very excited, continued, "I'm supposed to be here, too."

Sam couldn't seem to grasp what Angie was saying. But as she thought about it, she realized that since Angie's arrival, a whole lot more had happened both in her house and on the farm, stuff that seemed to be right up Angie's alley . . . but why? She didn't say a word.

The two tried to settle down and read some papers from both piles. After all, if some supernatural force designated papers for them to read, they were obliged to read said papers, but neither woman could concentrate and gave up. They were tired and emotionally exhausted so they decided to go to bed.

But so much had happened, and Sam was too keyed up to think about sleep. Instead, she spent time cleaning the mess the chaos had created hoping the hard physical work would tire her out. As she worked, she decided she'd take security precautions of her own. Angie's equipment inspired her, so had Noone. He too easily crept up on them in the barn earlier. She didn't want that to happen again. She made plans to buy a state-of-the art security system and have it installed, not just in the farm buildings, but in the fields as well. A complete monitoring system with television cameras to record everything over the entire farm would give her the same security Angie's video and audio system, gave them inside the house. She would hide the camera lenses so fastidiously they would become part of the scenery. With all the money she saved buying the place, the cost of an extensive security system won't hurt her pocketbook one little bit, she figured as she swept up broken glass.

"No—Noone isn't going to sneak up on me again, neither is anyone else," she said aloud. Maybe the security system could help solve her other problems as well. The work and the decision to add a security system did it; Sam climbed the stairs and fell into bed sleeping soundly.

The next morning, as the two sat at the kitchen table drinking their morning coffee, Sam fixed her sights on the paper stacks in front of her. Angie said, "Sam, have you ever done anything to find out who your parents are? I seem to remember something about that from college. Did you ever do one of those searches?"

"What?" Sam's mind was slow to register Angie's words. "No. I never did get around to that."

"Maybe you should."

"Why is that of any interest to you?" Sam's defenses flew into place instantly at the mention of the parental search, still a sore spot even after all these years. A sore spot Angie was well aware of.

"I think it has something to do with this place." Angie looked Sam in the eye ignoring her defensive remarks. She knew them for what they were.

Sam felt the blood drain from her head. She felt dizzy. Even though she was forty years old, she still secretly entertained the fantasy that one day her parents would find her, come back for her. Her heart ached at the thought of them. Their desertion had left her feeling as though she lacked something, that she was unworthy of receiving love. She knew it clouded her psyche in that she had a very difficult time with intimate relationships aside from Angie. She still threw her guard up at the slightest hint of intimacy or talk of that long ago desertion.

"It's been thirty eight years. I don't think there is any reason why I should look up the people who obviously had no desire to be near me. They left me—remember? They left me."

Angie looked at Sam from across the table. She said nothing.

Sam was thankful for that. If Angie tried to comfort her, she would break down, and she refused to show emotion in front of others. She would not appear vulnerable in any respect, not if she could help it. It was just one of the many devices she had contrived to protect herself from further pain.

Angie dropped the subject and the day passed uneventfully.

It was 9 p.m. when Sam stumbled up the stairs to take a bath, and lie down. She was asleep as soon as she put her head on the pillow. She had no dreams and slept so soundly she didn't wake until 10 a.m. the next morning.

The kitchen was warm when she came down to it. Fresh coffee awaited her in the pot. The house was quiet. She found a note from Angie on the table saying she had gone into town for a few things. She didn't expect to be back before evening.

Sam poured dried milk into her big coffee mug, poured the coffee and sat down with the morning paper in front of the kitchen window. Fuzz and Kitty joined her.

Kitty got up behind her and wrapped herself around Sam's neck like a mink stole, her tail methodically twitching, up and down, up and down. She wasn't crazy about Fuzz sitting so close to Sam's lap. Fuzz looked up at Kitty wagging his tail, oblivious to the fact that the cat wanted to swat him.

Sam ignored their interaction but enjoyed their company. Snowflakes drifted down like lazy feathers caught on a summer breeze. There had been snow storms already that year dropping 24 inches total at various times, but the area was due to get a significant amount in one fell swoop sometime soon, according to the weather forecast on the radio.

As she sat there Sam decided it was a good time to get at her paperwork attempting to ignore the two piles of papers that sat where they landed just the night before last. She got up and went to the den to retrieve her paperwork, but the pile of papers sitting on the kitchen table kept beckoning to her as if to accuse her for not looking at them yet. Instead of her fieldwork, Sam picked up the top paper from the stack of whirlwind papers, which is how she came to think of them.

"I might as well get this done and over with. Maybe I thought Angie could take a magic wand and wipe all this haunting business away; maybe I thought she could twitch her nose and it would all be gone . . . I don't know." She said to the dog as she sat back down, patting his head. The work, the stress of the threatening notes and of living in the haunted house, all were beginning to take their toll. Sam was exhausted, she realized as she seated herself once again. "I'm not going anywhere this weekend, nope, nowhere, not even if a bomb goes off in the basement and blows a big hole in the roof," she said to the cat who once again had wrapped itself around her neck. The cat reached over and touched her nose to Sam's as if approving her decision.

Thumbing through the papers Sam sipped a second cup of coffee while listening to the radio hoping to catch the full weather report. "A cold front will be moving southward next week. It's expected to bring cold temperatures and a lot of snow." The melodious voice from KJOJ droned on. "The National Weather service is predicting a major snow fall of twenty or more inches. It could begin as soon as Thursday; northern Minnesota can expect snowfall by next Friday or Saturday."

She shut the radio off and looked down at the papers in front of her. She picked one up and stared at it. A bound book drew her attention as she laid the fragile paper down. Three bound volumes rested among the other papers. Sam didn't remember seeing them before. The top one, she picked up and opened.

I think she's cheating on me, the first sentence of that volume read. *He comes over here when I'm gone. They don't know that I know that. I'm careful. I worry about the babies when I'm not here. Is she taking care of them? He's an awful man. He taunts me, throws hints out at me. He thinks I haven't picked up on what he's trying to say. I understand, all right.*

Sam wondered about the author of that entry. It was written in a refined hand. She imagined what he might have looked like, what his character might have been like. She forced her attention back to reading.

He showed me that photo of Janice . . . nude. She looked so happy. How could she do this to me?

Sam skipped through some of the journal pages that went on in the same vein.

He watched me pretty intently. He must be gloating over the pain Janice's betrayal is causing me, which he knew it would cause me. When I asked her what she was doing, she just looked away. Why Janice? Why? I know you love us. Why are you with him?

It was clear that the hand that wrote the journal was in a great deal of pain. The handwriting was shaky. Water spots stained the ink in places.

The journal upset her. Sam threw her jacket on over her sweats, put on socks and running shoes, grabbed a flashlight, and went out to the library in the barn. She hadn't been to the barn since the day she and Angie discovered it. Angie had though, Sam could tell as soon as she walked in the door. The room had been partially cleaned. Dust no longer clung to everything, although it still had a strong foothold on most of the books. The big cedar chest sat where they left it in the middle of the room. Sam walked over to it, opening it. She was surprised to see Angie hadn't made much of a dent in the papers that filled it. It was a gold mine of personal history.

Fuzz accompanied Sam to the barn, but wouldn't venture into the library. Instead, he sat at the threshold, with his back to the library facing the opposite wall emitting a low, barely audible growl. Sam paid him no heed. She rummaged through the cedar chest hoping to find a photo album. When there was none, she

scanned the bookshelves. Maybe something was there. She sat
down in one of the leather chairs and looked about the room. Her
eyes took in everything absentmindedly. She reached over to the
end table and turned the light switch on jumping when light
flooded the room. She hadn't expected it to work, which is why
she brought a flashlight with her.

She let her gaze drift again to a pile of junk on the south
side of the room, stuff that looked like it had been there a long
time, bits of broken, dusty glass, old, odd shapes of wood,
kerosene lamps, old harness. To the west, a wall was boarded up
with a piece of plywood. She wondered if there was a window
behind it.

Her gaze went back to the debris and although she
couldn't see it, she "knew" that somewhere in that pile of ruble, a
desk sat. She got up from her chair moving over to the ruble, and
tried to remove the board over top the window. She was rewarded
when rusty nails gave way to reveal a large glass pane facing the
house but blocked from view outside by overgrown brush.

Bits of daylight trickled into the room chasing away the
gloomy, oppressive dark that hid so much. Next, she moved over
to the debris pile and began to clear that junk out of the room.

Still, Fuzz would not come into the library. He did move
out of Sam's way as she went back and forth from the library into
the old stall area of the barn stacking rubble next to a ladder that
lead up the haymow. Fuzz kept his vigil and watched every move
Sam made as she came and went.

After a great deal of labor, Sam was again rewarded when
she discovered an old roll-top desk underneath the pile of debris. It
had long since been abandoned and was as dusty as everything else
in the room. The dust did not discourage her; however, as she ran
her hands over the oak veneer she asked herself how she had
known it was there.

The answer, of course, was the dreams although she hadn't told Angie about this one, not yet anyway. She found a key on the wall next to the desk and tried to open a drawer. When that didn't work, she tried the roll top, and with a little effort, it squeaked upward. An atomic cloud of dust spewed from the door. Sam sneezed furiously, and had to wait for it to settle before looking deeper.

Inside, she found an old photo album as well as old letters. She took off her coat, wrapped the booty up in it, looked around, saw Fuzz still sitting by the door, acknowledged, finally, the dog's peculiar behavior, shivered, then headed out of the library and the barn, running back up to the house with her treasures, and with Fuzz at her heels.

As she left, she noted a space heater in the library, something she hadn't noticed before. She would check to see if it worked some other time. Now, she wanted the warmth of her kitchen.

It was noon by the time she ran back up the hill. The day was dark even though it was midday, something not uncommon in Minnesota winters. Sam hadn't changed her clothes and didn't plan to. She got to the kitchen and was just setting the paperwork on the table beside all the others, when she heard a knock on the front door. She became immediately disgruntled.

I never see anyone unless I'm unprepared for it, she thought. Who calls on me any other time? No one unless I'm on the toilet or in the shower! You get an answering machine so at least you can call whoever back when you're done, but they don't leave a message. Too bad they can't make some kind of answering machine for the door so you could screen out guests, especially the unwanted ones.

By now, her grumbling was audible as she ambled from the kitchen, through the dinning room and across the front room to answer the door. She peeked out the porch window. Angie must have left the outer door unlocked because inside the porch looking through the glass pane back at her in her beat up old sweats was the sheriff.

"Yes sheriff, what is it this time? Is my dog barking too loudly? How about the cat? Maybe it's annoying the neighbors?" She said as she opened the door to him, angry because he caught her looking so shabby. She couldn't help herself.

Gilbert pulled himself up squarely. "Ma'am, I have an injunction here to serve you. It orders you to stop going through anything, let's see here," he stopped and read from the papers in his hand, "that you may find in a secret room in your barn?" Gilbert read the paper with detached authority implying he wasn't there to be friendly; he was on official business; he had a job to do.

Sam applauded his composure as he chose not to react to her barrage. She was fed up with his office continually ignoring her complaints about the notes being left in her mailbox. It took her a second to grasp what he had said about an injunction.

"An injunction? This is my property! Who can stop me from going through my own property?" She asked.

"Arthur Noone, Ma'am."

Sam wondered for a second if Gilbert was out of his mind.

"I have to lock up the barn Ma'am. Until this is settled, you're not to go in there."

"Are you kidding me?"

"Absolutely not, Ma'am. This is a very serious matter."

As he spoke, Sam remembered everything they had already taken from the barn and laid on the table. She wasn't sure if Gilbert could see any of it from where he stood. The open kitchen and dinning room doors certainly weren't concealing the papers. Of course, he had no way of knowing what the stacks of papers were even if he did see them, and she wasn't about to tell him.

"Ma'am. If you would take some advice, I could tell you that an attorney would be a good thing right now. Noone has some powerful friends around here. Maybe one from the Twin Cities . . .?" Familiar with the courts in the district, Gilbert testified in them often. He knew Arthur Noone had connections there, but didn't come right out and tell Sam that.

Sam looked at him for half a minute. Their eyes locked. "Alright, I will. I'll do that right away. Thank you." She sensed that something wasn't right here and that Gilbert was politely trying to clue her in on it.

"Ma'am," Gilbert decided to take advantage of her change in attitude, "I hope you lock your house up good and tight at night. I just walked in here, you know; that front door was unlocked. Lots of people living in the country don't lock their doors, but that's not smart. Lock it up tight. And when you drive down the roads . . . even the country roads . . . lock all your doors. This may not be the Twin Cities where they have drive by shootings, but just the same . . . There's plenty around here to be cautious of," Gilbert was so earnest, Sam shivered. He smiled at her then. It was a nice smile. She returned it.

Angie got home at 7 p.m. and listened intently as Sam told her what had happened throughout the day including what she found in the barn, Gilbert's visit, and Noone's injunction.

"I can't believe Noone can stop you from retrieving material from your own property!" she said, shocked. "Was there anything in the bill of sale that prevented you from having first rights to anything found here after the sale?"

"Not to my knowledge. He got the injunction, though; I have it in the kitchen. Probably got it through that judge friend of his Gilbert hinted at; he advised I get a lawyer from the Cities to handle it and that's what I'm going to do."

Chapter Eight

"Hey Pop, how ya' doing?" Skip Gilbert asked his father over his cell phone as he turned onto Highway 53 heading back to Eveleth after serving the injunction to Sam. His father had been trying to reach him all day, but Skip hadn't had time to return his call until then.

"I'm great son, but I been thinking," Stan Gilbert paused long enough to spit. Skip heard what he was doing and pictured his father with his old coffee can spittoon spitting the snuff he'd been chewing for years. "I get this feeling that something is going on up there. Maybe I can help?"

"Pop, I told you. Stay in Florida. It's nice there. I don't need any help." Skip tried to sound cordial but failed. He was tired of trying to fill his father's boots at work. If the old man comes up here now, I'll have an even harder time getting the men to accept me as their boss, he thought.

Stan wasn't stupid. He could tell Skip didn't want him there. He tried to keep the hurt he felt from transferring over the phone line. He prayed for static to cloud up the transmission.

"Okay son, I just had this feeling, that's all. How are you doing?" Stan wasn't expecting Skip to say much of anything to that question.

"The same Pop, the same. Why don't I call you on Sunday to see how you are then?" Skip didn't wait for a response; he flipped shut his cell-phone and put it back in his shirt pocket, immediately, consumed with guilt.

When he got back to the office, Gilbert checked in with the dispatcher who then buzzed him back to his office. As he passed by her, he barked, "Hey Harriet, get me the DNR on the phone. I want to talk to Phil."

Harriet Hornblower had her back to Gilbert as she busied herself with typing up deputy's incoming incident reports. She didn't want to do anything Skip Gilbert told her to, but she would; it was her job. She didn't like the way he treated Stan, though, sending him to Florida and all. Every time she thought about it, she got so mad at Skip, she pounded the keyboard with a vengeance. Harriet shook her head and stopped typing to dial the telephone number to the DNR. "You know, sheriff, Phil's probably in the field," she said sarcastically. Since Skip was already inside his office, she didn't think he could hear her.

I had better check and see if there's been any headway in that trap pulling business, Skip thought as he sat down behind his big oak desk, the one luxury he'd purchased for himself after getting the sheriff's position.

He knew the local trappers hadn't been lying when they told him their beaver traps were being pulled, but he was also sure Samantha Egar wasn't lying when she said she had only been pulling wolf traps. He had been so busy with the missing child investigation, he had neglected the Samantha Egar investigation, and she didn't even know there was one.

While Skip Gilbert worked his investigations, Arthur Noone worked behind the scenes with local trappers, especially Shorty Kivimaki. He invited Kivimaki to Tony's one night in

August of 2000 just before the City of Eveleth's big community picnic. The bar was packed. People were swarming into the area from Iowa, North and South Dakota and Wisconsin. Hotels were packed. Just five miles from Eveleth, Tony's attracted more than its share of the yearly visitors.

The picnic, a thing of legend, and Eveleth were the place to be in August for anyone who had ever heard of it. With the picnic's popularity, businesses in all the small Iron Range towns, especially the bars, had stellar weekends.

The Iron Range, known for its heavy alcohol consumption, attracted many with drinking problems on that weekend every year, the primary reason most folks flocked to town for the two-day event. A sanctioned orgy of over indulgence for many outsiders, it cost local taxpayers a great deal in overtime pay for police officers of every description, with vehicular accidents a common occurrence. It was not unusual for someone to end up dead due to drinking and driving, as well. The weekend was a nightmare for police officers and for Mothers Against Drunk Drivers. But for most businesses, it was business better than usual.

Franco and Botticelli loved August.

On that particular August evening, Noone sat to the back of Tony's bar by the bandstand. He sought out a spot where no one could overhear what he had to say to Shorty, his only reason for being in Tony's.

"Hey Shorty!" He threw an arm around the big outdoorsman's shoulders when Shorty arrived and said, as if an after thought, "Is that woman still messing with your traps?"

"Yeah, she's pulled a whole bunch of 'em. I'm starting to feel the pinch."

Noone could feel the tight knots in Shorty's shoulders.

Shorty grew taut whenever he thought of Samantha Egar

and his traps. The problem was he didn't know what he was going to do to stop her. She stood up to him as bold as she pleased when he challenged her. He was impressed with her, but she was hurting his finances. He didn't work in the mines. Trapping was his only means of support. It angered him that she didn't seem to understand the difference between a legal trap and an illegal one.

"I thought she was a scientist," he said, "aren't they supposed to be smart? What the hell is she pulling my beaver traps for?" he said.

"Well, she is a woman. How many of them do you know that can count to ten?" Noone asked as the two sat down in a booth.

"I go out there sometimes—in the woods, I mean. I've seen her there." Noone said as he sipped on a shot of scotch and pushed a beer bottle at Shorty.

Tony's was packed. It was 8:45 p.m., just fifteen minutes before the band would start playing and the price of drinks would go from happy hour prices—two for the price of one—to regular price. Four bartenders tried to keep up with the flow of customer orders before the price increase. Waitresses rushed to and fro from the bar with their little round trays full to overflowing with drinks.

"She must think she's special, with that college degree of hers. She can't be too smart if she doesn't know the difference between legal and illegal trapping." Noone taunted gauging Shorty's reaction.

"She's the one that's dumb!" Shorty responded as if on cue.

Noone smiled. "Wouldn't it be fun to teach her a lesson? You know? She's never been married. Maybe she needs someone to teach her about . . . things?" The woman aroused Shorty; Noone sensed it.

In the midst of their conversation, the band started playing and people all around them flooded the dance floor gyrating to the music the country/rock band played. Women, single and married, noticed the men sitting together with no women at their sides, so close to the door to the woman's bathroom. Many sauntered by them on their way to the latrine in an effort to catch the men's attention.

Both cheap and expensive perfumes lingered over the table, hanging in the air enticing Shorty's concentration away from what Noone wanted him to hear. Noone had to compete with sweaty body odors that wafted at them from the dance floor, and cigarette smoke so thick it was like fog.

Noone could smell the unmistakable scent of men and women in heat. He cringed. He hated the ritual. Women were tramps. He could see the lustful looks they gave him and Shorty. He didn't like it and didn't like it when they distracted Shorty from the conversation he was trying to have with him. As always with Noone, he bridled his temper as it dawned on him that he could use this evil environment to his advantage.

"It would be fun to win a fight with her, get her to spread those legs, don't you think?" Noone raised his eyebrows leering at Shorty and smiling a seemingly innocent smile as he spoke. If he planted a sexual seed in Shorty's mind that prompted him to approach, and, hopefully, molest the biologist, good. That's the way it should be. He continued with the suggestion when Shorty made no protest against his remarks. The barroom atmosphere was perfect for the tact he was taking. Where at first he was angered by the sexually aggressive women that came by the table, soon he was silently thanking them. Maybe they would stir up Shorty's lust so he would do something about the meddling bitch in the woods. All it would take, Noone reasoned, was a little more time before he would see results. He didn't know if Shorty would do anything like rape her, but the way he figured it, he would never know if he didn't at least try and find out.

"Hey boss, you need to see this," bartender Jack said to Franco who was in the middle of a hand of poker in the back room.

"Can't you see I'm busy here?!"

"But boss, this is something you've been watching for!" Franco lost his hand, glared at Jack, but followed him to the door to look inside the bar.

"There, in the back, by the band?"

Franco's eagle eye settled on the two men immediately.

He looked at Jack. "Yeah, it's been on," Jack said.

Franco watched a few minutes more then went upstairs to the office which overlooked the entire establishment. One way glass surrounded the hidden room and gave the two bar owners the ability to watch everything going on inside their bar without allowing anyone to see them inside. They had the glass surrounding the office painted black, which matched the paneling on the walls.

Once inside, Franco turned up the volume so he could hear what Noone was saying. The band was too loud for him to hear anything, however, but it didn't really matter. A technology buff, Franco would use his complicated sound system to erase all background noises, which would enable him to hear in detail everything Noone said to Shorty. The complicated recording system proved invaluable, especially when some mark didn't believe what he was telling them. The recording system was like taking out an insurance policy. After all, Franco never really gambled, except on something he knew he would win. Noone and Shorty were being video tapped as well.

Franco stayed perched upstairs watching the pair until Noone left at 10:30 p.m.

"Hey Jack, buy Shorty a beer. Tell him I want to talk to him." Franco barked at Jack when he went back downstairs.

Franco's cronies in the backroom razed him about leaving the game early. Franco ignored them. It was time for a different kind of game; a game they would never understand.

Franco decided long ago that the only way to protect himself from these same types of men was to use street survival tactics. He had seen way too much of life to be too trusting of anyone. He grew up tough learning how to be sure of himself, how to watch his back. He had to. If he hadn't, everyone on the street would have seen him as prey, and that was something he would never be.

He had a gentle spot in his heart for his employees though; watching many of them struggle with the same things he had to struggle with growing up. He was not a pushover for any of them, however, no matter whom they were. They did as he told them to do when he told them to do it even if he did not finesse them like Botticelli.

In return, most of his employees, especially the women, understood that he was one of them. They knew that the extra money at Christmas time and the anonymous gifts throughout the year all came from Franco. Botticelli never gave them anything over and above their earnings.

Franco's gruff exterior and cutthroat tongue did nothing to distract from his animal magnetism; he knew that, too. That was something else he had learned as a kid in the street. Women liked him . . . a lot. Men were scared of him, but they paid homage anyway and he sucked it up like a dry sponge. He knew husbands feared he would seduce their wives; they were right about their women, wrong about him. He never dated married women, held them in contempt if they came on to him, and they came on to him every chance they got.

That night in August was not different. As Franco stepped out of the backroom to seat himself at the horseshoe bar people fought for his attention.

"Can we buy you a drink Franco?

"We'd like to have you to dinner; can you come next Tuesday?"

"How's your mother, Franco?"

People always sucked up to him, asking him the same things over and over, trying to impress him. He knew they wanted his attention but were scared of him. They always called him Franco, never Anthony, or Tony; it got on his nerves. They were not his friends. He knew that, too.

The one exception was Sam. She had been on his mind a lot since they met. He couldn't get over how she had strong-armed him trying to protect herself. She had a lot of balls, he figured, and admired her for it. Of course, she didn't know who he was then. She wasn't trying to mess with anyone, really, which also impressed him. She could take care of herself.

That afternoon in July when she looked at him in the backroom, there was nothing of the wanton lust in her eyes that he had seen in so many other women. She looked him straight in the eye, too. Women out to play games never did. That's why he knew she was telling the truth when she said she thought he was Shorty's friend; she wasn't trying to con him. He couldn't remember the last time that had ever happened. He found himself thinking of her more and more and hoping to see her walk through the front door of Tony's.

In the meantime, he contemplated what Shorty and Noone might be up to. He'd find out. He'd also make sure nothing happened to the "wolf lady." When he learned she was getting threatening notes left in her mailbox, he took an even more active role in a private investigation to learn who was threatening her.

He'd find out just who was behind that bit of nasty business. He immediately suspected Arthur Noone was trying to drive her off but why? Noone always set his fine-honed street smarts to humming—Danger! Danger!

"Hey Franco, the boys are wondering when you're coming back to play?" Botticelli said as he stepped out front to get his partner. "They want some more of your money."

"Never mind, we've got other problems." Franco said to Botticelli leading him up to their office. "We got a bartender on the take at the back bar. I caught him on camera." They watched the bartender on the security system.

The back bar sat nestled away from the horseshoe bar in a corner by the south side exit. It was only open weekend nights when the bar featured live music. Attached to the back room, the bartender working it had to get permission to go into "the back" for needed supplies. It was always in his best interest if he used the house phone to call Jack up front, so Jack could deliver whatever was needed. The men in the "back room" wanted no one to know they were there and knew Jack wouldn't divulge their secrets, but he was the only one they trusted.

Franco and Botticelli watched as the bartender gave drinks to his friends without collecting from them.

"It's his last night," Botticelli said.

"You're damn right. I ought to kick his behind." Franco growled.

"He ain't worth it," Botticelli decreed.

"I think it's time to give Michelle a chance behind the bar. She's worked for us, what now—two years? Never has taken a thing," Franco said, the thief already dismissed from his thoughts.

"Get what we owe this jerk-off and give it to him; we can get rid of him right now. Put Michelle back there. She's familiar enough with the setup. We'll pay her a bartender's wage for the work," Franco told Jack over the phone. Franco knew Michelle would ask about the wage. She had too. She had four kids to raise and her ex-husband never gave her a dime in child-support. They watched as Jack went to the back bar to pay the ex-bartender off telling him to get out.

"You can't do that. You haven't got any authority around here," the bartender said to Jack just as Franco and Botticelli stepped down the stairs and around the corner into the back bar.

"We told him to do that." Botticelli said in a calm, quiet voice.

The ex-bartender froze, acutely aware of the two men's reputations. Botticelli was known to be brutal; unsure about Franco, he assumed he was too.

"All right, I'm going." The ex-bartender grabbed his pay from Jack's hand and slid out from behind the bar heading for the back door with his friends. Slinking away, none of them looked as if they wanted to tangle with the club owners or Jack.

"I don't think he needs to work on the Range anymore. I think he needs to move away," Franco said. The kid would never get a job on the Iron Range again; all Franco had to do was put a word in the ear of everyone in the backroom playing cards. They all owed him favors. He saw to that.

Franco turned his attention back to Shorty who sat waiting at the bar. From his perspective, Shorty couldn't see exactly what was going on in the back, but he watched as one of the bartenders headed out the side door, then as Michelle got behind the back bar and started pouring drinks.

Everyone in the club watched as the mini drama played out, tension hanging in the air like stale smoke. Cigarettes dangled from lips as hot ash fell onto unsuspecting flesh. Swizzle sticks slopped past mouths as ice sloshed out of glasses frozen in mid-air;

booze dribbled down a customer's chin; waitresses moved as if in slow motion; the band lost their beat and bartenders spilled booze on the bar.

It was the Franco mystique. He always created a stir. As he moved from the back bar to the main horseshoe bar, all eyes turned to him, most trying to watch from hooded eyelids. Everyone wanted to buy him a drink relieved that they were not the focus of his anger.

Franco stayed as polite as he knew how to be, after all, their money was going into his pocket, but he didn't have much patience for it that night. The bartender he fired pissed him off, royally.

He sauntered over to Shorty telling him to join him at a table behind the pull-tab booth, so they could talk. Franco gave orders and expected those he gave them to, to do as they were told without complaint. Shorty included, which he did. Most customers understood that if Franco took someone aside to talk to them, he wanted to be left alone. The smart ones kept their distance.

"I understand you're having some trouble with that dame, that one out there with them wolves. Is that right?" He said without preamble.

"Yeah, she's been pulling my traps. Man, I don't know what to do about it. I'm not trapping illegally, yet she told the sheriff I was."

"What makes you so sure it was her? I mean, she should know the difference between a wolf and a beaver trap and she keeps talking about pulling wolf traps." Franco paused looking long and hard at Shorty who said nothing. "You talking to Noone about it?" Franco watched Shorty's face intently expecting the man to answer his questions with his eyes rather than his lips.

"Why?"

"Something's wrong with the guy." Franco said matter-of-factly. He wanted to make sure the woman didn't get hurt. Shorty was capable of hurting women; Franco knew that. And though he didn't know exactly what Noone was up to, he knew he was up to something and suspected he would use Shorty if he needed too. Franco didn't trust Noone at all, but he liked Shorty.

"A couple years back Noone came to me, said some things that gave me the creeps. I've had my eye on him ever since. Besides, that woman keeps talking about wolf traps—not beaver traps. You thinking she don't know the difference?"

"Don't know, man. Just don't know."

Franco slapped him on the back, and whispered, "You watch out for Noone. He's more trouble than she will ever be." He left Shorty to his conundrum.

As Franco walked back up to the bar customers stepped over each other to get him to notice them. He stayed out front the rest of the night getting sloshed on whiskey. By 12:30 p.m. his glasses were askew on his face and he was telling dirty jokes to a rapt audience at the end of the bar.

Botticelli just shook his head when he realized Franco was drunk. He knew that meant he would have to close up by himself. Franco couldn't hold his liquor; Botticelli often wondered why he had ever wanted to own a bar.

Chapter Nine

Shorty left Tony's at midnight. While still there, he thought long and hard about what Franco had said. She should know the difference between traps. What if she wasn't the one pulling them? The thought hadn't occurred to him before, and he contemplated it the rest of the night. He was smiling as he walked out the front door, but his good humor didn't last.

When he got home, he found his girlfriend in bed asleep instantly igniting his hair trigger temper. His dinner was cold. He banged a metal pipe against the metal bedpost, screaming "Bitch!" Waking her up, his voice carried over the noise of metal hitting metal. "Who do you think you are? Get your lazy ass out of bed and fix my dinner!"

Grabbing her by her nightgown, Shorty threw Helen, the woman he had lived with for three years, out of bed still cursing her. He kicked her in the ribs as she tried to get to her feet. Grabbing her by the hair, he pulled her up on her feet hurling her into the kitchen where she fell against the porcelain sink.

She said nothing. She had been through this before. She knew if she said one word, she would be beaten even worse. She removed leftovers from the refrigerator heating them up on the

stove. To her surprise, Shorty calmed down and ate without
condemning her cooking or saying anything more.

When he finished eating he took her by the throat and
pushed her backward into the bedroom where she fell upon the bed
lying motionless. He undressed. She didn't move. He lowered his
bulk on top of her forcing her legs open and thrusting himself
inside, again, and again. She still didn't move. It wasn't long
before Shorty finished, rolled off, and fell asleep.

She lie awake the rest of the night. It wasn't as bad as the
last time when Shorty took the shotgun and shot up the house. She
thought she was dead that time and secretly hoped he would kill
her. She was tired. There seemed to be no way out. He would find
her if she left him and kill her anyway. A gun would be much
quicker than the constant beatings. Besides, who else would want
her now, what else could she do? She was too dumb to get a job;
everyone always told her that; she wasn't pretty enough anymore
to attract a man. Life with Shorty had made her old and she knew
it, so she lay there in bed waiting for dawn when she would get up
and it would start all over again.

As for Sam, she didn't see Skip Gilbert again until the
Eveleth community picnic. She had had such unpleasant dealings
with his deputies she was surprised to find the sheriff so nice.

Still, she felt paranoid about whom in authority she could
trust, so even though Gilbert treated her well the night he escorted
her home, she was leery of him, even more so his deputies.

Sam didn't recognize him at first for Gilbert had dressed
in shorts and a T-shirt. His blonde, wavy hair hung to his collar,
much longer than she expected to see it, especially since he was a
police officer. Sitting in the gazebo with a number of her new
friends eating a dinner of potato salad, fried chicken, baked beans,
corn bread and iced tea, she watched as he approached.

The meal smelled wonderful to Gilbert as he walked over to say "hi" entertaining the hope of an invitation to eat. Gilbert never married, so home cooked meals were a rare treat.

Sam had dressed for the occasion in a T-shirt and peach colored cotton summer dress with sandals. She swept her shoulder length brown hair up into a bun held in place with a hair clip. She wore no make-up except lipstick. Her skin, bronzed from all the time she spent in the summer sun, was smooth and soft thanks to the lotions she applied faithfully and frequently.

The ladies she lunched with watched in interest as the sheriff approached. There were few single men over 40 in the area, so they all kept special tabs on eligible bachelors.

Bernice's eyes danced with the possibilities. Happily married to John, and with five children, Earth Mother Bernice pronounced marriage as every woman's ultimate goal—as did the Spencer sisters—much to Sam's surprise.

Bernice made a point of inviting the sisters and Sam to eat with her family even though she knew it would rile many of her church friends who were also dinning in the large gazebo. When the sisters arrived, they sauntered over to Bernice's table like two lionesses ambling among the pride, confident, regal, and deadly. One dressed in bright orange, the other, bright pink. Many a mouth gapped as the women glided over the gazebo's hardwood floors in high heels as graceful as their animal counterparts wearing a subtle scented perfume that gently filled the air.

"Shameless," Sam heard one woman say as her lip curled up in contempt at the sisters.

"Old whores," another woman said. It was as if the sister's flamboyant airs were a bigger insult than their pasts. Most Iron Range locals knew what happened to Gladys and Inez as kids, and many hid a secret compassion for the two; what they found reprehensible was the two's attitude. How could they be so happy?

so full of life? How could they live the lives they had lived and not be down trodden, the way any good woman would be under similar circumstances? A good woman wouldn't wear flashy clothes among the upright, either. Since they were not "good" women, but still felt the need to dine among the righteous, then they should behave uprightly, and keep her eyes downcast. Didn't they know they were going straight to hell?

"How can those old biddies dress like that? Of all the nerve," one woman whispered to her sixteen-year-old daughter.

The daughter looked angrily at her mother and said, "I think they look nice."

"Nice?" Her mother's friend retorted while her head snapped forward accenting her double chins as she looked down at the girl, "those two old whores haven't got the decency to stay away from decent folks! Look at 'em, doesn't take too much of a brain to see what they are." She turned her nose up as the sisters passed hoping they heard her remarks.

If either Inez or Gladys heard any of the catty comments at their expense, they didn't acknowledge them. Instead they lifted their chins a little higher, threw their shoulders back ramrod straight and walked even slower through the gazebo looking even more majestic.

Gilbert could hear everything being said in the gazebo as the Spencer sisters crossed it. He shook his head in disgust. He knew most everyone sitting there. None of them had any business talking about anybody.

As the sisters moved over to Bernice's table, Inez muttered to Gladys, "I'll be damned if I'll hide my head in shame for anything I've done with my life. They can buzz off!" Gladys nodded her head in agreement. They fixed their gazes on their friends and didn't look back. Many of the men silently cheered the two women, glad to see their spirited souls waltz across the floor so magnificently even at their age.

Bernice heard everything, too, but chose to ignore the snide remarks. Instead, she tended to her children who were in and out of the gazebo demanding her attention. Bernice knew how many of her other friends and neighbors felt about the Spencer sisters, but she also knew she loved the two old ladies. If only her church friends could open their hearts a little and look beyond the sisters' pasts. Someday she prayed that would happen. She never spoke of this dream to Gladys or Inez; she knew they would just laugh at her.

Gilbert didn't know Bernice at all; he had seen her husband around, but didn't really know him either, except for the fact that he owned the infamous Steamroller and his reputation for handling the bull was solid among cattle people. When he noticed all of the women gathered together around Bernice, he wondered who she was. She had obviously invited the two old hookers to lunch with her. He liked her for that; and Sam was in the group, too, so Bernice earned more brownie points from him. However, groups of women made him nervous, so much so, his palms started sweating as he drew near.

Sam watched him as he walked over whispering to Inez that he looked like he was running a criminal check on them.

"He probably is." Inez retorted as she got up to get some iced tea.

"That one. I don't quite know what to make of him. He has a good heart. I've seen it in action, but sometimes he can be the worst pill on earth. Being around him is like being forced to have an enema when nothing's wrong," Gladys said, to which the group burst out laughing.

"He isn't always a horses' ass. When he is though, he's a big one," Inez filled in. "It's hard to believe that he's Stan's kid."

Gilbert moseyed even closer. That's how Sam saw him now, as a sheriff from the old west. They must have all moseyed, she imagined. His long lean legs, a bit bowed, looked like he rode a horse—often. No six-gun on his hip, it was still real easy to imagine one there. She wondered if he had one tucked away someplace else on his person. He didn't look so bad without the uniform, either, with his long blond hair loosely surrounding his face. His blue eyes were a little bluer than Sam remembered; his face was permanently bronzed from spending a lot of time outdoors. Put it all together and Sam admitted to herself that he was handsome for a forty-plus-year-old man who often acted like a horse's ass. She remembered that night at her house, when Sheriff Skip Gilbert went above and beyond the call of duty to make sure she was safe. She smiled.

"Ms.," he said to Sam emphasizing the Ms.

"Yes." Sam put on her sweetest smile fluttering her eyelids. She couldn't resist having a little playful fun seeing how Inez and Gladys were working hard to stifle a giggle.

"I just wanted to apologize for last week." Gilbert's face was a mask cast in stone.

Sam couldn't read it. The blue eyes were giving nothing away. "Apologize? What for?"

"My deputies. I know they haven't been taking your complaints seriously, but I want you to know that I have." Gilbert shuffled his feet as if he were uncomfortable in his own shoes.

"Thank you, sheriff."

He never said another word. Gilbert just turned and walked away. The women heard and saw everything but were as dumbfounded as Sam at his leaving.

"It's like I said," Gladys uttered, "sometimes he's as sweet as sweet potato pie, and at other times he's the worst horse's ass. Go figure." Everyone laughed once again.

By that time, the sheriff had passed out of earshot.

Across the small park, now filled to overflowing with visitors, Franco sat lunching with friends at a picnic table nestled close to the little lake at the center of the park. Under a weeping willow tree that offered cool shelter from the blazing August sun he and his friends ate in cool comfort. Even though the Iron Range is located so far north it is only a little over one hundred miles south of the Canadian border it gets hot in the summer. This particular day it was ninety degrees and climbing already by noon. The humidity was at seventy five percent and sweltering.

Fans waved as ladies tried in vain to keep themselves cool. With all the newcomers in town, the park buzzed with activity, which added to the temperature rise. Strangers walked through the crowd buying specialty foods from the many venders, sampling tastes from Finland, Poland, Russia, Yugoslavia, Italy, France, Germany, Sweden, Ireland, Norway, Scotland and more. It was like a small United Nations assembly had gathered in Eveleth to show the world they could all live together in harmony.

Franco had seen this same thing year after year, so he took no notice of it. What he sensed was Sam somewhere in the crowd and his heart beat a bit quicker, his pulse raced. He searched myriads of faces before he found her shortly after he entered the park. He had seen Gilbert amble over to her and wondered what they were talking about. He felt something he had never felt before, a pang of envy. Not to be undone, Franco started across the grounds toward Sam.

Sam felt a charge of excitement surge through the air. She sat with her back to the south, turning around sharply at the sense that someone was watching her. She too searched the crowd and saw as Franco passed charismatically through the crowd, where even total strangers bowed out of his way. He too had the grace of a big cat, but in Sam's estimation, he was much more like a tiger than a lion, singular, ominous. As he drew closer, Sam's body took on a life of its own. His eyes locked onto hers. She sat bolt upright. A slight blush colored her cheeks.

He moved toward her like tigers move toward gazelle. Everything about her excited him as he sensed her body responding to him, a slow smile crossed his lips making him even more appealing. The closer he came, the more electrical current passed between them. It was palpable.

Inez sensed the subtle changes in Sam and turned to see Franco approaching. No, she thought. It can't be!

"Miss Egar, we meet again," Franco said holding his hand out to Sam, smiling. She took it. "How are you enjoying the picnic?" His eyes locked on hers as he took her hand then lightly covered it with his other. She made no attempt to avert her eyes or retrieve her hand. She couldn't if she had wanted to.

"It's lovely. Did you have anything to do with organizing it?" She didn't know what else to say. His stare riveted her to the spot. So much heat surged through her she had all she could do to keep from losing her balance. Her knees felt like rubber.

"No, I don't do picnics," he said letting the corners of his mouth curl up slightly in the tiniest of smiles that caused her heart to leap. Still holding her hand, he said, "Tell me, have you beaten up any more men lately, or am I going to have to bear the brunt of my friend's jokes alone?"

"No, although I think the sheriff would like me to handle his deputies," she said smiling sweetly. Franco tensed ever so slightly, and in a flash Sam realized he had seen her with Gilbert.

"Well . . . if you need any help, let me know," he said as he continued to hold her hand and her gaze.

The words, uttered in jest, contained a tiny change in tone telling Sam he wasn't kidding. She shivered, in pleasure, not fear. No one had ever offered to protect her. There was something intoxicating about it and dangerous about Franco that drew her to him like a magnet. It was like she was dehydrated and he was the only water that could quench her thirst. Was it his power or his charisma? She didn't know, hadn't felt anything like it for anyone, and wasn't sure what to do with it. At forty years of age, she didn't think it possible that anything like that would happen to her.

As they listened to the exchange, Gladys and Inez were dumbstruck.

Bernice didn't know who Franco was, but she could tell the Spencers did, as did the rest of the town. So many eyes were turned in their direction it startled Bernice shifting her curiosity into overdrive. John watched, too, smiling. He knew Bernice wouldn't let him rest until she got the goods on Anthony Franco.

"By the way, it would be nice to see you and your friends in Tony's sometime. My treat," Franco said as he finally let go of Sam's hand. He knew everyone in town was watching them. Today was not the right time to move in on her.

"I think we could manage that," Sam said, smiling.

Franco said good-bye to everyone then turned to walk back to his table; "And remember," he said turning back once again and speaking to Sam, "If anyone gives you any trouble, let me know. I've got a little pull around here. I can help." Franco knew more than one person heard that remark. He was banking on it. That should keep her safe for awhile, he thought as he strolled back to his friends.

He smiled at Sam before turning his back on her once again and walking away. He wondered how she would handle everyone bomb basting her with questions about him. He wondered if she could handle it, the attention he always got. She'd hear plenty of stories about him, too. Would she believe them? If he did half of what people thought he did, he'd be in prison. He knew the stories were lies, exaggerations, but they served him, so he didn't dispute them. People left him alone, stayed out of his business. That's the way he liked it. As he walked back to his friends, he hoped the stories wouldn't scare her off.

No woman had ever stirred as much desire in him, and she, being a square, no less. If he wanted a woman—that was that—they were his. This was different, though. He didn't want her to be like everyone else, and deep down he knew she wasn't. He remembered the day she strong-armed him in the bar. What did he say then? Wasn't it, "throw the bitch outta' here?" He smiled as he thought of it, a smile that brought forth even more curiosity from his cronies, and the thousands of other pairs of eyes watching and wondering what the legendary Anthony Franco was secretly smiling about.

All Franco thought about as he sat back down at his table was that he wanted to be with Sam a little longer, talk to her in private, touch her. She was the first woman he had ever felt that way about, and he'd be damned if he'd let anyone get in the way. He sensed that nothing would stop her if she gave herself to him— that would be that—forever. He also sensed that he excited her as much as she did him.

Sam watched him walk away, wishing he would stay close just a little while longer.

The women among Sam's new circle of friends finished the picnic in high spirits laughing at everything. Sam felt almost giddy—a whole new experience for her. All of the women seemed to sense the electricity between her and Franco responding to it almost as much as Sam had. Eventually, even Bernice's church friends joined the group, an event that reinforced Bernice's belief that God works in mysterious ways and would reward her prayers.

It was an historical afternoon for the Spencer sisters, too. Women, who had only a few hours before shunned them, and had been doing so for years, were actually speaking to them as they joined the group at the Jennings' table inside the gazebo. The sisters were gracious enough to be polite in their responses holding back the quips they were famous for. They behaved themselves in deference to Bernice, whom they loved. The Spencer sisters in turn were discreetly plied with questions about their work. They, however, declined to share any information.

Although they didn't let on, the church ladies were relieved by the sisters' discretion. Most worried their husbands had visited the sisters a time or two and that the sisters would reveal that awful truth to them if they spoke to them.

Bernice kept her surprise at all the interaction to herself, although she was radiant. It was a start, she thought basking in the glory of God who, as she always said, did more to move people's hearts than she ever could. All she could do was pray for everyone concerned then know that God would have his way in the matter.

The church ladies, who also once rallied against Sam, admitted to her that they were intrigued with her work plying her, too, with questions. The church ladies found themselves basking in the joy of the electrical current that ran like wildfire through the group, too. There was something about Franco and Sam that had sparked their romantic imaginations, though no one broached the subject.

That afternoon, Sam kept glancing south to catch glimpses of Franco. At times, she could see him watching her, too. She noticed how many other folks sought Franco's presence, including women; it was easy to see, even from a distance that Franco was a man to be reckoned with. It made his offer of protection all the more valuable.

Sam saw Botticelli arrive later that afternoon with Tony's barmaids in tow. The girls couldn't stay long; they had to get to work, but for the moment Botticelli was treating them to anything they wanted. She watched as Botticelli, too, drew people to him like a magnet, but not of the same magnitude as Franco, although his popularity was almost as great. He carried himself in the same confident manner as Franco with many people seeking an audience. Maybe that was why the two were friends. They were kings holding court, she observed.

Botticelli made his way to the gazebo to say hello as well, and as he did, Sam's friends eyed him with the same interest they had shown Franco, only now the church ladies, too, eyed Botticelli as he ambled over. He charmed them as much as he had Sam that day at Tony's when she had her altercation with Shorty. He also invited everyone to Tony's.

When the church ladies learned he was single, they immediately set about to find who among their friends would be perfect for him. Matchmakers were always doing that to Tony Botticelli. Everybody's mother loved him and tried to marry off their sister's friend's little girl to him. He thought it was funny. He always got a good meal out of the set up. Folks invited him to their house for dinner and to meet the girl. He charmed the socks off her but nothing more. He broke a lot of hearts, but ate pretty well in the process.

As the afternoon wore on, Sam temporarily forgot her problems enjoying good conversation, good food, and interesting people, something she had been in dire need of. She spent so much time in the woods working she had forgotten how pleasant it could be mingling with her own kind. It was as if the dangers current in her life were put on hold.

She didn't see Gilbert anymore that afternoon and regretted not talking to him longer. She liked him. Something about him is as haunted as my house, she thought as she picked up paper plates and carried them to the trash working to clean up the gazebo with Bernice. As the day came to an end and it was almost time to leave, Sam wondered if Franco would call. Of course, he'd have to leave a message. She wasn't in much.

After the picnic, Sam spent most of her time in the field. She stayed with the wolves as they traversed the countryside, and watched the pack from downwind to keep her presence hidden. She found sign of a new den near her home. At times, it seemed as if the alpha female looked right at her as she worked quietly at a distance near the den. Sam reasoned that the wolf couldn't be looking directly at her because she was well hidden amid thick, impenetrable adder brush.

Unbeknownst to Sam, the alpha male and female did know she was there; they knew others were there, too. It was the first week of September and the pair was on the alert; Sam could tell by their actions. She wondered what had them so keyed up. She kept downwind, so there was no reason they should be on to her. What was it, then?

Shorty stealthily stalked Sam. He was what the wolves' scented. Shorty's scent was strong, dank; that of a hunter closing in on its prey; a scent the wolves knew all too well and were cautious of. As Shorty stalked Sam, Noone stalked Shorty. The wolves picked up on his scent, too. It was one they were all too familiar with; it meant death.

As the alpha male set out from the pack, Sam had no idea Shorty and Noone were closing in on her, and neither man knew the wolves were nearby.

The big alpha male wandered freely between them all, watching every movement the men made as he quietly made his way over fallen bramble, peeking out from behind thick under-growth. Like a vision, he was there, then gone vanishing instantly into the sun-speckled undergrowth, an apparition. He watched the men move about freely, taking note of the one creeping up on the woman, but sensing no real danger from him.

Sam wondered where the alpha male wolf had gone. She found herself scanning the deep alder brush surrounding her, but saw nothing but the bramble of fallen tree limbs, branches, tall cut grass and leaf leavings.

As she searched the bramble for the male, behind her the alpha female slipped away creeping up on her, getting close but keeping herself hidden, behind a tree trunk, under willow brush. Sam's scent was very familiar to her. It was on and around the steel contraptions hanging from the trees, the contraptions that when on the ground caught and killed many of her kind. She did not like the smell of the male that was on the traps, who was close by and getting closer. The she wolf crept closer and closer to Sam watching her out of curious, warm, brown-yellow eyes. The woman was no threat to her pups; if otherwise she would have already removed them from the den. But she didn't want the men getting any closer to her pups than they were now.

Shorty moved in behind Sam; as he did, the alpha female positioned herself between them, stealthily, as a predator. The scent of steel and gun oil permeated the air around the man making her wary, but not wary enough to back down. She saw the man stroke the gun lovingly.

Meanwhile, Sam grew restless, uneasy. Something was watching her; she felt it but couldn't see anything out of the ordinary. The hairs on the back of her neck stood up. She shivered. She periodically searched the dense undergrowth, but to no avail. There were just too many shadows. Sam jumped up, jerked around after a strong feeling of being watched permeated her being, frantically searching the undergrowth for signs of movement, causing the alpha female to lay herself belly down, so close to the ground, she seemed to become one with it.

At Sam's movement, Shorty quickly ducked behind a large tree trunk. Shorty set out to do the same to Sam as he had done to his live in girlfriend. But now, in her presence, he felt as if he had been dipped into freezing cold water.

Canine teeth were flashing in a noiseless growl as the alpha male crept up on Noone. Noone's scent was sour, full of hatred. The big male wolf knew it well. He lost his first mate to it. It was on the trap that had ensnared her. The man paid no attention to his surroundings; he was so intent on watching the other man, the wolf managed to come within inches of him. He snarled audibly at the man now, red hot hatred bringing him nearer and nearer the urge to take the man down.

Damn! Why doesn't he do something? Noone thought watching Shorty.

Shorty crept even closer to Sam.

The alpha female jumped up, moved quickly and noisily over fallen, dried debris back to the pups. Leaves and branches crackled underfoot as her ninety five-pound body sped out of hiding and back to the den.

Shorty pulled up immediately upon hearing the commotion, stood still squinting his eyes trying to find the source of the racket. Brush moved! His heart leapt in his chest; he pulled the gun up ready to shoot. Probably just a deer . . . damn! What's wrong with me? I'm jumping at the slightest noise! He thought once the racket subsided.

Sam stretched up to her full height scanning the forest for signs of life upon hearing the same racket. Since she was in black bear country, she wondered if she had surprised one.

She never saw Shorty. She was so engrossed in her work collecting wolf data when she heard the noise, she didn't think that whatever else was out there with her might be human.

The noise unnerved Shorty so much that he gave-up following her making his way back to his truck, which he had parked on a logging road not too far from Sam's property line. He wasn't aware that Noone was in the woods with him.

It wasn't just the wolves and Noone who had been watching him, however.

"Hmmm," Franco mumbled to himself as he rubbed his fingers across the steering column of his SUV, as Shorty walked up out of the woods and past his hidden vehicle.

As he came scurrying up the logging road to get to his own truck, Shorty didn't even notice Franco's big black 4x4, it blended so well into the dark under-growth of the statuesque pines. He never even glanced in Franco's direction.

That morning, as Franco made a pot of coffee in the kitchen of his Tudor styled home in Eveleth, a strong sensation had flowed over him. Something was going on in the woods, he knew, so he jumped into his SUV and headed out to forests close to Sam's house. Instinct told him exactly where to go; he'd hunted the area for the last thirty years and knew it well.

Although many locals didn't know Franco was an outdoorsman, in fact he was a skilled hunter and fisherman. He loved the outdoors. He liked being alone in the woods, too, getting away from the hustle and bustle of his own life, away from cloying people. He liked to take the time to get quiet, to commune with nature. The air in the back Minnesota woods was clean and fresh, too, a far cry from the cigarette smoke infested barroom odors of his daily environment.

Driving out there that morning, he never doubted that he would find a secluded spot where he could sit and wait for something to happen. He was on a hunting trip, just a different type of hunting trip. Patience was all it would take . . . something he had plenty of. When he turned off River Drive onto the logging road and saw Shorty's truck parked off to the side, he knew his instincts had been right on target.

Watching and waiting were a practice he had picked up as a young boy, both outside playing with neighborhood roughs and inside his own house dogging his father's drunken beatings, beatings that left him and his mother broken and bloody. It was how he had learned to stay alive and how his intuition had developed.

He told himself that it was because of Shorty's blind side that he watched the woods that day. He wouldn't admit to himself that it had anything to do with the "wolf lady" even though he felt anxious at the idea of her being hurt. His heart leapt as he hoped to catch a glimpse of her. He was not shy when it came to women. The wolf lady made him nervous though, he begrudgingly admitted to himself.

After watching Shorty walk up the road, get in his truck and leave, soon thereafter Franco saw Noone come skirting out of the deep forest at its edge making his way south. The hairs on Franco's neck stood on end at the sight of him. "What's he up to?" Franco wondered as he watched until Noone was completely out of sight. He guessed Sam was still out there in the woods someplace.

Noone was as oblivious to Franco's presence as he had been to the wolves'. His tall, trim body moved through the underbrush as gracefully as a white-tailed deer. Franco took extra interest in Noone because of his nephew Earl. Earl was in Stillwater State prison for life because of a murder he swore he didn't commit. Franco had no real love for Earl, but, "family was family" and he was doggedly determined to find out if Earl was telling the truth. Through some underworld investigating, he became suspicious that Noone had set Earl up for the fall.

Noone had no way of knowing Earl was related to Anthony Franco, if he had set him up, which made no difference to Franco. He didn't believe Earl was guilty, but he knew someone was. And he had no intention of letting whoever killed his neighbor's little twelve-year-old daughter get away with it.

He got angry every time he thought of Earl and that kid. The kid was a sweet little girl. He saw her all the time when he talked to her father.

He didn't think much of how the sheriff's office handled that investigation, either. It smelled fishy from the start. They couldn't find the real killer, so they set up Earl as the patsy. It didn't hurt Gene Trelavonti's feelings any that Earl was Franco's nephew, either. Trelavonti had tried his damnedest to get dirt on Franco over the years, but when he couldn't, he went after Earl who was a petty crook and an easy mark.

Be that as it may, Earl was no murderer or child molester, and Franco was not about to let the Franco name be tarnished with that type of a reputation. Earl would not spend his life in Stillwater State Prison, not if he was innocent, and Franco was convinced that he was.

Besides, whoever killed and molested a kid needed to be locked up forever, Franco believed. In his mind, any perverted son-of-a-bitch who could rape and murder a little girl should be tortured and fed to pigs.

After he watched both Shorty and Noone leave, Franco remained where he was on that old logging road thinking and still hoping to catch a glimpse of Sam. He chided himself for being so interested in her. So what, he said to himself, even if she was interested in me, what am I going to do with a broad like that? Is she going to be just a one-night stand? A casual affair? Someone who can be tossed aside when I get tired of her? I doubt it. So, does that mean I'm considering settling down? Can I? A new type of unease settled in his thoughts.

He hated to admit it to himself, but he was scared. His thoughts of Noone, Earl, that sweet little girl that was murdered, the newspaper's account of that other little girl that had just disappeared, and Shorty's reputation for violence against women, the threatening notes left in Sam's mailbox, none of it helped his unease as he continued to watch the woods.

What was happening on the Iron Range? It had always been a safe place to live, or had it? He remembered then the many kids that had gone missing over the years on the Range, and remembered the legendary haunted house just down the road from where he was.

It wasn't long before he grew so uncomfortable he started his SUV and left. It was dusk. He never did see Sam.

Chapter Ten

When Angie got home after Gilbert's visit to Sam with the injunction, she told Sam she spent the day in Eveleth looking up old property sales records. She found an old deed to Sam's property listing Arthur Noone as owner. Noone had attempted to sell the property in the late 1960's to a professor and his wife through a contract for deed; when the two disappeared the title reverted back to Noone through default.

Angie pointed out that the two hadn't missed a payment until they disappeared, so Noone would have already collected a substantial amount of money depending upon their down payment.

A check on Noone through old newspapers at the Tribune News' offices in Eveleth turned up some interesting information as well, she told Sam.

But Sam was too keyed up to listen any longer, restating the facts of the Sheriff's visit.

Angie said, "How can Noone do that?" She didn't expect an answer.

"I don't know, but apparently he can."

"Did Gilbert say anything about what we already have?"

"No. It was all lying on the kitchen table when he was here, too. He didn't come in any further than the front door, but both doors were open to the kitchen; he had a clear view of everything on the table. Of course, he had no way of knowing what was lying there. At least he didn't say anything about it."

"Good. I think we have more than we need already anyway. The only thing we need to do in the barn is clean it and catalogue the library."

Angie's eyes lit up as she smiled like a Cheshire cat. "I think we should invite the neighbors over for dinner. Maybe if we ply them with good food and drink, they'll tell us a lot more than we already know?" Angie raised her eyebrows to the question looking to Sam like the crazy old professor in ancient sci-fi flicks who always laughs as he rubs his hands together in glee at his monstrous creation and chuckling, "tee, he, he."

Sam still had to introduce Angie to her neighbors, and a dinner party would be just the ticket. "Yeah, I'll tell everyone it's a meet and greet party for you! That's a great idea—but look at you! You've got some dirt on someone, haven't you? It's written all over your face."

"You bettcha'. I've got copies of most of it, too. We're going to have to find some safe place to hide all this stuff." Angie went from mischievous to serious without stopping for air. "Noone probably suspects that we've already taken papers out of the barn. I'm betting, too, that the other day when he was here? That was the first time he'd ever seen that library. I suspect he thinks there's something out there that might incriminate him. The questions are, what and why?"

"Gilbert went down to the barn and locked it up, both the big doors and the doors to the library. There's even tape, police tape, in front of the doors." Sam said.

"You're kidding!"

"Don't I wish."

The two didn't dwell on it. They got busy with plans for the dinner party deciding to throw it the following Friday evening, six days away. They would invite the entire neighborhood sans Arthur Noone.

Angie didn't tell Sam everything she had learned in town. Sam was so caught up in the party plans, so happy she didn't have the heart to tell her she might have clues to the identity of her parents. It was too unbelievable to contemplate, anyway. What she hadn't told Sam when she brought up the dinner party, was that she hoped the neighbors had clues to Sam's real parentage, too, but didn't know it. She'd be able to piece it together without anyone really knowing before Sam. What better gift could she give her best friend, the real reason behind her Cheshire smile? When finished, the two wearily climbed the stairs to their respective bedrooms, both falling into bed and fast asleep immediately.

It was 1 a.m. when Sam awoke to loud banging noises coming from outside. She stumbled out of bed, and stubbed her toe on the bedpost as she fumbled across the floor to the second story bedroom window overlooking the barnyard. She rubbed madly at her sleep-laden eyes, but all she could see initially was the back lawn. A three-quarter-moon lit up the night. With great effort, she managed to focus on the barn door that was slamming back and forth against its door jam casings causing the racket that had awakened her.

I thought Gilbert locked the barn up? She thought, as she continued to watch the wind play with the door, slamming it back and forth. She crossed the room to her wardrobe, grabbed her robe, climbed down the stairs, put on her overcoat and started out the back door heading down to the barn, pulling her second boot on as she went.

She almost fell twice in the cold, wet snow. She tried to balance the flashlight as she walked, the one she grabbed from the kitchen drawer on her way out of the house, but she had no use for it, the night was bright enough without it. She liked the idea of the heavy metal object in her hands, though. With its long handle, it could be used as a weapon, she decided, noting its weight. It felt just right in her palm.

Angie, too, heard the banging. She walked up behind Sam once Sam reached the barn. Sam shined her light into the barn's interior. Nothing looked out of place to either one of them. When the light reached the library door, the women saw that it, too, was wide open. Sam knew Gilbert chained and locked both doors up tight, but there they were, open maws with padlocks dangling from loose chains before each door and police tape rattling in the wind against all of them. On the outside of the barn, the chain scratched against cedar shingles as it was hurdled at the outside walls by the door when it slammed against its casing in the wind. Angie looked around in trepidation.

Sam stepped gingerly between the barn doors as if playing a game of dodge ball to get inside. She stepped up to the library door tiptoeing up to the threshold. She was not aware yet of Angie being right behind her. Sam's flashlight beam lit up the library's interior.

Immaculate, the room was immaculate. Not a speck of dust lie anywhere; every book was dusted and neatly shelved. The leather chairs smelled of leather instead of dust, both freshly oiled. The old roll-top desk sat polished and gleaming. On the end table between the chairs sat a crystal ashtray. In the ashtray sat a pipe with smoke tendrils rising lazily from the red embers in its base. The smell of cherry blend tobacco permeated the room.

As both women looked on, Angie breathily whispered in Sam's ear, "amazing!"

Sam jumped, sucked in her breath, wheeled around to see who had spoken brandishing the flashlight over her head, and preparing to lay hold of her tormentor. She stared incoherently at Angie for a moment, trying to get a grip on the fear that gripped her.

"Sorry," Angie said blissfully unaware of the extent of Sam's fear, "I thought you knew I was right behind you."

"Now how would I know that? Jeez! You scarred me half to death! I darn near bopped you with this!" she shook the light at her causing eerie shadows to dance across the room. "You just took ten years off my life!" She fought to gain her composure.

Angie was struck dumb for but a moment then started to giggle. It wasn't long before Sam joined in. "Yeah, it is kind of funny. I must look a sight." Sam laughed. When she finally managed to stop, she said, "Forget that though, what is this?" She used the flashlight beam to make her point across the library interior.

Angie sobered up too, and said, "Maybe it isn't so wise, us being in here. What if this is Noone's doing? I think we should call the sheriff."

Sam reached into her robe pocket and pulled out her cell phone, a device she carried with her everywhere. She speed dialed Gilbert's number.

"Oh, he's on the speed dial?" Angie said as her left eyebrow rose. Sam ignored her, turned her back, and looked up into the haymow, seeing nothing as she exchanged a few words with Gilbert. She caught him as he was leaving the office. He had just put in another long day still trying to put together the pieces of the missing child puzzle.

Gilbert arrived at Sam's by 1:30 a.m. When they drove into the driveway, he saw two women standing inside the barn doors, and outside the library's double doors. He saw them intermittently through banging open and shut doors. He wondered who the second woman was.

He didn't like the looks of the doors being wide open. He had sealed them both himself. He and a deputy stepped out of the car. The deputy began noting everything in a notebook while Gilbert photographed it all, starting with the outside door lock and chain.

Gilbert scrutinized the floor just inside the outer doors, looked closely at the hanging chain to determine if the hasp had been pried away from the door jam. It hadn't. The chain hadn't been cut with a wire cutter either. The lock itself was not damaged. His eyes drifted over to the women now standing just inside the library out of the biting wind.

Sam and Angie watched as the two men went about their work.

Gilbert raised himself from the squatting position, as the deputy began dusting the library doors for fingerprints, and walked over to the women. "What time did you notice this, Ma'am?" he asked Sam.

"A loud banging woke me just before one. I went to the bedroom window and saw that the barn door was open and blowing in the wind. That's what made the banging noise. Then I came out to shut the barn door. When I did, I discovered the library doors were open, too, so I came in to close them. That's when I saw all this," she pointed to the clean room.

"I locked both doors earlier. Can you explain to me how they were opened? How did this room get so clean if you weren't in it?" Gilbert's gruff, professional, detached manner set Sam's temper on edge. She felt like she is being interrogated.

"No, I can't. I thought, maybe, you didn't lock the outer door? I was surprised to find it open, real surprised to find the library doors open." She fought to be polite

"The other day when we were in here, Noone was here. He came up on us real quiet like. We didn't even know anyone else was around until he spoke. He could have been here. Maybe he broke the locks," Angie offered.

"There is no sign of forced entry, Ma'am. Whoever was in here simply unlocked the doors. I'm the only one with the keys. There is an injunction on this piece of your property. If you two are violating that court order, there could be serious consequences." Gilbert looked at Sam directly. "When I was in here earlier, this room was dusty and dirty. What happened to it?"

"If you're trying to implicate me in anything, we'll just see about consequences." He made Sam so mad so fast, things popped out of her mouth before she could stop them.

But Gilbert was not about to be drawn into any argument. He ignored Sam's outburst turning his attentions to Angie. "Who are you?" He asked pointedly.

"I'm a friend of Samantha's, Angie Eckenridge. I'm visiting." She hated to admit it but Gilbert's scrutiny was unnerving her too, even though she dealt with police on a daily basis.

"Do either of you have enemies?" Skip Gilbert knew the name "Eckenridge" but it wasn't coming to him just how he knew it. She looked familiar to him, too.

"About the whole Iron Range!" Sam quipped. She couldn't help herself. He knew her wolf studies didn't please the locals, and he also knew her removal of wolf traps displeased a whole lot more. She called his office often enough about it.

"Oh, sorry Ma'am," the faintest hint of a smile crossed Gilbert's lips. "I forgot about that. What about you?" He turned to look at Angie. She seemed so familiar?

"Well, I suppose I've made quite a few enemies in my line of work."

"What do you do?"

"I help local authorities catch criminals."

"Oh," Gilbert wouldn't let his interest show. "How is that?"

"I'm thee Angie Eckenridge. Maybe you've heard of me? I've solved some unsolved murder mysteries in the Dakotas and Wisconsin, some in Minnesota, too, as a matter of fact."

"Ohhh! You're THAT Angie Eckenridge!" When he finally realized who she was, Gilbert couldn't believe it. He was a big fan and had read most of her books. He knew a lot of other cops felt that when it came to solving crimes by using a psychic, the cop doing it was daft, but Gilbert's theory was that most investigative cops were psychics themselves when it came to police work . . . at least the good ones.

"Well Miss Eckenbridge," he said slinging the camera he'd been using across his shoulder and putting out his hand to shake hers, "have you any clues as to what might be going on here?"

"I'm sorry to disappoint you, sheriff, but I have never been any good at helping friends solve any problems they might have. I'm too close, you see, just too close." Angie wasn't too surprised at the sheriff's reaction to her. Many cops liked to work with her, many didn't. She smiled. "But honestly, Sheriff, neither I nor Sam came out into the barn after you closed it up this afternoon. When I got home Sam told me you had been here and about the injunction."

Gilbert finally let go of her hand. "I see," he said, but didn't. "I guess we'll just finish up here and you two can go back to bed. It doesn't look like anyone pried these doors open or damaged the locks in any way. I doubt that Noone had anything to do with this. That doesn't mean you shouldn't lock your doors when you're safely inside. Until we know exactly what happened, my advice to you—both of you—is to be very cautious and take no chances with anything. Is that clear?"

"Yes, Sheriff, we'll take you advice." Sam's anger washed away once again at the sheriff's honest show of concern. She and Angie walked back up to the house.

"We'll finish up here and be gone shortly!" Gilbert called to their backs as they walked up the hill.

It took the police an hour to finish up and leave—an anti-climatic end to an eventful night. Neither woman slept much regardless of their late night foray to the barn. Too much excitement, too much time outdoors, all of it conspired against them as each lay in their beds rehashing the days' events.

It was 3:30 a.m., and Sam was counting the ticks of a clock. Finally, she drifted off into that Netherlands between sleep and wakefulness, so when the voice started she didn't stir in bed. She thought she was dreaming as someone called out softly at first, "Samantha. Samantha."

The voice grew more desperate, more demanding, with each utterance. "Samantha!" It screamed and she jumped up in bed. "Samantha!" the voice cried again. Her name reverberated from everywhere at once inside the large bedroom. It unnervered her so much, she ran for the door and out into the hall right into Angie, who stood across from her room, directly in front of the door.

Angie, too, had heard the demanding voice calling out to Sam. On her way to Sam's room, however, she stopped dead in her tracks after looking down over the banister into the dinning room. There, she saw what looked like a whirlwind gushing about counter clockwise. She grabbed Sam's arm and pointed down the stairs.

Sam looked down over to the railing glad to be away from the cacophony in her bedroom. The two stood there watching in silence. There was no question about it; a whirlwind had manifested once again inside the house.

Finally, their inertia broken, they ran downstairs to get a closer look stopping short at the dinning room threshold. Too terrified to enter, they watched as papers, dishes, wall hangings, and everything else in the room thrashed about. It was just like the miniature tornado that had swept through the kitchen the night Angie first arrived. Though they had been through it before, neither woman was prepared to go through it again. And as they stood watching, it stopped in an instant. Everything that had taken flight fell to the floor shattering the early morning household quiet.

Sam and Angie stood there barefoot, mouth's agape starring at the debris-strewn dinning room. An unnatural quiet permeated the surreal atmosphere, which crackled with electricity. Neither woman moved, as if held in suspended animation they waited for something else to happen. For ten minutes, Sam and Angie stood frozen to the threshold.

In all her research, Angie had never seen such a blatant display of telekinesis. She had heard of it, sure, but to actually experience it? She could feel the ebb of electrical current as it dissipated. Background noises, like the clock ticking in the kitchen, the refrigerator humming and the sink dripping, could be heard, which only moments ago had been drowned out by the eerie silence.

Taking one-another's hands, they crossed over the threshold into the dinning room proper, together. Amid the debris, neatly stacked on the dinning room table, were the papers Angie had brought home earlier that day from town. Though she said nothing, she suspected from this bout of telekinesis that she was on the right track concerning Sam's heritage because these were the papers atop the piles.

Sam caught the scent of cherry blend tobacco once again, and saw a waft of smoke lazily reach for the ceiling from an ashtray in the middle of the table, an ashtray she hadn't put there, an ashtray she didn't own. She nudged Angie nodding with her head at the phenomenon.

Angie turned to look at what Sam pointed at. At the same time, and ever so softly, Samantha's name was called out once again, though neither woman had uttered it.

It was just as Angie suspected; the event was not over. She listened intently, trying to determine where the voice came from. She motioned to Sam pointing at the basement stair, "There, I think it's coming from over there," she whispered and the two tiptoed over to the basement door in the kitchen. Together they clasped the violet colored glass doorknob pulling it open. As they did, the smell of cherry blend tobacco was so overpowering Sam gagged. The voice grew more insistent. Its plaintive cry summoning them downstairs, engulfing them as they stepped down the stairs side by side, arm in arm.

"Samantha," it demanded. "Down here!"

Neither woman spoke.

The basement stood exactly as Sam had left it—empty of anything other than the furnace, water heater, and washing machine, dryer and empty cardboard boxes. It was painted white, looked immaculate, and didn't appear to be able to hide anything.

"In here—down here!" They heard. Then the voice fell silent. As they reached the bottom stair, the women could no longer smell tobacco.

Angie had hoped the odor would lead her somewhere, clue her to the area she should be looking for. Disappointed, the women stood still in the middle of the room looking about for anything remotely out of the ordinary. Angie knew that whatever called to Sam wanted her to find something down there. But why her, and what was Sam supposed to find?

Angie analyzed what she had heard and seen in the past few minutes as she walked over to a wall—one that appeared to stand about three feet out from the outer wall. She laid a hand against the cool brick, and was immediately stung by a bolt of energy so strong she felt she'd been punched in the stomach. The wall pulsated, like it had a heartbeat.

Sam stood behind her, so Angie grabbed her hand thrusting it against the brick. Sam, too, felt the sensation, an accidental intimate brush against a stranger in a crowd, embarrassing, but multiplied a thousand times it was so intense. As if burnt, Sam yanked her hand away from the brick.

"I can feel it," Angie said whispering. "It's here; it's in here!"

Sam slapped Angie's hands away from the wall, "Stop it!" she yelled. "I've had enough!" Before Angie could react, Sam was upstairs walking across the kitchen floor overhead.

Angie was torn between the exciting discovery and the visible panic Sam was in. Reluctantly she went upstairs to find her old friend. She told herself as she climbed the steps that the phenomenon was not going away. She had plenty of time to research it. Right now, Sam needed her more. Angie walked into the kitchen to find Sam at the table, hands trembling as she tried to bring a water glass up to her lips.

"It's a little frightening, I know, but everything is going to be okay." She said rubbing Sam's back gently as she seated herself at the table.

"Is it? I'm not so sure." Sam thought of the stack of papers now on her dinning room table, neat and ready to be read. The papers Angie had retrieved from town. She feared the knowledge contained in those papers. Would they, somehow, have a great impact on her life? Something in the way Angie behaved since coming home had her on edge, too; it was as if Angie knew something she didn't. Something she wasn't sure she was ready to discover.

"What is going on here?" Sam asked. "I don't like it. It's not of this world, and I just don't like it!" She fought to hold down the panic that wanted to overtake her. "We don't know if it's evil or not, besides, we just shouldn't be dabbling with spirits!"

"I understand how you feel. All I can tell you is that I have dabbled in 'spirits, or ghosts' off and on now for the last twenty years. I seem to be able to pick up on them. I don't know why. Usually, it's spirits that have passed before their time, more often than not—violently. Most times, they want me to help them tell their loved ones where they are buried, or find their killer. I don't know why—I mean, why me? I pray about it. I ask for protection. I read the Bible, too, and don't understand this aspect of my life. I pray for guidance; that's all I can do. But I do know this—if God didn't want these victims found, or their murderers caught, I guess I couldn't do what I do. Remember, 'He said anything done in secret will be brought to the light. The earth will give up its dead.' Anyway, that's what I think is going on here. There's a spirit that needs someone to help it with unfinished business of some kind."

She wandered off into the dinning room, silently frustrated with it all, sitting down in front of one pile of papers looking at them as if they were alive, condemning her for her inadequacies, she angrily grabbed the top paper and slapped it down in front of herself.

"What's wrong with you?" Sam said after following Angie into the dinning room and observing her countenance as she stared at the paper in front of her.

"I have to go to the bathroom," Angie said, ignoring Sam's comment.

"Well go, for heaven's sake."

"I don't want to!" Angie said emphatically. She felt so compelled to read; she ignored her bodies' signals to use the latrine. As she read, she was more than a little surprised to find journal notes in among the paperwork that she brought home. She guessed that during the whirlwind some of the papers from the library became mixed up with the other paperwork. It was captivating reading.

Sam stood silently by watching her.

With no provocation from Sam, Angie slammed the paper she had been reading down on the tabletop hissing, "It makes me so mad! All those stories I heard in town about her, Janice, the professor's wife—I mean. Some actually insinuated she was having an affair with Arthur Noone! Can you imagine? But not according to this!" Angie picked the journal paper up off the table and shook it at Sam. "This is part of her journal. Read this." She thrust the loose-leaf paper at Sam.

"What are you so mad about? It isn't like she was anything to you!"

"How the hell do I know," she blurted in her frustration. "But I'll tell you this. I'm as mad as if someone where saying those nasty things about you. Go on! Read! I want to know what you think."

Angie ran to the bathroom as Sam read:

They are the sweetest little girls; they're only nine months old but already they can form words. Katrina takes after that delicious father of hers—brilliant. Cassandra is just like me—beautiful! Is my ego out of hand, or what? He's downstairs in the study reading. I can smell his tobacco; I love it, him. I'm so happy it's scary. How does anyone hold onto such blissful feelings? Can they? I have to go; I hear the girls upstairs. I can't wait to go hug them, rub their soft skin against my cheek, give them a bath, and get them all sweet smelling. I'll fix them up to show them off to their father. They always entice him out of his

books, even more than I can. If I weren't so happy that it's so, I
might be jealous.

The journal continued on in the same tone. If the woman
writing it was anything less than a loving wife and mother, it
didn't show in her writing. Sam had heard stories about the
professor's wife, too, the same stories Angie obviously heard, and
wondered—this can't be the same woman every one said ran off
with Noone—can it? And why was it so aggravating to Angie? It
made her angry, too, that people thought so poorly of Janice. She
loved her family! Sam couldn't see the woman running away to be
with Noone—no—never—it was an absurd idea!

Angie came back; Sam handed her the journal and told
her she agreed with her. The people in town were all wrong about
the professor's wife.

The two continued to work, saying little. It was a rough
night. After the early morning barn door incident and the voice
calling them to the basement, the quiet interlude was a welcome
relief. But it didn't last. It was late morning when they heard a
knock on the back door.

"I'll get it," Angie said and walked to the kitchen.

Skip Gilbert stood alone in the doorway. Without
preamble, he said, "I've read all your stuff" as Angie opened the
door to him. "What are you doing out here?"

"Why is that any of your concern?" Angie wasn't in the
mood for any fans, especially this one.

Sam joined Angie at the kitchen door. "Sheriff, why don't
you come in?" She had not heard their exchange.

"I'm sorry I was so abrupt," Gilbert said to Angie as he
followed her inside. "I didn't mean to come on like some star
struck fan. But the truth is I am a big fan of yours. You being here,
right in my district, and me getting to meet you, well, that's a big
deal to me. I have read a lot of your work and I remember some of

those cases. My dad was sheriff when that stuff went on in North Dakota. He was a good friend to one of the men you worked with out there—Sheriff Dan Gooseberry?"

"Oh yes, I remember him. I'm sorry, too, sheriff; I didn't mean to be so curt. It's just that so much has gone on and we still haven't gotten much sleep." Angie pointed to Sam as she talked and Gilbert took note of Sam for the first time.

"Hello Miss Egar; I hope we can clear that note business up for you soon, that and the barn door incident."

"Thanks, sheriff; I hope so too." But it wasn't the sheriff Sam looked at with interest; it was Angie. She hadn't paid much attention to Angie's work outside of her psychology practice. She knew Angie worked with the police, that she had a psychic gift, but not much more. Angie's books were on her bookshelf waiting for her to read them, but she hadn't gotten to it.

"You know, Ma'am," Gilbert said to Sam. "You have the best known profiler in the country staying at your house? Did you know that?"

"Profiler, what's a profiler?"

"I'm called into cases to use my psychological background; I give the police an idea of who it is they're dealing with. For instance, I can tell by studying a crime seen if a killer is a male, his ethnic background, the type of employment he is likely to have and a number of other factors. But I have taken it a step further. I use my psychic gifts as well. I've been pretty successful. It's also one of the things I do for a living." Angie resented the fact that Sam wasn't more aware of this. Sam and she, after all, were best friends.

Sam chided herself for being so insensitive. "I am sorry. I have a number of your books. I just haven't read them yet. I was planning on reading some over the winter, but so much has been going on, I just haven't gotten to it." She thought her apology weak, even to her own ears. She hoped Angie would forgive her in spite of it.

"I am disappointed, but I forgive you." The two hugged.

Gilbert stood to the side, just inside the kitchen door in his heavy winter clothing with his boots dripping snow onto the tiled floor. "I remember that case you worked on in Fargo. It was in all the papers. The local FBI was having a time trying to get a handle on that killer, Henry Albright. What was it that got him to killing? I don't remember."

They all moved over to the kitchen table while Sam got everyone coffee.

"He had been demoralized by his parents. He grew up being tortured every day of his life in new and horrendous ways by his mother and father. Anyone who remotely resembled either of them he killed in unique and varying ways. If they had kids, he didn't care. He'd torture them too. Police dubbed him the Mom and Pop killer—Henry Albright. He was tough."

"What was it like being around him?" Gilbert asked. He and Sam were captivated with Angie's story.

"He was hard core. Evil. One of three brothers, but we never could locate the other two. Their parents disappeared sometime after Henry turned eighteen; at least that's what an aunt of his said. They were never seen again, and the aunt, she felt that Henry, or one of the other brothers, killed them. She said they were all a mean bunch. Police learnt that the aunt suffered from senility, so they figured she was confused in her mind about Albright having brothers, since they could never find them. Anyway, Henry was hard for the police to catch and miserable for me to deal with."

"What do you mean, deal with?" Gilbert asked the question Sam was thinking.

"That's how I find them. I study the crime scene, to be sure, but I also pick up on psychic impressions. With some police, it's okay to talk about that, but it makes many others nervous, so I keep those impressions to myself. I usually confide in one investigator only, the one who called me in to begin with.

With Henry, the feelings were so strong I went into a trance right there at the crime scene. A number of uniformed officers refused to work with me after that, but your dad's friend, Sheriff Gooseberry, he paid even more attention to me and helped me through some awfully emotional scenes. You see, sometimes I have to witness what the killer has done, or is going to do, in my mind. It's very difficult. Horrible things happen, mostly though its empathetic feelings that help me locate a suspect.

Murderers, especially serial killers, don't start out life committing murder, things happen to them as they grow up, most of the time it's these things that I tune into. Emphatic feelings help me figure out what the suspect will do next, sort of guess where police should look for them to strike again. Of course, much of that is psychic awareness. I can see it. But it is never crystal clear; I get images, sometimes words.

Those can be difficult to interpret; an investigator might pick up on something I said, though. Perhaps a location I've talked about has meaning to them, and when they investigate, they find a clue or something that allows them to make an arrest.

The Mom and Pop killer, though, he brought me to a hard spiritual place where I could find little compassion for him.

When Gooseberry had me looking through mug shots, I zeroed in on Albright immediately. Relatives started talking about the family to me, things they never told the police. When I compared their information to medical information I had on Albright, I 'knew' he was the one."

Gilbert sat on the edge of his chair as Angie spoke. He remembered Gooseberry and his father talking about the case around their dinning room table, something his mother rarely allowed.

Angie continued, "He had a horrible life growing up. By the time Henry was twelve, the Mom and Pop killer in training was in plenty of trouble of his own with police. They had little compassion for him. The family was poor, what most called 'white trash' and no one did anything for the kid. According to his juvenile record, he had been in so many fights police lost count. The fights were serious too. One kid he put in a coma.

As soon as Henry turned fifteen he ran off and joined the Navy. Lied about his age to get in and got into a lot of trouble there, too. When he got out, he was a man, a very disturbed man. I think that he killed his parents time and time again with every murder he committed.

I don't have much hope for his siblings, either. The rest of his family has never been found and there are a lot of police who think Albright killed every one of them. I'm not so sure. I know he has two brothers, both younger, but investigators don't believe that. No one has been able to locate any of them. They may well all be dead, like the police suspect. I have a strong feeling, though, that his brothers, at least, are alive."

Gilbert was uneasy. Something fluttered at the back of his mind telling him she was absolutely right, but he couldn't grasp exactly what it was that convinced him so. He said, "Man, I just wish that once in my professional life I'd have to come up against someone that would take a lot of thinking to catch, someone with some intelligence whose arrest would be an accomplishment, a gift to society."

Angie looked at him for what seemed like an eternity sighing and shaking her head ever so slightly. "That may not be as far out of your reach as you think."

"What do you mean?"

"I mean, there's a real danger right here. I feel it. I feel it as much as I felt it with Henry Albright. It's evil—and tangible."

Chapter Eleven

On Friday night, dinner guests started arriving by 6 p.m. "Inez, Gladys, you two look marvelous," Bernice said as she greeted the Spencer sisters when they arrived shortly after she did.

"How good of you to say so, Bernice; your brood is looking good, too." Inez said as she gazed over Bernice's shoulder into the living room.

Bernice beamed as she turned to follow Inez's gaze. Vicki and Mike played Monopoly on the living room floor, while the youngest three, Josephine and Jasmine, twins aged nine, and Jeremy, seven, played Nintendo.

Sam had made a special trip to Duluth to buy games for the kids knowing that Bernice rarely went anywhere without them. She didn't have a clue as to what children might like. A clerk at Toys R' Us had been a boon of information, and from the looks of things, she was right on target. Sam went overboard purchasing everything the clerk said that kids might like; they were having so much fun, she was glad she had.

While they played the adults visited and moved about the

house getting a good look at it under normal circumstances, something few of them had done before. Bernice was determined to see just exactly what everyone had been talking about, especially since her son had told her those stories. It looked like any old house to her with nothing whatsoever to be frightened of, she thought as she walked its halls.

Bernice walked the upstairs halls without her husband, because John had stayed behind to tend the cattle. He'd be there later. Clem too, would arrive later as he also had to tend to his livestock. The women took the time away from the men to make a point of getting to know Angie as they toured the house.

Downstairs, Sam, having an eye for designing an appealing food tray, kept the trays filled as she bustled to and fro from the kitchen anytime a need arose. On one of her forays to fetch more food, Vicki quietly came in behind her to help. This was the first time she had broken away from the game of Monopoly she played with her brother to talk with the adult women. As they stood at the kitchen counter decorating, Vicki cleared her throat. She had yet to speak up and Sam wondered what was on her mind.

"Ms. Egar, Mike and I have heard rumors," she said shyly as they worked. "We wondered Mike and I—you know—the stories about this place? We've heard them ever since we moved out here. We even snuck over here once when no one was around. It was at night. We saw lights."

Sam looked into Vicki's young face and wondered about telling her some lie to cover up what really went on in her house at night.

"Are you asking me if the house is haunted?" Vicki nodded her head. "Yes—I think it is" Sam said, believing it was best to be honest, especially with children. "That's why I've invited everyone over. To see if they can help Angie and I put the pieces of this puzzle together. The house is a puzzle, you see, whatever happened in it long ago, I mean. We're trying to clear up the mysteries of the past. I suppose that sounds kind of strange."

"No, I don't think that's strange! But Mike and I are very interested in helping. Ever since we were kids . . ." Sam had to stifle an urge to grin, Vicki was so earnest. "We could talk to each other without speaking. Do you know what I mean? And sometimes we pick up on things." Vicki's eyes glistened. "The twins do, too. They often talk just by looking at each other."

"Have you told your mother this?"

"Oh, she knows . . . I think she's psychic. At least she is with us. We can't get away with anything. She's the same way with Pop. Worse even. But I gotta warn you; she doesn't like it, doesn't want us to discuss it."

"I'll see if I can persuade her to let you and Mike be included in the discussion. For now though, let's get back in there and mingle." Sam handed Vicki the tray and she took it into the living room to serve everyone. By then, John and Clem had arrived.

Inez and Gladys joined Clem on the couch sitting on either side of him. He looked happy as a lark to be the center of their attentions.

As she watched the three, Sam wondered if Clem felt safe with the ex-hookers, confident in his knowledge that neither lady had any designs on his bachelor-hood. Or did they? She remembered the conversation at the Eveleth community picnic. She smiled as she thought that perhaps Clem wasn't as safe as he thought he was.

John sat perched on the arm of the overstuffed chair Bernice occupied. Even in the winter, his skin was deeply bronzed with a farmer's tan. His arm muscles rippled as he used his hands to talk. The overall effect of his presence was one of endless vitality. When he placed his face next to Bernice's', as he did often, his tanned skin starkly contrasted against her milky white complexion. That night the quiet farmer, a man usually too busy to take time to visit, let the full force of his up-beat personality resonate within the room.

Sam discretely watched him looking from John and Bernice to the children and noting the resemblance between them all. Even a stranger would know they were family.

Vicki, after she finished with the serving tray, sat in a corner by herself listening. Overweight and shy, she didn't talk much preferring to sit quietly and politely listen to others. In contrast, Mike's hazel eyes twinkled as he spoke confidently with the adults. Sam could see that Mike overshadowed Vicki during family interactions.

Shortly after the men's arrival everyone's attention centered on Angie, and she started to tell them a bit about herself. Sam hadn't told her neighbors much about Angie's background, preferring that Angie do it herself. Angie grabbed and held her audience's attention easily as she spoke, while her gracious and warm personality charmed everyone.

"Sam has mentioned you from time to time. It's nice to finally meet you." John said.

"You know, honey, don't you, that you've walked right into a mess here?" Inez and Gladys said in unison. They already knew about Angie's other 'gifts' thanks to Inez's dreams.

"And we're glad you did," Gladys said without waiting for Angie's response. "We heard you have some special talents that might help Sam here with her problem?" Inez's right eyebrow rose knowingly. "We right about what we heard, honey?" She tested her to see if Angie would be forthcoming.

"Why don't you two let the woman alone?" Clem came directly to the point.

Bernice hugged Angie and told her not to fret over the curmudgeons she and Sam had for neighbors. "They are really quite harmless."

Mike said, "Aren't you the lady that helps police solve serial killings? I think I've read some of your books."

"Yes, I am." Angie said hiding her surprise that one as young as Mike knew about her 'other' work. "But what is someone so young doing reading about those killings? Most are pretty gruesome."

"I'm real interested in solving crimes," Mike said, pleased that the well-known psychic detective talked to him like he was grown. "I think I want to be a police officer when I get older."

"That's wonderful."

No one said a word. Sam had never mentioned that Angie helped police solve crimes, murders no less, since she herself hadn't kept up with that area of Angie's life.

"Well, from the look on your faces, I guess most of you are a bit surprised by what else I do. It is one of the reasons I'm here," Angie said turning to take in the whole room as she gauged reactions. "I think we'll be getting into that a little later on though." She fell silent.

Bernice took the pressure off Angie by starting a conversation with Gladys. John did the same with Clem, while Inez moved over to Angie asking her a totally unrelated question, and the kids went back to playing games. Most of the adults digested what they learned about Angie with grace, although Bernice wasn't too happy with Mike for never mentioning the fact that he had read Angie's books, or the content of said books. She knew why, too. She'd speak with him later.

The evening picked back up. The radio played softly in the kitchen as Sam went to and fro with food and drinks. She followed the weather reports as she went. The storm she first heard about last weekend was brewing, the broadcaster said, set to begin that evening. Forecasters were predicting twenty inches of snow, blowing winds, and freezing temperatures once the snow let up.

Blizzard conditions would prevail, the first big one of the season, she reported to her guests as she served them, but no one paid much attention. Tried and true Minnesotans, they were all prepared for the unexpected where weather was concerned, especially in the winter.

At dinner, everyone enjoyed food Angie, an accomplished cook, prepared. Not to be undone, Bernice, Gladys, and Inez had all brought along a favorite dish to share as well, as had Clem.

During their meal, Clem asked, "What on earth ever possessed you to buy that bull, John? That's something I never did understand. Does he make you any money? Is he worth the danger?"

"Steamroller has made me a lot of money, so yeah, he's worth it. But he is dangerous; I knew that from the day I bought him. I suspect I was better off that way, too, because I have never taken any stupid chances with him. I expect trouble from Steamroller, and if I'm not careful, he'll be more than happy to oblige. He won't catch me by surprise, not if I have anything to say about it.

And why I bought him? Well, the truth of it is I have a yen for the old west and he just seemed the ticket to getting me a piece of it. You know all those cowboys come up during rodeo season, and we sit and talk for hours, so I guess I just get to go rodeoing through them. One of these days when I get to take a vacation, I'm taking Bernice and the kids down south to a Dude ranch where we can go on a real cattle drive."

"I didn't know you had it in ya, John?" Clem said smiling, delighted by John's confession, "but does the little lady there share your idea of vacation fun?"

John laughed. He and Bernice had gone a round or two over his idea to take them on a cattle drive, but that's exactly where they'd be going the following winter.

Clem wasn't finished. He turned his attentions to Sam. He didn't care who was hosting the party, if he had something to say, he would damn well say it, he told anyone who would listen often enough. By the time he was well into his tirade against the kinda' pretty thieving sons-a-something he wouldn't name in front of the kids, meaning the wolves, someone knocked at the door.

Sam, relieved to get away from the table, hurried to answer it and was puzzled because she knew that everyone she intended to invite was already there.

As she got to the back door, she found Skip Gilbert and two of his deputies standing on her back porch.

"We've got a complaint about noise, Ma'am." Gilbert spoke in that professional tone that grated on her nerves so severely.

"Sheriff, I live two miles from my nearest neighbor, most of who are in my dinning room right now trying to enjoy a meal. Now who complains about a party two miles away?" With hands on her hips, she pushed her face in closer to the sheriff's and looked him in the eye.

A slight smile skimmed over Gilbert's lips, lightly, like dragonflies in the summer over tranquil waters gently rippling the calm lake surface. "That was a joke, Ma'am," Gilbert said watching defenselessly as her eyes stabbed him and her face-flushed red. His hat was in his hand. His deputies looked ill at ease. "May we come in?"

"I guess you can," Sam said, turning her back on the men inside her porch in order to force herself to shake off her feelings of intense irritation for the sheriff.

"Have any of you had dinner yet?"

"No Ma'am," the three men answered in unison. Kitchen smells were so enticing they knotted the men's stomachs with hunger.

"Come in please. Everyone is in the dinning room. There's plenty of food."

"Ma'am," Gilbert said, "I told the guys Angie Eckenridge was here, then I head about this little get together, and we have all heard stories about this house; we wanted to meet Ms. Eckenridge and check out the house." He pointed to his deputies. "There's a lot we might be able to help you with if you'll let us. I mean," he said stammering, "we've all heard plenty about this place, been out here a time or two on calls . . ."

Sam stopped dead in her tracks to look at all three of them. Too bad they aren't this helpful when it comes to the notes in my mailbox, she thought, then led the men into the dinning room shaking her head and fighting off the anger that seethed inside.

"And what are your names?" she asked the deputies as they crossed the room. "Gene Trelavonti," one said; "Jake Jackson," the other added. Trelavonti looked to Sam to be about sixty, Jackson, thirty or so.

"Gentlemen, meet the rest of my guests." Sam introduced the policemen all around. There was an uncomfortable moment as the policemen stood over the table with their hats in their hands that ended when John and Clem stood up to shake hands with the trio.

"Here, someone can take a seat here," Clem said moving his chair over, "let Skip sit next to me. You two, there's room on the other side of the table." Mike hurried to bring in extra chairs for the new guests. John made room for the two deputies next to him.

Skip was overjoyed that Clem offered him a seat for now he was sitting right across the table from Angie and right next to Sam who sat at the head of the table.

Most everyone knew who the deputies were except for Jackson. Jackson was new to the area and hadn't heard the rumors about Sam's house, but he was interested in anything the sheriff was interested in. He was the one deputy Skip had won over.

After dinner the women cleaned the table, put dishes in the dishwasher, served pie, coffee, brandy, and pop hurriedly, then sat back down at the dinning room table to tell and listen to stories.

Vicki and Mike remained at the table. The other children had fallen fast asleep in the living room watching a movie. It was 9 p.m. and the house was quiet except for the refrigerator running in the kitchen, the dishwasher going through its cycles, a dripping faucet, a clock ticking in another room, and the deep breathing sounds of the children sleeping.

Sam tingled with excitement sensing she was about to get a very interesting local history lesson. And it didn't pass without her noticing that this was the first real get together she had had since moving into her new home. For a brief second, awkwardness hung in the air as everyone wondered who would start the ball rolling.

"I guess you're wondering what we're doing here." Skip Gilbert took charge, as was his custom, pointing to himself and his men. "We've heard stories about this place, learned that something was going on out here tonight, and hoped we could sit in on it." He looked around the table briefly debating if he should tell these people about Ellen; in an instant he knew he should, but he didn't know why. He went with his instincts.

"I had a girlfriend when I was sixteen," he said. "We were just friends, although at one time we did date. I was crazy about her, but she didn't respond to me in that way. Oh, she liked me, but she saw me as a friend, period. Anyway, she went and got herself pregnant sometime after we quit hanging around together. The guy dumped her after he got what he wanted and she turned to her old 'friend' and told me about it. She didn't know what she was going to do. This was in the late 1960s

The next thing I know, she's gone, just up and disappeared. My father, Stan, in case any of you don't know, used to be the sheriff in St. Louis County; he investigated her disappearance, talked to her parents, and a lot of other people about her. The parents were members of some fundamental religion and wouldn't tell him anything. Her name was Ellen by the way.

You remind me of her," Gilbert said to Vicki, who blushed when everyone looked at her. The sheriff turned his attention back to the rest of the group.

"Every night when the old man came home from work I'd ask him 'did you find her?' He'd just say 'no.'" Gilbert looked down into his coffee cup as if deep in thought.

"That's the last I ever heard of Ellen. No one ever saw or heard from her again. When I became sheriff one of the first things I did was go through my father's old files on Ellen's disappearance. I am determined to find out what happened to her, you see, even if I have to keep looking until the day I die. In those old files I found out what my father really knew." Gilbert's deep baritone voice soothed nerves as he held everyone's undivided attention with his story.

"She disappeared off the face of the earth. Her parents claimed they didn't know anything about it. My father was suspicious of them, though, so he started snooping into their background. He found out Ellen's folks were friends of Arthur Noone and that they had her in their car the afternoon I last saw her.

Clem said he saw them leave Noone's later that day, but she wasn't in the car with her folks. It was after dark when he saw Noone leaving, too. He couldn't tell if anyone else was in the car with him. My pop wrote that Clem said he went to bed early so he never saw Noone return."Gilbert put his hand on Clem's shoulder, softly.

Angie watched Gilbert closely, hanging on every word, studying him.

Skip continued. "When we were kids, Ellen's parents wouldn't talk to me at all. I learned a great deal about them through Ellen when we were spending so much time together. From what she told me, they never would have tolerated an unwed pregnant girl living with them. They would have banned her from the house. They were also sure I was the one that got her pregnant. They had no clue as to what really happened.

I would have married Ellen even if I wasn't the baby's father. I loved her. I would have been a good father to the baby, too, but that wasn't good enough for her parents. I wasn't good enough. We didn't go to church, you see, so we were heathens in the eyes of Ellen's folks."

"I remember her," Trelavonti said. "You two were quite the item once, weren't ya'," he chided Gilbert. "She was a real looker. I'm not surprised somebody knocked her up." He remembered then the children at the table; "I mean . . ." his sentence drifted off.

Bernice gave Trelavonti a dirty look. Mike and Vicki didn't notice. They were completely caught up in the sheriff's story. A mystery, a kid their own age, they loved it! They hung on every word.

Without anyone noticing, Kitty came into the dinning room and sat underneath Sam's chair between her legs. No one heard her growling.

"Clem, do you remember who lived on the Waverly farm before John and Bernice?" Even though the family named Waverly hadn't owned the Jennings' farm in over fifty years, it was still called that by anyone born and raised on the Iron Range.

"Yeah. It was old Jim Rivers. He and Noone were buddy buddies if I remember right."

"Yep, that was him. It turned out Noone had something on Rivers and was holding it over his head to get him to do things for him. At least that's what my father figured. Rivers disappeared, too, you know."

"Yeah," Clem said, "I remember that. Rivers was a little slow in the head, weren't he? I mean no one thought too much of it when he disappeared. We all thought he'd gone back to the river and fell in, is all. That current can carry you away pretty quick. Jeez! I haven't thought of him in years. Damn near forgot the old bugger ever lived out here!"

"We haven't," Gilbert said ominously, his professional demeanor jumping to the fore as he took on an air of authority. As he did, his deputies' demeanor changed too. They sat up straighter in their chairs as an iron mask like veil fell over their eyes shielding their thoughts from observers. The change was instantaneous and in that moment everyone in the room felt like they were under investigation. In another almost visible change of mood, Gilbert remembered where he was and what he was talking about. His demeanor changed once again. He relaxed. As he did, his deputies did the same. Everyone in the room felt that change, too.

"My father didn't think old man Rivers drown in the river. My father thought Noone disposed of Rivers when he had no more use for him. My father turned up some other interesting things; for instance," Gilbert turned to look at Sam, "he found River's fingerprints in this house. Did you know that?"

"Well no, but I've never heard of this Rivers before. Who is he?"

Gilbert smiled. "Rivers was a mystery to most folks. Maybe that's just as well. He was more than just a little weird. The man stole into many of the neighboring homes and took things. Things he'd bring over to Noone. He was so bold he went into the houses at night when families were home in bed, and took stuff." Gilbert looked over at Vicki and Mike. He didn't elaborate on what types of things Rivers took. "My father found a lot of stuff at Rivers' house when they were investigating his disappearance. Nothing of any real value, mind you, just real personal belongings." Gilbert discreetly tried to tell the adults that what Rivers took were women's undergarments.

"You mean he stole women's underpants," Mike blurted out.

"Yeah, that's what I mean," Gilbert said.

Bernice and John raised their eyebrows as they looked at their son. Mike didn't notice. He was too interested in the sheriff's story to be concerned with what he had just said.

"My father found a lot of other stuff in Rivers' house, too," Gilbert continued. "Literature. Stuff on killing, things like that. He had a lot of guns, knives." Gilbert glanced at the children again and didn't elaborate.

"But he found out something a lot more interesting about Rivers. Rivers wasn't the man's real name." Gilbert paused and looked around the table, then turned to look at Clem, the one he figured it would have the most effect on.

"It was Noone. In reality, Rivers was Arthur Noone's brother, Joseph." The statement hung in the air like a lead weight.

Gilbert went on, "Arthur had the goods on Joseph alright. Joseph had been taking things since he moved out here. Police had no reason to investigate him before he disappeared and would never have known anything about him if he hadn't. He lived pretty quiet. And police never did learn what really happened to him, which bothered my father. He suspected Arthur of doing something to Joseph, but he could never prove anything."

As Gilbert spoke, Angie's mind flashed to something she had once gone through, the talk of Joseph and Arthur Noone triggering a memory, but it hung back in her mind just out of reach, and she couldn't grasp it.

"My father wrote copiously about what he suspected happened to Ellen and what he did find. I don't know if he ever guessed I would take his place as sheriff, but he wanted whoever did to have detailed reports about everything he knew," Gilbert said.

Trelavonti fidgeted in his chair. Everyone else was paying rapt attention to the sheriff and didn't notice—except for the cat. As Trelavonti moved, Kitty swatted at him from beneath the table but missed. Still no one at the table knew the cat was near them.

Gilbert turned to Sam. "That's why I want to make sure all of you know that Noone is no one to trifle with." He looked Sam in the eye. "You have to be careful. Shorty is no one to mess with either. He hangs around with Noone. And we suspect they work together in the woods. Who traps what, we don't know yet, but we're working on it. Shorty has a reputation for trouble. He's hard as nails," Gilbert turned and looked at everyone. He hoped he had made his point.

For the first time since Sam first started pulling wolf traps on the Iron Range, she felt fear about what was going on in her professional life. Regardless, she wasn't going to quit and she wasn't going to stop removing any illegally set steel leghold laceration traps. They were inhumane, nasty devices that put an animal in agony, should it get caught in one. Most trappers hadn't used the things in decades, and she'd be damned if she wouldn't stop springing them and tossing them up in trees every time she found one.

"Yeah? Well what's going on right now, here, in this house?" Vicki asked bringing about an audible sigh of relief from a number of the adults who were glad someone changed the subject.

"I've seen some funny things go on in this place over the last 30 years," Clem started the ball rolling. He told everyone about the lights, the voice; the same story he told Sam the night she had dinner with him.

"I came in here once, about a year ago," Mike offered. "A bunch of us guys were on our way back to the river. They dared me to do it—to come into the house by myself, I mean. I told them stories about the place. How it's funny . . . odd . . . you know?

Nothing happened when I was in here, but man it really weirded me out, like someone was in here with me, watching me. The hairs on the back of my neck stood up. It was creepy. I never made it to the other floors. I came as far as the kitchen standing by the pantry door—you know the one, Sam—when I got this real weird feeling, like I was in danger. It was so strong, I ran like hell to get out of here. The guys razed me about running out, but none of them had the guts to even come in here. But we did spend some time camped in the woods on the other side of the road watching the place. I can back up Mr. Johnson's story. I saw those lights, too, heard those cries. So did the guys. If you don't believe me, go ask 'em."

"Michael!" Bernice said. Mike just shrugged his shoulders. He was so engrossed in what was going on, he didn't care if his parents got mad at him. It would pass; besides . . . maybe he could help the police discover what was going on . . .

"Sometimes, at night, at home, I hear things," Vicki said. "It's scary. It happens most when I'm home alone. It sounds like names being called. I thought I heard the name 'Arthur' once." Her voice was soft, as if she was afraid to say anything out loud.

"That's happened to me too," Mike said. "I don't like it when I hear those noises. They don't feel right."

Vicki knew Mike had heard the same things she had and was delighted he spoke up in front to the adults to agree with her. Bernice was not delighted. Worry lines etched her brow. John didn't say a word, but picked up his pipe, lit it, and looked intently at their children.

Mike held his father's gaze. He didn't want him to think he was making up some story to look big in front of the cops. He and Vicki had been afraid to broach this subject with their parents. He was glad to finally get it out into the open. He looked over at Vicki who smiled back at him.

"I hear stuff in the barn," John said tapping his pipe in the crystal ashtray in front of him. Bernice's mouth dropped open and the children turned to stare at their father wide-eyed.

"I'll hear a 'huummmpppphhhhh' sound sometimes as if someone is frowning on the way I do things. It's nasty—feels threatening. I sense danger every time it happens, and it has happened more than once since we've lived out here. One time a pitchfork came off the wall and hurled itself at me landing at my feet. I was feeding the cows." John shook his head as if he still had a hard time believing the incident ever happened.

"You know, it has only happened a few times in all the years we've lived there, but lately it seems to be happening more. It makes me nervous, too, especially with that big old Brahma bull in the barn. If he gets excited, there'll be hell to pay."

Clem agreed. "That's one fine animal, John, but for the life of me, I don't understand why you bought 'yer self a bull that big. He must way a ton! You need to carry a gun with ya' just incase that big 'un ever does go crazy on ya."

"We hear footsteps. On the stairs." Bernice's nine-year-old twins Josephine and Jasmine said in unison from the living room threshold. No one had heard them get up. As they spoke from behind the group, everyone jumped. The twins ignored them. "It's like someone is coming down the stairs one step at a time. When they reach the landing to come down the last four steps into the kitchen, there's no one there."

Bernice was flabbergasted. "Has my whole family gone crazy?" She was more than a little agitated as she pushed her chair back from the table, grabbed the twins by the arms and practically hurled them up the stairs to a spare bedroom Sam had prepared for anyone who wanted to use it. It wasn't that Bernice didn't believe what her family was saying; she knew only too well that they were speaking the truth. What disturbed her was that she felt as if the devil himself was coming against them. She just had not realized to what extent he had been working his evil.

Upstairs, she got down beside the twin's bed after tucking them in and went to praying a prayer of protection for her family and friends. "Fear not" is the only thing that came to her mind. She knew the Bible contained that phrase time and again, she had read it often enough, so she recited Psalm 23: ". . . Yeah, though I walk through the valley of the shadow of death, I will fear no evil for the Lord is with me . . ."

Downstairs, the party continued.

John again shook tobacco from his pipe. "She's frightened." He said of Bernice. "I never told her about the pitchfork; I didn't want to scare her." He turned and looked at Vicki and Mike, "But it would have been wiser if you two had confided in us about what you've heard."

"We're sorry, Pop. Besides, it's so weird, we didn't think you'd believe us," Mike said.

"Well, we'll talk more about this when we get home. But if there is anything else to tell about strange goings on, I guess now would be the time to tell it." John loaded his pipe once again and lit it.

"We've heard that noise the twins were talking about, too," Vicki said softly.

"So have I," John said.

"What has all that got to do with what's happening here?" Sam wondered out loud.

"It's all related," Angie spoke up for the first time.

Immediately the sheriff and deputies sat forward in their chairs and everyone's eyes fell on her.

Angie was intrigued with the stories. She leaned her elbows on the table resting her head in her hands, and said, "It's Noone. He's the catalyst. Whatever is going on, he's behind it . . . He's got something to do with all of it, even your girlfriend, Sheriff." Angie looked at Gilbert. "I'm sensing some sort of spiral, as if someone here, in this house, is a catalyst to these events, events that are going to increase in occurrence until the mysteries surrounding this area are solved."

Angie said to Gilbert. "I think that wish you told me about the other day is about to come true for you, in a big, big way. That's why I'm here."

She turned to look at John. "You know, you need to be careful of whatever it is that's coming at you over at your place. That pitchfork incident tells me that you're dealing with a malevolent spirit and you need to take that seriously. I can give you some advice on how to do that if you like."

John shook his head, smiling slightly and said, "That's good of you to offer, but if we can't rely on God for protection, then our beliefs aren't as sound as we thought. What I'll do for you, as will the rest of my family, is pray for everyone here." He smiled at Angie then, a smile full of warmth and kindness.

"I've been having this feeling lately," Gilbert spoke up, "about this place. I don't just mean this house, but this area—you know? It's a feeling, like something is lurking behind the next bush. And the feeling just keeps getting stronger. When Sam showed up out here, I really got a sense of it. I escorted her home one night from Tony's and all the way out here, the feeling just got stronger and stronger. I hadn't thought of Ellen in years at the time, now all of a sudden I can't stop thinking about her. Sam is some kind of link, I think, but I don't know how that's possible; she's never been here before in her life, she said."

Oh, good grief, Sam thought, but said. "What? Are you going to blame me for the haunting too? Maybe I'm good for the disappearances you were talking about? Jeez!" She gave Skip Gilbert a dirty look.

Gilbert ignored her. "I'll tell you something from a police officer's perspective. Some of what I've heard, well . . . it's hard to believe. Any outsider listening to all these stories might think it's a bunch of . . . well, you know . . . made up gobbly gook." Gilbert wondered if he could convince a jury in a court of law that something supernatural was going on out there.

"Yeah," Jackson spoke up for the first time that night, "it might be hard to try and convince a jury of your stories. Personally, I'm not from around here, and all of it is a bit hard to swallow."

Chapter Twelve

The lights flickered—went out. No one moved. All held their breath in anticipation in a room so dark neighbor could not see neighbor. Blinded to their own fingers, they searched across the tabletop for reassurance hoping to touch one-another's hands.

Underneath the table, Kitty let out the infamous Siamese wail of anger so loudly the guests jumped up out of their chairs toppling them, screaming, falling backward or running headlong into one-another in their fright and flight in a feeble attempt to flee the house. The result: no one managed to escape the dinning room.

The air was so charged with electricity, it flashed repeatedly looking like tiny lightening bolts shooting spasmodically throughout the dinning room giving the guests intermittent flashes of the others in the room with them. The noxious smell of ozone permeated throughout. Slowly the air began to move swirling gently at first, but accelerating steadily until it was rushing about the group counter clockwise like a tornado. Sam's guests were at its epicenter as the winds and the static electricity drew the hair up off their heads to stand it on its ends. Faster and faster the air swirled hurling silverware, and grabbing heavy water goblets smashing them to the floor as it rotated furiously. Orange light rose from the center of the turmoil.

From the light came sobbing, barely audible at first, then growing in intensity until it reached such a crescendo, it seemed to come from every direction at once.

"Can't you help me," a male voice bemoaned. "Please! I need to find them." The words spilled out of the cyclone between bouts of heart wrenching sobs. The sound was so pitiful, so desperate, that tears fell from more than one pair of eyes caught in the midst of the strange orange glow and the whirlwind of chaos.

Once again, as abruptly as it started, the whirlwind stopped. Everything that was moving fell to the floor—without making a sound. For thirty seconds the room stood unnaturally quiet. No one moved. No one dared say a word. Inez and Bernice were crying quietly, Mike and Vicki looked terrified. Angie stood with her mouth agape. Sam's face looked as frozen as her body seemed to be. The deputies stood quietly, but with taut muscles ready to pounce on anything that moved.

In an instant the lights flicked back on blinding everyone with their unnatural intensity.

The quiet didn't last in the well-lit room. With a horrendous boom, the basement door banged open. Wham! It hit the wall. Wham! It slammed back shut again into its doorjamb. Again and again the door raged against the wall then against the door jam, so hard the doorjamb wood splintered.

Still, no one moved.

Gilbert's face was a mask revealing nothing. Jackson drew his gun.

"Put that away!" Gilbert croaked when he noticed. "Put it away!" He had to repeat himself.

Jackson holstered his gun.

"Take it easy kid," Trelavonti said grabbing Jackson's shoulder and looking about the room. "It's okay." But he didn't feel okay. Noone isn't going to like this, he thought.

Clem put a hand to his heart, grabbed at a fallen chair, righted it, and sat back down. The Spencer sisters rushed to his aid.

"You two got on-the-job training in CPR?" Trelavonti smirked as he watched the women hovering over Clem. He made no move to help the old farmer.

"Why don't you go downstairs and see what's going on," Gilbert ordered Trelavonti. "We'll handle what's going on up here."

Trelavonti glared at Gilbert making no move to obey his superior officer.

Immediately, Gilbert was distracted from Trelavonti's insubordination when with one more tremendous bang, the basement door wailed so hard against the door jam it shattered. So did the door. At the same instant, the electric current that was so palpable only one second before vanished leaving behind only the stench of ozone. The basement door lay shattered and askew against the stairs leading down into the basement.

The phenomenon just experienced was stronger than any supernatural phenomenon Angie had ever experienced either at Sam's house or in her other investigations. She was thrilled to be there, in the thick of things. She silently thanked Sam a thousand times over for the chance. While most of the other partygoers were frightened, she was ecstatic.

Gilbert moved fast toward the basement door unlatching his gun from its holster as he crossed the dinning room, going through the kitchen and nearing the basement entry. He flicked on the basement light switch. The room lit up. He started down the stairs, his gun drawn, looking in every direction slowly moving down one step at a time.

Angie eased in right behind him. She had to know; be there when things were most chaotic. Whatever it was, she knew it could manifest again at any second.

Since Gilbert had already gone before him, Trelavonti closed in behind Angie. As he moved, Kitty burst out from underneath the table, ran at him and leapt flying the last few feet to close in on him sinking her claws into the back of his right leg.

Trelavonti cried out in pain as the cat struck trying to swat it off his leg, but she leapt off disappearing before he could touch her. He wanted to get his hands around the cat's neck and squeeze so hard its eyes popped out. As it was, he had to fight from grabbing at his heart, forcing himself to stay to calm in front of the others. He wanted no one to know just how badly the cat had frightened him. He hated cats! He shook his head in disgust and approached the basement stair gingerly stepping down refusing to let the pain he felt show in his face. That damn cat better have its rabies shots, he thought as he fought off the pain and contemplated ways he could make Sam pay for the abuse her cat had caused him.

Gilbert was already at the bottom step. He stood there a moment, slowly lowering his right foot onto the concrete basement floor. He wanted nothing to take him by surprise. His long, bowed legs forced him to duck as he stepped all the way down into the room. His hat was still on the chair at the table, so his long, slightly curly hair fell in his face. He brushed it out his eyes repeatedly. As he did, he took in everything around him noticing that the basement looked like any other ordinary basement. He saw the washer, the dryer, empty boxes stacked in the corner. He stood quietly in the center of the room, slowly turning in a circular motion looking at everything in every direction. Facing east, he noticed that the room had an odd configuration on that side, not quite right, somehow. Upon reflection, he realized what the oddity was. One wall stood out from the others, about three feet further into the room, just enough so that upon casual observation, it wasn't immediately noticed.

Angie stood on the bottom step, watching as Gilbert stopped to look at the wall. She stepped into the room crossing over to him, continuing over to the odd wall, the one she and Sam had been directed to earlier.

He frowned when he noticed her for the first time, "Get back!" He spat.

She ignored him.

Gilbert made no move to stop her from continuing on over to the wall then touching it.

Trelavonti moved off the bottom step, and across the floor heading for Angie as if he were a heat-seeking missile and she, the target. It always angered him when women didn't do as they were told. It wasn't just that she was disobeying the sheriff. He didn't give a damn about that. But a dame needed to be put in her place whenever she stepped out of line.

Gilbert held up his hand stopping Trelavonti dead in his tracks. Trelavonti fumed. He wanted to light into the broad, so much he could taste it. But this time he thought it best to listen to Gilbert. He didn't wish to push him too hard.

By then, all the others, except for Bernice and the youngest children, were on the basement steps waiting in anxious anticipation for something else to happen. The room seemed unnaturally quiet.

Gilbert moved to the odd east wall behind Angie.

Angie continued to pass her hands over the brick, caressing them from one side of the wall to the other.

Trelavonti looked at Jackson arching his eyebrows, smirking, and tossing his head at Angie in a silent comment about

her sanity, while he rubbed the back of his right leg. It was
bleeding.

Jackson frowned.

Bernice quietly slipped in behind the others praying
continually for the Lord's protection as she watched Angie and the
sheriff. She watched Trelavonti, too, saw his gesture to the other
deputy, and decided she didn't like him much. She stood quietly
next to John, who hadn't heard her come up behind him.

Bernice didn't like any of what was going on, but what
could she do? Pray, of course and constantly remind herself that
she had nothing to fear; God was with her. But something evil was
going on. How was she supposed to deal with it?

The Bible expressly forbids Christians to traffic in ghosts
and spirits, was this trafficking? She doubted it. She certainly
didn't ask whatever it was to be there. She knew Sam hadn't
either. Firmly rooted in the word of God, she knew that He worked
in many ways, all supernatural. Yet, she knew this wasn't God
like. There was evil connected to these supernatural occurrences.

Whatever it was, it seemed different from the voice she
heard in the dinning room. Something in that voice was plaintive,
pitiful, begging for help, so desperate to get their attention.

Why? Whatever had caused that spirit—or whatever it
was—so much pain had to be evil, Bernice thought. But there was
another, more ominous force in the basement; it felt thick, heavy.
She fought to resist the urge to run, get away. "Resist the devil and
he will flee," she silently intoned. She sensed evil close by in
Trelavonti, too. In a flash of insight, she "knew" he was connected
with the evil force in the basement, somehow. Silently she prayed
for strength to "fear not." At the same time, she recognized the
first spiritual force, the one in so much pain. There was a war
being fought in Sam's basement. She shuddered, prayed for Angie
as she watched her across the room.

Angie continued caressing the brick block wall. She hummed, her eyes closed, her hands hypnotic as they moved over the rough brick slowly, back and forth, back and forth.

Mike and Vicki, perched on the bottom stair, were entranced with Angie's actions. Sam sat behind them. Inez, Gladys, Clem and John stood single file behind her. Jackson stood to the left of the bottom step. Trelavonti stood beside him still smirking as he watched Angie work.

The wall drew Angie's hands like magnets to one spot. Her hands moved in small circles about the whole wall, but kept returning to the same small spot at the center. Angie's whole body seemed to pick up a rhythm as if she were listening to music the rest could not hear. She swayed back and forth to that rhythm and began to hum. The humming grew louder. Her eyes were closed.

Gilbert, like everyone else, got caught up in the rhythm of Angie's movement. He stood by the washing machine captivated.

"Can you help me?" A strange male voice called out from Angie's lips. "I can't find them. Can you help me?" Sobs racked Angie's body. It was the same wail everyone had heard earlier in the dinning room and so wrenching Vicki began to cry. "I'm in here," the voice cried as Angie's hand continued to rub the same spot on the wall. "Help me!" With the last wail, Angie fell in a heap in front of the wall.

Gilbert reacted quickly by moving in and checking for Angie's vital signs. The palms of her hands were bleeding. "What the hell was that?" He asked no one in particular.

Angie's eyes fluttered.

"Huh. What happened?" She mumbled as she came to and slowly sat up.

Gilbert motioned to his deputies. They picked Angie up carrying her upstairs where they laid her on the couch. Jackson insisted on treating her bloody palms. Inez and Gladys found Sam's First Aid kit and brought it to him.

Angie sat up on the couch. She looked around at a sea of frightened faces looking back at her. "I realize that for many of you what you just saw down there was probably something you have never seen before. But it's okay, really. There's nothing to be frightened of," Angie tried to reassure the group.

They just stared back at her.

"You know I'm a psychic? You know what that means?" Everyone continued to stare blankly at her. "You heard my conversation with the sheriff? Surely, you have some idea of what that means?"

Inez spoke up and said, "I'm well aware of you, dear. It was just so interesting," she looked around the room at her friends. "I think maybe the cat got a hold of these people's tongues. You did give us quite a show, you know?"

Inez's comment set everyone to talking at once.

A wave of relief surged through Sam, who watched from the dinning room doorway. She had seen many things with Angie during their college days, but never anything like what she had just witnessed. She was glad to see Angie return to her old self.

Trelavonti watched too, still smirking. What are people going to think of the lovely sheriff now, he wondered in delight? This could be real bad for him come next election. That is once folks find out about it. As he stood there, Trelavonti mapped out the tact he would take to make sure everyone did know about it and just how he would win the next election and become the new county sheriff. Hell, this could be good for some green too, especially from Noone. He salivated at the thought of the money that would soon line his pockets as he looked around nervously for any sign of the cat.

Angie faced everyone sitting up on the couch. "Look folks, I deal in the paranormal all the time." She could tell most were still frightened. "There's nothing, and I do mean nothing, to be frightened of here. I'm fine and you'll be fine, too."

"Well, we don't deal in it all the time!" Bernice yelled. "I for one want to know a whole lot more about just what a psychic is and what you're doing here."

John placed his hands on his wife's shoulders. He knew she was frightened. He reached over and kissed her cheek from behind. Her anger banished with his kiss. "I guess I do deal in the paranormal, I mean nothing is more spiritual than Christ, but what I see going on here is not Christ like. Not by a long shot!" She still didn't like all the talk of psychics and evil spirits. Nobody, she believed, should deal with them except to cast out demons.

"I'm here, Bernice, to help Sam." Angie didn't want Bernice upset. "Maybe you didn't know about the trouble she has been having in this house. I can see you didn't know about your family's experiences. But there is nothing to be frightened of. In a case like this, where you see all of these manifestations, it's usually because someone has been hurt, badly, killed, maybe even murdered. Their soul is not at rest. They want justice, for whatever happened to be brought to the light, at least that's the case in ninety nine percent of these types of . . . well . . . hauntings.

I'm also here because I've been dreaming about Sam, the things that are going on here; we're friends from college; we have a bond that goes pretty deep. We tend to 'know' when one or the other of us needs the other. Sam does it to me all the time. I'll be thinking of her, and she'll call, things like that. Because of my background and our friendship, I came to help her."

Bernice smiled, tentatively at first, then completely. She was still uncomfortable, but she finally managed to relax and trust

God for help. Angie was such a nice person; she couldn't be trafficking in evil, could she? She asked in a silent prayer.

The beauty in Bernice's eyes drew Angie like a magnet. From what the sheriff had said about the Jennings' property, and from what John and the kids said had happened over there, Angie suspected that Bernice and her family could use her expertise, too.

"Sam, I really wish you had told me about this beforehand. I could have left the kids at home. I'm not crazy about them being here with all this . . . stuff! . . . going on." Bernice snapped at Sam. She did not want her family involved and no amount of cajoling from John was going to change that.

John hugged his wife's shoulder. "It's alright honey, the kids are safe. We're all okay. You know that." He kissed her cheek. Bernice was unnerved, which surprised him. She was always so fearless. He knew her to be a strong woman of faith, yet he could see she was experiencing doubts.

"Oh you," she poked him in the ribs, "you two are lucky he's here. I might have had a whole lot more to say about this." She smiled at Sam and Angie. "Day after tomorrow Missy, you are going to have to tell me a darn sight more than you've told me up to now," she said to Sam. "And you can do that at lunch. I'll expect you by one," she giggled, and her robust body shook. She turned to Angie, "And I'll tell you something you may not know. I have the power of the Lord on my side, and if there are any unclean spirits in this house, I am just as capable of casting them out as you might be, more so even because no one can do what God can do."

That said she went on to add, "Bring Angie when you come to lunch, Sam." Anyone as sensitive to the supernatural as she is, she thought, is a good candidate for the Lord, just like Inez and Gladys. She smiled.

While the women talked, Gilbert called Trelavonti and Jackson over and quietly told Trelavonti to go outdoors; when Skip finished speaking Jackson went outdoors to help Trelavonti.

Gilbert turned to Sam and said, "Why don't we take that basement wall down?"

"You mean tonight?" The idea had not occurred to her.

Outside, snow fell quietly. Wet and light, the light reflected off it and illuminated everything.

"What kind of tools do you need?" Sam asked sparking to the idea.

"A pick axe, wheelbarrow . . . not much. We have some stuff in the car," Gilbert said looking at Trelavonti and Jackson who had just come back into the house carrying tools from their police cruisers. Snow dripped from their uniforms. Jackson took his boots off in the porch, but Trelavonti came right in dripping melting snow on the hardwood floors.

"I've got some of those things in the shed right next to the barn. I guess we should take at least part of the wall down. Are you sure that's not a load bearing wall?" Sam asked as Gilbert started for the basement.

"No, it isn't," he said. "That's not something you have to worry about. Not tonight."

Gilbert noticed Trelavonti dripping all over the floor, so he sent him back outside to the shed to fetch Sam's tools. Trelavonti grumbled under his breath as he made his way though the falling snow. He returned with all the tools they would need. This time he took his boots off before coming back inside the house.

"Hey, boss," he said. "It's starting to come down pretty hard out there. Think we should check in? That wind is beginning to pick up, too." Trelavonti loved storms for one reason, it usually meant paid time off, and he could lay about the house and watch TV.

"Yeah, go ahead. Sam, do you mind if he uses your phone?"

"No, please." She pointed to the cordless phone on the table behind the couch.

"When you get done Gene come back downstairs and help. It's going to take all of us to get this work done."

"What do I tell them at the station if they ask what we're doing?"

"Just tell them we went to a party and that we're enjoying ourselves. No one needs to know anything else. We are off duty, remember? How much snow we talking about so far?"

"A couple inches already," Trelavonti said. "I thought this wasn't supposed to start until tomorrow?"

"It doesn't matter much for us, our 4-wheel drives will get us out of here," Gilbert said, "but some of you might want to consider the storm. I mean getting home might not be easy."

"Ah, hell," Clem said, "The Farmer's Almanac said we're going to get blizzard after blizzard this year, so I'm a staying. The way I figure it is that I'll be stuck home enough later in the season. I'm staying put. I ain't missing none of this action." Everyone else agreed.

Up until now, Sam never considered the idea of houseguests. It didn't matter too much; she kept plenty of provisions to keep them for a week, liking the idea of everyone spending a few days with her. She was enjoying the evening very much, regardless of the goings on. Her guests appeared to be, too.

It was 11 p.m. by the time everyone was ready to dig into the basement wall and find out if anything was behind it.

"We'll worry about getting home when the time comes," Clem said to the Spencer sisters as they climbed down the basement stairs. "We've all been through worse than this. I'll get you home; don't worry about that." Gladys tweaked Clem's cheek and he blushed.

Angie and Gilbert stood over by the wall speaking softly. Angie, once again, rubbed her hands over the brick. "He's grieving. He's angry, but I don't think he's dangerous. I can almost see him. He's in there," Angie pointed to the wall and trembled. "He's there."

Trelavonti and Jackson looked at each other. Trelavonti no longer smirked. The broad was creeping him out. He had heard about her all right, remembered some of the stories about how she helped cops all over the tri-state area solve crimes. No, he wasn't crazy about any of this, not at all. It wasn't funny anymore.

Gilbert wanted to accept what Angie said at face value and knew it. He knew, too, that Ellen's whereabouts were too important to him. He proceeded with caution, not because he didn't trust Angie, but because he wanted answers too much and didn't want to mess up any type of investigation because of his own needs. His mind was on Ellen as he worked, and it took great effort on his part to concentrate on what was happening at the moment. He prayed that whatever they found after they broke down the wall, it would not be her, as he secretly feared it was. Maybe I'll talk to Angie about Ellen before she leaves, he thought as he wielded the first pick ax blow to the wall. Maybe she could help me find her, put my mind to rest. I need to know what happened even if no one else is interested anymore.

Mike was the first to offer help. Gilbert gave him the pickaxe and let him help smash concrete blocks and mortar with it. Mike had been at it for a half-hour when Trelavonti moved over next to him pushing him aside and forcibly taking the axe. Mike begrudgingly let go of the handle, resentment marking his young features. He did not appreciate being pushed around, especially by Trelavonti.

"We'll take turns doing this," Gilbert said to Mike in an attempt to sooth the boy's feelings. "You've been at it quite awhile already while Trelavonti here has been doing nothing but flapping his gums." Gilbert looked Trelavonti in the eye letting his remark settle into the deputies' thick hide then turned back to Mike. "You rest awhile. We'll put you back to work soon enough."

Mike smiled as he walked over to the steps and sat down.

Trelavonti stewed at the open insult from Gilbert. He hated Skip Gilbert with a passion. The punk kid shouldn't have been down here in the first place. This is a police officer's job! He slammed the wall with the axe and more mortar fell away.

John watched from the doorway, smiling. He liked the way Gilbert had handled his son and the deputy. He was mad enough at Trelavonti to belt him one, something, he knew, Bernice would not be happy about.

Sam noticed, too. Mike could have lost face with Trelavonti's insult, but Gilbert saw to it he didn't. Smart man, she thought.

The five men, Trelavonti, Jackson, John, Mike and Gilbert all took turns swinging the pickaxe against the cement blocks and mortar that held the wall together. It was coming down brick by brick.

Sam and Angie sat together on the stairs. Sam grasped the handrail as she watched a small cavern come into view in front of the working men. She held her breath, waiting. She wondered what Gilbert's expected to find.

As the men worked taking out the first block, nothing was revealed except a gush of stale air with an offensive odor. Jackson removed the second block, and as he did, finger bones fell through the opening. The shock of the truth showed on everyone's—except the policemen's—faces. Bernice gasped. Inez and Gladys clung tighter to Clem's arm; Angie put her arm around Vicki's shoulders. No one said a word.

Gilbert seized command of the room from that moment on as his deputies moved in to work faster, blocking John and Mike for doing any more work. "This is now an official police investigation," Gilbert told everyone. "You will all have to step aside and let us do our job."

No one protested. By rights, Gilbert thought as he stewed over the situation, these people shouldn't be anywhere near this scene. Fact is, though, that it is an old crime scene and any evidence that might have been gathered when the murder was first committed vanished long ago. Still, he sent Jackson out to get police tape from the cruiser, which he used to block off the wall. No one could come within a few feet of the hole in the wall. He didn't know yet if the body inside was a murder victim, but since the skeletal remains were still chained to a wall, he felt safe to assume it was. By the time they had finished a complete intact human skeleton was uncovered. Secreted away in her heart, Sam knew they would find something like that once work began.

"The professor . . . is it the professor?" Sam whispered to Angie who sat next to her on the stair. "Are there two small skeletons in there? Where are the twins?" She asked Gilbert not waiting for Angie to answer her first question. She had already made up her mind whose bones had been blocked up in her cellar.

"Just one adult male," Gilbert said. He remembered the story of the professor's disappearance as well as everyone else and wondered the same thing Sam wondered, suspected that was exactly who it was that was once attached to the bones. Once he had seen the finger bone, which was easily discerned as adult, he expected to find two tiny human skeletons along side it, too and was surprised when he didn't. The exact identity of the one skeleton, however, would be determined in a lab, but Gilbert was confident of what that outcome would be. The bones were dry and dusty. They had been walled up a long, long time; he hoped forensic science could still identify whoever it had been. He took a closer look at the skeleton.

"Look Sheriff, this is my house; I've been going through a great deal lately concerning it, and I think—what you found there—I think I deserve an explanation!" Sam said emphatically.

"I can't tell you anymore than that it appears to be an adult male. It's been locked up in this wall for a very long time. We're treating this as murder scene. That means what we find here is confidential until we capture the killer, or killers." He spoke with authority, adding, "and I do think this is the professor who lived here forty or so years ago, if that's what you're wondering. That's just a hunch, mind you, so don't go repeating it to anyone outside this room; that goes for all of you.

We'll do some DNA testing, if it's possible; maybe check dental records, again, if it's possible. In the meantime, there is nothing else to say. But I do advise you and Miss Eckenridge that if you stumble across anything else that might aid our investigation; you are obliged to inform me."

Even with his little speech, Gilbert didn't attempt to make any one leave the basement. How could he? There was a storm outside; no one was in any imminent danger. They'd stay out of the way.

His men continued working. The partygoers watched as the entire wall came down. The walled in enclosure was only three feet deep; Gilbert measured it. The wall was a foot thick. The person inside would have had no room to move. The neck was shackled to the back wall. The man had stood on a solid concrete floor. There were no windows; the room was airtight. Inside, walled up, it would have been pitch black.

Sam shivered as she thought of the entrapment. Was the professor dead when he was put inside the hole? If not, how long had he stood there? Did his legs give out? Death had to have taken its sweet time before it finally relieved him of his torture, if he wasn't dead before someone placed him there.

"The spiral is starting. There will be no stopping them from coming through now. He leads the way. There are more. They all want to be found." Angie spoke quietly from her seat on the stair. She looked at the wall, through it. Her eyes turned inward so that only the whites were exposed. She saw something, something no one else could see. "There are many, and they will be vindicated." Her voice boomed throughout the basement as her body shivered with cold.

Trelavonti stopped working, turned to look at her, his eyes stone cold. She gave him the creeps. He didn't like being around her. He didn't like what she was saying. He had reasons for being unnerved. He hadn't expected an investigation, a body. Something went on out here long before he ever became involved.

"There are many who will be vindicated!" What the hell does that mean? He wondered as he watched Angie intently. "What others?" he snapped demanding to know what she was talking about. He moved over standing in front of her looming large, threatening.

"You'll see," Angie said, "you'll see." As quickly as it fell upon her, Angie snapped out of the trance she was in. She took in Trelavonti's expression and shuddered. It wasn't the first time someone had been frightened of her. Frightened people were often dangerous people.

Sam remained seated next to Angie on the steps keenly aware of the way Trelavonti stared down at her best friend. She took Angie's hand squeezing it, hoping to reassure her that she wasn't alone and that no one was going to hurt her.

"Get back to work, Gene," Gilbert said, aware of Trelavonti's veiled threat to Angie. Why? He wondered. Why would Trelavonti get so upset with what Angie just said? Interesting.

Sam wondered if the professor was warning them through Angie. He was the one that came to her in her dreams. The calling—my God, she thought, he's spent over thirty years calling out for help! She felt an overpowering sense of grief for the man. Her heart ached thinking how it must have been for him. Him thinking his wife was having an affair with Noone, and Noone taunting him with nude photos of her and who knew what else. Then to be locked up inside that coffin! She looked at the wall. He was probably alive when he got walled up, she reasoned considering that if Noone liked to torment him about his wife, perhaps he tormented him by killing him slowly as well.

Officers remained focused on the job at hand. Once the initial find was uncovered and documented, the deputies began a meticulous search of the room.

"This evidence is just that—evidence," Gilbert turned away from the wall when he was finished and faced the group, announcing, "It is not for public disclosure. I'm going to insist that none of you speak about what we've found here to anyone outside this room."

He knew as he said it that as soon as everyone went home, the news of the skeleton in Sam's closet would be all over the county. The story would escalate, too, with the telling of it. In his favor was a storm that he knew would buy him some time between no one knowing what they found and everyone knowing. Besides, if everything were made public every loony who wanted attention would confess to the crime.

Although he didn't say it, Gilbert put Noone at the top of his suspect list. Still, proving it wouldn't be easy. First, they'd need a positive ID on the skeleton.

The investigation turned to work bagging evidence, and hauling it all outside to the sheriff's vehicle. Jackson retrieved a body bag for the bones.

Sam didn't like watching police remove the body from her house. It didn't "feel" right to her. Something that she couldn't quite grasp was nagging at the back of her mind.

When the final load of evidence was packed safely into the sheriff's vehicle, the officers went back into the basement to make sure they hadn't missed anything. It was 3 a.m. by the time they finished. None of the partygoers moved to go home.

"Would you like some coffee, maybe a roll or something before you leave?" Sam asked Gilbert.

After righting the table and chairs and cleaning some of the mess, everyone gathered once again at the dinning room table, this time over coffee and rolls. It was exciting for the group to get a first hand look at how police worked and on such a 'big' crime, they enjoyed a few more minutes together. The policemen wouldn't admit it, but they enjoyed the positive attention they were receiving, as well.

But thoughts of the skeleton, which everyone believed was the professor, disturbed most of the partygoers. As Sam sat at the table with the others she could still hear his cries, saw him as he came to her in her dreams. Angie, too, could still feel his grief and his deep sorrow. It was as if the professor's grief permeated the whole house, which, she guessed, it probably did.

Clem said, "I often wondered what happened to that man. I forgot him for awhile. I can't believe I forgot him. God! How he must have felt locked in that wall waiting to die, hoping someone would come along and find him! I couldn't understand why he never said good-bye. I was angry at him for that!"

Clem remembered thirty or so years before when the professor walked out of his life. "If I had given it any thought, maybe I could have persisted and made the cops look for him, again. I should have done more!" No one could ease Clem's guilt over the professor's death. It wasn't his fault, but he wouldn't listen.

"What happened to his wife, daughters?" Clem asked once he could take his mind off the professor. "What happened to them? Are they buried here?" Everyone else at the table was wondering the same thing.

"I heard stories that she ran off with Noone to Canada," Gilbert said. He too was asking himself some of the same questions and wondering about his father's responsibility in all of it. "My father was active on the case. It always bothered him that he never solved it. There were no bodies, so he wasn't sure there was a crime, but he wrote in his notes that he thought something happened to the professor and the little girls—something like murder, I mean. It looks like I'll be finishing what he started."

"Do you think all that noise earlier, do you think it was him making it?" Vicki shyly asked.

"Probably," Angie said. "He wanted to be found. I think he's still looking for his family."

"That stuff you found in the barn—where is it?" Gilbert asked turning to Sam and Angie as he recalled the injunction.

"What stuff?" Sam asked innocently.

"Didn't you take some things from the barn?"

"You stopped us, remember? You came here with an injunction from Noone?"

"That injunction doesn't hold up now. I'll be retrieving material from the barn," he said matter-of-factly knowing he had probable cause to search it. He gave Jackson the keys to the barn door locks and asked John and Mike to help Jackson load the material into his vehicle.

"You stay here with me," he told Trelavonti. "Everything out there is now evidence," he added looking at everyone. "Evidence in a murder investigation takes precedence over any injunction Noone might have." Especially since Noone might be the prime suspect, he thought.

Gilbert hadn't forgotten Angie's comment either. He turned to her. "So," he said, "is all this tied together? Do you get anything on the children? And can you help with the investigation?"

"Yes, sheriff, I'll help you any way I can, and no, I didn't get anything on the children. I don't think they're here; or, more to the point, that they're dead. It's odd but there are no indications, for me psychically that the children have passed. I do believe the skeleton you found is that of the professor, and for some reason since Sam has moved in here, that she's the catalyst for all this paranormal activity. I believe that finding out why will solve the mystery."

"Why do you think Sam is the catalyst?"

"I don't know yet."

Angie turned to Samantha. "I'm sorry, kid. I know you didn't want to hear that, but somehow you are the catalyst, the reason behind this latest activity. But don't worry; I'm not going to leave you high and dry. We'll figure it out." She put her arm around Sam's shoulder.

"Do you think anything else, I mean anything 'paranormal,' is going to happen tonight? If it was the professor, we found him. Shouldn't that be enough?" Sam wondered.

"I don't think anymore will happen tonight. There are other problems here, more to this story, but this isn't over, not by a long shot." Angie's words did little for Sam's nerves. There was nothing more to say, nothing more to do.

Everyone in the room was tired as the excitement of the evening wore off. As Gilbert headed for the front door on his way outside, the others got their hats and coats preparing to leave as well.

They had to get home. John and Clem had to take care of their livestock. Bernice had a full day ahead of her just attending to the families' needs, and as for Inez and Gladys, they were looking forward to a long day's nap as were Angie and Sam. Everyone said their good-byes as one by one they headed out into the storm.

The storm had grown in intensity. Five inches of fresh snow lay on the ground. It wasn't enough to stop anyone from getting around, however. It was very quiet as the snow fell heavily and lazily in the early morning darkness.

By 4 a.m. police cruisers and assorted other vehicles were all leaving the yard. Sam felt better watching them go, knowing they would get home safely. The wind was supposed to blow so hard it would cause white out conditions later, but that wasn't happening yet. Sam and Angie watched until all the car lights were headed west down River Drive. They were glad they didn't have to go anywhere in the storm.

By 5:30 a.m. the women had cleaned up the mess in the dinning room and gone to bed. Sam could hear the wind whistling outside her bedroom window, but she was snug and cozy inside. Fuzz and Kitty lay on the chair next to the fireplace where a fire danced casting warm shadows on the bedroom walls. The sky was so dark she didn't bother drawing the curtains and drifted soundly to sleep.

Chapter Thirteen

Sam didn't get up until noon on Saturday. Groggy, she stumbled over to her bedroom window, looked outside, and saw snow coming down in torrents. Blowing, fierce winds rattled the windows pummeling snow against them. Sam embraced herself as cold blasts of air rocketed into the room through gaps in the ancient wooden window frames. "Brrrrrrrrr," she mumbled as she clumsily groped around the closet for her favorite beat up old sweater, and as she hurriedly pulled wool socks on to make her way downstairs.

Thoughts of a fresh cup of coffee enticed her into the kitchen, where she hurriedly ground coffee beans and started a pot brewing. No one was there as she flipped on the radio, and looked in the refrigerator for something to eat. Last night's leftovers looked pretty appealing. She lit a fire in the fireplace. With the smell of fresh brewed coffee wafting in the air, and the birch wood burning in the fireplace, she felt snug and cozy. The coffee poured, she sat on the bench to watch the storm from the warmth of her own kitchen, something that she still relished even after all that had gone on inside the house. The heat from the fireplace threw off just enough extra warmth to take the morning chill off. That and the hot coffee soothed her as she looked out the window at nothing but white lines horizontally blowing past her line of sight.

"The snow storm hitting northern Minnesota is expected to drop at least twenty inches while a cold front remains stationary over the area," the radio forecaster said as Sam sat quietly sipping hot coffee. "It will move out sometime Monday traveling east. Fifty to 80 mph winds are expected to continue well into the night. Unofficially, at least fifteen inches of snow has already accumulated." Sam absently wondered if he measured snowfall right at the station or if he read a press release from the National Weather Service. It didn't look good either way. She shut the radio off.

In a way, she was comforted by the gloomy weather predictions. Not only was she trapped in her own home, but everyone else was trapped where they were, too. Not much would be moving about in the accumulated snow. The county snowplows wouldn't get to her driveway until all the main roads were plowed. She paid a fee for her driveway to be plowed and expected results, but knew the county had everyone to consider, not just her.

Angie stirred in her bed upstairs to the smell of fresh brewed coffee that drifted up to her. She, too, made her way sleepily to the kitchen still dressed in her pajamas. She was quiet as she poured herself a cup and sat opposite Sam.

"Good morning," Sam said happily. "Looks like you got something on your mind?"

"Yes . . . I'm worried." Angie said through hastily sipped coffee. She was trying to get rid of the cobwebs inside her brain before she started thinking about everything. It wasn't working

"Why?"

"So much has happened and we haven't had time to think about what we're doing. We need to slow down. I wish the sheriff hadn't been here last night. Those papers are valuable to us.

Now he'll have a chance to completely look through them before we do." The look of worry on Angie's face only deepened as she gazed out the kitchen window at the raging storm.

"We weren't supposed to be reading them anyway— remember?"

Angie shot Sam a look that said, Yeah—right. Who are you kidding? "Hey, I just remembered. We had already retrieved a bunch of stuff from the barn before that injunction." Angie brightened. "Didn't the sheriff ask for that last night? He didn't take it though, did he?"

"Nope. He asked me once then apparently forgot about it, so I didn't bring it up . . . Relax awhile. We don't have to do anything right this minute. Let's just leave it alone for now, please!"

It wasn't but one minute before Sam added, "Can you believe what happened here? We have a party, invite friends over, the police show up, I guess, to join the party, and we end up telling ghost stories and finding a body in the basement. The police have already finished collecting evidence and are now investigating a possible homicide from thirty eight years ago! Could it have gotten any more Edgar Allen Poe-ish? I wonder if they'll be back out here today. Do you think?"

"In this weather! Come on Sam think about it. How are they going to get back out here, four wheeler or no, this storm is way too wicked for traveling, even for the police. I thought we weren't going to talk about this?"

"I can't help it. I suppose the police won't be able to get back out here." Sam looked a bit sad at the thought. Angie noticed. Then Sam perked up and said, "Come on. I'll fix us some breakfast and we can figure out what we'll do for the day—if anything. Leftovers from last night sound good to you?"

"Yeah! Let's have at 'em. I could eat a horse."

While they ate, Sheriff Skip Gilbert didn't get to his office until 2 p.m. He sipped coffee as he looked over material he confiscated from Sam's the night before. His thoughts drifted back to the previous evening. He tried to come up with a reason to go back out to the Egar farm, but could think of nothing. A bit dejected, he tried to concentrate on the material in front of him.

Already, regardless of the weather, Deputy Stanley Moran was transporting the bones found in Samantha Egar's basement to Minneapolis for forensic testing. Moran kept Gilbert apprised of road conditions as he drove.

If the storm was as bad as Gilbert thought it might get, he and his men would be pulling a lot of overtime. People were always going out in storm conditions when traveling was near impossible.

Moran called Gilbert on his cell phone while en route telling him that highway conditions were better the further south he traveled, and he had no trouble getting through the pilling snow in the department's 4x4 Jeep. The bones would make it to the Minnesota Bureau of Criminal Apprehension Department of Forensic Sciences with no problems.

Good, Gilbert thought. He worried that somehow the bones would end up in the wrong hands, which was why he assigned Moran to the task of getting them to the MBCA. He knew Moran was trustworthy. He could have sent Jackson, but last night when they got in, he gave him the day off to get some sleep. He gave Trelavonti the day off, too, only to keep him away from snooping into his investigation.

While Gilbert looked over the papers he confiscated from Sam's barn, his mind kept wandering back to thoughts of her. Something about her both intrigued and frightened him. As the afternoon wore on he started thinking about his father. He picked up his cell phone and called Florida to ask Stan Gilbert if he would like to join the investigation filling him in on everything, including Angie Eckenridge, Ellen, and finding the skeletal remains.

Stan seemed eager to come back to Minnesota and help his son with what looked like his old cases. What Skip didn't realize was that Stan looked forward to seeing him more than he did to helping in any investigation. Nevertheless, these particular mysteries had haunted him throughout his career, so they, too, grabbed at his imagination. Son and father had had a hard time seeing eye-to-eye on anything after Ellen disappeared, and Stan hoped, maybe they could finally get through that. Skip refused to dwell on it, but deep down he blamed his father for not finding her. Even though he had never said a word to his father about it, Stan suspected as much.

After finishing his conversation with Stan, Skip chose not to tell his men that Stan would be flying up from Florida to help once the storm let up. He moved around the office taking care of routine business just to have something to do while he mulled over events of the past few days, years. He liked to move about when something was on his mind. It helped him sort it out.

As he paced back and forth, Skip bristled at thoughts of Trelavoniti. The deputy paid no attention to anything he said, and hadn't since he became sheriff. He suspected Trelavonti considered him dimwitted when it came to solving crimes, too. Skip's statistical rate of almost ninety five percent solved crime since assuming the sheriff's office belied Trelavonti's assessment of him. Skip guessed that maybe that was what angered Trelavonti the most. He also knew Trelavonti watched him, caught the deputy peeking at him out of the corner of his eye often enough. Trelavonti reminded him of a sneaky junkyard dog getting ready to attack from behind, so Skip kept a wary eye on him.

Trelavonti had grown more and more confident since Skip took office, too. That was good, Skip concluded, because that was just how he wanted Trelavonti, overly confident. That's when mistakes were made and maybe, just maybe, he'd have reason to get rid of him once and for all.

As Skip mulled over the Trelavonti situation, Trelavonti was in his Virginia home making a few phone calls, one to Noone, the other to the Honorable David K. Wilkins, the judge who signed the injunction papers for Noone. Both Noone and Wilkins were very interested in the discovery of bones at the Egar house.

After Trelavonti's phone call, Noone spent the afternoon pacing back and forth in his living room. He was disgusted with Trelavonti's confidence. He had no misconceptions about Sheriff Skip Gilbert's ability to solve crime, especially this one.

"Hummmmpppphhhhh, so the professor finally got out. Ain't that a kick in the teeth? Well, what if he did? All they found were some old bones. That's it. Those bones aren't going to tell the cops anything. They won't even be able to identify him. I'd bet my life on that. If they figure out how he died, then they will still have to figure out why. They don't have a clue on motive." Noone was in the basement of his modest louse talking to his mother.

Gilbert's discovery brought back memories for Noone, memories of that day thirty eight years before when he and the professor had had their final confrontation. Noone tried never to think of Janice, but she was like a gossamer spider inside his head weaving a gossamer web that he couldn't escape.

"She should not have refused me; that's what caused her problems. She should have cooperated. She knew what was at stake; the stupid bitch. God, what a fuss she made when we dropped those kids off in Minneapolis. Did she really think I was going to raise those brats? Hell—no woman is worth that much trouble, and three of them? Not a chance," he said to his mother.

"I wonder if she ever grasped the idea of what was going to happen. How can a person be so dumb? Of course, I am good at convincing people of certain things." He smiled as he sat there in the basement next to his mother who rested atop a worktable in the middle of the room.

She listened without comment.

Noone remembered the many times he had convinced so many that he was doing things for their own good. "I'm surprised at how easy it was with her, though. She must have had her doubts about hubby before I came along. She would have been surprised at the fuss he made. She wouldn't have doubted him then, though. But that just made it easy for me, didn't it?

I should have known, though, that the other one would be nothing but trouble," his voice lowered to a whisper as he spoke of Sam. "Jeez! She looks just like him! Should a guessed the resemblance was a sign that nothing was finished.

You warned me, Mother. I know! I've got no one to blame but myself. But Mother, I just had to lure her into that house. You know that, too, don't you? You saw her. She looked so good. If she had moved just a little closer to the pantry door that day, just a little bit, I could have given her something she wasn't expecting. It would have been nice, all that flesh. I bet she's warm all over.

Yes mother, I know. I'll be careful. She's like her male counterpart. Now the other one is probably nothing but a slut like her female counterpart. You've said it all along, haven't you? And Mother, I've always listened to you when you've said I should have my fun and then get rid of them. I've done just that, haven't I?

Jeez! I have to quite thinking about this or I'll have to go over there. The storm is going to last for days. Think of it Mother; I'd have three days alone with two luscious women, just like when you and Henry and you and Joseph snuck off together, all alone, without me. Bet you never had Henry and Joseph at the same time, did you Mother?" He chuckled.

"Okay, Mother, if you insist, you can come along, too. Yes, dear, you can watch if you want to."

He paced the floor thinking about what to do next. Storm or no storm, he could make his way over to Samantha Egar's without too much trouble if he decided to go overland, which was what he would rather do. He was tired of going through the mineshafts. They were damp, cold, and drafty, full of spider webs and old dusty air. Fresh air would do him good. A little snow never hurt anyone, and, besides, he had no intention of taking his mother with him. She'd just slow him down. It was none of her business what he did anymore. She was lucky he let her stay with him.

Confident in his ability to navigate in the worst of weather conditions, Noone, as an experienced mountain climber, had been stranded in some of the worst storms ever recorded at elevations most climbers only dreamt of reaching. Still he survived. One little Minnesota winter storm wasn't going to stop him from doing anything he wanted to do, and as he thought about Samantha Egar, his desire to have her compelled him forward.

He threw on heavy winter gear and snowshoes to hike the two-miles through deep woods to get to the old farm. He didn't worry as he stepped out into the cold at 2 p.m. that afternoon. The wind had intensified since morning when he last stepped outside for stove wood, but he didn't care. Snowfall, too, had increased.

As physically fit as he was, Noone still found snowdrifts harder and harder to navigate as he hiked over open hay fields toward the forest line. Winds piled snow higher than he had ever seen it. Still, he kept going. It took him one hour and forty-five minutes to cross his fields and enter the dense pine forest that separated his property from Clem Johnson's, which bordered the Egar property for nearly two miles.

As he pressed on, he remembered the night before watching headlights move past his house and head to the Egar farm, and then come back out early in the morning. Cop cars too. Trelavonti told him police went out there to find out about the house and ended up finding a corpse.

Haunted house! What a laugh! He'd heard rumors about the old farm being haunted, but he'd been in that house millions of times and never saw anything odd. He was surprised so many others thought it was haunted, though, and at the things Trelavonti had heard about it. The Jennings' story of things happening at their place, Joseph's old place—that was real interesting, too. What was going on?

Noone considered Trelavonti shaking his head in disgust at the thought of him. The one time he tried to explain to Trelavonti the joys of living on the edge the mighty police officer, with his pistol in its holster, ran out of his house and practically had a car accident trying to get away from him! Noone tried not to laugh out loud at the remembrance.

Trelavonti's bullshit got in the way; but knowing all his dirty little secrets proved a great asset, helpful in keeping him in line at least. It was a good thing the mighty Trelavonti, to hear him tell it, liked young girls, and couldn't keep his hands off of them. No, Trelavonti wouldn't be turning him into his fellow police officers for any of his activities, not unless he wanted to be turned in for his own.

Noone kept trudging on through the woods toward Sam's.

It was a long time ago, but he remembered how Trelavonti made off with that teenage girl that had been offered up to him. The sheriff's girlfriend no less, he learned from Trelavonti's phone call.

The girl's parents thought I was a saint. Hell, they had to have known whom they were dealing with. That sanctimonious religious bitch with her wimpy husband? What'd they think I was gonna do? He shook his head from side to side in disgust. Snow caked on his wolf pelt hat that he wore draped down over his ears fell left and right.

Sixteen years old, knocked up, not a friend in the world, that girl was ripe for the picking; I asked the old lady about that eventually. Any man in his right mind would have lusted after her daughter, as sweet as she was. Couldn't really blame Trelavonti too much for not being able to keep hands off her with all that reddish, curly hair, round thighs, big hips, and breasts, hell, she'd entice a homosexual straight! She was only twelve weeks pregnant and already she was busting at the seams of her clothes. Mom was a little surprised when she found out the truth.

Her parents—they just knew God would deliver their darling daughter into hell for getting pregnant, but boy, were they were wrong. They delivered her there—in the name of God. What did they think would happen to someone as lush as she was? Shit, getting pregnant was probably the only way she knew of that would get her away from them! She should still be alive. There was nothing wrong with that kid that a little abortion wouldn't cure. I could have done that easy enough and she would have been as good as new, he thought as he continued with his trek. Hell, her parents knew that too, that's why they brought her to me. Wouldn't the pro-lifers of today just love that? Those Christians who abhor abortion are always the first ones to seek one when their little Janie gets herself in the family way if she ain't married. So what happened to this little darling of her doting Christian folks? Trelavonti got his lustful hands on her; that's what happened.

The man just couldn't keep his hands off. What did he think would happen? I mean, really? The girl knew who he was; at least that he was a deputy. Did he think he could do what he wanted to her then leave her to go tell his fellow officers? If she talked about him to the cops, what would he tell them about me? The man left me no choice. He had near finished the job before I got there, anyway. All I did was finish it.

Have to admit; it was fun playing with her. I wonder how long those Bible thumping folks of hers prayed for her to come back from wherever it was she went to have the baby. Never could get old momsey to tell me, no matter what I did to her. Betchua' they prayed a long time. Hell, she had the biddy's grandbaby the night they dropped her at my place, a boy. Since they didn't want to be proud grandparents, they should have thanked me for saving them from the responsibly of caring for a squalling brat. It didn't even cost them anything to bury him . . . or her! They should have thanked me for that, too! The grandma that wasn't, though, she didn't see it my way when she learned the truth. Too bad for her, I guess.

Noone struggled on through ever increasing winds and blinding snow. The storm didn't faze him; he just kept moving paying no attention to his surroundings. He walked bent at the waist against the steadily howling wind. He thought the wind would ease off when he left the house, but it hadn't; it seemed to be getting worse. The pine, poplar, oak and elm trees in the forest all appeared to hunker together against the cold driving wind, too, looking as if they had joined forces to stave it off. The wind pushed them so hard they doubled over, some cracked sounding like shotgun blasts before toppling to the ground as if executed. The screeching wind was so loud, the snowfall so heavy, that the breaking timber was the only thing he could hear above it.

He stopped to catch his breath. He could bear up under these conditions if he had to, but he did have a backup plan; he always had a backup plan. If it got too rough, he could hold up in one of his storm shelters and rely on the camping supplies he had cached throughout the forest.

He'd wait out the storm if need be. He assessed where he was turning slowly three hundred sixty degrees, shinning his flashlight over the trees and the snowdrifts to get his bearings. He was near a cache site, he realized. It was time to take a break. It couldn't hurt to rest awhile.

The others walking alongside him went unseen by Noone. He couldn't see or hear their soft padding in the snow. The wind howled too loudly. The snow came down too ferociously for Noone to see much farther than the hand in front of his face. But those padding alongside him caught his scent on the wind as soon as he left his house. They watched him often, never trusting what he was up to, remaining hidden for their own safety, but staying close enough to know where he was, what he was doing.

Noone was astonished when he recognized his location. He had been walking for two hours and wasn't even a half-mile from his own farm and for the first time in his life fear threatened to get him in its grip. He realized that no one knew where he was. As he took his bearings, he felt as if he were being watched, growing uneasy for the first time in his life by being alone in the woods.

The weather is playing tricks on me is all, he thought. Nearly whiteout conditions can play with your head. That's all it is.

Back in Virginia, Trelavonti sat on his couch watching a football game and drinking beer. He worked all night the night before and hadn't gotten home until early morning, so he didn't get out of bed until 2 p.m. Saturday afternoon. He knew the game was on, so he didn't waste energy showering or getting 'fixed up' because he wasn't going anywhere. He wanted to plant himself in front of the television and enjoy a little "down time" before his next shift.

His sweat pant waistband rested under his belly while his T-shirt bottom rested under his chest. Where the ends did not meet were the attributes of an unused body with full navel exposure. Trelavonti chalked his condition up to 'getting older.' He didn't work out anymore, and didn't care too much what he looked like. Hell, he often reasoned, he worked hard all his life. So what if he just wanted to relax some as he got older?

As he sat in front of the television dirty underwear lay strewn about the apartment, and sweat stained clothes lay across the backs of furniture, Trelavonti was oblivious to the aroma of both the room and his body.

By twilight, after he had tried to reach Noone once again, but couldn't; he worried. "He should have answered his phone by now. How am I going to go look for him in this storm? If he thinks I'm going to rush out there in forty below zero weather, he has another think coming. Damn him, anyway!" He said to the empty room as his mind strayed repeatedly from the game.

Out in the woods, Noone said to himself inside his shelter, "Damn this storm!" He was cold and tired. Once inside, he had unpacked a mat, his sleeping bag, and a small camp stove and set them up. He looked around for the cache of other supplies, and when he found them took out dried meat and fruits, a pan, a candle and dry matches. He set up a small pit in the ground in the center of his balsam bough hut and surrounded it with rocks he had also stored. He took out dried leaves, twigs and a few pieces of dried wood he had stored as well, making a fire after placing more rocks on the bottom of the pit. He cleared away a small opening at the top of the hut to act as a chimney. Once the fire got going, the rocks would throw off heat even after the fire went out. He wouldn't freeze to death.

Noone kept his cache in a metal, watertight, suitcase size container so no wildlife could get at it. If a human found it, they could help themselves; he didn't care.

The balsam bough shelter had been constructed around a hollow, fallen oak tree at the tree's roots, so it would be out of the wind. He could make the fire in the center of the balsam bough overhang then crawl into the hollow tree trunk. He had blocked off one end, so the large entrance came out into the balsam bough enclosure. The shelter was so inconspicuous among the fallen foliage debris to see it took an experienced eye.

Noone looked at his watch to find it was only 5 p.m. He turned on the portable radio he kept with him and listened for the weather report. It seemed Minnesota was in the throws of one of the worst storms on record. And it was just starting.

He tucked himself into the sleeping bag a bit worried by the weather forecast. His worry washed away by the fact that his feet were gradually warming in the dry wool socks he had also stored in his cache and as his whole body began to warm inside the bag. The fire threw off plenty of heat, too, and with its warmth, he grew optimistic once again. He congratulated himself for having the presence of mind to store dry clothing; including socks, long underwear, gloves and boots. You don't live long in the wild by being a fool, he thought as he drifted off to sleep. He was confident of his safety inside the tree trunk.

The wind howled on. So much snow fell that it blew up against the balsam boughs offering even more protection from the cold keeping the humble structure snug and warm.

Outside, the wolves paced around and around the log. They knew Noone was in there. The alpha male watched intently for him. His tongue lolled over his lips as he stared at the log where Noone hid himself. He lifted his leg and peed on the boughs.

Chapter Fourteen

Stan Gilbert arrived at the Twin Cities International Airport by 6 p.m. Saturday evening. He changed his mind after Skip's call that morning deciding to take the first flight north. He arranged to rent a 4x4 and was on I-35 heading north toward the Iron Range within an hour of touch down.

"Finally, I'm finally going to nail the bastard." The seventy two-year old ex-St. Louis County sheriff had a habit of talking to himself when he drove; it often helped him sort out things that were puzzling him. As he talked, he pulled a Camel cigarette from his shirt pocket and lit it with a Cricket lighter, the throwaway kind. He knew he shouldn't be smoking, "but what the hell, since I'm dying anyway, it doesn't much matter." The senior Gilbert learned he had terminal cancer shortly before his son's call that morning. He hadn't told Skip yet, didn't know how he would.

God must be helping me mend some fences before it's too late, he thought as he weaved in and out of traffic around the Twin Cities heading north.

By the time he got as far north as Cloquet, the storm Skip told him about was rearing its temperamental head. It would get much worse the farther north he drove, Stan knew, but he was accustomed to Minnesota weather. In fact, since moving to

Florida, he had found himself missing Minnesota winters where tangling with winter weather was a manly challenge.

Farther north, Skip Gilbert, too, was dealing with the storm. It presented a host of problems for his office.

"Yes, the department owns and operates emergency vehicles including two 4x4s, but even the county snowplows are pulling off the freeways because of zero visibility. Snow plow drivers can't see the road for crying out loud!" He yelled at the nineteenth caller. "How do you think we will be able to see? Or navigate our cars in all this snow? How on earth did you think you could?" Gilbert mumbled more about the problem with each new call.

Harriet Hornblower, the dispatcher, looked at him and shook her head slowly in agreement. The sheriff's office went through this every year with Harriet at the helm for twenty six of those years. She was now very skilled at dealing with just such situations, a skill Skip appreciated beyond expression.

All dispatchers could do over the phones was offer words of comfort to those stranded alone in their cars. They took locations as clearly as possible and noted them all. Some, those that were close to small towns, got help from that city's police department who sent out officers if the stranded vehicle was close enough to town. Those further out had to wait hours, sometimes days before help could arrive—that is if they had a cell phone to call in their location to the sheriff's department. Many didn't.

And since Harriet knew more about road situations during storms than he did, Skip used his time to go over the Egar murder investigation relaxing with Harriet at the helm. Looking over the paperwork, something nagged at him. There was something he needed to grasp, to see, but it fluttered just out of reach in his mind. Sitting at his old wooden desk, feet perched on its top, piecing together events of the last few days, he waited for the answer to come to him. He thought that perhaps it would be better to forget about it, then when he lest expected it, he would see what he was currently blind to. With that idea in mind, he tried to concentrate on the snow emergency efforts. He walked from his office out front to listen to Harriet direct traffic, sit alongside her as she controlled the switchboard.

She gave him a dirty look.

Being all too familiar with Harriet's looks, he got up and went to the windows to gaze out at the storm. He turned around to see computer screens flashing behind him as the state of the art office equipment hummed smoothly along. There was nothing for him to do there. He remembered that the office had back-up generators. He walked down to the basement and checked on those. Both were set up to kick in automatically if there was any kind of power outage. Finding them in perfect working order, he went back upstairs thinking about his deputies out on patrol. All of them were equipped with cell phones, as well as their cruiser radios, so they could call in if they needed to. They also used the cell phones as backup if the phone lines inside the office went dead. St. Louis County had opted to make sure their sheriff's department had all the latest equipment, considering it was rural and covered six thousand eight hundred sixty square miles, from Duluth to Orr and Hibbing to Ely. Skip was thankful for that because the devices did much to make his office more efficient considering the area they patrolled.

As the storm raged, Skip walked the aisles between the holding cells noting that the prisoners were tucked in nice and tight with nothing to worry about in the storm. As he walked, his mind wandered back to the murder investigation, still unable to grasp what lay just beyond his reach.

The injunction against Samantha Egar's property gnawed at him. She asked the right question when she wanted to know how

Noone could get away with that. He wondered too, and remembered how flabbergasted he was when he had to serve it and that Noone had instigated it.

Noone knew the women had been going through that trunk in the library, but how? He tried to remember if he had commented around the office to his men about that, and thought he might have. If so, that meant someone in his office had leaked information to Noone, but why? Trelavonti—what were those two up to?

As he reopened his office door and sat back down behind his desk, he propped his feet back up, and sighed in resignation. Not much had changed in the office since his father was sheriff.

Stan Gilbert had never trusted Trelavonti. Skip remembered nights as a child with his family at the dinner table listening to his father talk about work. It was a rare occasion for Stan Gilbert didn't believe in discussing business at home, neither had his wife.

Brenda Gilbert offered her support unequivocally to her husband. But she told Stan when he first joined the sheriff's department that she did not want the negative things he witnessed as sheriff voiced at their table during meals, something Stan respected. On rare occasion, if Stan needed to work on a personnel problem, Brenda didn't object if he did so at dinner. She knew that if she just let him talk about it, the answer he was looking for would come to him.

Skip always listened to his father talk about work during those times. He loved the stories and once in awhile Stan would tell him a few of the forbidden tales out of earshot of Brenda, omitting the worst of it. Those stories instigated his burning desire to be a cop just like his father.

Of course, that was all before Ellen.

It was during one of those personnel conversations his father and mother had that Skip first learned of Trelavonti. Stan told the family he suspected Trelavonti of being involved with Arthur Noone way back in the 1960s. Noone was allegedly paying Trelavonti for information concerning specific cases, or so Stan surmised. Nothing was ever proven. Trelavonti learned to cover his tracks pretty well. Stan Gilbert was real careful about what he said in front of him from then on.

Skip remembered those conversations when he joined the St. Louis County Sheriff's Department and learned Trelavonti was still on the payroll. Sometimes he said things in front of Trelavonti to test him and see if he had changed. He hadn't. Now, after thirty seven years in the sheriff's office, Trelavonti probably thought he had the run of the place . . . sometimes he did.

His problem was that there was nothing he could do as sheriff without proof and Trelavonti was real good at covering his tracks. He was getting up in age, letting himself go, Skip liked to remind himself. If Trelavonti let himself go too much, or got too cocky, he would slip up and Skip could get rid of him. He hoped his old man was around when he did.

Sitting there at his old wooden desk, Skip sipped his coffee and paged through his father's notes once again, this time looking through the pages covering the 1960s' disappearance of the couple that used to live on the Egar farm. They were special notes; notes no one in the sheriff's department knew existed until the night before, Stan's private stock. Skip had deliberately talked about the notes in front of Trelavonti. He planed to snare him and, hopefully, Noone too, although he didn't know what for with Noone. But the man was doing something illegal, of that he was sure.

As Skip sat there still sifting through the mountain of information, he remembered that Stan suspected Noone of something in the '60s, but he, too, could never nail him on anything. Noone was never questioned in the disappearance of that couple. By the time police began investigating the professor's disappearance Noone was in Canada. No body was ever found, so the case was handled as missing person's case, not a murder investigation. The professor was never heard from again, but that wasn't unusual. People dropped out of their own lives all the time. And, as Stan's notes indicated, maybe the professor was humiliated by the fact his wife ran off with another man and just wanted to disappear, forget he ever lived on the Iron Range. That thought didn't seem so unreasonable to Skip, either.

Now that Skip knew why no body was ever discovered and why the professor never got in touch with anyone, he doubted the thoroughness of his father's investigation. He tried not to. He reminded himself that things were different when his father ran the show. They had little or no technology to help solve crime, not like modern police officers.

With forensic science what it is today it's possible to make a positive identification on nothing but a skeleton, but even without that, Skip "knew" the skeletal remains found on the Egar property were those of the professor. He had learned the old fashioned way of doing police work from his father, and to trust his gut instinct on some things, but in court it was always good to have scientific proof.

After thirty eight years, the case that so puzzled his old man was coming together, a puzzle being solved without the picture guide. He wished his father were there to be in on it.

"Where are those twin girls? If they're still alive they would be something like forty years old by now," Skip said out loud. "They're probably buried somewhere in the fields out there. Someday some farmer will decide to till the land, land that hasn't been plowed in fifty years, and there they will be."

No one else in Skip's office knew about the papers left behind by the professor in the big oak chest Samantha and Angie found in the barn. He didn't want that information leaked to Noone. Still, Noone knew they'd been snooping through that library, tried to stop them from finding anything. Why? He asked himself for the hundredth time. What was in there that frightened Noone so much? What should he be looking for? Between the professor's papers, his father's notes, and the storm, it would be a long night.

Out on the road, Stan moved slowly north. "It's really getting hard to see." The senior Gilbert said to the empty cab, as he neared the highway patrol office on Highway 53 just north of Duluth fifty miles. The sheriff's department was five miles further up the road right outside of Eveleth. He eased his vehicle forward with caution on the isolated stretch of freeway. His speed dropped to 30 mph, then to 25 mph.

He engaged the 4-wheel drive mechanism just after leaving Cloquet, knowing it would be rough going as soon as he tried to climb the hill out of town. By then fifteen inches of snow made it hard for snowplows to clear the many miles of freeway roads they had to plow.

Highway 53 was still in pretty good shape, however. Plows had made at least one pass through. Even so, so much snow had fallen that the first pass through was quickly disappearing. Stan drove a Ford Bronco that sat high off the ground thanks to a lift kit, so its belly was well above the snowdrifts; it had new tires, was filled with gas, and made solid headway in the storm. He couldn't believe his luck when he found out the rental place even knew what a 4x4 was.

Because Stan grew up on the Iron Range and knew how precarious life could be if stranded in the middle of nowhere in a blizzard, he had stopped by a big chain store before leaving the

Twin Cities picking up enough supplies to make up a survival kit. He had food, extra warm clothing, blankets, flares, matches, candles, water and everything else he'd need to stay alive for a long period of time in the cold if he got stranded in his vehicle.

Truth was Stan sometimes liked taking on Mother Nature to test his skill against hers. He respected her though; if he didn't, she would make him regret it. And sometimes Stan just liked being alone with her when she was having what he called, a "temper tantrum."

Still, the six-foot six-inch former sheriff who had grown a paunch since his retirement was no fool. And though he liked her to misbehave, he knew Mother Nature would not pity him if he didn't acknowledge she was stronger than he was. He laughed as he drove thinking of all the times he had gone out in storms like this one, testing his mettle against hers.

Today was different, though. He no longer cared about testing his mettle. He just wanted to get to Eveleth to see his son. "Thank God for 4-wheel drives and cell phones," he said to the empty cab. He reached for his cell phone thinking he must be close enough to his old office to get a signal and dialed. Skip answered.

"Hey son, how are you?" Stan said.

"Hey Dad . . . I'm a little surprised to hear from you. What's up?" Skip thought his father was calling from Florida. "I haven't got anything new to report here."

"I'll be seeing you shortly. I'm on 53 now, just up the road a-piece. It's pretty bad out here. We can talk about the case when I get there." Stan couldn't keep the excitement he felt from his voice. He hadn't realized how much he missed his son, the chase.

"You're here! That's wonderful . . . I think. What are you driving? You shouldn't have tried to make it here during this storm!" Skip went from delighted to angry in thirty seconds.

"Hey, don't worry about it. Your old pop rented one hell of a 4x 4 that's hurling him right toward you. I'll have to tip that girl at the rental counter. This Bronco is something else."

"Well, that's good, but you still shouldn't be out there. Where are you anyway?"

"I'm just past the Townline gas station. I should be pulling into the office in about ten-fifteen minutes. It's rough going out here so it may take a little longer." Stan arrived safe and sound twenty minutes later.

"You know we should head out to the Egar farm and stay with those two women. I don't trust Noone," Stan said without preamble to Skip as he greeted his son in the parking lot. He had thought about everything Skip told him about the case earlier as he drove in, and now he had a real "bad feeling" about the women being alone out there.

"I was thinking the same thing. Come on in and help me carry these boxes of material out to your Bronco. We'll take it all with us." Stan and Skip went into Skip's office through a private entrance deciding that it was best that no one else in the office knew he was there.

As they worked gathering the boxes of information, the two men didn't bother to exchange family pleasantries. Both got so engrossed in their work they forgot everything else, especially on a case like the one in front of them. Skip often wondered if his singular focus came from his father naturally or if he learned it from watching him. Family business conversations came in spurts, an unexpected question here a comment there. They would not neglect their relationship altogether, although they approached it from odd directions.

No deputies were in the office when Stan arrived. Most of the men were out on calls. Dispatchers were working overtime.

The crew manning the jail cells worked in the back preparing to camp out at the office to relieve the dispatchers.

Since Harriet Hornblower was in charge of office management especially during emergencies, she prepared for storms. She made sure the building was stocked with food and ready for the long haul they all knew they would have to endure as long as there was a major blizzard in the forecast. She had even talked the sheriff into purchasing a stove and refrigerator for the break room, which she used to prepare many of the meals prisoners and personnel alike ate during long hauls. County commissioners had readily agreed to the request, once Skip presented them with the numbers showing how much they would save by doing so, numbers Harriet had prepared.

"Unless there's an emergency that no deputy can handle, don't tell anyone I am at the Egar farm," Skip told Harriet Hornblower as he prepared to leave. "That's where I'm headed now. You have everything under control here, as usual, so I won't worry about it. But, Harriet, if you need me for any reason don't hesitate to contact me. Okay?"

Harriet had seen the Ford Bronco pull up. Watched as the man who looked so familiar got out of it, watched Skip greet the man, watched the two go into Skip's office through his private entrance, then again as they hauled boxes back out putting them into the Bronco. She knew Skip was up to something. She also knew Stan was there. She worked for the man so many years she could spot him a mile away just by his walk. She was not happy that Stan had not stopped by her desk to say hello. She was peeved, but she still wouldn't tell a soul he was there unless he or Skip said it was okay. He wouldn't ignore her under normal circumstances. Harriet Hornblower, in spite of her name, found it very easy to keep a confidence, something both Skip and Stan counted on.

The boxes loaded, father and son climbed into the Bronco and headed out.

Trelavonti was still trying to reach Noone. He hated the cold, was overjoyed that he had the day off. He was worried about Noone, though. Noone always kept his cell phone with him even if he was in the woods. With such a storm raging, he couldn't travel out to River Drive to investigate. He drove a police cruiser. That thing would belly up in a blizzard. He would have to wait until the storm let up. That's all he could do.

Chapter Fifteen

Mike and Vicki Jennings watched the storm from the upstairs window in Mike's bedroom. "Do you ever wonder if that man, the one that used to live here, haunts this place?" Vicki asked.

"Yeah. Like this place has some sort of evil force that walks it, sees everything, knows everything. Something like that."

Vicki turned her head so Mike couldn't see her surprise. He had never admitted anything like that to her before. Fun loving, practical joker, Mike wasn't making fun of her like she thought he would. That really scared her. He made fun of her and laughed at her so often she didn't quite trust him. She watched him with a wary eye. "Were you surprised at what Dad said?"

"Yeah. Big time."

"Is that why you helped him with the chores when we got back? I mean, you OFFERED to help him!"

"I guess I've been giving Pop a hard a time lately. What he said about the pitchfork? Man that scared me. I got to thinking about 'what if he wasn't here?' So I offered to help; I don't want to see him get hurt."

Mike hated farming and the smell of the barn. He wasn't too keen on cows, either. The cows seemed to feel much the same about him for that matter, especially Steamroller.

Mike had more than one reason to hate cows and the barn. He took an awful lot of abuse at school from city kids because his father was a farmer. So did every other kid who lived in the country regardless of whether or not their parents farmed.

But sometimes, when Mike had to do chores in the morning before school, the smell of the barn lingered about him no matter how hard he showered afterward. Kids in school, the ones that didn't like him, used that as an opportunity to mock him, most of the time it was Ralph Kendal doing the mocking.

Once, while Mike sat in library during study hall reading, the principal, Arnold Kendal, Ralph's father, walked in, grabbed Mike by the arm and said, "you're coming with me young man!" Mike hadn't noticed Kendal until Kendal grabbed his arm and bellowed so loudly that everyone in the class, and every other class on the same floor, heard him.

"What's the matter boy, don't your folks make you wash before you come to school. I am sick of you stinking up my classrooms!" He said loudly enough so everyone could hear him. He drug Mike from the library to his office. When they got there, he made Mike change into some old clothes the janitor had found in an empty gym locker.

"You'd better watch your step around here, boy," Kendal said when he was alone with Mike. "We've been keeping an eye on you and know you're a troublemaker. You got that? If your parents want to discuss this, they know how to reach me."

The incident occurred in the morning, so Mike was forced to wear the old gym clothes for three more class periods before lunch. They smelled worse than his clothes had. Every footstep he took in those clothes reminded him of the humiliation he went through at the hands of Principal Kendal.

Ralph Kendal, a junior to Mike's freshman, was always looking for an excuse to harass Mike. Mike couldn't understand why a junior took such an active dislike to him; they had never exchanged words, had never laid eyes on one-another until that year, yet every chance he got, Ralph Kendal taunted and teased him, tried to break him down in front of his classmates.

Father must have told son about his morning run-in with Mike during lunch hour because Ralph Kendal was ready to add his own twist to Mike's humiliation just before the bell rang for students to return after lunch. He was hanging out in front of the school doors with his friends when he spied Mike coming up the walk. As Mike tried to walk past him to climb the stairs and go back into the school, Kendal started taunting.

"Hey, Jennings, smell like a barn, do ya?" Kendal said as his friends snickered. "Love your clothes."

That's all it took. Mike had had enough of the insults. He grabbed Ralph by the shirt, threw a strong left hook to the right side of Ralph Kendal's face, and laid him out quicker than a referee could yell 'one, two, three.' As it turned out, Ralph Kendal had a glass jaw. He had never learned to throw a punch, never worked out or participated in sports, all of which left him weak. With all the farm work Mike did, he was already strong, muscular at fifteen, and quick as a cat. Ralph never got up from that one punch, and none of Ralph's friends made a move against Mike, even though a couple of them were on the football team.

Mike's anger was not quenched with his round one knock out victory and he prayed old man Kendal had seen what happened from his office window, which overlooked the front of the school where the confrontation took place. Mike prayed the old man saw his son sprawled out on the front walk and knew it was him that put him there.

At the second bell that afternoon, which was Mike's free hour, he walked into Kendal's office and snatched his clothes off Kendal's desk. The secretary didn't try to stop him. Kendal wasn't in at the time. Mike put his own clothes back on at 2 p.m. and remained in them until the bell rang at 3:30. He wore them onto the bus where he sat silently until they reached home.

Ralph Kendal never bothered Mike again nor did his father, aside from dirty looks he gave Mike when they passed in the halls. Principal Kendal proved to be just as big a coward as his son, however. He was too cowardly to face Mike head-on, but he frequently spread lies about Mike to the other parents. Most did not take root.

The only effect the ridicule had on Mike was to make him stronger. He hadn't even finished his freshman year when more and more of his counterparts turned to him for advice, sought out his counsel. The mocking didn't have much of an affect on his popularity, either. Most of the kids sensed in Mike a leader, and his innate charm beguiled them all the more.

And even if his parents sometimes embarrassed him, as all parents do their teenage children, Mike loved, liked, and respected his mother and father.

Vicki never saw the incident, but other kids told her about it; Mike never said a word about it to her or their parents. He refused to insult his family with the ugliness of Principal Kendal or his son.

Vicki, however, as a source of embarrassment, was something Mike couldn't seem to rise above. He either could not, or would not, look past the twenty extra pounds she carried, and therefore he never saw how pretty she really was. He thought she lacked self-control, and to him, twenty pounds too much meant she was a tanker. He didn't want to be seen with her, didn't like it when his friends made comments like, "Hey man, you're so skinny, how'd Vicki get so fat?" or "How fat is she, anyway?" It got worse than that, and the more he heard, the more he was ashamed of her. When he looked at her, even in the middle of the snowstorm/haunted house crisis, those were the only thoughts he had of her.

"What are we going to do about this?" She asked.

"What can we do?"

"Well, we could call Reverend Wilson and see if he has some suggestions?"

"Not a bad idea, but he isn't going to be able to get out here in this storm," Mike said.

"Maybe Angie and Samantha can help? Angie is supposed to be a psychic."

That was an idea Mike could sink his teeth into. His eyes grew large as he said, "we could sneak over there later tonight on snowmobiles! Mom and Dad will be going to bed early; they always do. With this wind, they probably won't even hear the machines start up." Mike worked out a plan.

"Can't we just ask? I mean that's better than sneaking around," Vicki said.

` She got on his last nerve. "Can't you just once do what you're not supposed to? I really wish you weren't such a goody-to-shoes! Would it kill you to live on the edge a little?"

Vicki bit her lip to keep from crying.

"What are you two doing up there?" Bernice called from the kitchen. Her two teenagers were being way too quiet in light of everything that had been going on to be up to anything good.

"John!" Bernice yelled to her husband who was on his way into the kitchen, anyway. They both jumped as they met at the kitchen door and nearly collided. Bernice said, "Do you think we should talk to the kids about what they learned over at the Egar farm?" She spoke as she set the table for dinner.

"Yes. That's a good idea. Let's do it at dinner. The younger kids should hear too."

Mike and Vicki sat silently at the table while they ate. After supper, Bernice and Vicki cleared the table; Bernice took out a chocolate cake for desert and served everyone a piece. All took notice. Bernice never served dessert. Sugar wasn't good for their health she told them often enough, so they all knew something big was going on.

"People do awful things to each other sometimes," John started as everyone lifted a bite of the cake to their mouths. "Your mother and I don't understand it most of the time . . . but what I do know is this: If you're afraid of something, or if you sense danger, listen to that voice inside you that's giving you the warning. Don't be afraid of it. Use it. The Holy Spirit is guiding you. Your mother and I know that it is the Lord's voice shielding you . . . anyone who will heed him.

You saw how Angie uses her intuition, right? She has used it so much; she can hear it all the time, now. But what it really is is God speaking to her, shielding her. You, too, need to ask God for protection. He'll give it to you. He is that little voice. Heed it. Ask to be protected from evil, and you will be." John looked intently at his two teenagers. He wasn't too worried about the younger children that night. "You need to appreciate what evil, negative thoughts, can do to your life, but you have power over them and that power is the Word of God. Do you understand?"

Everyone nodded their heads yes.

"Now I know you are very interested in what you learned at Samantha's house, and that's okay, but I need for you to understand that you need the Lord's protection to sort it out. Much of it is evil. I don't think the voice, the one crying out for help is evil, but something is, or was, evil that stayed in that house," John paused, "and it may still be there. I don't know. Remember though, that nothing other than God is strong enough to protect you if you need it. That means you pray for guidance and protection then speak the Word against any type of evil you're faced with. Do you understand?"

All the children nodded their heads once again in agreement. Jeremy began to cry; he was frightened of the devil. John picked him up and cradled him while he finished eating his cake. No one else spoke until everyone had finished eating.

"Dad, do you mind if we take the snowmobiles back over to Samantha's house tonight; we'd like to see if there is more we can do?" Mike asked cautiously. He really wanted to go but he didn't want to defy his father outright.

John looked at Bernice. He could tell by the look on her face that she wasn't crazy about the idea. It was storming outside. "No," Bernice said firmly, "we need you here to watch the youngsters. We are going back over there."

John's mouth dropped open. "Since when?" He asked.

"Since I've been thinking about it all afternoon. Sam is in real danger, honey. I don't know what I'd think of myself if we didn't go back there and try to protect her. In this storm, we can't take the children out; besides, everyone is safe here, even if that old ghost is hanging around. Mike can handle it. I'm not so sure about Sam and Angie."

"Angie is a psychic, for crying out loud. If she can't handle it, who can?"

"God." Bernice answered matter-of-factly. "John, we can take that outfit you rigged to plow the driveway," Bernice continued as if the matter had already been decided. "It's got a cab with a heater in it so we can keep warm, something we can't do on a snowmobile. It also has that tread that will go over anything."

She's got this all planned, John thought as he sat at the table looking at his wife in disbelief. Bernice rarely behaved in a take-charge manner unless she felt something was terribly wrong. Twenty-two years of marriage proved to John that her instincts were well honed. He didn't argue with her.

Bernice could see that her two oldest children were keen on helping in the investigation, and were disappointed to be forced to stay home. She turned to them, and said, "We'll be back in the morning and then you two can go over there. We should try to do this in shifts. That rig you're father cooked up is strong enough for us to use in this storm. You can use it, too, when it's your turn. I know you two really want to be there to help tonight, but I think it's best if we do it this way. That way everyone will get a chance. But tonight, for some reason, I'd feel better if I knew you were all safe at home."

Mike and Vicki didn't like it, but they accepted it. They clung to the hope that tomorrow it would be their turn, and were satisfied with being given a chance to be of service.

Bernice packed a survival kit, everything she and John would need to cross the two and a half miles back to Samantha's. She worried about Sam and Angie as she packed, afraid they'd get hurt. Something was going on over there. She felt it, sensed it since early afternoon, which was why she was so adamant that Mike and Vicki stay home. She just hadn't figured out how or what it was yet, but she had a very strong sensation that someone was going to get hurt. As she packed, she prayed for everyone's protection.

Mike and Vicki went back to their rooms once they knew they wouldn't be going out. John went into his and Bernice's bedroom to the gun cabinet where he kept his guns under lock and key. John Jennings' stint in Viet Nam had taught him the value and danger of owning and handling guns. But he was not about to leave Mike and Vicki unprotected, so he readied his .357 Magnum for Mike and his .22 caliber pistol for Vicki while he armed himself with his shotgun for the trip to Sam's.

A nagging dread set upon him each time he thought of Sam's house, of going back over there. Something was warning him of danger, but Bernice was right. They couldn't just stay away and offer no help to the women. They were friends. He, too, prayed for protection for all concerned.

Bernice worked at packing an overnight bag, which was lying open on the bed. She saw what her husband was doing, and said nothing. She trusted his judgment.

John marched back out of the bedroom, stuffed the gun cabinet keys into his pocket, and called the teens back downstairs.

"You know you have to be careful with this," he said to Mike as he handed him the .357 Magnum. "Probably the most danger you will be in from this is little fingers picking it up and accidentally pulling the trigger. Make sure they can't touch it and that the safety is on. Don't leave it lying around. All right? And here's the key to the gun cabinet," he said handing it to Mike.

"Vicki, here's another spare key if you need it. You two have to promise me you will be very careful. Do you understand?"

"Yes, sir," Mike said.

"We'll both be careful." Vicki nodded in agreement. They were determined to be prepared for danger, be it animal, man, or spirit.

In the isolated farm country of the Iron Range, many parents prepared their children to deal with all kinds of dangers. It was a necessity. Parents knew it was possible for one of their children to meet up with a stray mountain lion, bear, wolf or even some lunatic who wandered out that way. It is not uncommon to find drunks lying in ditches, either.

Once, an escaped killer had made his way to the woods behind the Jennings' house making them his refuge. Every police agency in the state had representatives sitting on the perimeters of John's cornfields, watching and waiting, hoping to take the fugitive alive. The whole community was on alert, afraid they or their families would become victims to a man, police said, had killed his entire family. The man was captured without incident, but it instilled an even deeper need in the community to ensure that its children would be safe even if adults were not around.

As a consequence, everyone in the Jennings' household, once they reached the age of twelve, learned how to handle a gun. Local gun clubs taught gun safety classes utilizing police and DNR officers as instructors. The kids learned as much about responsibility and safety as they did about shooting.

So it was, that John Jennings prepared his older children before he and Bernice left for Sam's. He was confident the two would use the guns safely. He also knew they were level headed enough to use them with caution.

It was 6 p.m. by the time John and Bernice lit out for the Egar farm. Mike and Vicki watched from the stairway window facing south as their parents drove off into the night. The headlights on the crawler lit up the driveway. Snow fell heavy and the wind tossed it fiercely as John and Bernice were slowly swallowed up in the storm.

"You can go to bed. I'll stay up and watch the house."

Mike's superior tone instantly angered Vicki. "I'll do no such thing. Don't even think about it. I plan to stay awake and that's that."

She headed downstairs and into the kitchen and over to the stove where she put on a teakettle of water. They were never allowed to drink coffee, but Vicki didn't care. If they were old enough to stand guard, they were old enough to have a cappuccino, instant coffee Bernice kept hidden in the cupboard.

When Mike saw what she was up to, he said, "What do you think you're doing?" He was disgusted with her rebellion. "We aren't supposed to be drinking that."

"You don't have to. That's all the more for me. It tastes great."

"You would care what it tastes like."

"And just what does that mean?" Vicki faced him angrily.

Mike didn't say another word.

Vicki wasn't the only one getting ready to enjoy a cup of coffee. Angie too was brewing a pot in the kitchen.

"How can you drink that at night and expect to sleep?" Sam asked.

"Do you really think I'm going to be able to get back to sleep tonight?" Angie was incredulous that Sam would even ask her such a thing since she didn't get out of bed until early afternoon.

"Sorry. I guess I wasn't thinking." Sam said smiling realizing what she said.

Angie sat down in the booth in front of the fire beside her. They both stared at the coals burning in the grate. Neither woman had gone back into the basement since the early morning discovery.

"I called my sister the other day," Angie said out of the blue, "you know, the one I can't get along with, Karen? Even after all these years, she still hates me. You know what she said?" Angie wasn't really expecting Sam to answer, "She told me I was adopted."

Sam looked at her. The words hadn't sunk in. She thought she heard wrong. "What?" she asked.

"She told me I was adopted . . . So I called Mom and asked her about it. She confirmed it. Karen never liked me because she felt I was usurping her place in the family. That's why we had so much trouble growing up together. But that's not all." Angie paused a second. "Mom said they adopted me from the same orphanage that you grew up in, the Catholic one in the Twin Cities!"

"Get out of here! You're kidding! Right?"

"No . . . I'm not. I wish I were. It seems I was two and a half years old when mom and dad adopted me. They said I had a sister too; a sister they didn't adopt. Can you believe that? I'm forty years old and just now learning I'm adopted and have a blood sister, one I've never met. That astounds me! Do you remember that vision I had as a kid, the one I told you about?"

Sam nodded her head.

"I always planned on asking my mother about that. Its funny that I'm so surprised now."

"You know, there are way too many surprises going on here to suit me," Sam said in all earnestness. She had felt a kinship with Angie since they met in college, they became instant friends, something she never understood or questioned, but as Angie had come here to help her with her . . . situation . . . they found they had more, much more, in common than they had ever dreamed. She shook her head. If someone had told her two weeks ago this would happen, she never would have believed it. Now, Angie discovered for certain that she was adopted, and that the two of them had been in the same orphanage together at the same time! She couldn't believe it.

"How long have you known about this?"

"Two days. With so much going on, I didn't want to bring it up. Besides, I needed a little time to think about it. Usually I have such a handle on things, can read things intuitively if I can't figure them out otherwise. But I've so missed the mark on this I'm beginning to doubt myself."

"Hey, don't do that! You've been right on the money about everything else out here so far. What about those murders you help police with? Maybe you couldn't see the adoption thing because you're too close to it, but you sure as heck helped a lot of other families find their loved ones. I wouldn't let it shake my confidence in my intuition or psychic ability, that's for sure." Sam was thinking more out loud than speaking to Angie, but Angie appreciated her vote of confidence. "When this is over, and I bet it will be soon, we can look into your history and see what we can find. We'll find out what went on."

Angie felt relieved. "Don't you ever feel resentment because you weren't adopted?" She asked.

"I used to when I was younger, but I learned that I actually had it pretty good. You know you helped me learn that when you'd complain about your family. I guess it isn't easy living with a bunch of other people who want to tell you how to live. Correct me if I'm wrong, but I seem to remember you telling me that your family had a fit when you showed an interest in the paranormal. I also remember you saying how your parents tried to teach you that you shouldn't say anything about being able to 'see' things. How you were ashamed of it for a long time.

Yeah, I spent my childhood in the orphanage, but the nuns loved me. I knew that. So no . . . I don't resent not being adopted. It was a good experience growing up there."

"That's a good attitude you have." The two women sat quietly for another moment while the fire burned warmly in front of them.

"What do you think happened to the professor's twin daughters?" Sam broke the silence. "Do you think they could be buried inside this house? I can't seem to get them off my mind . . . they should be put to rest, I think."

"You think they're dead? I think the professor would have guided us to them if they were. I think he would have known; and I doubt he would have abandoned them in death. He's been trying for such a long time to get someone to find him. I bet if he could, he'd help us find them. The question is: why hasn't he?"

As they talked, Fuzz climbed up between them. The little mongrel dog that looked a bit like a fox terrier stared out the window toward the barn and growled. Sam didn't notice. She and Angie sipped their coffee then placed their cups on the table in concert, looking one-another in the eye, and saying in unison, "I'll beat you to the barn!"

Chapter Sixteen

The women ran for their winter gear dressing as they raced out into the storm. The snow came down in torrents. Sam determined to tie a guide rope from the house to the barn, unrolling it as she walked down the slippery slope tying the other end to a big cast iron handle attached opposite the barn doors. Angie walked behind her holding a flashlight. It took ten minutes battling the winds to reach the barn.

"There, we can use the rope to make sure we make it back to the house. Farmers do this all the time in the winter because they might get lost between their barn and their house in whiteout conditions. More than once a farmer has ended up freezing to death only feet from his own front door."

"That's a good idea," Angie said stamping snow off her boots inside the barn door. She knew of many instances of that happening, herself. "North Dakota is notorious for stranding people in blinding blizzards like this when snow whips across the prairie. This is actually better than storms I've been through there. At least here you've got the trees to stop some of the wind."

Sam looked at her friend. She was glad she didn't have to school a novice about the dangers of winter weather.

Inside the barn, out of the biting wind, the women crossed

into the library switching on the lights as they went.

As they did that, Stan and Skip watched snow blow sideways across the road as they drove down Townline Road to River Drive in silence. The more he thought about it, the angrier he got, so Skip said to his father as they turned down River Drive, "Why did you come up here in this storm?"

Stan said, "Didn't mean to ruffle your feathers son" as he looked across the front seat at Skip. "You can let me drive if you're tired."

"Jeez, Pop, you still don't think I can do anything, do ya?" Skip pulled the Bronco over, got out and bucked the wind to get to the passenger side door. Stan didn't say a word. He got out, too, making his way to the driver's door, got in and set the clutch pulling the stick shift out of neutral, gearing up to first and starting off down the road.

Skip was in a foul mood slapping the snow from his clothes much harder than he had to. He took a long hard look at Stan. He didn't like grayish cast of his father's skin. "You feeling okay?" he asked, his anger vanquished as quickly as it had risen.

"Yeah, I'm fine. It's just been a long night. Driving in this mess is harder than I remembered."

Skip said nothing. His main concern was for his father, but, he thought, he doesn't look that bad. Then he remembered the time ten years before when it was his mother who looked like that. She had been dying of cancer. Ever since, he had been skittish about loosing his father. He knew it would happen one day; he just didn't want to acknowledge that it could, one of the reasons he was glad the old man moved to Florida. He wouldn't have to watch if his health started to fail. He felt bad about that, thinking it was a lack of compassion for his father on his part, that he was weak. It made him feel like a fool, too, but he couldn't seem to rise above it.

Stan asked, "Are the Spencer sisters still living out here?"

"Yeah, I just saw them early this morning, as a matter of fact," Skip said. "Why?"

"I'd like to see 'em, is all," Stan said. "I always liked them. So did your mother. Did you know that?" He looked across the seat at his son then turned back to watch the road. "She even invited the two of them to the house for dinner on occasion." Stan wasn't waiting for Skip to reply. He was thinking out loud about two people he missed a great deal. "I've known those two since we were kids. Their lives were messed up then. They were the first ones to contact me, outside the family once they learned Brenda died . . . I'd like to see them."

"You will. They were there when we discovered the bones this morning, know about the investigation. Are we going to talk about that?" Skip said looking sideways at his father.

"Why don't we wait until we get out there then we don't have to repeat ourselves," Stan said. "In the meantime, I hope you will jump back into the driver's seat. I'm beat. I'd like to catch a little shut-eye. You don't mind, do you?"

Stan was exhausted. This investigation meant more to him than he wanted to let on and he wasn't going to let his health get in the way of it, so he'd take his rest where he could get it; he had too. If Skip knew just how sick he was, he would not let him help, period, and now since he had arrived, already the case was consuming him with a desire to solve it.

He pulled over and they traded places once again. Once the Bronco was back on the road, Stan pulled the visor of his baseball cap down over his eyes and leaned back in the seat to stretch his long legs out in front of him. The long drive from Minneapolis had cramped them, and the little exercise he had had since arriving had done little to ease the cramps in his feet that were agonizing. Stretching helped a little, that, and the warm cab, were all he needed. He fell fast asleep.

Skip drove on.

So did the Jennings. While they were still two miles from Sam's house, John and Bernice approached Clem's driveway in John's homemade crawler with its two seats, heater and covered cab. The little machine made it over the deepest snowdrifts with little effort.

"Clem, this is John. I'm fine, Clem. Listen, Bernice and I are going back to Sam's in the crawler. What do you plan to do on this evening?"

"Well, I didn't have any plans. The chores are done. I'm just eating supper."

"If you decide you don't want to stay home alone, why don't you see if you can make it back over there tonight, too. Both Bernice and I have this gut feeling, like maybe something is wrong over at Sam's. And if you're up to it, why don't you bring that Savage of yours? It can't hurt to have an extra gun."

"Ain't too crazy about the sounds of all that, but yeah, I can make it over there. How about I bring along two old ladies? They're always up for a little adventure." Clem winked at Gladys and Inez.

"Damn fool Jennings. He and Bernice are out there in this weather trying to go over to Samantha's! Can you believe that," he whispered to the Spencer sisters over the receiver he held covered with his hand. The women had not gone home earlier that morning. Instead they stayed with Johnson at his house; a tradition they began long ago when bad weather set in.

"We're just about to your place now. You'll be able to see our rig go by shortly. It's gotten a lot worse out here. Have you got something that will get you through this mess?"

"Yep, I've got an old snow plow, bought it from the county last year. It'll get through damn near anything. While I'm at it, I'll plow the road, too. Don't want Sam and Angie stuck back there with no way out. That thought makes me nervous."

"Sounds good, Clem. We'll be watching for you. By the way, you do have our cell phone number, don't you?"

"Yeah, I got it. Hey, I can see you now. I'm looking out the living room window. I'd know that rig anywhere, but with this blowing snow, I can barely make out your headlights."

"Well remember that when you're driving, and please . . . be careful. One more thing . . . I've tried to call Sam but I'm not getting any answer over there. I'm worried. Can you try to reach her, too?" As he finished talking to Clem, John Jennings snapped his cell phone cover closed. His unease grew with each failed phone call attempt to reach Sam. So did Bernice's.

At Johnson's, Clem stewed about John's comment. Glad to be with Inez and Gladys because they comforted him with their friendship, he thought he was getting too old for adventure. It didn't look like this one was going to pass him by, so he decided, with his friends, he might as well embrace it. They had already been through a great deal together. Why not something else?

As they prepared to go back over to Sam's, Clem finished dressing to go out into the storm before the women did. He watched his two friends finish pilling on their heavy woolen clothing.

"Okay, you old coot we're ready if you are," the sister's said in unison.

Once they were all piled into the front seat of the snowplow, Gladys said, "I thought I heard that Stan was coming up. Didn't Skip say that?"

"Yep, he did," Clem answered as he and Inez exchanged knowing looks. Gladys had had a thing for Stan ever since high school. They were all friends then. Stan often stuck up for the Spencer sisters, never caring much what others thought of him when he did. His defense of them carried weight, too, as Stan was one of the most popular kids in school. He graduated at the top of his class and he and Clem were on the football team together; that's how they met.

Others who had life easier often picked on them, so Inez and Gladys dropped out of high school. Not only did kids harass them, so did some teachers and the principal. They had both been smart enough to have graduated with honors if the school officials hadn't been so determined to keep them in their place, always misjudging them. Stan and Clem were right, in part, thinking the sisters dropped out because of that torment, but the other reason was something they never wanted to talk about, even to their close friends.

Raped by their father from the time they were little girls, all the two could think of when they got to be teenagers was getting off the farm and away from their folks and away from the small town that hated them without reason.

In 1945, when Inez was sixteen and Gladys, seventeen, they headed for the Twin Cities. There they fell in with the first man to notice them, a pimp. He plied them with loving attention and affection, and before they knew it, he had them working the streets of Hennepin Avenue. It only took two weeks.

Their first experience with a pimp was their last. One day, when he came to see them, once again to beat them up and steal their money, a vial of acid awaited him. Inez "knew" that day what the pimp planned to do the minute she opened the door and saw him standing there; she saw it in a vision that flashed before her eyes as they spoke. She silently signaled Gladys, so that she, too, knew it was time to carry out their plan.

They got the pimp into the bedroom where they had stored the small vial. Gladys slipped into the closet to get it while Inez enticed the man to shower his attentions on her. She endured another beating with a coat hanger for her efforts. As she lay bleeding upon the bed, welts popped out upon her skin as quickly as the iron hanger was brought to bear on her back, and legs. The pimp didn't notice Gladys slip into the closet; he enjoyed beating Inez too much, so he was more than a little surprised when she called to him sweetly with the hidden pot behind her back. She had dressed in lace panties and bra.

The pimp smiled, stepped away from Inez, and moved toward Gladys. As he did, Inez slipped off the bed. Gladys made sure Inez was well out of throwing range as she cooed to the man. He sauntered over to her. She waited until he stood directly in front of her then she hurled the acid into his face. He screamed horrifically falling onto the bed. The women ran from the apartment and called the police. The acid burned the pimp so badly it scared him for life. Police brought no charges against the Spencer sisters, deciding they acted in self-defense when Inez showed them her back and legs. Thanks to that incident, the girls earned a reputation for being dangerous.

On the streets, they no longer feared anyone because they carried weapons, and made sure every street hustler knew it. They made it their business to know who every pimp in town was, too, even drawing up acquaintanceships with the few who had sense enough to respect them. Most didn't.

Through all this, the women grew dependent on one-another for emotional support, independent of men. Through the abuse of their father, then the pimp, they had learned to hold men at arm's length, sharing nothing with them other than their bodies.

After six months on the streets, they called their mother hoping she would let them come home. They felt that they were wise enough by then to handle their father if he made any advances.

But instead of welcoming them home, their mother told them they had shamed the family by being whores. Secretly, she was glad they were gone. She no longer had to compete with them to get attention from their father, her husband. It also wouldn't do for the neighbors to find out what they were doing for a living.

As if that weren't enough, their mother hated them because Gladys and Inez reminded her of what she perceived as her failure—her husband's infidelity, something she dare not mention to him. How could she? If she accused him of infidelity with their daughters, she'd be admitting that she knew what he had done! He would throw her out of the house! What would she do if she had no husband to support her? She had no skills, no work history. She was too old at thirty nine to be taken in by some other man as a wife. She wasn't attractive. To look at her daughters after they had turned to prostitution? All that would do was shame her, so she did the only thing she knew how to do. She hid from the truth.

None of that mattered anyway because everyone on the Iron Range who knew the Spencer sisters knew they would turn out bad; after all, they put out for everyone. Their father was a thief who rarely held a steady job. There were his drunken brawls on Saturday nights, and everyone knew he beat his wife, so . . . his daughters? Well what else but prostitution awaited them?

Stan Gilbert had been different from everyone else, though. Even in high school he was nice to Inez and Gladys without expecting anything in return. It took awhile for the girls to grasp that Stan wasn't after anything. He liked them for themselves and they never forgot it. He was the one bright light in their lives when they were children, but it had not been enough to keep them off the streets.

As for Stan, after he joined the sheriff's office he learned much about the private lives of many families on the Iron Range, including the Spencers. Stan suspected what had happened to them at the hands of their father. He dealt with old man Spencer on more than one occasion in his official capacity. It pleased Stan to throw the man in jail every now and again.

He also discovered that the Spencer sisters were not alone in their particular tragedy. It went on a lot, even in the so-called "good" families, so most of the families that spent so much time ridiculing the Spencers had nothing to be ridiculing anyone about. Their private lives were worse than the Spencers.

Clem learned from Stan after they grew up about the girl's troubles. He once told Stan that old man Spencer had thrown him off of their old homestead on one occasion when he was a kid because he wanted to date Inez. The old man had told him to keep his "sniffing" to himself. He wished he'd have known back then, he had told Stan. He'd have kicked the old man's ass up and down the road every chance he got, and he still got angry just thinking about it even though it happened fifty years before.

As he turned the key in the ignition of his snowplow and prepared to carry his two friends over to Sam's house, he sighed with momentary regret as he headed down the driveway. The women sat quietly looking out into the blizzard paying no attention to Clem.

Back when they left home, it was twelve years later when, the elder Spencers were killed in a car accident. The sisters inherited their property, what there was of it, and came home. By that time, life on the streets had become a way of life for them. When they got back they put their natural intelligence to good use and invested some of their earnings in the stock market and in real estate. They grew wealthy. Their many contacts with men of power also freed them to continue their work protected both in the Twin Cities and on the Iron Range.

And since wealth always carries power, they gained a strong foothold in the political machine of the Iron Range, albeit a quiet foothold. Neither woman wished to make any public appearances. They made acquaintances with the rich and famous, as well, who, in turn, expected discretion. The Spencer sisters were renowned for it. To be discreet was like taking out an insurance policy. Whenever they needed help, they got it from those they helped by staying silent.

Stan and Clem, the only two people who always treated Inez and Gladys as friends as they were growing up, were the only two people in their lives that they fully trusted. Though Clem would never admit it, he secretly loved Inez and half suspected that Stan felt the same way about Gladys even though he'd gone on and created a life with Brenda.

Brenda liked the sisters and always treated them kindly. She was one of the only women from the "straight" world who ever did and the women never forgot it. Though she had loved Stan from the time they were pre-teens, Gladys never attempted to come between Stan and Brenda even if Stan had wanted to, which, Gladys sometimes thought he might.

When Stan needed money for bills after he had back surgery, it was Gladys and Inez who gave it to him. They would not let him pay them back, either. When he needed money for Brenda's mounting medical bills, then when she died, it was Gladys who made sure she had the best of everything both during her illness, then, at her funeral.

The sisters, though they were rich, did not live like they were. The women liked to use their money to help friends when they needed it. They secretly started a safe house in the Twin Cities to help stranded teenage girls, hoping to keep them off the streets and out of prostitution. In spite of the hardships of their youth, Gladys and Inez held no grudges against those who couldn't accept them for what they were. "It's just the way it is," both said often.

"What do you say we get back over to Samantha's," Clem said as turned the truck onto River Drive.

"When did you buy this damn thing," Gladys asked as she looked about the big utilitarian truck.

"I bought it from the county last year. Got it cheap. Been wantin' to try it out. Damnedest thing you ever saw. We'll be over there in two shakes of a lamb's tail."

Clem liked the idea of going back over to the Egar place. He loved a good mystery. "I sure wouldn't feel right if something went wrong over there. No sir."

"Well get the lead out you old coot, what the hell you waiting for, New Years next year?" the women said in unison.

As the three friends began the battle with weather conditions, inside Sam's barn library, Angie said to Sam as she looked through the roll top desk, "I wish you hadn't taken those photos to the house."

"Me too. I didn't even look at them! Can you believe that? I also forgot the cell phone up there. Did you bring yours?"

"Yes, it's right here," Angie said as she tapped her coat pocket. The room hadn't warmed enough to warrant taking off their over coats. "Look at this Sam; it's a notebook in the professor's hand writing. It must be notes for his novel; remember, the one Clem told you he was writing?"

"Yes, I remember. Can I see it."

Angie handed the notebook to Sam and she read:

The wolves travel in a pack with old Grey as the lead. He and Smokey are the alpha pair dominating the group. They traveled out of the Canadian wilderness and settled into Northern

Minnesota's Iron Range in the 1920s, according to DNR records. Hunters have systematically slaughtered most of the pack. Grey and Smokey kept alive by hiding deep in the Superior National Forest on the far southeastern edge of the Iron Range.

Grey is getting old, though. Young Savage has been edging him out as dominant male. Smokey, too, has seen better years. She had her last litter of pups two winters ago. The lone wolf, Savage, is edging into the pack and Grey can't seem to stop him.

Eventually, he and Smokey were banished, dying the next winter. But true to their nature, the pair stayed together until the end.

Savage mated with Sunset and the two took over the pack. Sunset is Smokey's daughter from three seasons ago. She's in her prime weighing one hundred pounds and is as fierce as any of her male counterparts. She chose Savage because of his strength.

Sam closed the notebook and looked at its cover to discover it was labeled "Field Study."

"That's so odd," she said. "He lived here, too, and studied the wolves just like I'm doing!"

"I agree. It is a strange coincidence. But look here. I've found something else. This is Janice's diary. Here, Sam, read some of this."

Sam took the leather bound book from Angie and read:

Dear Diary: It happened again today. I've seen things, things I don't want to think about, horrible things. It's as if my own future is set before my eyes and I can't do a thing to change it. Arthur Noone is going to destroy my family. My girls, they will be torn away from us, from each other. It's been coming to me in flashes. I see James locked up somewhere; somewhere that won't allow him to reach any of us. It's dark in there.

Dear God, should I tell him? How will he ever understand what I've been doing? How can he know I'm trying to save all our lives by taking Noone away? Noone can't take his hands off me. Maybe this way, I can keep him away from my family.

I've figured out a way to get the girls out of here, too; hopefully they'll be safe. That couple, the one whose daughter got pregnant and ran away, they will take them for me. They said they would raise them. They're not bad people. It's better than letting Noone have them. If I sell them the girls, Noone will be pleased. He thinks everyone is as evil as he is. He will think I've given over to him one hundred percent. It's the only way they will be safe."

That was the last entry.

"It sounds to me like she was trying to save her family by sacrificing herself; what do you think?" Sam asked Angie.

"Maybe the girls aren't dead. We have to find out who that couple was she referred to. It could be anyone. Just how many girls get pregnant without the benefit of marriage? That gives us a clue, but not much of one."

"For some reason Ellen comes to mind, the sheriff's old girlfriend? Her parents, I mean," Sam said softly.

"You know something I'll bet you're right! Now, Sam, please don't try to tell me you have no intuitive flashes. That's a stroke of genius!"

"Oh, please, please, not too much praise. It's just a place to start." Sam said blushing. She felt right about it though, and sensed it wouldn't be long before they knew just what had happened to the twin girls.

Angie took off her coat and seated herself in the big leather chair facing the bookcases. Sam sat across from her. "Have you been checking those videotapes at the house to see what's on them? The ones you have outside, I mean, the security tapes?"

"Frankly . . . no, I haven't gotten around to it. I have been collecting them, though and inserting new tapes each week."

Angie got comfortable in her chair. "Would you turn the lights low, and shut the doors. I'm going to read for awhile," she said.

Sam got up and headed for the library shelves reaching for Janice's diary. "I don't want to be distracted by anything, either." She shut the doors, turned down the stove, dimmed the lights, and sat back down across from Angie. Still, she couldn't concentrate as she looked about the room thinking of all she had learned thus far.

It wasn't long before she turned to Angie and noticed that on Angie's lap rested a pencil and a yellow legal pad. Almost imperceptibly, Angie's hand moved the pencil across the paper ever so slowly at first gradually gaining speed until it flew back and forth so fast the paper tore from the intensity. When it seemed Angie's hand could move no faster a husky, baritone, male voice hummed, droning hypnotically out of her mouth.

Sam swayed to the rhythm and cadence of the voice. "You're in danger," the voice hummed softly. "Things are happening now. What has happened in the past is still happening. Much blood has been spilt, will be spilt. Spirits seek retribution. The evil is close. Do not be afraid. Trust God. You are here for a reason."

As quickly as the rhythmic swaying of the pencil in Angie's hand had begun, it stopped. Her head slumped over onto her chest and nothing more came from her mouth. Her hands fell limp in her lap. The legal pad slid to the floor.

Sam jumped up spilling Janice's diary. She sat back down quietly, until Angie stirred and without preamble said, "That sounds like an engine. How can that be?" Sam witnessed

Angie go into trances before, so this one didn't startle her for long. She got up, pulled on her overcoat, dowsed the lights, fingered the gun in her pocket, and ran over to the barn doors to peer out into the night right alongside Angie.

As they peered out between the cracks in the doors, wind grabbed at the barn's timber frame shaking it. Snow had drifted up outside the door. They could barely see the rope that led back to the house. The driveway was visible only because lights approached, odd looking lights perched high up and pressed close together on some kind of strange vehicle, a vehicle that sounded like a snowmobile but didn't look like one.

The women grew fearful as the crawler pulled up alongside the house. With the wind howling and the snow blowing, they couldn't see who was inside the strange looking machine. A shape, unrecognizable to them, got out and started for the house. Something about the way the person walked seemed familiar, but it was so bundled up in outdoor gear, the women didn't recognize John Jennings immediately. Another shape exited the strange contraption and made its way to the house. Sam knew that walk instantly.

"Hey, that's Bernice! Can you believe it? That has to be John with her."

The women waved their flashlights toward the house hoping that the Jennings would see the light. They pushed and tugged at the barn doors enough so that some snow pushed aside letting them squeeze through a small opening. When they got outdoors, they groped for the rope and headed back up to the house.

Chapter Seventeen

"Watch out for the rope," John hollered against the wind to Bernice as they made their way up to Sam's back porch. The wind whistled with such force Bernice couldn't hear him and walked right into it.

"I told you to look out," John said as he bent down to help her up, looking down toward the barn as he did, exclaiming, "Hey!" at lights moving up the path. Bernice turned looking in the same direction jumping to her feet in fear at the sight.

John turned to her, "That has to be Sam and Angie," and with that he grabbed the rope and started down toward the women, after first saying to Bernice, "You head up to the house. I'll make sure these two get up there safely."

In the lead, Sam wasn't entirely sure that who approached her was friend or foe, so she pulled her gun from her coat pocket as the figure drew closer. They were face to face before she knew for sure that it was John Jennings because his parka shielded his face from the storm as well as from her. She said with an exhalation of relief, "John?" slipping the pistol discreetly back into her pocket.

"Yeah, it's me," he tried to say over the wind. He then helped the women make their way to the house. When they got inside the porch, they found Bernice there waiting for them.

Sam said, "What on earth are you two doing here in this weather?" She didn't know if she should hug them or tell them they were idiots for coming out in what had to be the worst blizzard in Minnesota history.

"We've . . . we've come to help," Bernice managed to say. "We felt we had to come. Even so, Sam, I'd really like to use your phone and check on the kids. Do you mind?" Bernice had been worrying about the children since leaving home.

"You certainly can, come on in. Angie, did you grab that tape and video before you left the barn? I didn't."

"Of course." She slapped her coat pocket to indicate where they were. "I brought the note pad too."

"Good." Sam smiled at her and headed inside to the warm kitchen, which was a welcome relief for everyone.

Outside the temperature continued to drop. Snow fell in sheets as it piled ever higher. As it grew colder, snowfall would stop, and the winds would grow stronger. Then below zero temperatures would set in, a typical winter pattern. With wind chills and forty below temperatures it could get as cold as eighty, even ninety below zero at times. In those conditions, exposed human skin froze in a matter of minutes.

"Can I plug the tank heater in on my crawler Sam? All I need is an extension cord." John knew that the small engine would freeze up if not properly cared for. Parked on the north side of the house, it was protected from the wind by the grove of pine trees, but the cold would still be too much for the small engine if not heated.

"Yes, John, I have an extension cord in the porch. Help yourself. It might also be a good idea to tie more of that rope up from the porch to your vehicle there."

John nodded in agreement and stepped back onto the porch to once again brave the cold and blowing snow. The wind made a concerted effort to push him back toward the house as he uncoiled the rope and extension cord to make himself a guideline to the crawler. When he finally reached it, he plugged the crawler in and made his way back to the house.

As a Minnesota native, John had had a lot of experience with unpredictable winter weather and knew the signs of an unusual storm. He watched the sky with this storm and guessed it would go down in his personal history as one of the worst he had ever been through. He hoped beyond hope that he had done the right thing by leaving his children home alone, but as he kept his furnace and house well taken care of, he reasoned they shouldn't have any problems.

He made sure the livestock had more than enough feed and water before he left, as well. They were housed close to the barn in covered feed lots, which would shield them from the wind. The big round hay bales were perfect for storms, and water tank heaters worked to keep the animal's drinking water from freezing. He even put the big Brahma bull inside the barn to keep him out of trouble. He was so unpredictable John didn't want his children handling him in any way, including feeding him.

Dressed in fleece lined Sorel boots, woolen mittens, and a down filled snowmobile suit, John hoped the blizzard would do him no harm either as he worked his way back to the house. His heavy clothes made the simple task of walking difficult because of the wind. He bent over into it clutching the rope. The snow stung his face feeling like pebbles pelting him, so he lowered his head even further blindly following the lead rope back. Climbing the five steps up to the porch took all the energy he had left. Standing just inside the porch door, he tried to catch his breath as he shook his head and lifted the hood from his face.

Inside the house, Bernice talked on the phone to Mike and Vicki, telling them to make sure that they and the younger children stayed inside until they got home.

With Bernice on the phone and John standing near the door, Sam filled the teakettle and put it on the wood stove in order to make everyone hot chocolate. Angie started a fire in the kitchen fireplace. John struggled out of his boots and snowmobile suit, and in stocking feet made his way to the table to sit in front of the fire rubbing his hands together to warm them. Bernice hung up the phone and sat down beside him.

Sam brought two steaming cups of hot cocoa to the table placing them in front of her guests. She went back to the stove to fix two more cups bringing them back to the table for herself and Angie, who sat with the Jennings there.

Cold air steamed off John. "Brrrrr, John, you must be freezing," Angie said as she tried to shake off the chill he brought into the room.

"I'm just glad to be inside in front of this fireplace! I don't feel a thing," he said, then paused for a moment to sip on his cocoa. "You know," he began again, "I think some of the things going on here, in your house Sam, are meant for us, too." He used his finger to indicate Bernice and himself. "I mean it feels like we are supposed to be here, to help you. Does that make sense?"

"I agree," Bernice said. "And we are going to help you put a stop to it!" She tried to sound more confident than she really felt.

In a quiet tone, she added, "Once when Vicki was lying outside sun-tanning, you know how our driveway goes around in that circle? Anyway, she was lying there on the grass in the middle of the circle reading when she felt as if someone were watching her. She turned around and a man in his late fiftys or so was looking down at her. He asked if John was home. She told him 'no' and he smiled at her. She said that when he did, she felt the hairs on the back of her neck stand on end.

She ran inside to tell Mike and me. She even drew us to the living room window to watch the man as he walked down and out the driveway. He was right there in plan sight, she said . . . only thing was . . . we couldn't see him. I accused her of lying," Bernice said softly, tears welling up in her eyes. "I'd never done that before."

"Yeah, I remember that," John said putting his arm around his wife to comfort her. The incident had caused a lot of strife in the Jennings' household. Vicki refused to speak to Bernice for quite some time after it. No one had every questioned whether she told the truth before. She had a reputation for being honest and straightforward even when it wasn't in her best interest to do so. Bernice's accusation hurt her deeply. Apologies were made, but the words couldn't be retrieved. They clouded the air in the Jenning's household for a long time.

"What do you think you can help with here?" Angie asked.

"I don't know," Bernice said, "but there is something. I just know it! It has something to do with the man Vicki saw, something to do with our place and yours, together . . . somehow?"

"Do you hear that?" Sam said. "It can't possibly be someone else—can it?" Everyone hurried to the south facing front room windows and looked out as Sam pulled back the drapes. Up the driveway, through blowing snow, they could see headlights moving toward the house. Sam and Angie ran for their guns.

It wasn't Clem's plow coming up the driveway, either. John hurriedly told the women that Clem and the Spencers were coming over, but he didn't know whose vehicle it was that was driving up her driveway right then. It wasn't Clem's. He dowsed the lights as the foursome traveled throughout the house using the vehicles' headlights as guides. When whatever it was pulled up behind the crawler and stopped, the doors opened, and the dome lights came on illuminating the sheriff and another man.

"It astounds me that I can get so much company in the middle of one of the worst storms the Iron Range has ever seen," Sam said shaking her head in disbelief still staring out the window. Someone flicked the kitchen light switch back on and the room was once again set aglow.

Driving from his house to Sam's, John had managed to clear a narrow pathway on the roadway. That path proved to be a boon for Skip and Stan Gilbert as they made their passage down the same road. Even so, as winds blew with gale force, the road had drifted over quickly. It would be hard to retrace the tracks, Skip thought as he stepped out of the Bronco. He also agreed with Stan about Stan's rental. It got through everything laid before it. Skip decided to chip in on that tip Stan planed to give the girl who rented it to him. He couldn't have received a better vehicle, not for travel in this storm.

As Skip approached the crawler through the snow, he recognized it as belonging to Jennings'. He caught the kids using it on a main road last year and warned them about doing so again. If he caught them at it, he told them then, he'd give them a ticket; they knew that. Even more upsetting was the idea of two youngsters out in this storm.

"The Jennings' kids must be here!" Skip pointed to the crawler. "That's odd," he yelled to Stan above the roaring winds, "that all the lights are off in the house." As he spoke every light on the first floor came to life and the front door opened.

"Hey Sheriff," Sam called, "come on in."

He could barely see Sam's form through the blowing snow and couldn't hear a word she said guessing that she welcomed him in by her arm motioning them inside. As he looked at her waving to him, a wave of relief surged through him. Right beside him, Stan noted with interest his son's reaction to the woman at the door. The faintest of smiles crossed his lips. The two men groped their way to the house. When they reached the crawler's guide rope, they too used it to get to the porch.

On the porch, Skip and Stan stomped the snow from their boots. "Here, use this broom and sweep some of that mess off. You can hang your coats on the rack over there," Sam said handing the broom to Skip. Earlier, she had placed an electric heater on the porch, so by the time Skip and Stan arrived the room was comfortably warm compared to the outdoors.

"Thanks," Skip said, "maybe you're wondering who it is with me and why we're out here in the middle of a night out of hell?"

Sam then took a good long look at the man standing beside the sheriff and knew the two had to be related. The resemblance was amazing.

"Dad, this is Samantha Egar; she owns the place. I told you about her."

"You didn't tell me she was so pretty." Stan laid on the charm. He liked feisty women and from what he's heard, she topped the cake. He smiled and held out his hand. She took it and led the two into the kitchen.

Angie stood by the stove watching the men as they came through the door. Stan recognized her immediately. He thought his son had hit pay dirt. He'd be hard pressed to choose between these two women if he were in Skip's shoes. He hoped Skip was interested in one of them at least. Skip's single life had always puzzled Stan. He wondered if his son was much more in love with Ellen than he had ever suspected. With regret, he looked at Skip and wished he could have solved that case, given the boy some peace. Now, on observing the look in Skip's eye as he gazed at

Sam, hope rose in Stan's breast. Finally, he thought, Skip needs a good woman in his life.

"Dad, this is Angie Eckenridge. I know you've heard of her. She's the one that has worked with police all over Minnesota and the Dakotas on cold cases."

Stan didn't need an introduction; he met Angie Eckenridge when she worked a case with a fellow sheriff in the Dakotas. He took both Angie's hands in his, covering them.

"It's been a long time. It's good to see you, dear," Stan said still holding Angie's hand. "I've read all your stuff since we first met."

"Thank you. It's good to see you again, too, Stan."

"You two already know each other?" Skip asked completely unaware that his father had ever met her.

"Yes, son, Angie and I met when I helped with that case in South Dakota, the serial killer there? You weren't around here then, so maybe you missed it, but Angie here did a hell of a job on that one." Stan still held her hands.

Angie pulled them free. She didn't like what she saw when he held her. Skip's father was deathly ill.

"Now I remember!" Angie said looking at Skip. "That's why you looked so familiar to me when we met and why your name resonated so. It's your father I met long ago. My, you two look a lot alike."

Stan beamed at the observation and at everyone in the room. It was like this everywhere he went. Most people took an instant liking to him just like they were now. He was full of vitality and good humor.

For no apparent reason, Skip grew angry. "You know, I told your kids last year that if I caught that vehicle of yours out on the road, I'd ticket it. Did they tell you that? What in God's name are you doing over here in weather like this in that little contraption!" Skip asked John Jennings angrily.

"Hey, lighten up son," Stan said.

Skip only grew angrier, but said nothing. What the hell was he supposed to do—encourage people to risk their lives just because they wanted a little excitement! He was not keen on his father reproaching him in front of strangers, either. He was not a little boy! He sat down at the table and asked for something warm to drink. He was freezing.

"We're sorry sheriff," John said. "We came over here to help. We thought the women could use some, especially tonight." John stewed in his anger at the sheriff for speaking to him like he was a child. "Besides, sheriff, you know I've been through a few of these Northeasters, and I do know how to take care of myself." He looked Skip in the eye.

"Sorry, John, I didn't mean to give you a hard time. I thought those kids of yours were here and I guess I had to blow off steam even when I found it was you instead of them." Skip regretted speaking to John the way he had, but was relieved that John accepted his apology without any apparent hard feelings.

"So . . . sheriff . . . why are you here?" Sam asked.

"Why the hell do you think?" Skip snapped. He was still in a sour mood. He hadn't slept in two days, and didn't expect to get any soon. "We're here to help you, of course, me and my father, here," he said pointing at Stan, "who was the St. Louis County Sheriff before me! Of course he didn't tell me he was coming up here in the middle of a blizzard to help, but so what. I mean, no one tells me anything anyway, now do they?"

"Have you had any sleep since yesterday?" Angie asked Skip guessing at the reason for his foul mood.

"No. I've been working since 7 a.m. yesterday," he admitted, "and I didn't get any the day before, either. So?"

"Sheriff, you can go on up to the bedroom on the left at the far end of the hall upstairs," Sam said. "You might as well get some rest. I doubt if much is going to happen tonight. Besides, the rest of us are going to stay awake. We can wake you if we have to. You can't keep pushing yourself like this," Sam said.

"That's a good idea, son. We can wake you anytime, and since I'm here, I can help. I know the routine." Stan had no prior knowledge that Skip was running on empty. "The women are okay, they have lots of friends here, and two police officers; you can rest."

As exhausted as he was, Skip had to agree. On top of everything else, the trip out to Sam's had taken what little reserves he had left. He couldn't go on. He was simply too tired.

"Alright, I will, but Stan is in charge of anything concerning the investigation. Is that understood?" He turned to look at everyone other than his father. "I mean don't disturb anything without his consent. We brought what we took from here last night and old files from our office and some of that paperwork that the professor left behind. Although it's unorthodox, maybe some of you can read some of it and offer some input. If anything pops out at you, jot it down. Okay?"

They all nodded their heads, surprised that Skip Gilbert was letting them read precious investigative material. Skip went upstairs without another word. Once in the bedroom, he took off his shoes, grabbed a blanket he found lying on the back of a rocking chair, laid down, and was asleep within minutes.

Stan and John went outdoors and made their way from the house to the Bronco using the guide rope. The boxes were heavy and it was tough going trying to carry them and use the guide rope to get back to the house at the same time. The snow was already an inch deeper than when Stan arrived. With the added weight, it took the men over twenty minutes to bring both boxes into the house.

Stan was winded by the time he finished. Sam insisted he sit down. Angie helped him off with his boots and Bernice got him some hot chocolate.

"Are you hungry," Sam asked. Stan hadn't eaten since leaving Florida. He was famished.

As Sam cooked, her mind drifted to thoughts of Anthony Franco and the way he made her feel. She hadn't seen him since the community picnic, and because he never contacted her, she believed it was her imagination telling her he was interested in her. She had never experienced such a primal attraction to anyone like the attraction she felt toward Franco. One half of her was dying to try out the experience to its fullest, while her sensible side warned her away from him, telling her he was dangerous, in a whole different league. A league she could never be part of. At the same time, she knew there was something decent about him, something wonderfully honorable. And in that way, he and Skip Gilbert seemed similar.

She tried not to compare the two men, so as she continued to work she forced her thoughts to center on how good it felt to have so many people in the house with her. She had more friends than she ever realized. It was pleasant to hear their voices sounding around the table and to know Skip was upstairs asleep. They distracted her from the fear that was growing inside her. She finished cooking, turned off the stove, and took the food into the dinning room where every one had gathered.

As the group sat at the table safe and snug inside Sam's warm house enjoying a meal, drifting snow piled high in front of the barn doors once again. Snowdrifts piled high about the windows, as well, reaching up to the lower casements and piling high on the roof.

Regardless of the snowfall, Noone kept walking. When he awoke from his unscheduled nap, the cold had incited him to get dressed in a hurry. The weather wasn't going to get any better. It was 9 p.m. He had slept for hours. He felt rested and ready to take on the weather once again. He restored his cache to its hiding place. He could hear the wind whistling outside as he worked knowing that instead of dissipating, the storm was getting worse.

He climbed out of his resting-place to start once again on his trek, but the wind hit him with gale like strength pushing him backward. He worked to place one foot in front of the other thereby steadily making headway in spite of the winds as he determined to reach Samantha Egar's house that night.

Unbeknownst to him, the wolves walked alongside, just out of sight, behind the trees, in the brush, hidden from view by the blowing snow. It was 12 p.m. when he finally squeezed his way into Sam's barn through the barn doors. He was hardly able to open them for the snow. Once inside, he looked around for a comfortable place to rest and wait. He decided on the haymow upstairs, but was so tired once again, that he almost had to crawl up the ladder into it. He burrowed into the hay after taking off his wet outer clothes and hanging them across ceiling joists at the back of the barn. Dressing in warm clothes, he draped himself in woolen blankets he had found in the library, swigged from a flask of whiskey and settled into loosely stacked hay to rest. He ate beef jerky and string cheese to ease his hunger. Almost immediately, he fell asleep. The hay, dry clothes, and blankets were more than enough to keep him warm. The well-built barn was not drafty. It smelled of dust and fresh hay.

Outside, his walking companions stationed themselves around the barn to keep vigil on both the barn and the house.

Chapter Eighteen

Sitting inside Tony's, the empty nightclub afforded Franco a lot of time to think. He decided he wasn't going to let a little thing like the weather stop him from checking up on the dame and Noone. Something about that situation gnawed at him and he couldn't get the broad off his mind, even though he wanted to.

Samantha Egar, a college-educated woman, turned him on; he didn't want to admit that, but she did. He excited her too; he could tell whenever she was near to him. Was he supposed to behave differently just because she was who she was? He doubted it. And how different could she be? Imagine, someone like that falling for me, he thought and smiled at the idea.

Botticelli noticed, sensing that a woman had something to do with that smile. He was glad to focus on something other than the rotten night they were having. It was so bad that he and Franco decided to close up shop by 11 p.m. The place was completely empty. No need to pay the help for doing nothing, they reasoned, disgusted by people's reluctance to come out in a storm. Such a little thing like the weather stopping people from having a good time! It was ridiculous. The two long-time Iron Range bar owners were in complete agreement on the issue.

"So what if it's snowing," Bottecelli said over the phone

to one of his cronies. "What kind of a pussy are you? You let a little thing like that keep you home? What's the matter? Scared I'll go home with some of your money?"

Neither bar owner had a family, or wanted one, and they could not comprehend the desires of their family men friends who wanted to stay home with theirs, especially during bad weather.

"Since nobody's around, I'm going to find out if the wolf lady is okay." Franco said as he grabbed his coat and got ready to head out the door, "I got this feeling. Something is going down out there and storm or no storm, I'm going to find out what it is."

"You want some help?" Botticelli asked finally figuring out who the woman was that Franco had been smiling to himself about. He could use a little action and knew Franco had good instincts about that. Besides, he kinda' liked the 'wolf lady' himself. She had balls.

"Nah, man, stay here and secure this baby. I'll be fine," Franco said over his shoulder as he opened the door and walked out into the snowstorm. It took five minutes to wipe all the snow off his SUV. But before he did, Franco jumped in and turned the key in the ignition. The big motor roared to life immediately, and was nice and warm by the time he finished clearing it and climbed back in. He headed out onto the highway, and south down Townline Road.

Franco was completely unconcerned with the ragging storm. He could reach Sam's; she only lived ten miles from the bar. No storm could stop him from doing anything he wanted to do.

Back in Virginia, Trelavonti had problems.

"Hey, Shorty," Trelavonti said into his cell phone. "Have you heard from Noone? I've been trying to reach him all afternoon." Trelavonti didn't really care if Noone was lying dead somewhere, he just wanted to make sure he was. In fact, he was praying that the old buzzard had gone out during the storm and gotten himself killed, somehow.

"Why don't you quite worrying about it? You know he knows his way around even if he is caught out in this storm. He stores stuff out there in the woods. Didn't you know that?"

"What do you mean? What kind of stuff?"

"Supplies, man, supplies. He keeps all kinds of stuff out there; food, tents, blankets, clothes, things like that."

"No, I didn't know. So . . . he's probably okay then?"

"Probably. I'll tell you what. If you don't hear anything from Noone by tomorrow morning, you and I can go looking. Okay?"

"Sure, that sounds okay." Trelavonti said as he slammed his phone shut. He should have known Noone would have survival kits stashed all over. "Damn. That old bastard thinks of everything."

He went into the kitchen, slammed shut an open cupboard door, then grabbed a beer from the refrigerator, popped the top, and took a swig. He went back into the living room, sat down once again in front of the TV, and tried to turn his attentions back to the football game. There was nothing else he could do. He might just as well enjoy himself a little.

Outside, above the High Noon Bar on Chestnut Street in Virginia where Trelavonti lived, the worst blizzard the state had seen in thirty years raged on. Trelavonti didn't care. He had everything he needed. The remote control, a freezer full of frozen TV dinners, beer, and cable television hook up. He belched.

Out on the road, Franco had reached River Drive. He had no extreme weather condition supplies with him as weather conditions simply never concerned him. Things always went his way and he was confident that they always would, weather, included.

As he crawled along River Drive, he asked himself why he was so interested in Samantha Egar. *I can have any woman I want, young ones, too, and worst of all she is independent and can strong-arm me.* Once again, he wondered how she could go for the likes of him. *Man, she doesn't even go to bars. What am I doing?*

He gave up thinking about it. If, for some reason he was compelled to drive out to her house in the middle of a storm, well then, so be it. His heart beat a little faster as each mile brought him closer to her house.

Ahead of him and unbeknownst to Franco, a snowplow made good time over the snow-burdened backwoods roads.

"Clem, whatever possessed you to buy this thing? I'm not complaining, mind you'. It's wonderful." Gladys reached over to turn the radio on.

The cab was so warm Inez had taken off her coat. "I've never ridden so high. You can see everything!" She said as she leaned closer to the windshield trying to see into the blowing snow.

Clem beamed. He wasn't too sure when he bought the old 1985 snowplow that he was doing the right thing, but as it turned out it was a stroke of luck.

"Saw something go by when you two were packing the supplies." Inez said to her companions. "Can you see any tracks on the road Clem?"

"I think you've had too much to drink, Inez." Gladys said.

"Don't you wish."

Clem kept his eyes fixed to the windshield continuing to plow, and was so focused on what he was doing, he didn't hear Inez's question. "There sure is a lot of snow. I've never seen this much come down at one time. It's hard for the plow to move it. Man, if I didn't do this, those county guys would never get through out here . . . course, no one else would either.

When it finally registered, he said, "Inez, I don't see how you could have seen anyone going past my place in this. You aren't talking about John and Bernice, are ya'?"

"No, it was after they went by, so watch for tracks, please." She sat back in the seat and said no more.

They reached Sam's at 10:45 p.m. Clem continued to plow right up the driveway. They didn't see the Bronco until they reached the north side of the house.

"Whose rig is that?" Clem asked Gladys but didn't expect a reply. He backed the plow up, straightened it, and plowed forward so he wouldn't bank the Bronco in with snow. He edged his plow to the side of the Bronco and cleared a space there as well.

"I told you something drove past while you two were packing." Inez said. "Let's get to the house."

Clem parked next to the Bronco and the trio struggled to get past it finding the guide rope when they reached the crawler. They used it, too.

"Hey! Is anyone home?" They yelled as they stepped onto the porch through the unlocked porch door. The kitchen door was bolted, but the porch was nice and warm.

Sam, Angie, Stan, Bernice, and John were in the dinning room reading when Sam thought she heard someone calling. They had not seen the headlights. Clem knocked again, harder this time, and everyone looked up, startled. Sam crept across the dinning room floor. The lights were all on, so anyone inside the porch could see into the house easily. The porch lights, too, were on, and Sam sighed with relief when she saw Clem, Gladys and Inez standing there waving hello and smiling. They had all forgotten that Clem and the Spencers planned on being there too.

"Hey! It's cold out here; let us in!"

"I can't believe I'm getting so much company this time of night in the middle of this storm. Now what do you three think you're doing? I mean . . . really!"

"Hey, just thought we could offer some support," Clem grinned.

"Who else you got in there?" Gladys asked.

As she spoke, Stan came around the corner from the dinning room into the kitchen. Their eyes locked and held.

"You big galoote! You couldn't tell me you were coming?" Gladys ran to Stan embracing him tightly.

"You look good, Gladys. You don't look a bit different than you did in high school." Stan's big arms encircled her little frame.

She sucked in the smell of his flannel shirt, enjoying the scent of him.

"You're still a liar."

"Am not. That's the honest truth." Stan released his hold on her and grabbed Inez. "Now don't think you're going to get away from me."

She laughed. "You're the one who hasn't changed from high school, you old flirt." She slapped his back as he grabbed Gladys again holding a woman in each arm; he drew them both to him for one big bear hug. "You two feel so good, I'm never going to let you go!"

"You old fool."

"Howdy Clem. It's good to see ya'." Stan said releasing his hold on the women..

"You too Stan." The men grasped hands and shook slapping each other on the biceps with their free hands.

Their greeting tickled Angie as she watched. Stan had a way about him that made them all feel safe.

Angie's attention was focused more on Inez, though. Something about the old woman captivated her. They had yet to have a private conversation.

Inez looked back at Angie who was standing in the doorway. Their eyes meet and held. They responded to one another silently, as if they had known each other for a long, long time. Neither woman said a word.

"John Wayne" Bernice whispered to Sam as she pointed discretely at Stan. "He reminds me of John Wayne."

Sam smiled, nodding her head in agreement.

"Come on, you three. You can help us out here." Sam said to the new arrivals helping them off with their coats and escorting them into the dinning room.

"I get the feeling that no one is going to get any sleep tonight." Angie said as Stan and Gladys seated themselves across the table from her. There was something between them, a shared intimacy, she sensed. Inez seated herself next to Angie.

"Most of us seem to be assuming nothing will happen because of the storm; am I right?" Stan was serious and not really interested in a verbal answer. "You do understand this is a dangerous situation, don't you?" He looked around the room at everyone. "Someone is dead. There is no statute of limitation on murder, and from what I've seen so far, this is a homicide investigation. Skip filled me in on some of the other things going on out here, too. There are also some things going on in the county that I'm not at liberty to talk about just yet. But I suspect we're going to find a relationship that connects them all."

John looked at Bernice, then around the room at Angie, Sam, Gladys, Inez, Clem, and Stan. "Everything will be okay as long as we keep our heads and ask for the Lord's help," John said, in an effort to sound confident. Inside, a foreboding had settled upon him.

After a long pause, Stan said, "There may be more than one murder to consider here." He decided to speak in general terms about the missing children.

"What do you mean?" John asked.

"There have been children disappearing in this county since way back when I took office, maybe even before; Skip's been working on just such a case, the most recent one. But I think we'll talk more about that once Skip wakes up and can join us. I don't know how much of that he wants me to share, so for now, let's look into what we can about the professor and his family."

Uneasily, John picked up an old newspaper clipping, one of the articles Angie retrieved from the newspaper office in Eveleth. He glanced over it, but he wasn't concentrating. He had been uneasy from the start. He knew he was supposed to be there, but the feeling of uneasiness grew instead of dissipating like he had expected it to once he arrived at Sam's. He looked at Bernice and smiled, but he was worried about her, too. It was almost like she had a shadow surrounding her. He felt an overwhelming compulsion to protect her, but from what? He had never experienced anything like it in their twenty plus years of marriage.

"Two year old girls, father missing," the headline read as John finally focused his attention on the task at hand. The story, written by Eveleth News staff writer Diane Dell, reported the chronological events leading up to the disappearance of the professor, his wife and his daughters. John read it to the others, "Since the story of their disappearance broke, reports of the little girls being seen in the Twin Cities had come into the newspaper, but the article went on to say that the sightings had never been confirmed. The disappearance, police told the reporter, was domestic in nature.

"Our investigation found that Mrs. Janice Browne left her husband Alfred for another man taking their twin daughters with her. They are thought to be in Canada. As for Alfred Browne, we don't know where he is, but believe that he simply moved away from the area. We do not feel there is anything strange in the fact that he did not call into work before leaving, or that he took no personal belongings from his house," Officer Gene Trelavonti of the St. Louis County Sheriff's Department said. "Hey, the guy was embarrassed."

"I remember that," Stan said to John. "Trelavonti was never authorized to talk to the press. He took it upon himself to do that interview and damn near lost his job because of it. You bet we found the whole thing odd, about the professor, I mean, and you can bet that we weren't done with the investigation. Trelavonti was finished working on it though; I'll guarantee you that. He can be a braggart and I swear he's an idiot." As soon as he said it, Stan regretted it. He did not believe in talking about personnel matters in public.

"Skip was telling us about a girlfriend he had as a kid. She disappeared? Is that connected at all to this? I get a feeling that it is," Angie said. "The deeper we dig, the more she pops into my head."

"Yeah, like Joseph at our house. I bet he's connected too." John said.

Damn, he's still thinking about Ellen? Stan sighed knowing Skip still pined for his childhood sweetheart. "You're right, both of you," he looked first at Angie, then John. "Back when I was sheriff, I suspected Joseph was involved with Noone in some way, criminal, I mean. After awhile we discovered they were brothers so my suspicions proved true on that account. He disappeared, too, you know, and his disappearance was as strange as the professor's. I still think Noone had something to do with that, too. As far as Joseph was concerned, he and Noone had problems over a woman. I say that because Clem here heard them arguing in the woods just before Joseph disappeared. Isn't that right Clem?"

"Yup. They was out there hunting, like they always did, Noone and Joseph, course, at the time, I didn't know they was brothers.

Anyways, I heard them talking just before Joseph dropped out of sight. Arthur was yelling at him.. Them two boys was going at it in them woods that day, all right. Sounded like two ole' tom cats a fight 'en."

"Did you know Joseph was stealing women's undergarments?" John asked Stan.

"No. Nobody ever reported anything. After he disappeared, we found all kinds of women's underwear in his house. Then we knew. Even if we had known back then, we didn't know about sexual deviance, how it often leads to more serious crime, so we probably wouldn't have done anything anyway. It wasn't like grand theft auto; we're talking about items costing less than five bucks. Today though, police would take it seriously, but there wouldn't be much they could do unless they caught the culprit in someone else's house.

It was shortly after Clem heard the fight Arthur and Joseph had that we learned Joseph disappeared. We never found any sign of him anywhere, but we were pretty sure he was dead. Some thought Joseph just fell into the St. Louis River, drowned and got swept downstream by the current. We figured the same thing. That current can take you pretty far before anyone will find you, if they ever do. It's fast and treacherous. And without a body, you can't prove much of anything, including that someone is dead, unless you have a lot of circumstantial evidence. We didn't. One overheard argument was not enough."

Aside from Stan telling everyone about events that occurred in the 1960's, Sam's house was eerily quiet.

Out on River Drive, driving conditions were getting worse. "This is bad," Franco mumbled. It was half past midnight when he approached a curve in the road just a short distance from the Jennings' farm. He could see lights on inside a house, but the whirring snow was such that they were only dim fractions of their true intensity. Franco knew who the Jennings were by name and their proximity to Sam, but that was all, so he drove on knowing that he was close.

As he reached the Spencer and Noone road, he lost his bearings completely. "Maybe I should stop, try to figure out where I am." He spoke out loud, a habit of his whenever he felt uneasy about something. He rarely drove down River Drive and didn't know who owned the houses he saw straight ahead, off the main road, but in his situation he decided to go toward the lights, maybe get directions.

Pulling onto the gravel access road, the front wheels of his SUV grabbed into the snow dragging it into a ditch on the left side of the road where it lodged tightly in the snow bank. Franco tried to extricate it by stepping on the gas, throwing it into reverse and gunning it. He just dug himself in deeper. He had never used the 4-wheel drive mechanism, and had no understanding of how helpful it could be in situations like the one he found himself in. He didn't even know how to initiate it. As he sat there alone in his SUV, it dawned on him just how precarious a position he was in. He couldn't walk far. It was too cold and he wasn't dressed for it.

I saw houses. They can't be too far up the road, he thought as he stepped out of the SUV and started walking down the road that led to both the Noone and Spencer houses. He didn't have far to go, but the snow was deep; each step was a struggle. Years spent in a smoke filled bar room hadn't helped his lung capacity either, so each step grew in difficulty.

Wet snow seeped through his dress shoes and the thin socks that covered his feet. The fierce wind chilled his hands, as well as his feet, as he slowly moved up the road. Frostbite gnawed at his toes. He had no hat on either. He was in trouble. The alcohol he drank earlier numbed him to the pain, but the cold kept working on him. Finally, he made it to the top of a small knoll and looked left. There he saw Noone's house; it looked closer than the other one, so he made his way toward it. He had no idea where he was.

Standing on a wooden porch step, Franco tried the doorknob. It was locked. He could see a dim light inside through lace covered, and shaded windows, but no one came to the door no matter how hard he pounded. It was difficult making his hands and arms work. Even sheltered from the wind as he was, the cold grasped Franco in its chill. His ears and face were numb. He felt an uneasy touch of panic as he comprehended his dilemma. He looked around the porch, found stove wood tucked into one corner, took a piece, and smashed a small glass pane in the door. He reached in and unlocked the deadbolt lock.

The house was warm. Immediately, tingling sensations stung through his feet and hands. His legs felt like they were burning. He stood with his back to the door, and sighed with relief even though it felt like thousands of needles were being stuck throughout his entire body. Thankful to find warmth and shelter, his frost bitten fingers and toes screamed at him, making him realize just how close he had come to freezing to death.

Still, Franco wasn't going to let that stop him from making sure his surroundings were secure. Too many years living with his unpredictable, alcoholic father had taught him to never be too trustful of anything and to watch where he stepped.

Small and neat, there wasn't much to see inside the house. Comfortable that he was alone and safe, Franco accessed his own immediate needs. In the bedroom, he found men's woolen socks, a sweat suit, long underwear, an undershirt, and some warm outer winter clothing. He put every thing but the outer garments on hanging his wet clothes over the shower rod in the bathroom.

The heavy parka, boots, and other outerwear he took into the living room and placed in an easy chair. He wasn't sure about holding up in a strange house to wait out the storm, but couldn't work up the energy it would take to walk back out into it, no more that night; he was too tired. He would assess his condition in the morning before going out again, besides, it was doubtful the homeowner would return in the storm anyway.

The tingling sensation in his hands and feet eased a bit, and he realized he wasn't as seriously injured as he had feared. Still, it would be best to stay inside until morning. I'll leave some money for this stuff, he thought as he sat down on the couch.

Sitting there, his stomach growled in hunger, reminding him he hadn't eaten since noon. He was famished. He went to the kitchen, looked through the refrigerator, and found roast beef, apple pie, milk, and bread. He made a sandwich, ate it, and two pieces of pie after returning to the living room. He fell asleep immediately.

The next thing Franco knew it was morning, that he was in a strange house wrapped in a wool blanket and it was still dark outside regardless of the time, 4 a.m. He stumbled to the window, and looked out into the blizzard that blew snow so violently about the yard he couldn't see more than five feet out into it.

Chapter Nineteen

Vicki and Mike watched as their parents headed down the driveway in the crawler wishing they were going to the Egar place instead of their folks.

The blowing snow mesmerized Vicki who continued to stare out into it long after her parents passed from sight. She liked storms. Snowstorms were as electrifying as summer storms even without lightening.

Still watching, movement from the corner of her eye caught her attention. She turned looking down toward the barn, but couldn't see anything other than blowing snow. Unsure if it were real or just her imagination, she pressed her face to the windowpane, shielding her eyes from her own reflection, wondering if perhaps a cow had broken through the fence. The bull often did such things. She prayed it wasn't him. Mike would insist on trying to pasture the animal. Steamroller was dangerous and could easily overtake a grown man, let alone Mike.

Vicki stared intently into the blizzard as she tried to figure out if something was really moving around out there or if she were just seeing things. After awhile, she was sure something was there, but it wasn't a cow.

"Hey, Mike, come here. Something's out there . . . What is that?" She whispered pointing out the window at the sea of blowing snow down toward the barn.

Mike, too, found it difficult focusing because of the horizontally blowing snow, so it took awhile before he could see what Vicki was talking about.

"I'll bet that old bull is out again. Damn him!"

"Mike!"

"Well, if I have to go out in this weather and try to put him away, well, I just don't know what!" Just the thought of the bull exasperated him. Mike didn't want to go into the storm. He and Vicki kept their vigil at the window, watching, peering through the snow, and trying to identify what they were looking at. Whatever it was, it was approaching the house. It wasn't big enough to be the bull, which brought Mike much relief. It looked like a dog.

The form moved up under the yard light, sat on its haunches, lifted its head to the sky, and howled.

Vicki and Mike looked at one another. "Wolves!" They said in unison, even though there was only one. "They're probably down there raiding the herd right now! Dad can't afford that!" He grabbed his coat and a rifle.

"Mike, wait, there's only one and he's right here. We only saw one!"

Mike came back to stand by Vicki. The wolf moved over to the step just outside the kitchen door. It looked in the window at the two teenagers who were staring back at it; the animal laid down on the step still staring at them.

"Damn," Mike said, "what do you suppose this is all about?"

"I don't know, but I know you shouldn't go out there."

Mike agreed, but decided to hang onto the rifle just in case, a rifle he had retrieved from his father's gun cabinet no sooner than the elder Jennings was out of sight. Mike had retrieved another one for Vicki. She was as good a shot as he was. He laid the loaded weapon on the kitchen table then went back to stand next to Vicki who still watched the wolf.

"Look at him just lying there," she said.

Snow began to cover the animal's back. As they watched, the wolf slowly got up then lay back down at the foot of the stair turning his back on the children and focusing his gaze on the barn. Vicki followed with her eyes hoping to see what it was watching. Through the wind and blowing snow, she thought she saw a light on inside the barn.

"Did you leave any lights on down there, or did Dad?" She asked Mike.

"No, and you know how he is about the lights. He never would have left any on. How many times have you heard that lecture about not giving his hard-earned money to the light company? That does look like a light though, doesn't it?"

"Yeah, and I know this, too, it's going to stay on. No way are you going out there with that wolf on the front porch step, and I know I'm not going." Vicki said as they looked at each other.

She was right of course, Mike knew. He couldn't confront that wolf without the gun and he didn't want to have to shot it. It wasn't doing anything, but he knew if he went outside that it might just come after him.

That old wives tale about wolves never attaching a human being in North America was just that, an old wife's tale, and he knew it. North American Indians and Eskimos knew that wolves would attack people if given an opportunity because they suffered from those attacks. The only reason there hadn't been any record of wolf attacks in the modern world, Mike knew, was that when settlers came to America, they brought guns and the wolf soon learned to fear their guns and them. They stayed away from humans for the most part. But the wolf outside his front door wasn't staying away. That was not a good sign.

"What's going on?" Jasmine asked. She stood in the stairwell looking at Vicki and Mike. "Where's mom and dad?"

Vicki ran to her, picked her up, and told her that their parents had gone to Sam's house. "Come on, you need to get back to bed." She carried Jasmine upstairs tucking her under her covers when they got to the girl's room. Vicki checked all the windows making sure they were locked, and looked in at the other children to insure that they were asleep.

As she walked through the bedrooms, she prayed for protection then went back downstairs. When she got there, Mike was sitting at the kitchen table still starring out the window. The barn lights were off, and the wolf remained on the steps with his back to the window, staring off in the direction of the barn.

"Maybe we should bring the kids downstairs, have them sleep on the couch so we can keep a close eye on them. Maybe we should keep an eye on the barn, too, just to be on the safe side," Mike said.

When the youngest Jennings children were tucked safely in the makeshift bed on the couch, Vicki went to sleep in the easy chair across from them. She was exhausted. Mike took the first watch staying up until 4 a.m. when he woke Vicki. She took over then and didn't mind doing so. The wolf hadn't budged during the night, not until dawn when, to Vicki's surprise, it disappeared in a blink of an eye.

The storm raged on.

During the night, neither Mike nor Vicki saw Franco's SUV as it drove past their house.

Just a half mile away, Franco, too, was getting up. He was warm, rested and ready to get back on the road. He didn't understand what was prompting him, but he had an overwhelming urge to get over to Sam's house and make sure she was okay. He dawned all the gear he'd found in the house, made his way to his vehicle without too much discomfort, got in, pulled the visor down, found the instructions on how to use the 4-wheel drive mechanism and started the SUV. He let it warm-up, then engaged the 4-wheel drive, and managed to back himself out of the ditch with few problems. Slowly he crept back out onto the road to continue his journey down River Drive. A trip that normally took less than five minutes took Franco eight hours.

At Sam's, Skip slept until 6 a.m. Tip-toeing downstairs, he found everyone else asleep in chairs, on the couch, even on the floor. He smiled when he saw Stan sitting in the recliner next to the fireplace. Man, this is just like home, he thought. He went into the kitchen, made coffee, lit a fire in the fireplace, and sat down in front of the blaze sipping a steaming cup of hot, strong brew. It was so peaceful, the quiet house, listening to the wood burning, he liked it. Storms forced everyone to stay put. People communicated with one another during a storm, got to know each other better. They had too. That's what he liked most about storms. Maybe I'll have some time to communicate with Pop, too, he thought.

Skip stayed in front of the fire until 7 a.m. The cat and the dog kept him company, had kept him company all night. Even Kitty, the testy Siamese, took a liking to Skip sleeping on his pillow with him and growling anytime Fuzz had a notion to join them.

The first one of the others to wake, Angie stumbled into the kitchen. "Good morning. Did you sleep okay?" She looked bleary eyed as she sat next to Skip on the bench.

"Yes. I slept real well." He said still staring at the fire.

"Nice, isn't it?"

"Very." Skip stroked the dog's head, stretched, and then went upstairs to dress.

"I'll fix us some breakfast," Angie said as he left the room.

Stan was next to stumble into the kitchen following his nose as he scented fresh brewed coffee, bacon sizzling, and saw pancakes cooking on the grill. "You need any help, Angie?"

"No, Stan. Why don't you help yourself to some coffee and sit down. Skip is up. He went upstairs to dress. He should be down shortly."

"When did he get up?" Stan asked.

"I don't know. He was up and in here when I got up."

Soon, Sam, Inez and Bernice found their ways into the kitchen, too. Angie finished cooking for the whole crew by 7:45 a.m. They all sat around the kitchen table watching the storm, enjoying a second cup of coffee, and mentally preparing to continue with the investigation. As they did, snow hurtled past the kitchen windows under the direction of fierce winds from the northeast.

Outside and amid the pine grove next to Sam's barn, seven pairs of eyes watched the group through the windows. They were comfortable in their fur coats burrowed into the deep snow with the pine trees for protection. The alpha male sniffed the air. He was moving about, the wolf could smell him.

Noone awakened as those in the house were finishing breakfast; he relieved himself, looked through the small window of the haymow then lay back down. Not too much was happening up at the house, he thought. He might as well get more rest. He ate from his rations, then drifted back to sleep. He was tired. He slept in peace totally unaware of the vehicles parked next to the house.

Throughout the night, snow had worked to cover all of them. They were not visible to the naked eye.

The alpha male relaxed once again.

While Noone slept, snowshoes and skies rattled against the barn's exterior wooden walls as 40 mph winds whistled around the structure. He was oblivious to the whistle that often sounded like a teakettle about to blow. It was 10:30 a.m. before he awoke once again, this time to hunger pangs. He fumbled through his supplies deciding on beef jerky and string cheese. His thermos of coffee from the day before was still hot to the touch. It tasted better than he could have imagined.

The barn, though, was cold. No haymow could keep the cold out regardless of how well it was built. "It must be forty five below out there," Noone spoke to the walls as he rummaged around his knapsack for his cell phone. When he couldn't find it, he mentally retraced his steps from the house trying to remember what happened to it. "Where did I use it last? I talked to Shorty, then laid it down on the kitchen counter. Didn't I pick it up again? Yes, yes I did. I slipped it into my jacket as I headed out the door. I bent over near the woodpile. I thought I felt something slip. Shit! I bet it dropped out there, by the woodpile. What am I going to do now? I can't stay in this barn much longer. It's too cold to go back home . . . Hey! The library . . . seems to me I remember seeing a heater in there!"

Noone scurried to the window to look over at the house. Was anyone moving toward the barn? He couldn't tell because he saw nothing but blowing snow. The cold drove him downstairs. He was careful not to make much noise as he climbed backwards down the ladder to the first floor of the barn. He crept silently over to the outer barn doors to peer through them. Maybe there he could see the house better, but all he saw were lights on inside the house and mounds of snow piling in the yard. He did not see the lead rope tied to the barn wall. "Hell, even if they could make it down here; I bet they won't try. Not today." He rubbed his hands gleefully both at the thought of being alone in the barn and to warm them.

He slipped into the library looking around until he found the space heater. "Yes!" He exclaimed, "I will have some heat!" He lit the stove and stood in front of it trying to glean some heat from the still cold hearth. Soon enough warmth given off by the stove was a balm to his chilled body. He laid out his clothes on chairs next to it to warm them before putting them back on. Regardless of the hour, the day was dark with clouds, so he used his flashlight to see being very careful with it. If anyone from the house saw light in the barn, they would come to investigate, he was sure.

"Yes, Mother," Noone said as he dressed. His clothes were toasty warm and felt good to his body. He was annoyed with his mother, though, had tried to leave her home, but she harangued him like a harpy until he relented and took her with him. She liked to make sure he did things the way she wanted them done. Even so, he was glad to have someone to talk to.

"Everything is fine. I told you not to worry. Haven't I been careful?" He pulled dried fruit from his pack eating it in front of the stove along with warmed bread. It all tasted wonderful. He was content to eat breakfast alone with his mother. He remembered the many good times they had had in the barn together over the years.

Imagine, he thought, I didn't even know this room was here! I have to give the professor credit for that one. How many other things did he get away with that I wasn't aware of? The question hung in his mind, convicting him that he had to be more careful.

"Yes, son, you need to think of those things. You know, you can't be too careful. Folks just wouldn't understand you like I do." His mother's double-edged words stung, as usual.

"Yes, mother, you're right. I'll be more careful."

He heated what remained of his coffee on top the stove. He sipped it starring out the window at the house. Now he could see people walking about in the kitchen. He couldn't make out who they were, but it seemed like there were a lot more people up there than he had anticipated.

The wind howled.

The wolf pack stayed where it was, watching.

Inside the house, with breakfast over, the men decided to clean the kitchen. The women went into the dinning room."I can't believe this. Did you know that Janice Browne sold her daughters to Ellen's mother?" Inez asked. Angie looked at Sam. Bernice sat beside them listening.

"Joan Simpleton was her name; she was married to Randolph," Gladys said.

"How could she sell those kids?" Inez said.

"How do you know that? Is there some documentation?" Sam was offended by what Inez said about Janice Browne.

"They don't come out and say she sold the twins in the adoption papers; it just says that the Simpletons were given custody of them. Janice wrote that she sold them. Remember? It was in her diary." Inez said, surprised by Sam's reaction.

"Did you find anything that said what happened to the kids after the Simpletons took them in?" Sam asked Angie.

"I asked a couple of people in town, at the grocery store—you know—if they ever heard of the Simpletons. One woman at the check out stand said she remembered them. Her kids were friends with their daughter, Ellen. She remembered Ellen's disappearance but nothing about two little girls." Angie said.

"How could the Simpletons live around here all those years with no one noticing if they had twins living with them?" Sam had a hard time dealing with the fact that not one person seemed to care enough to wonder what happened to the two little girls. "What, did they all do, turn their heads? I don't get it!"

"Good question. When I was in town, I also learned that the Simpletons lived in Virginia until Randolph died in 1980. Joan moved to Florida then, and I guess, she is still down there."

"And no one ever saw those kids grow up?"

"Nope, not from what I could learn. I got the feeling though, that some of those folks in the grocery store knew a whole lot more than they told me. I couldn't get anyone to open up."

"I remember Joan," Inez said. "She hated us, Gladys and me. Remember that Gladys? She would drive by our house on purpose hoping to catch a glimpse of us." Inez pointed to herself and Gladys who sat next to her at the dinning room table.

"She and our mother were friends, although Joan was much younger. She wasn't much older than us."

"I remember that. You know," Gladys started to say something casting a sidelong look at Bernice, but forged ahead anyway. "Our mother wasn't too fond of us, either. Once Inez told mother dear about our father, it took me a long time to come to grips with her reaction. I've thought about it a lot. I was angrier with my mother than my father if you can believe that. He may have sexually molested us, but it was our mother who turned her back on us.

She would say and do things to put us down in front of others—perfect strangers—every chance she got. More than once she suckered me in by being nice to me only to get me out in public and humiliate me. Once, before we ran away, Inez and I went to town with her. We were at a restaurant. Do you remember that Inez?"

"Yes," Inez picked up the story. "Gladys and I were overweight then. Mother made all these cheap pasta dishes and if we didn't have second helpings, she would accuse us of not liking her cooking and shun us or pout until we ate more. We didn't want to hurt her feelings. After we gained thirty extra pounds, she'd chide us in front of neighbors saying we couldn't control our eating habits, said we were pigs at the troth always coming to the table for a second helping at supper.

When we were at that restaurant together, Mom said to the waitress after she told us to order banana splits, 'I sure wish my daughters could restrain themselves and look more like you. You have a wonderful figure, dear.' The waitress smiled at dear old mom and thanked her for the compliment while she smirked at Inez and me . . . right along with mother dearest.

Man, she hated us! I'm guessing it's because we took away her perfect family life fantasy that she liked to wallow in. No wonder dad acted like he did. Course, there's no excuse for that, either. We were his daughters."

"The gist of the story being, Joan was just like mom." Gladys took up the tale. "Don't bet on her ever having raised those kids. She didn't think too highly of anyone other than herself, although she professed love for everyone. She had to have thought Janice Browne was a whore. She never would have wanted those kids around her."

"Where could Joan have taken the twin girls, then?" Bernice asked. "We have to think about that." Though she spoke of Janice Browne's children, Bernice was thinking about Vicki and how hurt Gladys and Inez were at their mother's ridicule. She silently vowed never to do the same to Vicki about her weight.

"You're right, Bernice. We do have to consider what happened to them. I doubt that the Simpletons killed the girls. I bet they dumped them someplace." Angie said then pulled Janice's diary from the pile to read.

"Where's the nearest orphanage?" Bernice asked.

"Twin Cities," a choir of voices answered.

Angie and Sam looked at each other.

"How old would they be now, Gladys? Have you figured that out?" Bernice asked.

"I guess they'd be about forty by now, if they're still alive."

Just then, Stan and Skip Gilbert, along with John and Clem came into the dinning room with a fresh carafe of coffee and one of hot chocolate.

Without preamble, Angie said, "Here's some of the stuff that came from the barn. You might as well start reading." She handed out stacks of papers to the men. The women were already back to work and deeply entrenched in the paperwork.

"Hey, no thanks for cleaning the kitchen?" Skip grinned. The women smiled at him, pointed to the chairs, and motioned for him and the others to sit down.

A bit chagrined for the apparent lack of appreciation, Skip sat, turned to his father, and asked, "Hey, Pop, whatever happened with that investigation into Ellen's disappearance?" He looked through his father's old investigative reports for the hundredth time. "I mean, did you learn anything new about what happened to her?" Skip knew the reports, had read them often enough, but he also knew that sometimes a cop got a hunch, and it didn't always get entered into the official report.

"Nothing I could prove in court. I think Noone and Trelavonti had something to do with it, though. I suspect she's dead and buried son, sorry to say." Stan saw no point in misguiding Skip.

"You should have told me that thirty years ago!" Skip snapped at Stan.

"No son, I shouldn't have and I didn't. You were too hot-tempered then. I know you. You would have done something stupid." Stan sat between Gladys and Inez across the table from Skip, and as he spoke, he leaned in closer to his son.

"I've read your reports. I know what you thought. Did you think I wouldn't find them?"

"I knew you would. I also know that you are strong enough now to handle them; I expect you won't fly off the handle. Son, I just didn't know what to tell you back then. Some things aren't meant for public knowledge, you know that. I couldn't tell anyone . . . not even you, especially you, everything I suspected. That's not professional and you know it."

"Where do you think she is?" Stan was wrong, Skip believed unequivocally. He hadn't entirely left behind his childhood temper; he had not forsaken his hope of finding Ellen alive someday, either. As far as his temper was concerned, he had to work very hard at times to keep it in check, like now. He didn't wish to say anything to his father that he would later regret.

"My guess is she's buried somewhere on Noone's farm. That's probably where we're going to find them twins you've been talking about, too. I'm guessing we're going to find a whole lot more there than we ever bargained for, that's what I'm guessing," Stan said.

"If you thought all of that, why didn't you do something about it a long time ago?" Skip sounded like a petulant twelve-year-old.

"Look, son. You know how it is. Trelavonti and Noone are friends. Noone has friends in high places. Each time I tried to do something, I hit a brick wall."

"There have been a number of disappearances around this area over the years, like I told you last night. Mostly it's been young women, but once in awhile, a young boy turns up missing, too. Something ugly has gone on out here for a long, long time, and I'd sure like to see it stopped," Stan said to everyone in the room.

Skip cast a sidelong glance at his father. Why does his skin look so gray? He wondered.

"So far Ellen, the twins, their mother and their father (who we're pretty sure we already found) and Joseph are missing. Who else Mr. Gilbert?" John asked, engrossed in the story.

"In my time, which covered twenty nine years on the force, fourteen others besides those you've named, have disappeared. Remember some of those son?"

"Yeah, I remember some of the girls. Wasn't there a disappearance in '78 and another in '79?"

"That's right. There was also one in 1968, as well as one each in "69, '70, '71, '72, 'seventy three, and '74, up until 1984. Joseph disappeared in 84."

"There's been more since," Skip said shaking his head. "All kids, mostly girls about sixteen years of age, at least one a year, every year. I know they're all connected. I just know it. I just don't know how, why or by whom."

Bernice shuddered, as did John.

"Weren't their parents concerned? Out looking for them?" John asked.

"Yeah, sometimes, most of them though didn't come from around here. The kids, they were runaways, or from bad homes, or one-parent homes, you know, their mom's on welfare and can't afford to go looking for them. I got more than one call from a home like that. The mom would be pretty upset. She didn't know what to do."

Inez placed her hand atop Bernice's. "Don't you worry none, dear. We'll be damned before we let anything happen to your children." It was as if she had read Bernice's mind.

"That's right," Clem added. "Shit, Stan, you should have said something to me. I could be on the look out, you know. I am his neighbor!"

"Calm yourself, Clem. You probably know more than you think you do right now, which brings me to my question. How much tramping around do you do in those back woods of yours?"

"Considerable amount. Sam here, she does even more than me."

Everyone looked at Sam.

Inez grabbed Angie's hand saying, "Why don't we see if we can read anything? I bet together we would be pretty powerful."

Angie felt the pull of Inez's spirit.

Until then, Inez had not had an opportunity to get Angie alone to talk to her. She knew the moment they meet that they were sisters in spirit. Inez had always been able to "see" things beyond the physical. For years she had longed to communicate with someone like herself that could look deeper than the physical, see things others were too afraid to look at.

Angie turned to Inez and smiled hugging her in a warm embrace.

"Well," Inez said. "Are we good to go?"

"Good to go," Angie whispered squeezing her hand.

"How can a bunch of grown ups think that some spook is going to speak to them?" Clem said, still skeptical of anything paranormal.

"I seem to remember it was a . . . 'spook' . . . that helped you uncover a corpse. Isn't that right, sheriff?" Sam said, looking at Clem but talking to Skip.

"What do you say, Miss Eckenridge? Are you up for helping this group to solve some crime?" Gladys said jumping to Inez's aid and poking Clem in the side. The old coot knew Inez could read minds, that she saw things, had seen things about him! She couldn't fathom him being scared of Inez, of all people.

Neither Angie nor Inez paid heed to Clem's comments.

Chapter Twenty

In Virginia, Shorty dialed Trelavonti's telephone number once again. It was 7 a.m. Sunday morning.

Gene Trelavonti wasn't happy to hear the jarring ring. He picked it up anyway.

"Have you heard from Noone yet?" Shorty asked.

"No, nothing; how about you?" Trelavonti feigned concern.

"Me neither. I think it's time for us to get out there and go look for him. We need to go check on him."

"How are we going to get out there?" Trelavonti wasn't the least bit interested in traveling out in a blizzard.

"I've got my 4-wheeler. We'll be okay. Dress warm."

"Don't tell me what to do."

"We can be out of town in ten minutes."

"Alright." Trelavonti begrudgingly agreed getting up and dressing for the storm.

It had grown in intensity. With wind chills, temperatures had fallen into the sixty-degree below zero range. Experienced outdoorsman that he was, Shorty kept his pick-up in the garage when the temperatures and wind chills were expected to go below zero. The big V-8 engine fired up as soon as he turned the key.

Cardboard covered the front grille to protect the radiator and keep the engine warm while moving. Shorty didn't want it to freeze up out on the road. The idea of being stranded out in dangerous weather held zero appeal.

He also kept the back seat of his extended cab loaded with survival gear.

As a boy Shorty witnessed what frostbite could do to the skin when one of his friends got caught out in a blizzard. The kid had to have a hand and a foot amputated. He was never the same although he was plucky and kept right on hunting even with his disabilities. Nevertheless, Shorty couldn't abide the idea of loosing a hand or a foot, so he made sure he was always well prepared for unexpected contingencies. He didn't solely rely on weather reports either, not when it came to judging for bad weather. No forecaster ever predicted the weather correctly one hundred percent of the time, with or without Doppler radar.

The Frostbit Kid listened to a forecaster the day he went and got caught out in a spring storm, and look what happened to him! Shorty always shuddered at the thought of it. It was April then, and still the temperature dropped to well below freezing. All the Frostbit Kid wore that day were pants, shirt, sweater, light socks, and tennis shoes. He hadn't even worn gloves! Memories of the Frostbit Kid haunted Shorty every time a blizzard hit.

Trelavonti's idea of survival meant staying indoors. If he absolutely had to go outside, he put on long underwear, wool pants, a heavy shirt, heavy overcoat, and two pairs of wool socks, heavy winter boots, a hat and gloves. He carried his gun inside his jacket, but it was hard to reach with all the outer clothing.

When Shorty picked him up, Trelavonti was waiting for him outside on the sidewalk in front of the tavern.

The two men traveled in silence until turning off Highway 53 onto Townline Road. The roads were bad all the way out, but got a whole lot worse off the main road. Plows could hardly get through on the freeway, but they had made some headway there at least.

What if we get stuck! Shit! How are we going to get out? Trelavonti worried. "Can't we go back? It's horrible out here!"

Ignoring him, Shorty drove on in silence.

Trelavonti sat against the door brooding. Maybe I can stay inside Noone's house if the old man isn't home. I'm no outdoorsman, and Shorty knows it! Why is he so concerned with Noone anyway? Hell, that old buzzard wouldn't go looking for him in a storm. "How's business?" He asked so he could hear himself talk. He didn't like to think, or to be quiet for too long.

"Fine; how's yours?" Shorty didn't have much use for Trelavonti and didn't want to know anything about him. He was happy Trelavonti kept his trap shut most of the time. But driving was slow and Shorty grew uncomfortable. He started to fidget. His legs cramped. His big frame forced him to push the seat back as far as it would go. Still, his long legs needed more room. Dressed in heavy winter gear, he was even bulkier behind the wheel and grew more uncomfortable as they crawled up the road.

With a five-speed standard transmission, he was forced to downshift in order to keep the vehicle pulling through the snowdrifts. That meant he had to use the clutch, so his feet and legs moved some, but as they did, millions of needle-like pricks of pain shot through them. Cramps spread to his feet and he wanted to scream. He couldn't take off his boots to stretch his toes and he couldn't stand up to put pressure on his legs to relieve them. He tried to do both as he drove, but found little comfort; he grew sick of the snow and the length of time it was taking them to get to Noone's house. He considered pulling over to get out and stand up, but didn't. They plodded along.

"Man! Can't we go any faster than this," Trelavonti whined.

"No, we can't." Shorty snapped as he worked to keep the truck on the road. It was difficult to see, let alone handle the big pick-up in all the drifting snow. He didn't need to listen to Trelavonti's whining on top of dealing with the storm.

They were two miles from Noone's house. No plows had traveled the back roads at all, so Shorty downshifted into second gear, pulled into the snow filled road, and barged through the snowdrifts like a tank. He feared shifting down into first and stalling out, but the snow was so deep he had to use the low gears to hold the road. The lift kit he put on the truck had the box as high off the ground as the law would allow, which worked wonders in the heavy snow. He managed to get through the impasses that would have stranded a standard vehicle. Still, it wasn't easy. There were no tracks on the road to help him keep his bearings, either, not until they reached the Jennings' place.

Shorty knew John Jennings. During hunting season he made a point of talking to every farmer in the community, so he could go onto their property to hunt. Some farmers said no, but not John Jennings. Shorty made sure Jennings never had a reason to regret that decision, either. He was careful of shooting anywhere near the house or barn.

"Well, I'll be damned. It looks like someone has been on this road," he said out loud, but more to himself than his companion. Shorty studied the tracks and could tell someone had been stuck in the ditch of the access road, that whoever it was had gotten out of their vehicle, walked toward Noone's house, walked back, and left. The blowing wind had not completely wiped out the evidence.

Trelavonti didn't notice. He was overwhelmed by the amount of snow piling up. "Look at this mess!" He said as they started up the road. Snowdrifts on his side of road reached eye level.

Shorty fixed his sights on Noone's yard stepping on the gas to make sure his rig would climb the little incline to put them right in front of the house. With the whinny Trelavonti at his side, he did not want to risk getting stuck and having to walk up to the house with him.

By the time they pulled up in Noone's yard, it was 11 a.m. There, they saw the same things Franco had seen the night before. No sign of life about the house, snow piled high on the porch, a light on inside. While still inside the truck, Shorty noticed the broken window on the front door. He guessed that the person caught in the ditch broke into Noone's house. He and Trelavonti got out of the truck and made their way to the porch.

"Doesn't look like anyone's around, does it?" Trelavonti said.

"Where could Noone be? You don't think he's hurt do you?"

Trelavonti secretly hoped he was, but said, "Nah. That old buzzard! Shit, nothing can hurt him. Ain't you the one that told me he keeps survival caches out in the woods?"

"Yeah, I did, but he's still old. This snow is deep."

"He ain't that old. I can get around in this stuff just fine." Trelavonti bragged, offended at the age comment. "I'm out in this kind of weather all the time. I shovel the walks at home, at the department, go skiing, snow-shoeing, all kinds of stuff in the winter."

Shorty doubted it. He guessed Trelavonti didn't get any exercise, summer or winter. "Since you get around so well, you can come with me. I brought a couple pair of snowshoes. We're going to have to go look for Noone. It isn't going to be easy. Since you're a deputy, you can do it in your official capacity."

"What! I'm not going out searching for that old man in this weather! Are you crazy! No police department would send anyone out to search for a missing person in a storm, at least not until the storm passed! You have to know that?" Trelavonti hoped Shorty believed him as to what an official search would be like. But then what he said wasn't a complete lie.

Shorty ignored Trelavonti. He looked at the house, shivering. It wasn't from the cold; there was something about the place that gave him the heebie jeebies. He didn't like the idea of going inside if the old man wasn't there, but he had to check it out before setting out in the storm. Hell, Noone could be lying on the floor inside, dead of a heart attack!

When Trelavonti noticed the window, he discovered the glass had fallen inside confirming Shorty's theory that Noone's house had been broken into.

Shorty watched Trelavonti investigate the door guessing he was at least sixty pounds overweight; he knew he smoked cigarettes and figured he probably drank way too much beer. It would be best if Trelavonti stayed put; he would make better time without him.

Over at Sam's and inside the barn, Noone pondered his next move. The library, toasty warm, was just the way he liked it. Periodically he shut the heater off just in case someone did come down to the barn. That way they wouldn't immediately guess they weren't alone because of the heat. He could stay hidden if someone surprised him. After all, he'd owned the place for fifty years. He knew every nook and cranny of it, except for the library.

"It sure is nice of you to come with me, Ma. It'd be awful lonesome if you weren't here.

Joseph? Why do you keep bringing him up? Now why don't you just hush up about him? I'm tired of listening to it."

As usual, his mother was getting on his last nerve, and he was bored with watching the house from the barn. He turned around to look at the shelves of books. Absentmindedly, he ran his fingers over the many volumes until they brushed against rough cardboard like stiffness poking out from one of them. He pulled the book down to find an old photograph tucked between the cover and the first page. Its stiff edges were frayed and yellowed with age.

"Janice?" He turned the picture over in his hands, touching it gingerly; "You should have listened to me. I told you that. Didn't you think I'd find out what you did with those brats? The Simpletons loved me. They told me everything. Joan, Miss Upright, sanctimonious Christian had a 'thing' for me. Surely, Janice, you could see that? We did so many things together, Joan and me. More than you would ever do.

Why is it that we want most that which doesn't want us? I'll never understand it. But Janice, dear, you certainly should have known I'd get what I wanted, whether you liked it or not. Dear woman." His hands stroked the picture as if it were living flesh. He tucked it inside his shirt then looked about the room for other things that might remind him of those days, forty years earlier. He found nothing.

"I should go up to the house, see what they've taken from the library already, don't you think so mother?"

Underneath the snow, the wolves were on red alert, watching. The alpha male periodically sniffed the air to scent him whose smell permeated the traps that killed so many of his kind. The big male watched the barn through a hole in the snow he fashioned with his nose. The pack stayed close to one another keeping warm through mutual body heat, snow cover and their fur coats. They were in fine shape. The winter had not yet been a struggle for any of the group of seven, the two adults, two sub-adults from last year's litter, and three spring cubs.

The pack patriarch scented the male, and saw as he squeezed out from between the barn doors. He watched as the man found the rope then trudged uphill to the lighted house. He saw the man reach the porch, then veer to the right toward the basement entry. He watched as the man crouched low against the side of the house.

The wind howled its furry hurtling snow in front of the basement door, stinging the wolf through his fur, as he stood close behind the man.

The man, too, felt the sting of blinding snow as he brushed it from his face and struggled to open the old coal shoot door.

The storm took on its own persona as it lashed out at the Northern Minnesota landscape. A persona the wolf had never seen before—nor had Noone.

Even through the snow-blanketed abyss, Noone found what he was looking for. He had gone through it too many times not to be able to find it in any kind of weather. He could do it blindfolded. The door wouldn't budge, however, behaving as if it were locked from the inside, something he hadn't counted on. Most people never noticed the door was even there. Noone tugged on it while the wind did its best to hold the door shut screeching around him and muffling any noise that he made.

It also muffled the approach of the pack. The big alpha male signaled the others to follow once he had secured his position behind Noone. They circled about Noone forming a crescent moon shaped barrier blocking any retreat to the barn Noone might try to make.

Noone still didn't notice them; he was completely focused on the door. The snow blinded him as it hurled against his face. His only thoughts were of getting inside out of the wind and cold. The sky overhead remained dark gray. It looked more like evening than day.

Just when he felt like giving up, the basement door gave way. The tire jack worked its magic, as Noone knew it would when he used it to pry the door loose. He always carried tools with him for emergencies. "You just never know," he said often enough to anyone who had the gall to ask him why he carried tools with him into the woods.

When the big alpha male saw the door give way, he moved in closer emitting low growls and bearing his teeth. Noone slowly turned at the sound of the snarl to see the big male right behind him. The animal weighed over a hundred pounds, and looked to Noone to be in his prime. It moved in even closer silently bearing his teeth at him. Noone backed up. He had never seen a wolf behave like that before. They weren't supposed to bother humans. He'd been told that a million times. He stepped backward looking behind the big alpha male to see the rest of the pack moving in on him, too. His heart screamed inside his chest. He edged further backward once again hoping to touch the door that he let drop shut at the sight of the big male. No one inside the house had heard him; they wouldn't hear him even if he cried out for help. Besides, he didn't want them to know he was there. He tried to calm himself as he bent backwards blindly groping for the door handle.

The wolves slowly, kept moving in, following the alpha's lead.

Noone found the door handle fighting to pull it open without turning his back on the pack. As he did, the wind fought to hold the door shut. Noone struggled on watching as the wolves got closer and closer tightly blocking any means of escape.

Finally, Noone managed to slip through a small opening into the basement and to pull the door shut behind him just as the alpha male snarled and leapt. Noone gripped the door tightly to keep the wind from grabbing it open letting the wolves in. He could feel the weight of the big male as he landed on the door. Noone looked around, found a 2x4 within reach, groped it, and then slammed it into the lathes on either side of the door to secure it tightly. His heart raced, his breathing came in short gasps. With the 2x4 secured, he sat on the steps listening for any movement inside the house and out, as he tried to slow his heart rate.

The wolves howled—and howled—and howled—just outside the basement door in their frustration.

Noone remained seated on the steps, trembling at the sound.

Upstairs in the kitchen Inez was running water into a teakettle as the howling began. She thought she heard something, but the wind screeched so loudly, she had to turn her ear toward the window to make sure. She finally recognized the sound, yelling at the top of her voice, "Jeez!" She dropped the tea kettle on the floor with a thundering clash as she ran for the doorway into the dinning room, crying, "Wolves! Wolves! They're just outside the house!" Grabbing Gladys by the arm; she pulled her into the kitchen.

Everyone else followed suit. Sam reached the windows first. She couldn't see out of the frost-covered glass. The screeching wind and blowing snow prevented her from hearing anything. But by then, the wolves were no longer howling. Stan, John, Skip and Clem all looked out the windows; they, too, neither heard nor saw anything but the blizzard.

"Are you sure you heard wolves?" Skip asked Inez as he moved away from the window. "I couldn't see or hear anything other than the storm."

"Yeah! I heard them! I wasn't born yesterday, you know." It peeved Inez that Skip didn't believe her.

"Hey Sam! You might want to come check this out," Stan said in such a way that Sam ran to the kitchen door. He stood there looking out its little window pointing out at the back lawn.

Sam stepped up to the window to see the big alpha male wolf standing on the steps just outside the porch door looking inside at her. When he saw her, he threw his head back and howled. Once he started, the rest of the pack joined in. Everyone in the kitchen heard and saw them then.

Angie shook her head in disbelief. She wondered what it all meant. It couldn't be good, she decided. "That is the eeriest noise I have ever heard," she said. "

Noone heard the wolves, too. He warmed himself still sitting on the stair, letting the heat from the house seep through him. He could tell the pack had moved away from the basement door. He made sure the 2x4 was secured, regardless. Now he felt safe.

"Do you think they're warning me of something?" Sam asked Angie.

"That's got to be it." Angie said.

"But from what? Do they know something we don't know?" Sam looked nervously about the kitchen, her gaze drifting to the basement door.

"Maybe that's why I'm having those dreams, why the professor came to me. Maybe we're sympathetic souls or something; he studied wolves, too. Maybe they're as tied into this as we are? I mean maybe that's why I'm supposed to be here." She looked around the room hoping for some affirmation. All shook their heads, wondering, too, what it all meant, but no one had anymore answers than she did, including Angie.

After a long silence Angie said: "We're in the middle of a big jigsaw puzzle, but we've only just begun to assemble it, and without the big picture as a guide. It's going to be a challenge to complete."

No one else had anything to add, so the group slowly and silently made their way back into the dinning room, except for Sam who continued to stare out the window at the wolves.

"Why don't you know more about what's going on?" Skip asked Angie as they seated themselves at the table. "You're the psychic." He wanted answers to questions he had had for forty years! Angie was his hope of getting those answers and he was growing more and more frustrated with her lack of insight. How long was he supposed to wait?

Skip's questioning her psychic ability didn't faze Angie. "I am picking up on some things around here. It has more to do with people that have disappeared, more so than with the house, the professor or his family. I know you want to know about Ellen sheriff, I can see it in your eyes. And I'll tell you this; I have been seeing a young, white female—in my head—ever since you got here with your father. She's standing at your side. I get the overpowering impression she is trying to reach you."

"What?" Skip asked. "What do you mean, she's beside me?" Skip wanted so much to know what happened to Ellen, he was afraid to believe that he might finally find out.

So was Stan.

"Was she a brunette with shoulder length hair? Big hair, what we would call big hair now? It has a bow, a little bow in the front and it's flipped up at the ends. She wears a plaid, pleated skirt with knee high stockings, white tennis shoes, and a white cotton blouse. It looks a bit like a school uniform.

I can hear 'Sugar Shack' playing in the background."

"That was our song! That sounds like what she used to wear. We didn't have school uniforms, but all the girls dressed like that. They used to "rat" their hair so it was 'big'. She was a brunette. And they all wore pleated skirts like that then and those dumb white tennis shoes." Skip recalled.

"She's beckoning to me." Angie sat down facing the dinning room windows staring blankly outside. "She's holding a man's hand," Angie continued. "Yes. Yes, I can see them, but I can't see the man's face; his back is to me. She's walking with him into the woods. Wait! Her face—it's changing. Her mouth is opening; nothing is coming out. She's screaming! Jeez! Wait now; I almost see him, he's—yes! He's wearing a uniform. He has a gun belt on. A badge, I see a badge! He's pulling her so hard, she trips, she's on the ground; he keeps right on pulling. They're going away from a house down a grass-lined road. You can see the road a little; it's covered in grass. There's a house; they're walking away from a yellow clapboard house. He's pulling her and as he does, her skirt rises. The man grins. He likes her resistance—a lot. I still can't see his face, but I can sense what he intends to do, her fear! She digs in her heels, tries to stop him. He isn't going to be stopped. He's much bigger than she is."

John grabbed the small tape recorder from the dinning room table as Angie started to speak, turned it on, and started recording.

Enthralled, everyone hung on Angie's every word. No one heard the vehicle pull up outside and come to a stop behind Clem's truck. No one noticed when the headlights came up the drive.

Inez sat close to Angie, watching. She wasn't listening to Ellen's story. She was seeing the professor's story, visually, just as Angie was seeing Ellen's. She saw things, things that some people in the room with her were going to find hard to bear. Both women listened with their spirits, a skill they had fine tuned over many years of use. The only downside was that the things they saw were not always pleasant.

"She's big busted, this girl," Angie said. "A lot of men lust after her. She's pregnant. I see a fetus—a little boy." Angie still stared out at the howling storm.

The wolves had not left off their back door vigil. The seven sat on their haunches forming a crescent around the door as snow swirled about them.

Angie said, "They pass farm machinery. I see hay racks, mowers, tractors, and lumber. He has her by the hair as she falls to the ground. He's pulling her into the woods. She's terrified. She weighs about one hundred pounds. He's a big man, real big. Older, much older than she is."

Skip's hands opened and closed into fists as Angie spoke.

"She thought she was safe with this man—at first. She doesn't understand why her parents left her there, with that other man. He's creepy, she thinks.

How could her parents do that to her? They wanted her to kill the baby. Her father beat her, called her all kinds of names, and shoved her down into the basement until they dragged her out to that farm where they cast her welfare into the hands of those two evil men. They were, are evil. I feel it," Angie whispered hoarsely. She was getting weary but refused to stop.

"Ellen wants to protect her baby. She loves the baby's father. She's thinking these things as the man drags her deeper into the woods. She's frightened for the baby, herself. She's leaving a psychological mark on all her surroundings. The man thinks they're alone, but they're not. Everything in the woods is watching, the trees, the grass, birds, rocks, animals, everything. Ellen and the man are now deep in the forest. Its daylight, but it's a real dark, cloudy day and the trees hide what meager sunlight there is. The girl smells moss, balsam boughs, and earth.

Can you smell it?" Angie asked. "I can. It's right here. Right here in this room." She didn't expect an answer.

"The man, he throws the girl to the ground, out there in the deep woods, and gets on top of her, lifts her skirt. She screams. No one hears. He slaps her about the face as he rapes her. Between rapes, he beats her. It stimulates him. The more she fights, the more he wants her, and the more he beats her, the more she fights.

But she grows weak, can't fight anymore. He's already raped her three times. He picks her up, shakes her, tries to get a rise out of her, but she falls limp, her head lolls to the side, dribble coming from her mouth.

She looks dead to him. He runs back to the house when he realizes what he's done. He's left her lying there in the woods. He's never gone this far before, never killed anyone.

Two men now; I see their backs. They walk side-by-side back to the site. They're carrying shovels. They dig. She's buried there. She's between two big oak trees, the only ones out there in that part of the woods. She's buried closest to the one on the east side. Her baby is thrown in the grave with her. She gave birth then died. She managed to lift the child to her chest. The baby lived long enough to gaze up at its mother. They died together."

Angie fell limp. She had experienced all Ellen and the baby had gone through when they were murdered. Now she was drained emotionally and physically as she looked about the room at the group who stared back at her.

"I know just the place you're talking about," Clem said. "It's on my property. That road, that's my road. It goes from my house to the woods out back. I drive tractor on it all the time."

"You recognize this place?" Stan asked, as he and Skip looked intensely at Clem.

"We're talking about someone who was real familiar with those back woods, and had no compunction about trespassing onto Clem's property," Angie said.

"So, the man hurting Ellen wore a badge." Stan pondered.

Whoever hurt Ellen—Skip couldn't think of her as murdered—would pay for it. No matter whom it was.

"Well Ma'am," Skip said looking at Angie. "It looks like you've been a bigger help than I ever thought possible." Angie had to look away from the steal gaze of Sheriff Skip Gilbert.

Chapter Twenty One

Franco was surprised to see so many vehicles. He stepped out of his SUV. His body, now well covered with winter outerwear, was nice and warm, and the storm no longer fazed him. His frostbite of the night before was minor and with two pairs of socks on his feet, one pair wool the other cotton, they were snug and warm, as were his hands in rabbit fur lined gloves. He parked as close as he could to the plow using it to make his way to the next vehicle, the Ford Bronco. In front of that, he found the crawler, the likes of which he had never seen before, and after that, the guide rope, which helped him find his way to the house.

As Franco slowly made his way to the house, the pack picked up his scent, and moved back into the shadows. It was easy for them to hide amidst the blowing snow and wind as the lone man moved closer to the house.

Franco fought his way over and through high snowdrifts, glad to finally reach the porch. The wind was horrific. He caught his breath before knocking. He rapped on the door just as Skip finished speaking.

"What was that?" Sam said tiptoeing into the kitchen and over to the door. Everyone in the room quietly watched as she moved through the room silently. As she looked through the small kitchen door window and her eyes adjusted to the porch light, she found a pair of human eyes staring back at her.

"Ahhhhhhhh!" She screamed falling back away from the door into a utensil crowded cupboard scattering metal spoons, pans, bowls and canisters all over the kitchen floor.

Everyone ran for the door.

Skip opened the door to a grinning Franco. "I've had some strange greetings in my life, but I must say, never one quite as strange as that," Franco said as he threw the hood of his coat off from around his face and let his infamous half-smile dazzle onlookers. He looked Sam in the eye as he spoke oblivious to the others as he watched her being helped to her feet by Angie.

She stared back, her heart fluttering at the unexpected surprise and flustered because of her reaction. Franco had to pull his eyes away from her to look about him, surprised to see so many other people in the kitchen looking back at him.

"Well, can I come in or do I have to go back out into that storm?" He asked Sam. "I think it's illegal to send someone out in weather like this, isn't it sheriff," Franco grinned at Skip noting Stan's presence. He didn't know the others, except for Clem and the Spencer sisters. He turned his charms on all of them.

No one could resist Franco's affable personality, not even Skip or Stan. It wasn't long before everyone sat drinking hot cocoa telling Franco all that had transpired thus far. Everyone wondered why he had traveled out to Sam's in the middle of a horrific blizzard, but no one called up enough nerve to ask him.

Just down the road, Shorty and Trelavonti were entering Noone's house. Trelavonti walked through it taking in everything. It was small so it didn't take long. He found the note Franco left along with a $500 bill for the clothes he had taken.

Franco most not have known whose house he was in. Good, let the old man think somebody stole the stuff, thought

Trelavonti as he pocketed the cash and the note and caught up with Shorty who sat on the living room couch.

Trelavonti was plenty familiar with Noone's house; he had been there often enough in the past. It was cozy. A fireplace sat on the north side of the living room with wood piled next to it. The two bedrooms on the east and west sides of the house both had ample blankets on the beds. Going through the kitchen cupboards, he found plenty of food there and in the refrigerator. He could do just fine there for a few days.

"Hey, we ought to just hold up here." He said to Shorty.

"Noone must be in the woods someplace. We're going to go out and look for him," Shorty said ignoring Trelavonti's comment.

"What! How the hell do think we can find him in this? It's eighty below with the wind-chill! Have you lost your mind? I'm not twenty one years old, you know." Trelavonti decided he wasn't going anywhere.

Shorty didn't care. He headed out the door.

Trelavonti refused to budge. If he is so damn dumb that he wants to risk his life to save that old fart's life, well, he deserves what he gets, Trelovinti thought as he looked for the remote control to the TV, found it, and seated himself on the overstuffed couch to get comfortable. Channel surfing brought him to a football game, which settled the issue for him. He wasn't going anywhere. He was staying right where he was to watch the game.

Shorty was just as determined to find Noone, but it wasn't out of any great love for the man. It was simply the right thing to do. Noone could be hurt. He was relieved Trelavonti was not going to tag along. He wouldn't get far in the storm with the old weather beaten deputy tagging along and he knew it. He would make good time on his own. The cold was not a problem, the way he saw it. If anyone understood the rigors of severe weather, he did. He had covered every inch of his flesh with clothing. He'd been out in winds like these before and knew it could be rough, so he had prepared for it. A knit facemask covered most of his face and goggles covered his eyes. Overtop his layers of clothing, Shorty dressed in polypropylene, a substance designed specifically for Arctic air. He wore a fur cap with earflaps on his head, as well as a hood. He also wore numerous pairs of wool socks on his feet, well lined winter boots, and stored extra dry clothing in a backpack along with matches and a few tools. He strapped snowshoes on his feet outside next to his truck then headed out over the snowdrifts to make his way into the deep woods.

It was rough. For every few steps forward he took, he was pushed back three when 40 mph wind gusts shoved his two hundred twenty five pound body around as if it were a plaything. He had yet to reach the woods and already he wondered about the wisdom of trekking out in this particular storm. He had never seen anything like it.

Regardless of the weather, or perhaps because of it, Shorty thought back to the days when he worked in the Eveleth mine pits of Wary Mining Company, in Aurora, Minnesota, not more than thirty miles from where he walked.

He hated the orange grit from the taconite pellets that clung to his clothes and skin everyday when he got off work. He hated the look of the man-made-mountains and the open pit mines thinking they destroyed the landscape. The ore had an odor to it, too, that clung to his pores and regardless of how hard he scrubbed, he couldn't seem to get rid of the smell.

The taconite tailings clogged up his washing machine at home, so his so-called wife made him take his work clothes to the Laundromat in town. "Let that taconite ruin their machines!" she'd scream until Shorty finally complied.

He hated to listen to the shrillness of her voice when it reached that high pitched crescendo every time she felt a need to beret him about something, which she did often enough. She sounded like a shrew. It was easier on the ears to do his own wash in town than to listen to her.

He remembered the day in March of 1988 when he finally called it quits at the mine. Her voice reached an especially high trill that day. As he walked through the storm, he laughed at the memory. She was not a happy camper; not that day, that was for certain.

He also remembered the overwhelming joy that filled him when he walked away from that dirty mine. He hadn't even planned to quit. He headed out for work as usual that day. He got up, made coffee, sandwiches for his lunch box, ate breakfast and headed out the door, same as always. It was one gorgeous spring morning, too. And with every mile he drove, he yearned to be out in the woods. By the time he had driven the thirty miles it took to get to work, he knew he couldn't stand it one more day. He walked into his foreman's office, told him he wasn't coming back, and walked back out again. Nope, no more swing shifts working days, afternoons and midnights. No more looking at four days off as if it were the best thing that could ever happen to him, no more working for anyone else; he'd be his own boss.

Mary, his so-called-wife, left him shortly thereafter. She said she wasn't living with any man that would quit his job to leave her wondering where money to pay the bills was coming from. After all, they had two children to think about. She didn't like the idea of him working for himself, either. She wouldn't know where he was every minute, he guessed. She wouldn't know how much money they had coming in on a regular basis, either. Nope, she didn't like his quitting one little bit, so she packed her bags; that was the last day he spent living with Mary.

The day he left Wary Mining Co. was a good day for him no matter how he looked at. He learned that day just exactly how Mary felt about him. She wanted a meal ticket, and that was about it. She did not care how he felt, wouldn't listen to him as he tried to explain about his need to be in the woods. She took the kids to go live with some man she had been having an affair with all along. He had had no idea.

Now, she rarely let him see the kids. The courts backed her up allowing her a restraining order against him. She told the judge he threatened her; he had not; but the judge believed her.

Threaten her? How could she tell a judge that? In all the time they were married, no matter what she did, he never lifted a finger against her. Now he couldn't seem to stop hitting Helen. Maybe Mary found out about that and was using it against him, he thought as he trudged onward.

Mary went to live with a foreman from Wary who made better money. They deserved each other, Shorty felt, but the kids didn't deserve either one of them. How could he ever get the judge to see that and change his mind? Yep, the day he left the mines had been an eye opener; Mary leaving was a good thing, but he missed the kids.

Regardless of the weather, Shorty spent as many as six days a week in the woods, which is how he liked it, just him and Mother Nature.

He couldn't help but turn his thoughts from the outdoors over to Sam. How can she think I'd trap wolves? He asked himself as he walked. She had been on his mind a lot lately. She wasn't so different from any other women he met except for the fact that she spent most of her time in the woods, too. He couldn't help but like that about her. He didn't want her to think badly of him, one of the reasons he found it so disturbing that she thought he'd do something illegal. He was no angel, but he loved nature every bit as much as she did, and that included the wolves.

Why do I automatically think badly of her? He wondered.

The storm grabbed his attention. He bent at the waist to battle winds that were trying to force him backward once again.

Back at Sam's and secreted inside the house, Noone climbed the basement stairs up to the kitchen to listen at the door and heard as Angie related what she had seen in her vision of Ellen. She spoke as if she were there the day he and Trelavonti buried the pregnant bitch. How many years ago was that? He wondered as he squatted on the top step. She would have been a little kid then. She couldn't have seen it—but she knew! This roused his curiosity to a fever pitch.

At Noone's with the football game over, Trelavonti found himself at loose ends. He had no interest in reading any of Noone's books, so he started looking around, again.

He went downstairs to the basement stopping halfway down when he smelled a sweet and cloying odor. He gagged. Something about the smell seemed familiar but he couldn't recall where he had smelled it before. He held his breath and continued on, looking around, taking his time. He covered every brick of the neat walls with his eyes looking for anything out of place. He noticed the wall close to the washtubs, by the chimney. He moved over to it feeling along it until he came upon a loose brick. He pulled it out finding a cigar box tucked inside. He lifted that out and discovered photos; he took them over to the light to get a good look at them. He couldn't believe his eyes. After taking one out and tucking it inside his shirt, he replaced the cigar box and went back upstairs.

Upstairs, he went into a bedroom hoping to find something else of interest there, and had no compunction about snooping through Noone's belongings. He noticed an old suitcase inside a closet on the top shelf and pulled it down. There he found a picture of Angie Eckenridge, which was odd because it looked extremely old.

"How the hell did that old buzzard get this," he said aloud as he turned it over. Even though he was lazy, Trelavonti was a trained investigator and a good one. His instincts were finely honed. "That can't be her. This picture is way too old. She's no spring chicken, but this looks like it was taken in the '50s or '60s or something." He found the name, Janice Browne, written on the back.

"Hmmmm. She looks just like that Eckenridge broad." He slipped that photo into his shirt pocket as well and went back to searching through the contents of the suitcase. You never know when something might prove useful, he thought as his fingers picked through the contents.

Noone made Trelavonti nervous, although he never admitted that to anyone. Noone had the goods on him about a lot of things, but he had nothing on Noone, nothing—well nothing before this. He was cautious of Noone and well aware of all the friends Noone had in high places. It would be best to have something to set the scales in balance, an insurance policy, so to speak, and now I do, he thought.

Trelavonti found more photos under a compartment at the bottom of the suitcase. They were real old, too. One was of a man standing against a brick wall; the next photo showed the same man against the same wall, but bricks were up to the man's knees. The rest of the photos showed the progression of the same man being bricked up into a wall.

"Hey! This is must be the guy we found over at Egar's!" Trelvonti could barely contain his excitement. He pocketed those photos as well, and continued his search rummaging through the clothes inside the suitcase where he found two children's lace bonnets, a woman's slip, and a pair of women's shoes, some dresses and a pair of slacks. He rubbed the lace bonnets between his fingers.

"Funny . . . nothing else in here for a kid."

Over at Sam's, Franco could tell by the look on everyone's face that his arrival had interrupted something important. And though he was real happy to see Sam, those he found in the kitchen with her also intrigued him, Stan especially. He didn't like him. Stan Gilbert sent his nephew Earl to prison on trumpeted up charges. Franco's cool gray eyes took in Stan's demeanor finding it anything but menacing. He was still angry about Earl, but Stan Gilbert wasn't giving off a bad vibe. He'd watch and listen. He'd learn something, he knew.

Stan, more than a little surprised to see Franco, tried hard not to show it. He knew who Franco was all right, but never in a million years had he expected to see the bar-owner at Sam's in the middle of a storm. He could tell she was pretty straight laced. Not someone he'd expect Franco to be interested in. But by the look in their eyes, there was some hot and heavy chemistry going on between the two of them.

Stan remembered when he locked up Franco's nephew for that little Eveleth girl's murder. Franco was beyond angry over it. Stan never did think Franco's nephew had anything to do with the girl's death. Trelavonti railroaded the kid, but Stan could never prove it. So Franco's nephew went to Stillwater State Prison, and was still there the last Stan heard. As far as Franco was concerned, he had never been implicated in any crime.

The others in Sam's kitchen were mostly people Franco didn't know. Sam introduced him to everyone. The Jennings and Angie had never met Franco, but Franco knew of John Jennings because of the infamous Steamroller. The others knew who Franco was by reputation only.

Skip was real interested in this turn of events. He didn't like the way Franco and Sam looked at each other.

Sam was shocked. She had fantasized about what it would be like to be alone with Franco inside her house, but never expected him to show up at her door, especially during a raging winter storm. Besides, she wasn't alone. Her heart raced at the thought while he stood beside her a bit too close so that his cologne discreetly wafted up her nose.

"I got this feeling something was wrong, out here," Franco said to everyone. "I had to come and check up on you," he turned and looked Sam in the eye. "It looks like you've got plenty of help, though."

"Yes, I do, and you're right about something being wrong, first and foremost, the blizzard outside? Did you notice it as you drove in?" She couldn't fathom what would compel a relative stranger to come out in it to try and help her.

Franco said nothing.

He made her uneasy, but she continued, "I hope you're not afraid of ghosts."

"What?" Franco wasn't sure he heard her right. "Ghosts, did you say ghosts?"

"Yes, you came in just as Angie was in the midst of a vision concerning a young girl the sheriff was once in love with. The girl disappeared 40 years ago.

Angie's a psychic from Fargo."

Sam invited Franco to join everyone in the dinning room. The others seated themselves around the table turning their attention back to Angie.

Franco kept silent trying to pick up on what he had missed before getting there. He sat quietly sipping his hot cocoa. While the others talked, he remembered his mother telling him about ghosts and how she said that when she died she would watch

over him from Heaven; that he would know she was there. He
never did, though. He took another sip of cocoa as a strange
looking dog jumped up against his leg then crawled up into his lap.
Franco made no attempt to unseat Fuzz. He scratched the little dog
behind the ears, absentmindedly.

Angie sat in the middle of the table and tried to slip back
into a state of quiet to recapture the vision she had seen earlier. She
was well practiced at getting quiet and had no trouble meditating
even in a room full of people.

Franco nudged Sam who sat next to him, "What's going
on with her?" he asked not taking his eyes off Angie.

"She's meditating. Trying to get a vision, see things. "

"Oh." Franco said.

Stan whispered, "She helps police officers all over North
Dakota, South Dakota, Wisconsin and Minnesota track down
killers police can't get a handle on. She's helped find victims, too.
She's the real thing, alright."

Franco hid his surprise. He never pegged Stan Gilbert for
someone who would use a psychic for police work. He kept silent,
not wanting to judge the man too hastily. If a gritty cop could see
doing something like this, he'd keep an open mind.

"I thought forensic science was a big help to you guys,"
John said. He had taken a real interest in police work since Mike
had shown such an interest in it.

"It is," Stan said. "But sometimes, especially in cold
cases, it can be tough. If there's a body, then forensic science is a
big help. I mean we can identify killers from a strand of hair. Learn
the time of death through bug-infestation even learn how someone
was killed by the pattern of the blood splatter at a crime scene.
Sometimes, though, even science can't determine if someone has
been a crime victim. Especially, like with that body found in the
basement if there is no violence visible on the skeletal remains, or

if a body has not been recovered. Then, once in a great while, someone comes along who can see things. Like Angie here," Stan pointed to her and smiled. "She's not the only one. There are a lot of people across this country that 'see' things we can't see. And even they have their doubts about how 'good' this thing is that they have that allows them to help us."

"Is it hard? I mean to become a policeman?" John wanted to know just how difficult it might be for Mike.

"No, not too hard. You have to go to school nowadays. We didn't when I started. But school's not too difficult. Not if you apply yourself," Stan said.

"Most days on the force, though, are nothing but routine and boring," Skip added. "There isn't that much crime out here. For the most part it's stopping drunk drivers, busting up fights, and coming between a husband and wife brawl."

"You just happened upon the biggest unsolved mystery case this county has ever seen," Stan added, "an unsolved mystery that is probably a murder mystery."

This time Angie wasn't getting anywhere with her meditation.

Inez said, "Well, gentlemen, I think that's enough for now. Let's get some lunch."

She took Bernice's hand and pulled her to the kitchen. As they worked, the phone rang. Inez picked it up and said hello.

"I'd like to talk to my mom or dad." Mike Jennings said.

"Your mom is right here." Inez handed the phone to Bernice mouthing the word, "Mike."

"Hi Mom! What's up?"

"Is something going on over there Mike? Did someone get hurt? Did that bull get loose again? If he did, you just let him stay loose. Do you understand? Your father will handle it when he gets home." A thousand horrifying scenarios raced through Bernice's mind as she thought about her children.

"No, he didn't get loose, and we're all okay. We were wondering when you were coming home is all." Vicki stood behind Mike crossing her fingers, hoping they wouldn't have to spend another night alone in the house.

"Do you need us home now, Mike?" Bernice pushed. "We can get in that crawler and be home in a few hours. I know we promised you two that you could come over here, but really, son, things are going on over here that I don't want you involved with. I hope you can forgive me."

Mike was disappointed. He did want to go over to Sam's but he wouldn't tell his mother what was going on at home, either, not over the phone. It was too hard to describe; besides, he didn't want his parents out in the storm anymore than they wanted him out in it.

"No, Mom. You and Dad just stay put till this storm passes. We're all okay here. Really, Mom, there is nothing for you to worry about."

Bernice hung up the phone. She called John into the kitchen then took him aside to the kitchen table.

"Are the kids are okay?" John whispered in Bernice's ear.

Bernice touched his shoulder and said, "Yes."

John stared out into the storm. His whole body wound tighter than a top.

Bernice, standing beside him, stroked his shoulders, rubbed them. "The kids will be okay," she whispered as she bent down to speak in his ear. She put her hand on his shoulder as he held his up to cover hers. They stayed that way, praying, for a long time.

John's face was immobile. Something about this whole situation tugged at him from the start. Not just the professor being discovered downstairs, or the strange things happening in theirs' and Sam's houses, but something else, something unthinkable. It was as if he knew something tragic was about to happen, but he was powerless to do anything to stop it. His fears lay with his children. He felt completely safe at Sam's and wasn't worried about himself or Bernice.

Bernice ran her fingers through his curly, black hair and kissed his cheek. "It's going to be okay. No one is going to hurt the kids." She said this even as she worried.

"I had this dream last night—Joseph, was in it. He was laughing at Mike and Vicki as he tied them up to a chair. He was fondling Vicki watching Mike squirm as he did," John said so quietly Bernice wasn't sure she had heard him correctly.

"John that was just a dream, come on now, relax." Bernice decided she wouldn't tell him she had had the same dream. "Let's pray that they're okay and that the storm will let up so we can go home and they can come over here like we promised them they could."

"If our prayers aren't answered, there's going to be hell to pay." John's voice was cold, calm.

"Yeah, though I walk through the valley of the shadow of death, I will fear no evil for the Lord is with me." Bernice kissed the top of her husband's head wrapping her arm lightly around his neck and squeezing gently.

At the Jennings farm, Mike wasn't feeling so hot. He thought the phone call to his parents would ease his fears, but it hadn't. He stood by the sink, lost in thought.

Vicki looked out the kitchen window. She could see a shadow moving about in the snow. The wolf had moved away from the house and was starting down the driveway. Vicki ran into the living room opening the plantation shutters to watch as the wolf sauntered over the snow.

"Hey, you guys. There it is! There's the wolf!"

The younger children rushed to the window in hopes of seeing it. As they watched, the solitary animal made his way down the drive crossing into the forest across the road. It headed northeast in the direction of Sam's house.

As Mike watched, he was prompted to move about the house checking all the locks on the doors and windows. He wished the wolf had stayed put, but didn't know why.

At the same time over at Sam's, Bernice watched a similar sight. As she looked out the kitchen window, she saw what looked like shadows rise up out of the snow and start moving down the driveway. What is that? She wondered as she watched. The blowing snow played tricks with her eyesight, so she waited before mentioning it to the others. When the shadows moved out of sight in the kitchen, she ran to the dining room windows, then the living room windows to watch as the wolves climbed the snow-banked driveway and headed south. She yelled, "It's the wolves! They're moving away!" Everyone rushed to the living room windows to see.

Inez stared mesmerized by the storm and the animals when an unbidden vision loomed on the horizon of her mind. She could almost see it through the murky mists, almost put together one big piece of the jigsaw puzzle they were all involved in, but the vision remained on the horizon amid the mists in her mind. It would not come forward to illuminate itself.

Sam said, "It amazes me sometimes, even after watching wolves full-time for three years, how they can get around so easily in the worst of weather." She was speaking more to herself than to her companions.

As she spoke, the vision walked out of the mists of Inez's mind and she grasped the piece of the puzzle fitting it into place. She gasped.

"Don't worry, dear. They're not coming in here," Gladys said attributing Inez's gasp to the wolves. Inez patted her sister's hand, but said nothing.

Downstairs, Noone crept over to the wall, his movements as silent as a cat's. The cops had made nice work of clearing it out. He looked closely at the room. No, they hadn't discovered it. He wondered if it would still open after all those years. He pushed in a brick at the top of the wall. Slowly, a solid brick door laboriously moved groaning and scraping across the concrete floor so loudly, Noone kept one eye on the basement stair to see if the noise had alerted anyone upstairs. They either hadn't heard it because of the storm, or they weren't listening because no one came downstairs. Relieved, he went back to studying his handiwork of days long past.

He had constructed the passageway throughout the house in case he would need it to get out of tight spots. It served as a vantage point through which he watched the entire house. Once he had walled up the professor, however, he hadn't been able to use it. That was just before he and Janice had left for Canada.

Noone fondly remembered building the hiding place some fifty years before. He hadn't been in it since he returned from Canada. He hadn't given the professor a moment's thought, either, not until the day Trelavonti told him police found a skeleton in a small room in the basement of Egar's house.

The passage, which was right behind the room, led throughout the house, a small secret corridor barely wide enough for one average sized adult to pass through. Noone knew when he constructed it that it had to be that way otherwise anyone looking at the house would notice an oddity, investigate. He didn't want that—ever.

He had another hidden passageway to use, too. The underground mine shafts, the ones directly under Sam's house leading to the barn. He would use that to make his escape when the time was right to carry out his plans, which he had yet to work out. He'd use the mineshafts to make his way home. No one would ever be able to place him at the Egar house afterward.

He had hidden the doorway to the mineshafts so well behind a false wall painted to look like the rest of the neat, clean interior of the basement, that it went unseen by everyone who didn't know to look for it, like the cops the other night. Noone moved the false wall easily deciding to make sure it would be ready when he needed it. The doorway and the tunnels were well constructed. Nothing blocked the tunnel, no cave-ins, and it was still water tight. Dust and cobwebs were all Noone would have to battle to get through to the barn.

He traveled the tunnel length to the barn to ensure the entire shaft was all right. When he reached the barn door entrance, he marked it with chalk, so if he were in a great hurry he could still find his way back quickly. When he finished, he slipped back down the tunnel and scurried back into the basement and over to the wall climbing through the secret corridor to the top of the house. He stopped periodically to look through tiny pinholes in the sheet-rocked rooms all along the corridor. The holes allowed him to see what was going on in each room. Some were caked over with dust and paint, which Noone cleared carefully, listening for any sounds before moving on. He made his way up the stairs doing the same thing at each room. He wanted each and every spy hole ready when it was time to use them.

"Joseph loved this place. It's too bad he can't be here now, Mom. You would be so proud." He chuckled as he scooted along the passageway like a gigantic cock roach scurrying away from noise and light.

When he got upstairs to the attic, Noone rested. It was nice and warm upstairs.

Chapter Twenty Two

Neither Shorty's bulk nor his forty five years slowed him as he made his way through the forest; not even the raw winter weather fazed him. Still, though, he wasn't making good time. Wind gusts forced him backward as he walked into it, so he had to redouble his efforts to simply take one step forward.

He realized by the time he reached the edge of the forest behind Noone's house that it was too cold to be out searching for Noone. He shouldn't have tried it. He worried about making it to the Egar place himself. When he reached the forest edge, he hunkered behind a big pine tree to escape the wind and assess his situation.

Squatting behind the big tree Shorty started to topple throwing out his left hand to steady himself. It struck something solid under the snow. He cleared the snow away to find a makeshift shanty made out of balsam bows. It was so well hidden; he wouldn't have seen it if he hadn't fallen into it. Shorty crawled inside the snug shelter, and was relieved to be out of the blasting winds.

Inside, he felt around the dark enclosure hoping to find one of Noone's caches. He did. Two big plastic storage bins at the far end were a welcome relief. One contained a sleeping bag, air mattress, and pump. Shorty pulled them out rigging up a bed that not only would help keep him warm, but it would keep him off the freezing ground. Inside the other bin he found food including dried fruits and beef jerky.

Shorty helped himself. He was hungry. He found a flashlight that he shinned around to find something to light a fire. He discovered a small stove behind one of the plastic storage bins. With it was a supply of dry wood, even matches. He lit the stove. He would be okay inside the shelter for awhile.

Fitting, he thought, that I should come upon Noone's survival stuff but not Noone. I sure hope he's okay.

He fell asleep waking three hours later to a storm that still raged on. He peeked outside to see just how bad it was. It wouldn't be letting up for a long time, he decided, so he would leave after he ate. While chewing beef jerky inside the cozy shelter, he took a good look around his immediate surroundings. He could hold up there for a week, he decided. It was nice and warm and the bins were packed with essentials that would ensure his survival.

He found a small pan and went outside to gather fresh snow from in front of the entrance. He brought the pan with the snow back inside and melted it on the stove. He didn't let it get too hot before he drank it. He found tea bags and made himself a cup of that, too. There was even dried milk to sweeten it with. Shorty stayed inside the balsam tent until his bladder was so full he had to relieve himself. He didn't relish going outside but he did, staying near the dugout and taking a good look at the sky. The dense forest shielded much of it from view.

As his hot urine sprayed the balsam boughs to the left of the dugout, the wind howled, shaking the trees. Inside the forest, going should be easier, he thought, scanning the woods. With all the trees, there would be some shelter from the wind. They were heavy laden with snow, but he saw that he could get through the ground cover even though it was heavy. He expected that when he reached the hay fields surrounding Samantha Egar's house, he would have a more difficult time. In his heart, he already knew that was where he'd find Noone. He zipped up his pants, and made another 180-degree turn scouting out what he was up against.

Even in the heart of the fierce storm, he felt as if something were watching him.

Something was—the wolf pack. Shorty didn't see them. The alpha male drew closer to the shelter when the man went back inside. He scented the human's urine and headed back to the pack. The pack moved in closer until they encircled the dugout.

Inside, Shorty, in no hurry to face the storm, let his mind wander to thoughts of his father. He would have loved it there in the dugout during the storm. Born and raised on the Iron Range, Shorty spent his entire childhood in the woods with his dad while the elder taught him how to trap game. His father loved the woods. He loved everything about the wild. He and Shorty had sat in front of many campfires over the years, where his father regaled him with tales of wildlife hunting trips he took part in when he was a child.

Through all his tales of bravado about treks into the forest, Shorty's father instilled a life long love of the great outdoors in Shorty. He also taught him to respect it. The old man never hunted more than he needed. He didn't even like the killing; sometimes it was just necessary to survive.

So engrossed in the memories of his father, Shorty didn't notice the strange noise outside the shelter. When he finally did hear it, he thought, Nothing . . . no, wait . . . what is that? He drew nearer the outer wall to listen. With the wind raging, and tree limbs groaning, it was hard to hear anything other than the storm itself. But when Shorty heard a twig break right outside the dugout entrance, he froze.

At the exact same time, not much was happening at Noone's house that Trelavonti couldn't handle. He was nice and warm and by 3 p.m. Saturday afternoon, he had polished off a quart of Chivas Regal while rummaging through Noone's cupboards looking for more. His shirttail hung loose from his pants. His heavy rimmed eyeglasses were askew on his nose. His blond, naturally wavy hair was mused up and out of place.

He had a hard time focusing on anything. He stared out the window both bored and drunk. He hated winter weather with the wind howling and the snow blowing. He looked across the road and saw the old whore's place through an occasional lull in the winds. He thought he saw lights on over there, but he couldn't be sure and it was too damn cold to go find out. Besides, he thought, they're just old whores. Who gives a damn if they're dead or alive? He sure as hell didn't.

By that time the storm had deposited fifteen inches of snow and in some places where drifting snow piled up it was two and three feet deep.

Trelavonti felt old and tired. He didn't want to deal with any storm. He spat on the floor weaving over the couch. He was sick of it, all right, damn sick of it.

"I'll just watch some TV . . . hiccup!" He said to no one as he fell into an easy chair and punched the remote to turn the TV back on.

As the storm raged, and Shorty waited it out in a makeshift shelter and Trelavonti got drunk, Bernice washed dinner dishes at Sam's, with John alongside her drying them. It was one of his favorite things to do with his wife. He liked being close to her, helping her. There was something intimate about a kitchen that he especially liked. He couldn't help but share time with her in it.

He had never said in words to her how he felt, but she knew; he could tell she enjoyed those moments with him just as much as he did. She even enjoyed slapping him with a towel on occasion, or pinching his backside when no one was watching or stealing a kiss. He wasn't above giving Bernice a pinch, either. There was no pinching that night, however. It wasn't their house; other people were steadily coming in and out of room.

Angie and Inez talked at the kitchen table. Angie told Inez of her sister Karen and all the problems they had had in their relationship over the years. She spoke of a brother with whom she was always fighting. In her family, she felt like she was an interloper and constantly strove for positive attention from her siblings. Her parents had always been good to her; something she suspected drove her brothers and sisters to distraction.

"I wish I had had a brother growing up." Sam said to Skip and Franco who were all standing around the fireplace with her. They were listening to Angie speak with Inez, and now turned to look at Sam as she spoke. "It would be nice having brothers, sisters and parents that love you. I was raised in an orphanage, you know. I never had anyone that was mine to fight with." A wistful look crossed Sam's face.

Neither man knew what to say. They didn't know anything of Sam's past and found it interesting. Franco moved a bit closer to her. She could smell the faint scent of his cologne. He was tempted to put an arm around her shoulder but didn't. He wished the sheriff would find something else to do.

"The nuns made me do chores, all the time, but it wasn't bad," Sam said, with no idea why she was telling these two her life story. "No one got out of those. What I meant was I didn't have anyone I could rely on, lean on, or talk to growing up. Not the way family can talk to one another. Family knows all there is to know about you and they still love you."

"Yeah, but family also hurts you, makes fun of you, treats you like dirt," Franco said remembering his own childhood.

"And look at what the Spencer sisters went through," Bernice added, turning from the sink when Franco and Sam finished speaking.

John put his arm around her shoulders. He knew how much she loved the two old women, although he thought they were unlikely friends—her a Christian zealot and them being whores, well, ex-whores. He liked 'em, too, but for the life of him, he couldn't understand why. They were bossy and contrary minded, never mind what they used to do for a living.

"You're right Bernice; there are no perfect family relationships, but there must be comfort in having blood relatives around to share your life with. Look at you and your family. Sometimes it's hard not having anyone you can turn to." Sam said.

"You have us," Franco said pointing to everyone in the room. And he was right. He may have only just arrived, but he sensed something between everyone in the room that was bonding them together tighter than any family ties ever could. He wanted to be part of it.

"Yes, and that's wonderful. I guess I'll have to adopt you all as my family!" Sam smiled looking at Franco and Skip. Franco touched her hand.

No one else said a word. The house was quiet. The normal conversation was a welcome respite. They needed the break that the after dinner chatter afforded them. But it didn't last. Too many things needed sorting out.

Franco sat among them taking it all in. He was surprised at his reception. They all welcomed him, yet they were all so different. No one seemed to care. No one treated the prostitutes or farmers like second class citizens, either; a scholar, farmers, prostitutes, police, a psychologist and a bar owner, sitting together listening to one-another like it was something that happened every day, he shook his head.

Skip looked at Franco and cleared his throat. Like his father, he was well aware of Franco's reputation. He also knew there wasn't one scrape of evidence to support that reputation. Oh, everyone on the Iron Range knew how Franco grew up, knew his father. But they did not know the enigma known as Franco, not really. Franco's reputation for being a tough guy was justified to a degree, he knew. He played with his prey, like a cat, clamping his jaws about their necks to asphyxiate them, metaphorically speaking, when he was determined to make someone pay for a mistake. But it was the prey that needed consideration. Who were they?

Franco had gone after some of the so-called elite businessmen for double-dealing their employees, stealing their wages, benefits. He'd gone after the low life's who preyed on the elderly and the weak, seeing to it that victims got all the help they needed to get back on their feet. He had even gone after prosecutors who were reluctant to try criminals who attacked the vulnerable. He made phone calls, contacted superiors, in general made their lives miserable until they saw the light.

He supported political movements that gave the disenfranchised and poor help, like heating assistance, and food stamps, and supported legislators who fought for the "little guy." But he never relied on violence to do what needed to be done. He didn't have to. He used his head and his considerable influence. If there was one thing Franco couldn't seem to stand, it was seeing people tormented by those in power no matter whom that power might be.

Skip wondered if that was the reason Franco kept his cronies close; those men that sought his counsel in the back room. Skip suspected he watched them like a hawk maybe wondering when they would try to take advantage of someone that got in their way, including him if he gave them the opportunity.

Skip also learned things about Franco through his dealings with state officials, and was often surprised by what he learned considering Franco's reputation at home.

At home Franco was a tough guy, an underworld character, someone the police had never arrested for anything, ever, and not because he was a master at covering up dirty dealings, but because he wasn't engaged in any. Franco's manner was gruff and no nonsense. At the same time, Skip saw first hand the charitable things Franco did. He'd also heard many of the elderly fools he had helped talk about Franco like he was dirt because of the family he came from. If they had half of Franco's conscience, they wouldn't have to talk about anyone, Skip thought.

Skip wondered, too, why Franco was at Sam's, on that day of all days? "I find it real interesting that you should come out in this storm," he said to Franco. "I mean it's really coming down, and you living in town and all?" Skip didn't like the way Franco was hanging around so close to Sam, either.

Franco detected the edginess in Skip's voice. "What do you mean Sheriff? You want to know why I'm here? Just ask. I don't play games."

"Okay, then—why are you here?"

"I don't know. I felt compelled to be here. That's all."

"How long have you been on the road," John asked Franco, curious about the road conditions and trying to ease the tension between Franco and Skip.

"I started out last night actually. I got hung up a couple of miles from here and held up in someone's house just off River Drive. That's where I got this winter gear," he pointed to his heavy clothing.

He turned to look at Skip, "I left $500 for what I took," glaring steely eyed at Skip daring someone to call him a thief. Franco had never stolen a thing in his life.

"Whereabouts was that house?" John asked.

Franco realized then that no one there considered him a thief; they were simply interested in him. "Just up the road. I ended up on a little side road. I should have made that turn but I kept going straight. Got stuck in a ditch. Walked up the road, up a little hill; my feet and hands were freezing. I took a left at the top of the hill where I saw lights and knocked hard at the door, all the while my hands and feet were aching from the cold. I had to break into the place, a little house. Has a little porch on it, wooden, with a woodpile at the end of it. I left there early this morning. Took a few hours to get this far."

A hushed silence fell over the room. Everyone knew where Franco had spent the night.

"Can you tell us anything about the place," Stan stood in the doorway to the dinning room with Gladys staring at Franco. He, too, was real interested in what Franco had to say.

Franco still wasn't keen on talking to Stan, but as he looked about the room he sensed that Stan had captured what was on everyone's mind, and it went far deeper than their reaction to him. "Whose house was I in?" He asked before he said anything else.

In unison, they all replied "Noone's, Arthur Noone's."

Shit! Franco thought immediately wishing he'd checked the place out better. He tried to recall all that he had seen. He felt odd there; he remembered that and told the group as much, as if some presence had been watching him, something that didn't like him. That feeling set on him no sooner than he went inside the house. That same pall hung in the air when he got up in the morning. All he wanted to do was get out of there. He was surprised to have slept at all now that he knew where he had been.

Franco told the group that he saw guns on the wall, traps on the porch, a freezer full of wild game. When he was in the kitchen, he saw a picture of a woman, about thirty five, hanging next to the basement door. Recalling that picture, he remembered seeing a resemblance between Noone and the woman. She must have been a relation, he said. She had a smile that looked . . . well . . . mean, thin lips that curved downward, more like a leer than a smile, emptiness in the eyes. She looked tough. It was also an odd place to hang a portrait. It hung just above the lentil of the doorway leading to the basement, or what he supposed was the basement. He had not gone down there.

"I found these in the coat pocket," he said getting up and walking out onto the porch, pulling photos from his overcoat hanging next to the kitchen door. Everyone moved in unison to look over Franco's shoulder or to his side at the pictures when he stepped back inside the kitchen proper.

"That's the professor," Clem whispered. He and Stan were the only ones there to remember what the professor looked like, to have met him.

"So, is anyone going to tell me what's going on?" Franco asked innocently. "It looks like the guy is being walled up or something."

Skip and Stan filled Franco in on what Skip and his deputies had found Friday night in Sam's basement.

Franco shook his head in disbelief as he wondered, right along with everyone else, why he was led to be there. He hadn't told anyone yet, but he had a strong feeling, a compulsion almost, to drive out to Sam's in the blizzard. It was overwhelming. He couldn't have denied it if he had wanted too.

Franco thought of his nephew and blurted out, "What about, Earl, my nephew? You know damn good and well he couldn't have done that murder you sent him up for. He's not bright enough. "Yet, Sheriff," he said glaring at Stan, "your boys locked him up. Tight! Set him up would be more like it."

Stan shook his head in dismay. Franco was right and he knew it. "It was one of those times—and there were a lot of them—when Noone pulled his weight around the county. That's why Earl is in prison. I did what I could to help him."

"You mean Noone had something to do with it? I find that hard to believe." Franco said staring at Stan even though he had always suspected a Noone connection to Earl's imprisonment.

"Yep, somehow, someway Noone and Trelavonti put that nephew of yours away. And don't take this the wrong way, but anyone meeting that kid knew he didn't have the brains to tie his own shoes let alone take that kid out and kill her the way we found her. It was real pat, the way we found her, I mean. They earmarked your nephew for some reason, and there you have it.

The powers that be sent him off and threw away the key. But it ain't over till I say it's over," Stan bent down looking Franco in the eye. "Yeah, the kid may be where he don't want to be today, but who can say what tomorrow will bring? Eh?"

Stan's statement befuddled Franco. He didn't expect it, didn't realize that the sheriff didn't think Earl was a killer anymore than he did.

"Hey," Angie piped up, "what say we get back to our detective work?"

With the gray skies of winter wagering an assault outdoors, inside Sam's old farm house rooms were dark enough that lights had to be turned on as early as 3 p.m. So when the group traipsed back into the dinning room, they had to turn on all the lights to hold back the gloom.

Angie sensed that something was about to happen. She slipped into a quiet meditation no sooner than she sat down in an easy chair out of the way of foot traffic and waited to see a vision. Whatever was going on needed to be put to rest. She could feel the growing intensity of the situation.

Fuzz and Kitty refused to come into the room. Kitty stared at Angie with menacing eyes.

Angie's eyes closed. Her chest heaved up and down, slowly, rhythmically. She began to sway, ever so slightly at first, then faster rocking from side to side. Seated across from her quietly reading one of the papers, Sam didn't notice Angie's movement until Angie dropped a pencil on the floor.

"Hey?" Sam said when she noticed. She knew from their college days what was happening.

Out of Angie's mouth a melodious tenor voice said, "Hello."

Sam responded with, "Hello?"

"It's good to see so many." The voice paused for half a minute then continued, "There is danger in this house. Alfred is still here. He has found his children. They are here too." The voice paused as Angie continued to gently rock to and fro.

"There's danger inside this house and out," the voice repeated. "He'll hurt the children if he gets a chance. Not Alfred, the other one, he has hurt Alfred's children already, and many others besides. He's interested in Sam now, the one they call Sam."

Kitty's body arched; every hair on her back stood on edge as she hissed at Angie from the kitchen doorway. She moved into the room sideways threatening her.

Sam jumped up, grabbed the cat, and tried to calm her down. She locked her in the bathroom then ran back to Angie gently shaking her shoulders.

"Are you alright?"

Angie slumped into a heap as sweat beaded across her forehead. She sat up feeling groggy, like she was coming out of a deep sleep. "Yes, yes, I'm fine. Did you get anything?" She asked as she looked around the room wiping her palms on the legs of her jogging pants.

Everyone stared at her. They were so concerned for her the last words spoken by the voice hadn't sunk in yet.

"We sure did Sugar," Gladys said.

"A voice. A deep, man's voice said we are all in danger," Skip said. "It also said the professor thinks he's found his daughters. He said they're here." He looked at Angie expectantly, waiting for her to say more. The others did, too.

"I don't know anything," Angie said watching their faces and realizing what they are thinking. "I'm not here when an entity comes through. That's why you have to take notes, tape everything. I can't help with that myself."

Bernice and John held up their notepads and pencils in affirmation. "It said we were in danger," Bernice said, her voice shaky.

"Did it say anything else?" Angie asked, hoping for other clues.

"Yes, here, why don't you listen to the tape" John handed it to Angie. Angie went into the kitchen to listen in private. When she walked back into the dinning room, she saw little Fuzz cringing next to the bathroom door, whimpering. She moved over to him, and heard the cat on the other side of the door hissing. She patted the dog on the top his head. She didn't open the bathroom door.

"I think we need to make sure the kids are okay," Gladys said to Bernice who was dialing the phone before Gladys finished her sentence.

"I'm wondering what kids he is talking about? Seems to me there have been a lot of kids hurt. I mean they've been disappearing for forty years out here. Was that what the voice meant?" Stan wondered out loud. If he could do anything worthwhile with his life right now, he would solve those missing kid's cases. He hated that they were still unsolved. He hated the idea of kids vanishing off the face of the earth, of their parents forever wondering where they might be. If he could only give them closure! He had always wanted to be able to do that.

Skip looked sidelong at his father. The elder Gilbert didn't look good. There was an ashen color to his skin. Skip pushed those thoughts aside to wonder if his father was right. Was the voice talking about all the kids that had mysteriously disappeared over the years? He grew excited. The more he thought about it, the surer he became that that was exactly what the voice meant. It would be great to have Pop here to solve those cases, he thought. Nothing would make him happier.

"What kind of danger do you think that voice meant?" Bernice asked Gladys while she waited for someone to pick up the phone at home. "Do you think someone else is here with us, or is it a ghost we should be worried about, or is he talking about my kids? For Heaven's sake! And what about the professor's kids? Are they buried in the house, or out in the fields somewhere? Why hasn't he led us to them? He led us to him!"

As a devout born again Christian, Bernice was well aware of negative spirits and the damage they could do. She relied on God to keep her from those spirits. She prayed constantly that she and her family would be kept safe from evil.

She wasn't crazy about Angie's trances, either. One should never open themselves up for spirits, because any kind of spirit could come and dwell on the inside of them. Angie should be asking for protection from the Lord. His Holy Spirit would help and that's a darn site better than an unholy one, she thought as she tapped her foot impatiently waiting for the phone to be answered at home. She didn't' really care if Gladys didn't answer any of the questions she had posed. She had merely been thinking out loud.

"It doesn't seem likely someone else is in this house," Skip said. "Still, you never know. With this storm, though, I have my doubts. Maybe the professor's kids are here? Maybe they are buried here? Maybe there is a . . . ghost . . . or something we need to be concerned with. I don't know. It did say the professor found his children. Is he going to lead us to them, too?"

Inez shivered.

"Ya know, looks to me like someone could hide in this house pretty easy if they had a mind ta'. The walls are too thick. The rooms ain't big enough fer' the frame, ya' know, like there might be som'en behind 'em?" Clem hoped the officers would catch his tone. Ever since he was frightened by Sam's house, he had been studying the way it was built. It was peculiar. Something was off, just a little bit. It had taken Clem awhile to put his finger on just what the oddity was. "Ya don't suppose we have any secret rooms in here, do ya?"

Everyone turned to look about the dinning room. Skip and Stan couldn't detect anything odd. The walls looked fine to them.

Just then, a whiff of a breeze tickled Clem's cheek. "Hey, what was that?" It brushed against Gladys, Inez and Stan then, too.

"Did you feel that!" Inez screamed. "Something just touched me!"

"Me too," Gladys and Stan yelled in unison. She grabbed onto Stan's arm and he, hers. A tiny breeze brushed past the others, then, too. Their hair and clothes gently rustled. Bernice's hair stood on end as the breeze hovered over her. Angie stepped back into the living room at that moment and immediately the breeze rushed at her, hitting her full force, swelling through her. Everyone could hear as the wind "whooshed" at her. She fell to the floor.

"We will watch over you," a deep, husky voice emanated once again from Angie's mouth as she lay in a heap. "Revenge is ours, not yours. We will handle what needs to be done. Watch your step; you are not entirely safe here. We can only do so much, but we will warn you." With another whoosh, the breeze rushed out of Angie as fast as it had entered and disappeared from the room. She sat up dazed and disoriented.

"You know. I'm getting a little tired of this. What happened this time?" She said.

"It warned us again that something is inside this house, but it told us to stay out of its way. It's seeking revenge. It wasn't the same voice as the first one."

"I thought this might happen. There's more than one entity here. Something is really wrong. When the professor's body was found, it unleashed a lot of turbulence that hadn't manifested before, even though the professor had. He's still here. Finding his body was not enough. His work here isn't finished."

Angie was still on the floor getting flashes of visions as she spoke. She could see a myriad of spirits rushing in and out of the room in synchronized formation heading south and west away from Sam's house. It was like they were trying to show her something, but she wasn't able to see what.

"Damn," Skip said. "Personally I find it hard to believe that anyone could be in this house with that storm that's ragging outside, but I guess we better check it out. We all managed to get out here in it, so it's possible someone else did, too.

I think the women need to stay down here, in the kitchen or dinning room, though. The rest of us can search the house in teams. Stan, Clem and John can start in the basement, and Franco and I can go upstairs to the attic. We will all meet right here again when we're done. Okay?

Sam, I know you're pretty good with a gun. You can come with me and Franco."

Franco smiled. He didn't know much about spooks, but he was glad to be on Sam's team.

"Hey, if we're in danger whose going to stay here with us?" Angie wanted to know.

"Well how about when we find the son of a bitch, we knock him out with a night stick, or maybe use that cast iron skillet we saw in the kitchen to brain him," Gladys said.

"Or how about I pull this here stun gun out of my handbag and zap him with that?" Inez offered.

"Or maybe we can burn the asshole with some hot grease we'll get ready on the stove," Gladys added.

"Or I could just shot him with my .22 pistol," Inez continued.

"Or I could use my Colt 45," Gladys offered.

"Okay, okay, so you got us covered," Angie got up laughing.

The men raised their eyebrows, gave the older women a wide birth and made their way to their prospective search areas, as Skip said, "Well, ladies, I guess you don't need us in your hair." realizing the women carried more firepower than he did.

Stan smiled. He already knew; so did Clem.

Sam smiled at the men's discomfort trailing upstairs to the attic behind Skip and Franco. Gladys and Inez should be the ones up here, she thought as she climbed the steps. Hell, sounds like they're ready to kick butt.

Chapter Twenty Three

Noone heard everything through the heating ducts. It was amazing how crystal clear voices carried, he thought.

He bided his time in an old heat duct that was tucked behind the chimney in the attic. No longer in use, it was so secluded he would be surprised if anyone ever discovered it, which is the way he planned it when he had the new heating system installed. You never knew when you might need to hide away. He learned that as a kid. So as he sat tucked away from prying eyes, he learned of their plans to search the house and who was going where; he felt completely safe from discovery, so much so he was almost complacent about his safety . . . almost. He heard their footsteps as they climbed the attic stairs, then the door opening when they reached the top. He heard muffled voices as three people entered to search the attic room he hid himself in.

So, they have a medium with them, Angie Eckenridge, Egar's friend; he shook his head in mild surprise as he listened to the trio moving about. He knew Eckenridge all right, by reputation. Hell, anyone who did what he did, knew who she was. They were destined to meet he figured remembering his brother Henry. I wonder how she'd feel if she knew who was in the house with her, he thought. He almost laughed out loud.

His mother said, "shhhhhh."

And whose voice was that that warned them someone else was in the house? He wanted to know.

"You've gone and done it this time, you little fool! How long do you think it will be before they find you out, boy? I've told you a million times to be more careful, but you never listen."

Noone was sick and tired of his mother's constant nagging whispers in his ear. Would she ever leave him alone? "No one who knows what I've done is here mother, so why don't you just shut-up?"

"You watch your mouth, boy. I've done plenty over the years to keep you out of trouble, although, for the life of me I don't know why. Now, just keep your mouth shut, or them fools out there in the attic are going to find you, do you hear me?"

Noone didn't say another word. No one who knew him knew he was at the Egar farm. Not even Trelavonti knew where he was. Trelavonti was the only one who really knew too much about him anyway, but he wasn't a problem. Noone had more than enough on Trelavonti to keep that son of a bitch quiet for the rest of his life.

But, he decided, his mother was right. They were too close to finding out the truth, so the real problem was—how could he get rid of all ten people without coming under suspicion? He pondered that thought for awhile until it came to him.

If a fire broke out in the old farmhouse, no one would see that as unusual considering the age of the place and the weather. Stuff like that happened all the time in Minnesota, especially in older homes during the worst winter weather. Say a faulty furnace blew up or an electrical outlet shorted out and started a fire, any number of things could happen during a bad winter.

Everyone inside would die of smoke inhalation; that is if they're asleep and don't know the house is burning. I'll set a fire at night. During a major winter storm—what could be better? Firemen won't be able to get out here until it is way too late. It'll be easy to get rid of ten meddling fools, course with the sheriff here some sort of investigation is likely, but all they'll find is faulty, old wiring. Perfect, he decided.

      With the Jennings there too, things could get a lot more interesting for him at home, he figured. Their kids would be fair game once the folks were gone. The girl was a bit younger than what he normally went for, but she would do nicely just the same. Her age might make her all the more enticing. The boy was just right.

      Maybe it wasn't such a bad idea having Trelavonti around after all, Noone thought as he wiggled around trying to ease his cramped muscles being careful not to make noise. He had opened my mind to whole new possibilities. Mother will hate it, too, another plus.

      He was so busy considering his situation; he didn't hear the footsteps approach the chimney. When he finally did hear them, they stopped right outside the big heating duct where he hid. Someone ran their fingers across the metal pipe. He held his breath

      "What's that Sam?" Skip asked.

      "An old heat pipe, I guess; I don't really know. I haven't been up here much; just peeked in as I was moving in."

      Noone tittered with excitement realizing Sam stood right next to the duct. It would be easy to grab her, take her away. Nobody would catch him. He knew the area so much better than they did; he could pull it off easily.

      Sam's attention focused on what looked to be much more interesting than the old heating duct. There were boxes of stuff pilled high to the rear of the opposite end of the attic.

      "What's all that stuff over there?" Franco asked, his eyes following Sam's.

"Let's take a look."

As they moved away from the duct, Noone breathed a
sigh of relief. That was way too close for comfort. He realized in a
flash how it would be better for him to stay put and find out who
wanted revenge. He'd continue to listen through the duct to find
out from the renowned psychic just who it was that was warning
the meddling bunch. He'd learn everything he needed to know.
Wouldn't Henry love that! Of course, he didn't really give a damn
what Henry would love.

Henry and Joseph weren't around to bother him anymore.
But it didn't seem right not to try and avenge Henry since the
bitch that put him away was right there, family loyalty, and all
that. Yeah, he thought; I'll make sure the bitch knows whom she's
dealing with, how highly regarded Henry is among his kin. It
might be fun.

Outside the storm raged on. Inside Noone's dugout Shorty
remained relatively snug and warm. He was prepared for
everything . . . except the wolves. He knew by then that they
surrounded him. He was extremely uncomfortable and a bit
frightened. He'd never been seen as prey before by a wild animal,
and he was sure that was what was happening. In the storm, by
himself, he might have a very difficult time defending himself
against seven wolves. He shuddered knowing what they did to
their prey before killing it.

As the late afternoon set in he berated himself for not
having left earlier, which he had planned to do. He wondered if he
should try and get some sleep, but doubted he could, with a pack
of predators just outside the flimsy dugout. They could get at him
anytime they wanted to. So, why didn't they? He didn't know, but
fingered the butt of the pistol he had strapped to his side just the
same. He had never killed a wolf in his life. He didn't want to start

now. But what if they attacked? He knew he would do anything he had to do to survive.

The alpha male kept a close watch on the dugout door. He wanted the human to come out.

At 7 p.m. Shorty could stand it no more. He stepped outside and looked around for the wolves he knew were lying in wait for him. They can come and get me now, he thought. Let's get this over with, but they better know some of them are going down with me.

Shorty packed his gear onto his back, ready to finish the trek. He saw the alpha male just as he jostled the backpack into a more comfortable position; the wolf looked him in the eye. They stood staring at each other for two minutes. The wolf tossed his head and padded off into the woods, stopping to look back at Shorty. He took two more steps, turned and looked back at Shorty once again; again padding off further into the woods, taking two more steps then stopping and looking back at Shorty. The alpha male started and stopped that action almost a dozen times before Shorty realized that the wolf wanted him to follow him. The rest of the pack hung back, almost out of sight behind the trees so that Shorty only caught rare glimpses of them. He knew they were there, though. When he did start to follow the alpha male, relaxing in the knowledge that apparently the wolf meant him no harm, the rest of the pack moved in front of him creating a path for him to follow by stepping in behind their leader. Shorty was stunned. In all his outdoor exploits, he had never witnessed such behavior in a predator.

Man, no one is going to believe this! He thought as he followed them. No one! As he walked he hoped one day to be able to tell everyone. What a story!

Back at Tony's, Botticelli opened the bar in spite of the cold and the wind and the fact that it was Sunday. Not one customer showed up; the help didn't even come in, except Jack, who always showed up. Even Franco was a no show. Where the hell is he? Botticelli wondered. It isn't like Franco not to come down, even in a storm. He worried. When and the storm let up, he'd be sending some people out to look for him. At least he knew where Franco had been headed.

Jack sat at the horseshoe bar playing solitaire. He too wondered where Franco was. Isn't the same if he isn't here, the place has no pizzazz, that's for damn sure, he thought.

"Hey Jack, if you want to get outta here, you might as well. Nothing's gonna happen today."

"What are you going to do?"

"I'm gonna wait here for Franco to call. He should be calling in anytime now."

"I'll wait with ya."

Out at Noone's, Trelavonti was busy digging in the basement. He didn't like what he found. It was the smell that kept nagging at him. It was familiar, smelled like something he had smelled in the course of investigating crime. When it dawned on him that the smell was that of decaying flesh, he started digging. It didn't take long for him to uncover the source of the stench.

I knew the old son-of-a-bitch was into some strange shit; I'm into some myself, but this! No way, man!

After he found them, he was filled with doubt about how to proceed. If he squealed on Noone, his own ass would be grass. There was no way people weren't going to think he had something to do with this mess. No matter, he knew the criminal process all to well, and had seen less circumstantial evidence convict those he knew were innocent.

Maybe I won't go to prison if I use the find to bargain with . . . maybe. It's about the only chance I've got to save myself. If I don't reveal what I've found, it's a good bet Noone will accuse me of being an accessory. No way am I going down for this shit!

He found Noone's cell phone outside by the woodpile; tried it and discovered the battery had not gone dead. It was a good thing, too, because the regular phone lines were. At 4 p.m. he was still debating on whether or not to call the sheriff's office. Damn! He thought, if I squeal on Noone, he's going to blow the whistle on me, but look at this! How can I not talk?

Trelavonti estimated that he had found at least five bodies so far; he had counted five human skulls at least. But he was tired and the work grossed him out. The skeletons looked small, so he supposed that whoever they had been, they were pretty young when they died. One was so small Trelavonti figured it was a baby. It didn't dawn on him at first; he didn't recall that day so long ago when he had molested Ellen then killed her. When he did remember, he decided that it couldn't be the same baby. That baby was buried out in the woods alongside its mother. He knew; he helped bury them. He knew, too, that Noone used to perform abortions for the local ladies and wondered if the tiny skeleton belonged to one of them. Probably, but Noone wouldn't bury it in his own house, would he?

He went upstairs to the bathroom and showered. When he finished, he sat down on the couch considering what to do next. Finally, he picked up the cell phone and dialed. But instead of calling the sheriff's department, he called Noone's friend, Judge David K. Wilkins. By the time they finished talking, Trelavonti had already made a deal. He wouldn't serve too much time, the judge assured him, and what time he would serve would be done right there at home; no Stillwater State Prison for him.

After all, Trelavonti reasoned with the judge as they spoke, he could say a thing or two about the judge himself if no strings were pulled on his behalf. But, as Wilkins explained, there was no way Trelavonti could get off scot free. That was okay with Trelavonti; he knew he could do much worse than one year in the county lockup right there on the Range.

"I'm fine Harriet; I'm out at the Noone place, got stuck here because of the storm. But, Harriet, there's a problem, a big problem. I'm going to need some help. I've found something." As Trelavonti spoke, some of the weariness that had driven Harriet Hornblower for the last forty eight hours washed away in a flood of energy. It was always like this when a major case rolled in, and that's what was happening now; she could feel it in her bones. She checked the duty roster as Trelavonti talked preparing to call in deputies to drive out to the Arthur Noone residence immediately.

"Hell, most of the guys are lucky if they can make it across the road in them cars!" She told Trelavonti when he asked for help. Help would not be quick. She couldn't stand Trelavonti anyway, but the idiot needed help out there at Noone's in the middle of the worst winter storm Minnesota had ever seen, and she'd do her best to get it to him. The sheriff would be real peeved if he found she had hesitated on something like that. Besides, she'd been around cops so long she could smell a big case faster than they could half the time.

"Look, Harriet, this is big, real big. Some way, some how, you're going to have to get me some help, quick!" Trelavonti was already thinking of what he would look like on the evening news. He planned on getting complete credit for this find, for solving the biggest case in St. Louis County history. He liked that idea. His mind spun with the possibilities. He didn't care if reporters connected him to Noone. That would give him more airtime and his name would be forever connected to the case. He'd be famous. Imagine, me on TV, he thought.

"You at Noone's place? That right?" Harriet didn't like Noone either. She was hoping maybe the old bastard was dead or had to be put away for something. He had always given her the willies.

"Yeah, that's right; I already told you that! Why don't you write this down so you don't forget?"

"You just go into his place uninvited, did ya?"

"Yeah, what of it?"

"Well, that's real interesting. You always go into places uninvited?" She couldn't resist needling Trelavonti. He got on her last nerve. She waited to hear from the other officers before she let him get off the line. If they couldn't make it out there, he needed to know right away.

"Just don't worry about that. When they get here, they'll find something else a whole lot more interesting than me breaking into someone's house in the middle of a storm. Something, I did, by the way, to keep from freezing to death. And by the time they're finished out here, the rest of the force will be thanking me, not arresting me for trespassing! Thank you very much." He was getting peeved. Couldn't she hurry up?

Harriet wondered what Trelavonti was onto, sensing something enormous, but he wouldn't say much over the cell phone and that's as it should be. Too bad he had to discover it, whatever it is, she thought. One by one three other deputies called in and once she relayed Trelavonti's information to them they told her they were on their way to help him. She relayed their information back to Trelavonti. She also gave the three deputies Trelavonti's cell phone number. He would fill them in on the details when they got there.

After he finished talking to the exasperating Harriet, all he had to do was wait. Trelavonti went back inside the nice warm house periodically running to the windows watching for help to arrive. He hoped to see headlights coming down the road even though he hadn't been off the phone more than ten minutes. With the storm, help wouldn't arrive for awhile, but he was itching to get out of the house. He had been inside it with all those dead people for way too long. It was creeping him out. He paced around upstairs while waiting; when he tired of that, he went back downstairs to the basement to dig some more. He kept Noone's cell phone in his shirt pocket so he could get to it quickly. As he dug, he occasionally stopped to run back upstairs and gaze out the windows watching for the help that he was sure would be there any minute.

The storm raged on. Temperatures dropped as high-speed winds increased bringing the wind chill factor to sixty below zero. Snow blew across roadways, blocking passages all over the county.

Only two 4-wheel drive sheriff department vehicles were on the road. The three deputies were stranded on Highway 53 just shy of Townline Road thanks to snow filled roads. They radioed in. Harriet relayed that information to the highway department hoping to get the big trucks out onto those back roads and get them plowed so the deputies could get out to Noone's.

The back roads weren't normally the first to be plowed, she knew, but this was an emergency and she had friends in the highway department. She'd get help out to Trelavonti even if she couldn't stand the sight of him.

At Sam's house, Sam was enjoying her time with Skip and Franco, and wasn't taking the warning that came from Angie's lips too seriously. She had a hard time believing anyone, or thing, would venture out in this weather despite the fact that she had a house full of company, all of whom had ventured out in said weather.

"Look at this," she said as they approached the trunk at the opposite side of the room away from the heat duct concealing Arthur Noone. "I've never seen it before."

"Have you ever been up here before?" Skip asked.

"Well, once . . . and all I did was peek up the stairs."

Franco stood near her. Skip stood opposite the two and looked down at the trunk. He was tired. Sam saw it in his face and her heart went out to him. Thirty years, she couldn't imagine anyone being in unrequited love for thirty years, but there he stood; a man whose heart must have broken anew every day, she romanticized. She reached out and touched his arm. Skip felt something akin to a bolt of lightening flash through him at her touch.

It was just a friendly gesture, he told himself. Why did she do that? He didn't ask her; he just said, "Come on, let's get this thing open and see what's inside."

Franco noticed the gesture Sam made to Skip. He stepped over to help Skip open the trunk. It was not easy, so they grabbed hold of the lid and in tandem forced it wide. Inside, they found nothing but old clothes.

Skip pulled garments aside digging to the bottom of the trunk. The clothes smelled of mothballs. Must have been up here for a long time, he thought as he hurled many of them onto the floor. He stopped. "Jeez!" he said, "she looks just like Angie!" He pulled a single photo from the bottom of the trunk and stared at it then showed it to Sam and Franco.

"It's remarkable," Franco agreed. He turned from them and looked to see what else was at the bottom of the trunk. He too pulled out a photo.

"Hey, this one looks just like Sam!" Sam and Skip moved over to Franco to look at his photo.

"Family photos, do you suppose?" Franco asked.

"Yes, but whose family?" Sam looked at Skip.

"It looks like yours," he said quietly. Franco stared at her. The women don't look much alike, but they sure resemble who ever owned the trunk. Could it be, he wondered? Are they the twins?

"Are you upset that you haven't heard from Ellen? I mean I've heard the dead will often speak through mediums. Angie is the real deal—you know—a medium, I mean. What she said down there, about that girl, with that deputy? She had to have been talking about Ellen." Sam rambled she knew but couldn't stop. The photos unnerved her. She was fighting to keep certain thoughts out of her head. She wanted to change the subject.

"What makes you so sure Ellen is dead?" Skip's icy voice chilled her.

"I . . . well . . . from what Angie said, and, well . . . I get this feeling. That's all. I just thought that's what you believed."

Skip couldn't hide the anger from his eyes as he stared at Sam. Who the hell was she to even mention Ellen's name, he thought, and how the hell was she going to know if Ellen was alive or dead.

After thirty years, Skip still couldn't bring himself to consider that possibility. He didn't give a damn what Eckenridge said; he wouldn't believe Ellen was dead until he saw her dead body, or what remained of it, that was the end of it.

Skip brought his hard, cold, blue eyes over to stare at Franco. "You seem pretty angry at my old man. What happened between you two?" Skip wasn't so old that he had completely forgotten his youthful nature, the one that was always spoiling for a fight. Right then, he wanted to hurt something, and as long as Franco was there, what the hell, he'd do just fine.

Franco was an old hat at discerning trouble, however. He calmly told Skip what happened between his nephew and Stan, thereby leaving Skip no place to put his anger. Talking about Earl and Stan was not as hard as Franco thought it would be. As he spoke, he found his anger with Stan was gone.

"Oh, that jerk-off is a rat, all right, Earl, I mean, but he's just not mean enough to have killed that kid. He wouldn't have. I didn't believe it when they arrested him and I still don't believe it. You know how it is, sheriff. When you know somebody, you know what they're capable of, how far they will go. The boy's an idiot but he has never been into little girls. I mean who ever killed that little girl raped and tortured her first. You know that, don't you?"

"Yeah, my old man told me about it. It was one of those cases he was never comfortable with the outcome of. So, you think the old man let whoever committed the murder set up your nephew?"

"I did. I don't so much now. What I mean is, yeah, somebody set up the kid, but I don't think Stan did or had anything to do with it now that I've meet him, talked to him. I did think that, though." Franco refused to rise to Skip's baiting. This was no place for a fight. The sheriff would have to exorcise his demons on someone else.

Skip shook his head trying to get rid of his own doubts about his father. The fight had gone out of him. "Well, I'm making a promise here, in front of witnesses," Skip nodded at Franco, "that I'll look deeply into this. I don't know if anything will come of it, but I'll give it my full attention."

"Thanks, sheriff, that's all I ask. You know that one deputy of yours, Trelavonti? He's got it in for me and hassles me every chance he gets. Maybe you could look into that too."

"My pleasure."

Franco was surprised by that response, but kept his surprise to himself. He eyed the sheriff with skepticism.

Sam sensed a shift in the tension realizing the men's exchange had brought them to an amicable understanding. She thought for a moment that Skip might attack Franco. She was relieved that they seemed to have patched up whatever it was between them. It was with reluctance that she followed the men back downstairs. She really didn't want to leave their company, the cozy attic room and intimacy they shared there. Before descending, however, she picked up the photos, and shoved them into her pants pocket not caring that she was creating creases in them, and wondering how Angie would respond. Odd, the way those people look just like Angie and me, she thought as she climbed down the stairs. Still, she refused to dwell on the resemblance. If it hadn't been for the men, she might not have even noticed it.

When he heard the attic door shut, Noone stepped out of his hiding place. He tiptoed over to the trunk. The contents were as Skip had left them, all over the floor. He hoped to see the photos they talked about, but couldn't find them. He rummaged through the trunk futilely. He heard everything the threesome had said.

I know where Ellen is! He wanted to cry out. He wanted Skip Gilbert to know exactly what had happened to her and in detail, just what he had done. Gilbert's attitude toward him had grated on his nerves for some time, like a burr underneath the saddle on a horse's back. Stan Gilbert was just as bad. Franco was another matter all together. Noone never could get a handle on him, so he steered clear.

He also now knew for sure that Angie was THE dame, THE psychic instrumental in putting Henry away. The idea of her being right where he could get at her gave him a great deal of pleasure. It was as if the gods were offering her up to his whole family. Henry may not have been able to deal with her, but he would be only too happy to do what his brother couldn't. He felt superior to both Henry and Angie.

What was it the broad said? That Ellen was in this house? In this house? Why would she be here and not at my house, Noone thought. According to what he'd read on the subject, spirits tended to hang out where they had been killed, so how could she be at Egar's? It didn't make sense. But what if she is here and wants revenge? Can that be?

No, he refused to believe in any afterlife. Bullshit thought up by religious folks to scare people from doing what they really wanted to do, was the way he saw it. He wouldn't mind having the voluptuous Ellen back to play with, though—not at all. But nothing like that was going to happen to him, or to anybody else. Dead was dead. No one could accuse him from the grave. It'd never happen.

He crept over to the heat vent overhanging the dinning room. He wanted to know more about the other houseguests. He heard Bernice Jennings talking but couldn't make out what she said. The so-called Christian, he thought. I wonder if her God is going to save her now. Where was He when I took those kids? THEY didn't see Him. No matter, I know her God isn't going to help her or her family, either. Believing in something supernatural? How can she be so stupid! She deserves what I'm going to give her, so do the rest of them.

As Arthur Noone sat there in the attic listening, he worked out just how to set the fire and make good his escape. He sat in front of the duct, warm and cozy, enjoying himself as he listened; he knew that they didn't have a clue that he was right there among them regardless of Eckenridge's warning. He gloated over his position, confident that he was in complete control. He knew their every move. The heat vents had only one disadvantage; he couldn't see anybody from there.

He got up, stretched, and then crept stealthy down the secret passageway to the fireplace in the dinning room. The borehole there allowed him to see just enough so that he could watch anyone sitting at the dinning room table. Since the room was small, that meant he could see most everyone.

Stan, Clem and John came upstairs from the basement. They joined everyone else in the dinning room.

Bernice sat on a bench in front of the windows while the others gathered around the table. John was the first one up. He said nothing to Bernice, which set off her alarm bells. He had never done that before. She suspected he found something he didn't want her to know about. She was already uneasy about the children. She had already called them a number of times, and they kept telling her they were okay, but . . . she wrung her hands and sat quietly on the bench.

"Something's funny around that death chamber," Clem said. "It looks odd."

"I don't agree," Stan said. "It looks like what it is. A small room built to hold one body, that's all."

"The wall to the east has lighter brick in one spot. I didn't want to go in there, so I didn't touch it, but I bet if we did som' 'en would happen."

"Clem, I think you've lost your wits; that's what I think," Stan said.

"What you in such a huff about, Stan? You were right here when we got that warning about some 'en else being in this house with us. If some 'en is in this house, it can't be in the regular part, we're in the regular part and ain't nobody we don't know about here with us, therefore, whoever else is here has to be in a secret room or som' 'en."

Stan wasn't too sure himself why he felt compelled to argue with Clem.

John agreed with Clem. It had to be a secret room! He saw the bricks Clem was talking about. Why did Stan think that possibility was so unreasonable? John contemplated all that had gone on thus far, spiritually and otherwise, as he tried to fit the puzzle pieces together.

In his spare time, or when he sat alone on his tractor working, John solved hundreds of mysteries. Of course they were all in books, but so what, why couldn't he help solve this one? He was almost always right when solving fictional puzzles, figuring out the ending before getting to it. The more he thought about it, the clearer it became to him that Clem was onto something, and he said so to the others not understanding why Stan refused to see it.

Angie sat at the end of the table in a wing chair with her arms hanging listlessly over the armrests and with her legs pulled up on the seat. Sam paged through photos on the table then got up, walked over to the wing chair, and dropped the two Skip and Franco had found in the attic in Angie's lap.

Angie appeared to be sleeping, at first, but then said, "Is Skip here? Hey, Sugar! It's been awhile." Her body sat bolt upright and took on a youthful glow. With rosy red cheeks, Angie looked twenty years younger and her manner became flirty. She sauntered over to Skip, who sat at the far end of the table, and plopped herself in his lap running her fingers through his wavy hair.

No one in the room moved, dumbstruck by the complete change in Angie's demeanor.

Spellbound, Sam watched her best friend act like a schoolgirl with a crush, behavior she had never witnessed in Angie before. She didn't like seeing Angie in Skip's lap flirting with him, either. A flush of anger spread through her like wildfire, but she kept her mouth shut realizing that something very unusual was going on. It wasn't really Angie in Skip's lap.

Skip didn't move; the color in his face washed away.

"It's been such a long time Sugar; I thought you forgot about me. You never did come looking, now did you?" Angie kept running her fingers though Skip's hair looking him in the eyes and smiling coquettishly.

"Ellen?"

"You have to ask that, Sugar? My, you do have a short memory." Angie's eyelids fluttered as she feigned hurt feelings. She didn't get out of Skip's lap, and he didn't move her.

"Now Sugar, I've got news that you aren't going to like, even though I know you know it's true. It's about how I got over here. You know I'm gone, now admit it." Skip nodded his head in the affirmative, slowly. "Well, I didn't get over here on my own. I had some help.

You can thank that lovely deputy of yours, sheriff," she turned to look at Stan. "He couldn't keep his hands off me. You know that too, don't you, Sugar?" She said turning back to face Skip, still cradling his face in her hands. She tweaked his nose.

Skip knew it was Ellen speaking to him through Angie. He saw her there in his lap; gone was the psychic from Fargo and in her place was his high school sweetheart; the woman he was still deeply in love with.

"Well, one night my lovely parents, who you know didn't approve of me, they sent me out to Arthur Noone's place. You know—that saintly pillar of society that lives out here?

My Christian parents hired that saintly pillar to perform an abortion on me. You know my saintly church going parents, when they found out I was pregnant, that's the first thing they wanted me to do.

Well, anyway, they brought me out to Noone's. He was supposed to take me to Duluth the next day after I'd had a good night's rest. Sometime after my parents left his place, Trelavonti showed up. Noone knew Trelavonti had this thing for me, for young girls, even back then; I was only sixteen and he was probably thirty or better at the time. Well, Trelavonti, he gets me out into those woods and decides to have his way with me.

He did just that too, let me tell you, but I didn't make it easy for him. I kicked him in the groin once so hard he darned near puked on me. That just made him mad. He started slapping me and wouldn't stop. I fell against a tree root and was knocked out. He thought I was dead, I guess. He ran back and got Noone. Noone finished the job for him.

I was two and a half months pregnant at the time. I went into labor. Noone, he could see this happening and he gets this idea, something, he told Trelavonti, that he read about in a man's magazine about what Hitler's men did to concentration camp women during the second world war. He tied my legs together and let the birthing continue. I don't know what they were expecting, but Noone and Trelavonti watched as the labor progressed, enjoying my pain, I think.

Finally, it was over. I was covered with blood; I managed to pull the baby onto my chest, surprised the hell out of those two pieces of filth staring down at me. All they did was grin, although when I reached for the baby they jumped.

By that time, I was past caring. There was nothing I could do. I wanted to die. The last thing I remember was Trelavonti masturbating in front of Noone as I lay there on the ground in my own blood with my dead baby resting on my chest. He cast his seed on the soiled dirt as I breathed my last breath."

Sam's dinning room was unnaturally quiet. Skip was as still as a statue. Angie quit speaking then, too. Her eyes fluttered back in her head and her head lolled to Skip's shoulder. Slowly she moved it once again, and sat up. When she realized where she was, her cheeks flushed red; she jumped up and stood back. No one said a word.

Ellen wasn't finished speaking yet, though. Out of Angie's mouth, Ellen's voice echoed throughout the room.

"Now, Sugar. Don't you go getting all riled here," Ellen said as she dropped Angie's lithe body back down into Skip's lap once again. "Noone, Trelavonti, they owe me, and it's me that will make them pay. It's not for you to even think about. I know you loved me. God is not going to let their sins go unpunished." Angie/Ellen didn't move. Skip tried to push her off his lap and get up, but she was like a dead weight. He couldn't budge her. "Samantha!" Ellen yelled, "You come here and take my place. He isn't to get up. Noone is mine and so is Trelavonti. I will handle both of them. Stan, get over here, too, you and John. You can all help. Don't let him up until he calms down!" Ellen's voice boomed throughout the room as she barked orders like an army sergeant with everyone jumping to.

Stan, so familiar with his son's temper, was there before Ellen finished speaking. He wasn't going to let Skip go off the deep end. He couldn't bear the thought of it; not after all Skip had been through, already. John, too, insured that Skip stayed seated.

Bernice rushed to help Angie for after she moved away from Skip she collapsed onto the floor in the middle of the room.

"I'll get those bastards!" Skip roared from his chair. "They'll pay for what they've done!" Every muscle he had bulged as he fought to free himself from his captors. Frustrated, he gave up his battle to his grief. Depleted, he broke down, weeping. Something he hadn't done since Ellen had disappeared. All of his fears confirmed, there was nothing more he could do.

Franco watched in disbelief. He heard Ellen's voice, saw how Angie acted when that strange voice came out of her mouth, yet he couldn't comprehend how someone else could speak out of her mouth, and it was someone else, of that he was sure.

Too, he tried not to be moved by Skip's grief, but failed. Damn, he loved some girl for thirty years and he hadn't seen her in all that time . . . or knew whether or not she was alive or dead!

Skip's sobs wrenched many hearts. The men tried to fight it off by holding Skip down, and saying things like, "get a grip, man" and "forget about that bastard, Noone. You can pay Trelavonti back when you get to the office." Most of them had the urge to beat the daylights out of Trelavonti themselves for thousands of different reasons, including Ellen and her baby.

Behind the fireplace Noone listened and watched in stunned silence. He saw her, Ellen. Heard every word she said. That was her! How can that be?

He got as close to the borehole as he could, trying to see more. Eckenridge was helped to the couch, but moved out of his limited line of sight. He knew that it was Eckenridge in the house, not Ellen. Ellen was dead! But everything she had done seated in the sheriff's lap, Noone remembered seeing Ellen do when she was alive. The girl was a flirt. And now she wanted revenge? How the hell can she take revenge if she's a spirit? He still wasn't convinced there was anything spiritual in the world to consider, let alone be afraid of.

Ellen didn't go through shit compared to what I've been through. She had nothing to complain about, so what if she's dead? Hell, that ain't the worst that can happen to a person, he thought; he knew that from first-hand experience. None of them knew what having it bad really meant.

"Now, Sonny, you quit belly aching about the past. If I told you once, I've told you a thousand times, we was doing it for your own good! You know that. You know I did nothing that you can say was abusive, so just shut your mouth, now!"

"Shut up, you old battleaxe! You abused all of us and you know it. How many mothers make their sons their lovers, huh? Ma?"

"You're just jealous cause I never went for you, and you know it!"

"Shut up!" Noone hissed at her as he tried to get away from her cloying, whining mouth. He wouldn't be bothered with that nasty old crow right now. He had too many other things to think about. He wondered if Eckenridge was using some sort of witchcraft or something to scare him. Well, she ain't scaring me! She might be able to see stuff, but so what? I'm able to do stuff!

He knew better than most what Eckenridge could accomplish; he read about her in the newspapers, about her crime solving exploits in detective magazines, devouring everything ever written about her and Henry. He loved the irony of her being there with him hidden behind the wall. Imagine, the country's best serial killer psychic detective right here in this house. I wonder if she'll connect me to Henry.

After a short time, he decided to leave this hiding space and creep back up to the attic. He had things to plan.

Chapter Twenty Four

It was a long trek, but Shorty made good time following the wolves. They actually allowed him close enough, so that he could have reached out and touched them if he wanted to. He didn't. That closeness was the only way he could make it through the blinding blizzard, too, for he could barely see. The wolves seemed to know the easiest routes. He could also walk much faster following their trail than if he had to break a trail of his own. He wouldn't have made it otherwise.

The wolves guided him to Sam's kitchen porch then disappeared into the background of the early winter evening. Already it was pitch black at 5 p.m. Sunday afternoon. As he knocked on the door, Shorty turned to take one last look at the animals. They were no where to be seen. He strained to peer through the falling and blowing snow, but to no avail.

"Is that the door?" Sam asked no one in particular.

Gladys went to the kitchen to check. She peered through the window to see Shorty on the other side of the curtained glass. Unsure about letting him in, she did anyway after considering all the lawmen seated in the dinning room. Shorty still had a lot of snow covering him. He swept most of it off in the porch after Gladys silently handed him a broom. He then followed her into the kitchen, and on into the dinning room.

Shorty stood on the threshold to the dinning room towering over Gladys, bringing the room to utter silence. Astonishment washed through Sam and her guests.

"I would never have believed it if I hadn't seen it with my own eyes, but those wolves, they led me here," Shorty said to the group as he stood there staring back at everyone feeling like a fool and so nervous sweat beaded on his forehead.

Shorty hadn't expected a warm welcome, hadn't considered what might happen when he showed up at Sam's, never would have dreamt to feel as he did that moment. Panic threatened to force him to run when he realized that he was stuck there whether anyone in the room wanted him to be there or not. The realization chilled him to the bone. If she throws me out, I've got no place to go, he thought. It's too cold out there to survive for long.

Sam got up, never taking her eyes off Shorty. She was livid at his audacity thinking: how dare he come into my house! She didn't want him there, was sure he was the one threatening her with the notes; she faced off with him. "What are you doing here?" She demanded remembering what Franco had told her about him.

Franco quietly moved into place next to the pair. He was well aware of the animosity between them and determined not to let it get out of hand.

Clem perked up at the interesting turn of events, and shook his head in disbelief as he looked up at Shorty. He too moved in closer. You didn't have to be a brain surgeon to know Shorty and Sam were enemies. Everyone on the Range had heard of their feud over the wolves.

Shorty stood facing Sam looking sheepish. While making his way there, he was so focused on finding Noone, he hadn't considered the fact that he might not be welcome, and was not prepared for it.

"I came here looking for Arthur Noone. Have you seen him?" He blurted out looking at Sam. He was captivated by her challenging manor, although he wasn't going to let her know that.

"How the hell would I have seen him?" Sam's hands perched on her hips as she got ready for a fight.

"I don't know where he is; he isn't home. I thought maybe he came over here." Shorty was so uncomfortable he wanted to rush back out to the porch and into the storm with the wolves, no matter what might happen to him.

"What do you mean, he's not home," Skip asked hanging on every word Shorty uttered.

Stan let the implications of what Shorty said sink in, too. Noone wasn't home. He wasn't there the night before, either, when Franco spent the night. There was a raging storm outside. Shorty came through a raging blizzard to Sam's because he thought Noone might be there. What was going on?

"I'm out looking for him." The defensive edge in Shorty's voice interested Skip.

"I followed some wolves over here. Stayed in one of Noone's dugouts for a few hours after leaving Trelavonti at Noone's place, earlier. We haven't heard from Noone since the day before yesterday. I was worried about him. He's an old man. I thought I'd try and find him."

"You followed wolves over here?" Sam said, incredulous. "Why would they go anywhere near you?" She still believed he was the one who trapped and killed them.

"Look, Lady, I don't trap wolves. Got that? I don't trap them! I trap beaver," Shorty said as if reading Sam's mind. "That's legal. Ask the sheriff." She pissed him off royally. He was so sick of the hoity-toity broad saying his traps were illegal; he'd heard it all over town! He loved wildlife every bit as much as she did, including wolves! He pointed a finger in Sam's face, bending down to look her in the eye, hissing, "I've been out in the woods longer than you ever have lady, yet you seem to think you know everything there is to know about the outdoors. Well, maybe you do have yourself a college education, but you ain't as smart as you think you are. So—get off my back, check your facts, and leave me the fuck alone, got it?!" He no longer cared if she threw him out of her house. He'd gladly go back to the dugout if need be. Anything was better than staying under the same roof with the idiot who thought he didn't know what he was doing.

"If you're so smart, Bucko," Sam's hands held firm to her hips as she stared Shorty down, so close the two were eyeball to eyeball. She prayed he'd make a move so she could flip him about the room, something she would dearly love to do, "Why are you hanging around that sick old bastard, Noone? What kind of trouble you two hatching?" She judged Shorty by the company he kept, and didn't give a damn.

"Trouble! The only trouble I've had around here is with you! You're the one pulling my traps! Why don't you just leave me the hell alone? And another thing, Noone's not some stupid bitch running around pulling legally set beaver traps. He knows the difference between a beaver and a wolf. I may not have a college degree, Lady, but I have more brains than you do!" Shorty hoped he was pissing her off but good, but he couldn't tell for sure; she was still in front of him with her hands on her hips and eyes flashing. His own were flashing daggers right back, as they glared at each other nose to nose.

Franco stood just to the left of them making sure neither of them made it a physical confrontation. He was leery about getting too close to Sam; he did not want to get man handled by her again; he'd never live it down. He didn't want to get in front of

Shorty, either. The man's reputation for fighting was legendary; the big trapper could toss him about like a feather. Franco's worries were short lived as much to his surprise, Sam backed off—first. Shorty seemed to finally be getting through to her.

"Correct me if I'm wrong," she said, "but I do know the difference between a beaver and a wolf trap. I have not once pulled a legally set trap, but I have pulled a number of steel jawed wolf traps and will continue to pull them as long as you, or whoever, is stupid enough to set them. Got it?"

"You're the one pulling our legally set traps! Everyone around here knows it. Who are you trying to kid!" Shorty was still furious and getting madder by the minute as Sam continued to deny pulling his beaver traps.

"And just how do you know that?"

"Some have seen you out there in the woods doing it! That's how."

"Saw me pulling beaver traps? Oh, I don't think so!"

"Prove it."

"I'll do just that. Hey, Angie, where are those security videos?"

"In the den. I'll get them."

"Now, we can all watch and learn." Sam turned her back to Shorty with a look of victory in her eyes.

He wanted to challenge her immediately, but if she had taped evidence, he wanted to see it. If she wasn't pulling his traps then who was? Maybe he would find that out. He still didn't believe anyone other than Samantha Egar had touched them, but he would watch . . . with a wary eye.

Angie returned with three videos and put one in the recorder as everyone else moved though the dinning room into the living room to watch television. The battle brewing between Sam and Shorty had them all sitting on the edge of their seats waiting to

find out who would be the victor. It was clear that they all
expected the videos to settle the fight once and for all.

Skip thought that the tapes, (something he knew nothing
about before then) ought to be real interesting, so he settled down
on the couch beside Sam to watch.

Gladys and Inez made room for Shorty and he sat next to
them on one of the two couches in the room. They had heard about
Shorty, how he abused the woman he lived with. They weren't too
keen on him for that. They knew what it was like to be beat by a
man. The elderly sisters had placed too many flowers on too many
graves not to know that a woman being abused had to get away
from it; the man doing the abusing had to get help. And if there
were a way to help a man stop his bad behavior, they would
support it.

Something about him, however, called them to him rather
than repelling them away. As Shorty sat next to them, he looked at
them and smiled slightly. The sisters smiled back in unison and
wondered what his story was.

No one paid any attention to the little mongrel dog that sat
in the dinning room growling up at the wall.

Shorty was too keen on seeing the tapes and looking for
answers to his trapping problems to fret long about his nervousness
at being in Samantha Egar's house. He made himself comfortable
on the couch next to the old ladies, and wondered if Egar had
rigged the cameras in any way. He raised an eyebrow in skeptic
anticipation. He looked out of place sitting next to Gladys and
Inez. He was so big, and so masculine, he looked uncomfortable
amid the frilly pillows and floral decorated throws that surrounded
him. His bulky frame took up at least half the couch; and his
weathered countenance gave him the appearance of wisdom in
spite of the anger that rolled in waves off his body. His presence
added a huge psychological force to the room. He was proud,

independent man who preferred the company of wildlife to human beings. He made almost everyone uncomfortable, all except Skip, Franco and John, who, in many ways, admired him.

Skip watched Shorty as discreetly as he could. This battle between Shorty and Sam had been brewing for a long time. He hoped the tapes would cool it off before it got any worse. He could tell that there was a communication gap between the two. It was almost as if they couldn't hear what the other was saying.

With the video in the VCR and everyone seated around the TV, Angie hit the play button and the TV screen filled with snow just before the video started. It was eerie.

The camera eye was fixed on a single spot in the deep forest on the edge of Sam's property line. The first tape they watched showed nothing other than a few birds as they pecked for seed near the camera lens.

"Let's try the number three camera, Angie. That's set up near some traps."

Angie pulled the first tape out of the recorder then inserted the number-three-camera tape. Again, nothing happened for a long time except for wildlife crossing the camera's path. Samantha was about to pull it, too, when a white tail deer came into view. "Wait!" Everyone yelled as they watched the deer sniffing around the traps and the camera.

When that tape played out, Sam said, "I've got a video here that should be interesting. I found a wolf trap near this camera a few weeks ago. I pulled the trap. I also saw other traps near it, all legally set. I didn't touch them." The number two-camera video went into VCR. Sam hit the play button.

"I think this is just a stall," Shorty said, convinced she was lying. He didn't feel like sitting through another boring video. As he spoke, the next tape came into focus showing Sam working to release a trap. She held it up clearly showing that what she had was an illegal steel jawed wolf trap, the kind trappers had stopped using some forty years before; she threw it up over a tree limb and walked out of sight of the camera. After a few minutes, another figure came into view from the left. Clearly a male, the figure crept through the underbrush looking as if he were trying to remain hidden. Sam had not yet seen the number two-camera video. She was as surprised as everyone else to see a figure skulking through the underbrush behind her. She let out a gasp as she watched the figure move slowly in her direction. No one could see the figure's face. After five minutes of creeping forward, the man finally stepped out of the brush and into the foreground.

It was Arthur Noone.

Shorty sat as far forward as he could in his seat on the couch when he saw Noone. Along with everyone else, he watched as Noone bent down and dropped one of his beaver traps underneath the trees, leaving it where Shorty would find it. "Damn," Shorty said. But the tape wasn't over. Noone moved off screen, apparently following Sam, as yet another figure crept up from behind them both. It was a wolf.

"Shit," Sam and Shorty said in unison; it was the big alpha male. The wolf sniffed around the area of the wolf trap looking up into the tree where Sam had tossed it; then looking off in the direction that Sam and Noone had gone. He too moved off screen. In a few moments, six other wolves traversed the trail behind their leader and in front of the camera. There, the tape ended.

Sam got up and pulled the tape from the VCR. "I had no idea he was out in the woods with me." She whispered, barely audible. "No wonder I've been getting so much static from the locals. Noone's making it look like I'm the one pulling those other traps. He's following me!" She thought about that. She shouldn't have been surprised. He always seemed to show up where she was.

"Jeez!" Shorty, too, was dumbfounded. "I swear I thought it was you. Noone said it was you! Damn! You know—it was the wolves that led me here. I mean led me—literally. They walked me here, helped me find my way through that blizzard out there." Shorty leaned back with his backside straddling the edge of the couch and his legs spread wide. Dressed in winter wool, his long underwear could be seen at the bottom of his pant leg, shirt cuffs, and through the v-neck of his shirt.

"You might as well make yourself comfortable, Shorty. You can't go back out in this weather, wolves or no." Sam said, again more to herself than out-loud. Her mind was on Noone.

"Didn't you say you thought Noone might be here, that's why you're here?"

"Yeah, I was at his house. He ain't there. I left Trelavonti there. Don't suppose Noone went back there, Trelavonti would have called me . . . I think?"

"Where are they now, the wolves I mean?" Sam asked. No one had an answer. They must have gone to Shorty when they left the farm this morning, she thought. "And where did they find you?" She turned her attentions back to Shorty.

"I lit out from Noone's place today after Trelavonti and I got out there, must have been around noon. Even so, it was pretty dark out with the clouds and all. He has a cell phone and usually calls me to let me know if he's going in the woods. Since he didn't call, I thought something might be wrong with him. The storm was so bad though, that I holed up in dugout that Noone set up in the woods. It's packed with supplies. He has a bunch of them out there. After I found that place, I planned on holing up in it until the storm let up, but the wolves, they got there and settled in around the camp. They made me nervous. Finally, I decided to get out of there and continue on. If they were going to attack me, I thought then let them. But they did no such thing. They helped me get here."

"Seems like a lot of things are helping all of us to 'get here,'" John said. "It's like an unseen force is determined that we find answers to some of the questions that have been hanging in the air over the area for the past forty years."

"He's right." Stan said nodding his head in affirmation. He was seated on the arm of the chair Angie sat in.

"Are you telling us," Gladys said, "that Trelavonti is in Noone's house?"

"That's where I left him. I haven't seen a trace of Noone anywhere. Course, I haven't checked all his dugouts, but I'm guessing he's here someplace. He comes over here a lot."

"What?" Sam asked, "He comes over here a lot? Wouldn't we have seen him?"

"Not necessarily. You saw him in that video. If he doesn't want to be seen, you aren't going to see him. He's lived out in these woods for eons. He can hide or hole up anywhere."

"Why were you so sure he was telling you the truth about me pulling your traps?"

"Well, Ma'am. You're new around here. I know him. He never lied to me before that I know of. I guess I trusted him more than you, you being a stranger."

"Snap judgments about strangers, not a good idea." Sam said.

"Yeah, you're right. Maybe we should both be more careful. Maybe not, but this is our land too you know, and you march in here acting like you can tell us what we can and can't do with it. You pissed us all off!"

"I'm sorry if I came across like that. I was upset over the wolf traps. You were upset because of the other traps. I guess we both jumped to conclusions." Hoping to change the subject, Sam asked, "Where do you think Noone might be now?"

Skip stood up anticipating the answer; Stan, Clem and Franco were all real interested in it, too.

Shorty stood up too, towering over them all, saying, "Anywhere, I guess."

"I think you know exactly where he is. Come on, tell us what you know," Skip said.

Shorty knew nothing of Ellen or how she had communicated to Skip through Angie. He didn't know Skip was determined to find Noone and find out what had happened to her.

Stan moved in to stand between the two, watching Skip closely, "Come on son. This guy knows nothing about what happened back then. I can tell."

"Yeah, like you can tell so much," Skip turned on Stan, some of his anger toward his father rushing out before he could cap it off. "Like you knew so much you could solve Ellen's murder; like you knew so much you put that Franco kid away for a murder he didn't commit; like you knew so much you were able to solve all those disappearances over the past fortyyears! You haven't been able to solve anything." As soon as he said it, Skip regretted it. The color washed from Stan's face looking to Skip as if he were about to cry.

Stan had no idea Skip harbored such intense anger at him. It hurt him, but it was a relief, too. He knew something had been broiling just beneath the surface between him and his son. He was glad it was finally out in the open, even if it did hurt. "Well . . . finally," Stan said resignation in his voice. "You've finally come out with it after all these years. Son, I haven't got all the answers for you, but as far as my police work, it's been impeccable. I was up against forces you've probably come up against since then. Noone being one of them, and he is one smart son of a bitch.

You'll find that out first hand, if you haven't already. Maybe, when you do, you'll understand." Stan stood there looking at Skip wondering how he could have been so blind not to know Skip loved Ellen so much.

"Look son, you know Shorty here has always been on the level with us. If he says he doesn't know where Noone is, he doesn't know." Stan managed to bring the conversation back to the topic at hand hoping Shorty would get the message and keep quiet even if he did know. Someone else needed to find Noone right now—not Skip, Stan thought. Skip was way too emotional to be rational.

Shorty's presence was commanding even as he faced off with the sheriff and the sheriff's father. He had a reputation with authorities as being dangerous. Even so, that reputation was tempered some if he respected his advisories. Police rarely had to quarrel with Shorty if Shorty knew he had done something wrong. He'd been arrested for domestic abuse, and an occasional barroom brawl. The barroom brawl always presented the biggest challenge to authorities. They found it hard to slap handcuffs on his enormous wrists, which seemed to get bigger if he'd been fighting. Too, Shorty enjoyed a good fight from time to time resenting anyone for interrupting what he thought of as an innocent good time, innocent for him; jaw breaking for his opponents.

And it was always the same. Strangers mistook Shorty's size as a sign of low intelligence, although Stan could never understand why. By the time they realized their mistake, it is usually too late and they found out the hard way they had tried to take advantage of the wrong man. Stan suspected that it was the duplicity of his would be detractors that set the big outdoorsman into a rage.

Regardless of his reputation for being a fighter, Shorty was also well known for being honest and straightforward in his dealings with others, something Stan came to respect over the years. Most of the sheriff's department deputies felt the same, except, of course, for Trelavonti.

I wouldn't want to be in Noone's shoes about now, Stan thought to himself remembering what he had seen on the video. If Shorty finds him, he's toast. If Skip finds him, the same could be said. Guess I'll have to keep the two of them out of trouble.

"Franco, man, you're about the last person I ever expected to see out here. You got something going?" Shorty asked the one person in the room who had never been hostile toward him. Franco said nothing, but glanced fleetingly at Sam telling Shorty everything he needed to know.

"You might just say I'm helping out," Franco said smiling; hoping to deflect Shorty's curiosity he continued, "Didn't I tell you not to trust that lousy old man?"

"Yeah, you did, man. Thanks—guess you were right." Shorty had the overwhelming desire for a drink. He turned to Sam and asked, "You got something to wet my whistle? Something with a little bite?" Shorty gulped the shot of brandy Sam brought him and let it warm his insides.

He turned to John. "Hey, John. How are you?"

"I'm good Shorty. How's Helen?"

"She's okay, I guess, least she was last time I saw her. What you doing out here in this storm?"

"We're here to help Samantha. A lot of stuff has been going on out here. We found a body buried in the basement just the other night," he added.

"A body? You found a body?" Shorty looked at Skip posing the question to him instead of John.

"A skeleton, to be exact," Skip replied. "It's been here a long time."

"Where did you find it?" Shorty asked, fascinated.

"In the basement. Walled up inside a narrow brick wall."

"Can you show me?"

"Sure, come on," Skip, Stan, John, Franco and Clem all went with Shorty downstairs where he looked intently at the wall's construction. He stepped inside the small room.

"Hey, don't do that!" Skip commanded.

Shorty ignored him. Once inside the tiny room that had held the professor captive, he rubbed his hands gently against the brick, much like Angie had done earlier just before they uncovered the skeleton. Shorty's big stature swallowed up the tiny cubicle.

"Give me a flashlight," he ordered.

John handed him a big one.

Shorty scrutinized every crevice in the wall. He paid special interest in the right side of the small cell. He shut the light off, and with his big, beefy hands, he caressed the top of the wall near the ceiling. There, he detected a loose brick. As he gently removed it, a brick door slowly creaked open across a threshold into the tiny cubicle. Shorty had to jump out of the room so the door could swing all the way out.

"Shhhhhhh!" Shorty placed his index finger to his mouth and motioned to the others to keep quiet. He peered inside the dimly lit hallway behind the door, seeing nothing but dust motes and a staircase. The others came forward one by one to gaze at the hidden stairwell, the one Clem had guessed earlier was inside the house. After everyone had viewed the dimly lit hallway and stairs, Shorty again motioned them to be quiet. He moved his hands back over the wall replacing the brick and marking it with a green felt pen he always kept in his pocket. If he marked the loose brick, it would be easier for them to find again later.

Shorty eased out of the cubicle. He wondered how sound proof the hidden stairwell was. Noone may well be in there somewhere, he thought as he climbed the stairs with the others back up to the kitchen. He couldn't wait to get his hands on him. Once they were safely upstairs with the basement door shut behind them, Shorty said, "I think I know where Noone is."

"I'll go," Inez said after they all determined they would investigate inside the hidden stairwell.

"No. This is no job for women," Skip said.

Inez gave him a dirty look. She said nothing.

"Rather than send anyone in, I think it would be better if we waited him out. No one knows what he's capable of," Shorty said. He thought of Noone following Samantha silently through the woods. He remembered all the times Noone baited him about her, probed his mind about his feelings for her. He remembered what Noone said about her needing a man, what it would be like. He realized what Noone had hoped he would do. "No," he said again, "you women can not go into that tunnel. We can't risk it," he looked to Skip and Stan for support.

"Shorty's right," Franco said immediately. "Nobody knows for sure what Noone is capable of."

Shorty was happy to get Franco's support. Skip and Stan nodded their heads in agreement.

Inez relented remembering Gladys' run in with Noone.

"He's mine." Ellen's voice poured out of Angie's mouth as Angie stood quietly behind everyone. All eyes turned to her. Angie's face had changed once again taking on a youthful glow as Ellen's eyes shone brightly back at them.

"Hey?" Bernice said as Angie grabbed her hand and clutched it tightly.

"Shhhhhh," Inez said as she placed her arm around Bernice's shoulders. "She wants' to tell us . . . you . . . something."

"Don't let him near the children," Ellen's voice warned. "He wants them." Angie held onto Bernice with one hand and pointed at John with the other.

The couple exchanged looks realizing that she was talking about their kids. Their kids were in danger from Noone, but as long as Noone was in Sam's house, (Bernice now desperately hoped he was) and they were at home, the kids were safe, she reasoned. She was relieved that the children didn't get the chance they had been promised to be there to help. Never before had a broken promise brought her so much joy and relief.

But Ellen wasn't finished; "He will hurt them just like he's done the others. Someone was in his house. That person has found scores of bodies, mostly kids; he's digging there now!"

"Trelavonti?" Shorty questioned out loud.

"Yes, that's him, the man with the uniform, badge, the one that raped me, killed me. He's Noone's friend, but he's turned Noone in, already called authorities on the bodies. He doesn't want to be implicated. I see him there, he's digging; help will be slow in coming. The weather is bad. And no one likes or trusts the digging man."

"The other one is here! He's waiting. I feel him. He's going to try something—tonight! Something that he thinks will destroy everyone! I see fire! He's playing with fire!" She continued, saying there were other forces there, too, forces that were going to handle him. But she wouldn't say how, just that they had to trust her; she'd protect them. She sounded like a young girl trying hard to get adults to listen to her. She spat words out as if making sure they were said before she could change her mind about saying them; then her eyelids fluttered and she slid to the floor.

They ignored Angie on the floor, and formed a plan to stop Noone; they would not depend on some spirit force they weren't sure, in spite of everything, existed to protect them. It was too much.

It was only 6 p.m. but all of the lights were on inside the house. Because of the cold weather the furnace worked harder than usual, a common occurrence for Minnesota residents in the middle of a severely cold winter.

As the group gathered in the living room, Skip was filled with memories of Ellen, how they had been together, but it wasn't long before he was forced to think about the here and now. What was it that Ellen and Inez had told them? Fire, how could Noone use fire against them? It didn't take him long to realize that the easiest way to get rid of all of them in one fell swoop would be to set the house on fire. He gasped at the realization, and Franco, who stood next to him, picked up on his thoughts.

"We better go check out the furnace—now!" Franco hissed to Skip as quietly as he could hoping to convey the urgency he felt, and at the same time not alarm the others.

Skip motioned to Stan, John, Shorty and Clem and the men followed him and Franco back downstairs, not because they knew what was going on, but because they wanted to be doing something. The furnace was running smoothly, looked like it was brand new and the men found no evidence of tampering. They breathed a collective sigh of relief.

"Maybe someone should stand guard?" Franco muttered not expecting anyone to hear him thinking out-loud.

"I'll take the first watch," John offered determined to do something. There was no way he was going to let Noone anywhere near his children. Maybe, if he kept watch, Noone would come to him. If he got the chance, he would stop him; he could do it. He had worked hard all his life. He was quick, agile and strong not to mention thirty years younger than Noone. Farming was good to the body, worked every muscle. He didn't know what Noone had done to other kids, but he wasn't about to let anything happen to his own. Ellen's warning was not lost on him, or Bernice.

When they went back upstairs to the living room, Skip pulled Bernice aside and told her where John was and what he was doing. She slipped downstairs herself to sit with him. She didn't like the idea of her husband being alone with Noone somewhere inside the house. Besides, she hoped for a chance to bop Noone over the head with a piece of wood herself. She had never been angrier. As the two sat together, they prayed, "Yeah, though I walk through the valley of the shadow of death, I will fear no evil for the Lord is with me."

Inez and Angie sat on the couch holding hands.

Gladys sat across from them in Sam's rocking chair staring intently at her sister and rocking back and forth. "It's time the truth came out, Inez, and I'm the one that's going to tell it! You men sit down. I have something to say."Everyone sat.

"Inez here has been hiding a little known fact from you all. She is, was and always will be just as psychic as Sam's friend here, Angie" Gladys threw her finger up pointing at Angie. "I don't know why she never tells anyone about it, I guess it's because when we grew up things were different. Maybe that's why she tries to hide it, her being psychic, I mean, but she has kept the two of us safe for a lot of years because of it.

It started just after daddy beat her bad once when she was resisting his advances. He hit her in the head. Every since that day, he never managed to get his hands on us. Inez here knew exactly what he was up to at all times. It pissed the old man off, let me tell you, but he could never touch us again. We were sixteen then."

Gladys knew that everyone in the room was familiar with their background. Stan learned about it through his police work. Skip learned about it through old files. The women assumed from hearing gossip that most everyone in the county knew.

"She's been keeping us safe all these years. Now she's trying to protect that kid, Ellen. I can tell because Inez here would empathize with someone like her, being pregnant, alone, being raped and trapped in a horrible family situation."

Gladys stared at Angie and Sam who stood behind Inez. "And you two need to know that she has something REAL important to tell you both." Gladys looked quietly at Inez impatiently taping her foot on the floor.

"Now you go on, honey. You got nothing to be afraid of here. No one is going to mock you." Gladys looked at everybody daring someone to challenge her. "Come on, honey. No one is going to hurt you," she cajoled.

After what seemed like an eternity to Gladys, Inez spoke, "I've been dreaming about the two of you," she turned her head to both sides looking at Angie and Sam, motioning them to come, sit beside her, patting the cushion of the sofa. Inez held Angie's arm then took Sam's, too after she sat down. As she spoke, she continuously patted their hands.

"You two are more deeply connected than you know if my dreams are correct," she said gauging their reactions then proceeding slowly. After a short pause, she said, "I think you two are the twins. The professor and Janice's daughters, I mean, the little girls that were left at the orphanage in Minneapolis."

The room went deathly quiet.

"What are you talking about," Sam said flabbergasted that Inez would think such a thing. "We don't even resemble each other! Look at us! How on earth could we even be related? Sisters! Let alone twins?" Even though she couldn't believe it, she liked the idea of Angie as a sister. She held her breath waiting for Inez to continue, as did Angie.

"Fraternal dear, fraternal twins. They don't necessarily look alike. Gladys and I have been going through a lot of those photos, looking at the old records. You two bare a striking resemblance to both the professor and Janice, one to the mother, the other to the father. Even your lives are running parallel paths to your parents. Look at you Sam, you're doing the same work your father did as a hobby. And Angie, she's as psychic as your mother was, and Janice was very much the psychic; her diaries verify that fact.

Now boys, that's what you get for leaving two old ladies out of all the action. They'll find some of their own." Inez didn't let anyone interrupt her before she continued, "then there's the dreams. I've been dreaming of the two of you, seeing you in the same womb; watching as you both were born. I think the professor is trying to reach me, so you will know.

For instance: I know, Angie," she turned to face her, "that you can't psychically read anything if you're too close to it, that, I think, is why nothing is coming to you on this. But it's coming to me, loud and clear. And you, Sam, you have been guided here by your father; the one you are most alike. He wants you two to know who you are in relation to one-another. He wants you two to know you are family, and that your parents never deserted either of you. Even the way your lives have turned out has been orchestrated so that you would end up here, together."

"That's the Lord's doing, he said so in my dreams." Inez heard Bernice speaking in her head and thought she was in the room. Inez spoke to Bernice in response to what she heard.

"Bernice, I know you and John are scarred for those kids of yours, and something is going on over there, I know that too; but they'll be okay. You've taught them well. They have powerful spiritual energy protecting them. I see that too, so try not to worry too much."

Bernice and John didn't hear a word. They sat downstairs talking quietly in front of the furnace.

.

Chapter Twenty Five

Two and a half miles away, Vicki and Mike watched as the pack of wolves returned and deposited themselves at their front door. Worried, Mike said, "First, there was one wolf, now how many are out there? Seven! What do they want?"

It was early evening when the wolves paced up the driveway. Mike had been staring out the window, watching, he didn't know for what, so he saw them first as they trotted up, the big alpha male in the lead.

He recognized the wolf that had watched over them the night before; he was at the rear of the pack. He, too, was big, almost as big as the alpha male. They fascinated Mike. What were they doing there? As the storm raged on it was hard to see clearly as the wolves padded up to their position under the kitchen window, settling down just outside the patio doors.

Vicki shook her head. She didn't know what the wolves wanted, but she had the feeling they were all safe from the predators. She wasn't afraid. She did wish her parents home and not because of the wolves, but because she missed them. She always felt safe when they were around. She stood at the window wishing the storm and the night would end. Already she was tired. Last night seemed like it happened years ago.

Mike walked through the house checking locks, even on all the windows. He prayed that his fear would leave him, not let him cower away from trouble if it arose.

The younger children were filled with pent-up energy. They were bored, restless, and cranky, so they whined and whimpered complaining about not having anything to do. As Mike stood there watching the wolves, the younger children came to the window and saw the animals circle a spot, then lie down.

"Oh Mike," they cried, "look at the dogs! I want to go pet them!" The girls said running for their coats and boots with their youngest brother in tow.

"No!" Mike yelled.

The three children paused, looked at him, terrified by the anger they heard in his voice. "Those aren't dogs!" Mike yelled. "Those are wolves, wild animals! They kill things! You can't just walk up to them to pet them!"

Jasmine and Josephine started crying, as did Jeremy. Mike realized he had scared them, went over, and hugged all three. "It's okay," he said. "They can't hurt you if you're in the house. But you can't go outdoors with them in the yard. I don't know what they might do. It's too dangerous."

The twins stopped crying then, happy just to be hugged by their big brother. Jeremy wanted to show that he, too, was brave, so he threw back his shoulders and put his arms around his sisters' shoulders, as far as he could reach, in an effort to show Mike that he would help protect the family. Mike smiled, but Jasmine turned her nose up, slapped Jeremy's hand from her shoulder as if it were a stinky rag, turned and walked over to Vicki.

"I can take care of myself, thank you very much," she said as she walked away. Not to be undone, Josephine was right behind her with her nose high in the air.

Immediately bored with acting like a grown-up, Jeremy ran to catch up with his sisters and the three youngsters dropped to their knees on the thick rag rug in front of the patio doors to watch the wolves. The animals didn't stir after arriving and were being slowly covered with snow. The alpha female did lift her head to look in the window at the three faces peering back at her. She stared at them for a time before nestling her head back into her belly fur.

When boredom overcame the children once again, Vicki started a guessing game to see which wolf would be covered with snow first. The younger children found the game great fun as they argued over which animal would win. Vicki left them to it.

Mike was wondering why, at different times during the day, he had heard the cattle bellowing down in the feedlot. They shouldn't have been. Everything had been set up to take care of their feed and water needs, so he wouldn't have to go down to the barn. Now, though, he had this gnawing gut feeling that something was very wrong down there. He vacillated between going out in the storm with the wolves to see if something was wrong, or staying inside the house where it was safe and warm.

Something has to be wrong for the cows to bellow that way, he reasoned. Maybe the heating element in the water tank quit working and their water is frozen over. Finally, he decided that he had no choice. He had to go outside even if a pack of wolves sat at his front door; he had to check on the cows. They could starve or die of thirst if he didn't. He decided to take a gun.

"You have got to be kidding," Vicki yelled as she watched Mike put on his winter gear. He tried to tell her what he had to do. "You can't go out there!"

"Don't you hear them bawling? Something's going on down there! I have to check it out. Look, I'll take the gun. You watch here from the house. If any of the wolves move, like to come up behind me to attack me, you shot them. Watch my back, sort of."

"I don't like this."

"Neither do I, but I don't see as I have a choice. We told dad we could take care of the place. What are we going to do, let a bunch of wolves stop us? I don't think so."

"I guess you're right, but I still don't like it. I'm scarred."

Vicki and Mike stood in front of the kitchen door away from the children to keep from frightening them again. They didn't want the kids to know Mike was headed outdoors, either. They would start whining to go out with him, and they couldn't.

"Look, when you go out that door, look back at the patio. I'll be there watching the wolves. I don't think they're here to hurt us, but still, I'll keep a gun at hand. You take that lantern and I'll be able to see you through the blowing snow. If any wolf moves, I'll fire a shot in the air so you'll know it's up and about. You can shoot it if it tries to attack you."

"Yeah, that's a good plan. I don't want to shoot it either, but if I have to, I will. And if I find something in the barn, I'll fire a shot. I'm not sure what you should do, but hopefully nothing is wrong. I guess you better call 9-1-1 if I do fire a shot. Don't come down to the barn though, no matter what; do you understand?" Vicki nodded her head.

Mike headed out the door. Vicki grabbed her pistol off the top of the buffet and ran to the window. Josephine demanded to know what was going on, as Jasmine and Jeremy listened intently. "Be quiet!" Vicki whispered never taking her eye off the wolves. The youngsters continued to protest as Vicki opened the patio doors a crack and cold air rushed in. The kids scrambled back hiding behind the kitchen table. Good, Vicki thought.

John had rigged a guide rope from the house to the barn much like the one Sam rigged from her house to her barn. The rope

insured that when he or one of the kids went to the barn in a
blizzard, they could make their way back up to the house safely.
He spent countless hours schooling the children about the
importance of using a guide rope in the winter from the time that
they were tots.

Mike was thankful it was there. He remembered his
father's lectures on Minnesota winters as soon as he stepped onto
the back porch, so he clung to the rope with one hand, and inched
his way down to the barn. He held the rope in the same hand as he
held the lantern, keeping his gun hand free. He figured if an animal
attacked, he'd drop the lantern then fire.

The snow was deep. Even with his strong fifteen-year-old
legs, Mike struggled to get through the drifts. With each step, his
uneasiness grew. If any of the wolves wanted to attack him, he was
in no position to fight them off. One, maybe . . . but eight? He
didn't look back. If they were coming, Vicki would warn him;
besides, it was hard enough to see to get to the barn.

Halfway there, he heard a shot and turned around, his
heart pounding in his chest. He saw Vicki in the window, the
kitchen light burning warmly behind her, and wished he were there
with her. As the wind driven snow lashed his face, Mike also saw a
black figure creep over the snowdrifts toward him. One, it was just
one of the wolves. He had a chance. But the animal was acting
oddly. It kept its distance behind him.

Mike's mittens became entangled in the lantern handle
and rope, but he managed to stumble down closer to the barn
getting almost to the door. Before he could reach it, however, the
wolf jumped ahead of him starting up the hill at Mike baring its
teeth as it came. His open mouth revealed huge canine teeth
flashing danger in the lamplight.

Mike still heard the cows bellowing behind the barn, and
knew he had to get to them. He was so close to the barn he didn't

think he could make it back to the house before the wolf attacked. It dawned on him then that maybe the cows smelled the wolves. Maybe that was why they were bellowing. He wished he had thought of it sooner.

Now, outside in a ragging blizzard, he had a wolf snarling at him and stopping him from what he though was his only means to safety, getting into the barn. The way he saw it he now had only one recourse; he took a tentative step backward. The wolf stopped. Mike took another step back, the wolf took a step toward him, and as Mike inched his way back to the house, the wolf silently inched with him baring his fangs, pushing him back every time Mike stopped.

Mike had already broken a path alongside the lead rope, so going back was easier, and he reached the house quickly. The gun wouldn't do him much good because his mitten-covered hands were too clumsy to operate it.

With every step backward, Mike kept his eye trained on the wolf. As he climbed the concrete stairs to the back door, the wolf halted. Mike couldn't turn the doorknob; his hands were so full.

Vicki saw everything from the kitchen window and was at the door opening it for Mike as soon as he reached it. The wolf made no attempt to lunge as Mike stepped quickly into the house. It retreated back to the pack. Mike swallowed hard as he leaned against the closed kitchen door looking at Vicki. "Did you see that?" she said.

Mike smiled; he understood her excitement. Of course he saw it; he was the main attraction! Both of them were pretty happy not to have had to shot the animal, and Mike was extremely happy he hadn't been attacked. "I never thought of this before I went outside, but the cows probably smell the wolves. That's why they've been bellowing. Jeez, that was stupid! Me going out there,

I mean!" Mike was harder on himself than Vicki felt like being. "Did you see it from the house? The wolf wouldn't let me go into the barn! Did you see that?"

"Yes. Why? I mean, why would a wild animal stop you from getting into the barn? What's down there besides the cows, and aren't most of them outside anyway? I don't think the wolves have been bothering them; do you?"

"No," Mike said as he pulled off his boots and hung up his coat. "Maybe they're protecting us from something. Samantha is in the woods with them all the time. They don't bother her. Maybe it's nothing, or, who knows, maybe Steamroller has gone off his rocker down there. Maybe the wolf was just warning me to get inside because of the blizzard? I don't know! But I'll tell you this, Vicki. I'm not as scared as I was. I think we have some protection. That's why I think they're here."

Over at Noone's, Trelavonti was agitated. He wanted to get out of Noone's house. The basement was gross even for him. In his agitation, he ran to the window repeatedly hoping to see car lights coming up the road. He hated this storm. All the snow, the drifts, it'd be damn near impossible for the other deputies to get out there, he knew and cursed it. With all those bodies in the basement, he was uneasy and didn't want to be alone.

It wasn't like he'd never seen a dead body before, either. He had, more times than most, but this was different. He and Noone had done some pretty funky things together, stuff most people were too repressed to ever try, but now, if anyone associated him with Noone, they were going to associate him with what was downstairs, and he had nothing whatsoever to do with that!

In one split second, Noone had become an albatross around his neck. He wished he had known what the old man was really like before hooking up with him. I've never killed anybody! Never! He conveniently forgot his role in Ellen's death.

Things he'd done to insure innocent people went to prison for things Noone had done popped into his head bringing to mind Earl Franco. The little girl—did Noone kill that kid, too? He wondered. He remembered Noone repeatedly suggesting Earl Franco was the culprit. He remembered, too, that Noone knew he didn't like the Francos, especially the son-of-a-bitch Anthony; he had thought that if he could get rid of at least one of them, he'd be doing society a favor.

As he paced the floor in yet another flight to the window to watch for car lights, Trelavonti started to wonder about divine retribution. Was there such a thing? He went to church every Sunday. He knew what the preacher said about it. He brushed the thought aside. He didn't want to think about spirits when he was alone in a house that was bound to be full of them. Unhappy ones at that! Besides, God is just a crutch for the weak, the poor and wretched who can't do anything for themselves, those are the ones clinging to God Almighty. Nobody in church really believes in God's retribution and I know that most don't really believe there is a God anyway, he thought.

He peered out the windows yet again, shading the glass so that the light from the lamps didn't throw their reflection back in his eyes. He wanted to see car lights, was trying to will them into view; he didn't have time to waste on false images. He just wanted someone from the sheriff's department to show up so he could get out of the morgue he was trapped in.

It was during one of his window watching vigils that he first saw the lights in the distance. The blowing snow obliterated them periodically, forcing him to stare harder into the storm, but he was sure he saw house lights as he stared out into the blizzard. He remembered the house they had passed on River Drive just before taking the exit up Noone's access road.

Jennings, yeah, John Jennings owns that place. He knew who John Jennings was, a farmer with a wife and five kids. Ordinary, the Jennings are ordinary people, he recalled. Ordinary was just what he wanted right then. Ordinary was perfect.

He was so tired of being cooped up in Noone's house with all the dead bodies, Trelavonti considered going out into the blizzard wondering if he could make it up the road to the Jennings' house. It was not that far, surely. Besides, he needed to talk to someone.

"Them Jennings are pretty straight people, so maybe they would let me stay there awhile," he said out loud to the empty house. "I'll have to tell them a bit about what I found over here, but that'll be okay. They're farmers so they're pretty simple. Not like they'd go out and tell anyone else, not in this storm anyway. I'll just give 'em the bare essentials, something we'd tell reporters at this stage of an investigation—get them intrigued enough to invite me to stay longer. Yeah, that'd work!" The idea of talking to someone was more than Trelavonti could resist.

He donned his winter clothing and headed out into the storm. He was not crazy about going outside, the snow being so deep, but his only alternative was to stay inside until back-up arrived. Something he couldn't stand the thought of anymore.

He tried calling the sheriff's office once again before going out, but to no avail. He suspected Harriet knew who was calling and ignored him. She had caller id on her phone so she could check on any incoming anonymous calls. She knew Noone's number, too. He gave it to her and told her where he was. "Damn her," he said to the blowing wind as he walked out onto the porch and into the driving snow of Noone's driveway.

The storm took his attention away from Harriet and turned it back to Noone.

"How could he have done that?" he mumbled as he walked. Trelavonti wished he had been wiser about pairing up with Noone. He got angry with himself all over again, not because of what Noone had done, but because of how those actions were going to reflect on him. He hunkered down, bent against the wind and struggled forward.

He knew why he and Noone had become cronies. It started with Ellen, but how many more had there been since her?

I couldn't help it, they were so young, so luscious, they knew I wanted them and still they teased me beyond endurance. Hell, any man would do what I did if they had the chance. Can't tell me they wouldn't lust after the young stuff, especially if they'd been married a long time! Its them girls' own fault, too, wearing those short skirts and little shirts, flaunting their boobs in my face. What am I supposed to do? Hell, I'm just a red-blooded, all-American male! They should have stopped me!

Trelavonti hated the idea that he did not know Noone as he supposed he had. I was not aware of any killing. He doesn't seem like no killer. Course, if I had thought about it, fit those missing kid's reports together with some of the things Noone has said over the years, maybe I should have guessed. We were too close . . . I just didn't see it. I took it for granted that he was like me, hell; Noone liked girls!

There was Ellen, he remembered, but those boys—many of the bodies he dug up were boys. What went on with them? How did he kill them? Why? I can understand why he'd want too oft a broad, I mean they're all broads, no matter how old they are . . . but boys? Man what's his problem?

Trelavonti didn't count the female remains as he dug them up. He threw them into a pile in the corner of the basement and never marked their gravesites. He took each male skeleton and placed it neatly in front of its respective grave site so investigators would have no problems making determinations about the manner of death and so on. It didn't occur to him that they would want to do the same for the females. He assumed they would feel as he did, that they would think as he did.

As the wind howled around him, Trelavonti struggled through the blowing snow to the Jennings farm. Each step through mounting snow banks exhausted him. Temperatures slipped down to thirty below zero, while winds gusted up to 40 mph. It was seventy below with the wind chill factor. He stumbled along.

Drifts were up to his thighs in places. He had to crawl over the crusted snow to move forward at times. In other spots, to his relief, the wind had nearly cleared the roadway making the going easy, but relief was spotty at best.

Finally, he reached River Drive. There he stood for a moment with his back to the wind trying to catch his breath. He was almost sixty years of age, overweight and smoked, the cold and wind were having an affect on his exposed face; his feet and hands grew icy cold regardless of their coverings.

He could still see the lights, though, so he pushed forward. River Drive was much as the access road had been, clear in some spots, very high drifts in others. Trelavonti's eyes grew accustomed to the darkness, but winds slapped snow against his face with gale force. He could barely keep his eyes open trying to protect them from the stinging snow that flung itself at him. Tears stung his face and froze there. He hoped, as he walked, that he hadn't wandered off the road and into a ditch. It was too hard to tell for sure.

After only a few steps, he rested again but not for long. It was hard to breathe now as the cold air seeped into his lungs. Still, he stumbled up the road heading for the Jennings' driveway. He put one foot in front of the other as he climbed and crawled through and over more drifts.

At times, he lay prostrate across a snowdrift catching his breath and thinking how nice it would be to just fall asleep. His life style habits all worked against him hindering his efforts to get to the house whose lights so enticed him.

Still, he was glad to be out of Noone's house. "Damn, that place smelled awful," he said to the storm as he half crawled, half walked up the road. He was winded. Again, he stopped to rest.

As the wind howled about him, Trelavonti heard nothing else. Besides, his head was covered with a fur-lined cap with the earflaps pulled tightly over his ears. Blowing snow continued to beat against his uncovered face. And once again, the lights of the Jennings' household spurred him on. And once again after only a few steps, he had to stop and rest.

When he finally reached the end of Jennings' driveway, he was so relieved he didn't see the figure there with him. He had been out in the storm two hours by then; it had taken him that long to get through the drifts.

He was winded; his heart raced in his chest. It thundered in his pounding ears. He hoped he wasn't having a heart attack as he cursed his luck. He saw the figure then and thought he was hallucinating. It was there to his side one moment, in front of him the next.

Funny, he thought, it looks like its floating. Trelavonti stood at the end of the driveway for some time watching the floating figure. Looking long and hard at the driveway, he saw that the quarter-mile up to the house was through more snowdrifts higher than those he had already crossed over.

As his heart raced in his chest, he wondered once again if he could make it. And who the hell is that next to me! Damn!

The figure beckoned with its finger at Trelavonti as if to entice him to follow it up the driveway, smiling and floating over the snow. Trelavonti liked the look of the figure, whatever the hell it was, so he followed it.

Trelavonti was close to freezing to death at that point. He didn't care. He was no longer thinking clearly, and wasn't feeling the cold, either. He was warm and just wanted to lie down in the snow; it looked so fluffy and comfortable. He was tired. He no longer felt the tingling pain that raged through his nose earlier, which was a relief. His face was his only exposed flesh, yet his legs and hands were cold, too. He thought he put on enough clothes to keep from freezing when he donned long underwear, two pairs of wool pants, fur lined mittens, and wool socks.

If he could only walk faster, he'd be okay; so he tried to follow the figure up the driveway, but lost his effort to keep up with it. I will get through this storm, he thought. He had gone too far to turn back now, besides, he couldn't, no, he wouldn't, go back into that morgue by himself!

He started to sway in the wind. The free-floating figure moved in closer still enticing Trelavonti to follow it with its finger, encouraging him on, smiling at him. Trelavonti stared hard trying to understand what the figure was, but the snow blasted his face so hard he had to squeeze his eyes almost shut. He was no longer thinking clearly and just wanted to get out of the cold. If his eyes started to water again, his eyelids would freeze shut, still, he thought he needed to look, to see who it was out there in the storm with him. "Maybe someone has come to help me!" A warm ray of hope raced through him. "Help, that's what I need."

As if on cue to his thoughts, the form moved in closer until it was eye to eye with Trelavonti. "Joseph," Trelavonti said, "I thought you were dead! You've come to help me through this? Thank you! I am so tired."

The form took Trelavonti's elbow guiding him over the snow. Trelavonti no longer had to lift his legs to get through the snowdrifts. He was warm, too.

"Thank heaven," he said as he and Joseph made their way into the Jennings' barn. Inside and out of the cold, Trelavonti sank into some sweet smelling loose hay and passed out. As he did, the shadowy form disappeared.

When Trelavonti came too, he found that the shadowy figure was real, not just in his imagination. It left behind it a steaming mug of hot coffee. He savored the brew with shaking hands. He felt the cold now all the way to his bones. He wasn't quite sure where he was; his thinking, a bit foggy; he couldn't remember what day it was.

Funny, he thought as he looked around, how can all these people be in this barn with me? So many smiling faces, he thought as his face and limbs warmed, feeling like thousands of needles piercing his flesh.

"I'm a cop," Trelavonti said to the group, taking on an air of authority in spite of his vulnerable position. "I'm sure glad someone else is out here besides me. No one should be out in this weather."

"You got that right." One voice said.

"Did you drive out here, man?" Trelavonti asked.

"No. I came out years ago," the voice answered.

Trelavonti was suddenly uneasy. "So, you've been out here for years?" He said, wondering why there were so many people in the barn. He didn't understand.

"Yes, years. Tonight I saw the lights and thought I'd stop by. You know, it can get a little crazy when you're alone in a storm with no one to talk to," the voice said in ultra soothing tones.

"Tell me about it. At least here I've got some hot coffee. The barn is nice and warm too."

"So you know this fellow Noone, do you? Did you know Joseph? He was a fine man, at least until he died."

"What do you mean, died? He brought me here, got me out of this storm." Trelavonti said, coughing and feeling an unfamiliar pounding in his chest. It was so loud he wondered if anyone else could hear it.

"I'm old. I can't go traipsing around in storms like I did when I was younger," the voice said changing the subject.

"Whose place is this?" Trelavonti asked.

"I think it's that farmer. They keep a nice place, I'll give 'em that." Another voice said.

"They are way to Christian for my tastes—and those kids? Inside the house right now they're praying like crazy. They think something bad is out here in the barn, like a bogeyman, I suppose. Can you believe that? I mean really . . . bad? What's bad about us?" The group smiled at Trelavonti.

He shivered and picked up the coffee mug to take a long draw of the hot liquid as he looked out over the top of it at the group. He felt like he'd regained his senses some, but when he saw the figures grinning at him, he had his doubts. They looked funny, kind-a transparent, creepy. He set the mug down on an old wooden crate next to him, and remained seated in the midst of the sweet smelling hay, which blocked the wind from coming through cracks in the barn walls. There weren't many of those though; the place was well built and cozy. He was glad no cows were inside. He hated the smell of cow shit, hated the thought of stepping in it. Right now, the place smelled sweet and clean, just the way he liked it.

"Where you all from?" he asked no one in particular. There were an awful lot of young people there. What were their folks thinking, letting kids stay out in weather like this? He wondered as he looked closely at each individual.

"It's pretty cold. The wind is horrible. We barely made it over here." One of the youths told him.

"What do you mean, you idiot?" Another one said angrily. "Hell, we had no trouble at all getting over here."

"Shut up, you fool! He's not ready for that yet." Another young male said.

Trelavonti wondered what they meant. He didn't understand.

"Hey man, did you know this place used to belong to Joseph? Well, it did, and did you notice those wolves up there by the house? You came right past them. They won't let us get by them. They know we're here. They've been sniffing at the door. I want to go up to that house and introduce myself to those kids. That would be real nice. You know, get inside their heads, that kind of thing. It'd be nice and warm up at the house, I bet."

"Damn, but I miss being warm. I'm never warm anymore!" Another voice said.

Trelavonti trembled. Still, he said, "No, I didn't see any wolves. Where are they?"

"Right up there by the house. Now really, you couldn't have missed them." A young woman said as she approached Trelavonti. She was pretty and seemed somewhat familiar.

Trelavonti noticed what he always noticed about young girls, her breasts, which were huge. She had legs that went on for days. His interest grew more with each step she took.

She sauntered over close to him, undoing the buttons of her shirt as she walked exposing herself to him. All the others watched what she did without saying a word. A few tittered.

Trelavonti wasn't going to stop her. Hell, anything she wanted to do, he was game for it. After being out in the cold, he could use a good warm roll in the hay to warm himself. He smiled as she drew closer. Now her breasts were completely exposed. Trelavonti could feel the heat rise inside of him.

"Don't you remember me?" She asked sweetly.

"No, Dearie, I don't, but I think I would if I ever met you." He grabbed her arm and pulled her against him. He felt her warm flesh next to his cold skin and started to sweat with anticipation. He pushed her back for a moment so he could stare at her breasts, which were firm with rock hard nipples and cold dimples that speckled her ivory colored skin. He boldly rubbed his hands over them.

She didn't flinch, but said sweetly, "Not so fast, Sugar. Take your time." She turned her body away slightly; just enough, so that he couldn't caress her. He no longer considered that other people were in the room. He knew what she wanted; he wanted it too and pulled her close to him again, forcibly, nuzzling her breasts.

"My name is Ellen," she said, as his tongue tasted her flesh.

He didn't hear her; he didn't give a damn what her name was; he was too excited.

Back at the sheriff's department, dispatch was being flooded with calls about the weather, but that wasn't what was worrying Harriet Hornblower. It was Trelavonti. She tried to call the sheriff and tell him something was going on out there, but she couldn't reach him. Nobody was answering their phones!

The storm wasn't letting up, either; deputies were in and out of the office trying to help stranded motorists. The deputies she sent out to Noone's house couldn't make it even in their four-wheel drive pick-ups because of all the snow. According to the National Weather Service, it wasn't going to get much better and someone should have been at Noone's hours ago.

All else considered she knew she had to call for help. Harriet dialed the number to the highway department. She didn't trust Trelavonti with whatever was going on. Trelavonti was such a boob he'd probably screw up the crime scene.

When she finally reached the highway department head she called in a few favors, and he agreed to send a convoy of plows to clear the road out to Noone's farm. On their way, they would pull the sheriff's department pick-ups free, so the deputies could follow them out to Noone's in the plow's wake. Still, the highway department head told her, even the plows were having trouble getting through the roads. No one was going to get there quickly. That was okay, Harriet thought, as long as they got there. While she was at it, she asked to have the plows sent out to Samantha Egar's. She had this feeling that maybe the sheriff was in trouble.

"We'll try, Miss Hornblower, but I can't guarantee anything, not unless it's a dire emergency. Is that what you're saying is going on out there?"

"No, I guess I can't say that yet," she mumbled wondering if she should lie to the man deciding against it in a split second.

"Well, don't worry none about it. If we can make it over there, we will, but don't bet on it. Course, you can always call me back if you find there is an emergency out there. Ya' hear?"

County plows and sheriff deputies descended on the Noone property by 11 p.m.

Inside the Jennings' house, Vicki kept vigil at the kitchen window, so she was the first to see a convoy of lights roll down the road past their house heading towards Noone's. The flashing lights of the snowplows lit up the night. She sighed with relief. Now her parents could come home . . . soon! That meant that she and Mike could go over to Samantha's house, too. She was tired of being cooped up in the house.

As three snowplows passed, Vicki saw the revolving lights of the police vehicles as they came into view. What was going on, she wondered? The plows didn't stay on River Drive as she assumed they would, though. Instead, they went straight down the access road to Noone's place.

"Hey, Mike!" she yelled. The other children were upstairs in bed. "You have to see this! A bunch of plows and cop cars are going up the road to Noone's house! Come look!" The siblings stood side by side staring out the patio window that faced Noone's property to the east. They watched red and blue lights flashing and lighting up Noone's yard through blowing snow.

Jackson, the rookie, was the first officer on the scene behind the plows. He was surprised to find the front door of Noone's house wide open. Then the highway department crew made fast work of Noone's yard clearing it so the other deputy vehicles could enter.

The whole of River Drive, up to Noone's house, was plowed as the highway crew headed back to the county garage in Eveleth. The crew chief, Steve Crawford, gave Jackson his cell phone number before pulling out, telling him to call if he needed help getting back to town, and that he'd back him up if anyone said anything about the door. Crawford had not been notified about plowing the roads to the Egar farm.

Behind the plows were three sheriff's deputies, two in 4-wheel drive vehicles, and one in a squad car. Jackson stepped through the open doorway as the other deputies pulled into the yard.

Jackson is in over his head, longtime deputy Mark Stringer thought as he pulled his cruiser up next to the porch. What the hell is he doing going into the house already? Jeez! Didn't he know he was supposed to wait for backup? Jackson in charge—he shook his head at the thought. That had to have been Hornblower's idea, he figured. Wait till the sheriff hears about this. Stringer stepped out of his cruiser and walked up to the house crossing over the porch and stepping into the living room where Jackson stood looking around.

"We've got a warrant, Mark." Jackson moved in close to Stringer starring him in the eye. "You got a problem with that?"

"Why are we out here in this weather snooping through some old man's house, anyway?" Stringer did not want to be out in this particular storm, and it showed. "By the way, you aren't leading anything here Rich; no rookie is leading any investigation." He paused, "except maybe one looking for a lost dog." He laughed then stepped around Jackson to examine the house for himself.

By now, the other officers were on site and inside. "Don't pay any attention to that fool," Deputy Dave Thompson said to Jackson. "He's almost as bad as Trelavonti."

Thompson and Ace Smith trailed Stringer, watching him. Stringer got so engrossed in the search for Trelavonti throughout the first floor of the simple ranch style house that he momentarily forgot office politics.

Jackson was the first one downstairs into the basement. What Trelavonti had uncovered assaulted his eyes midway down the steps. Any thoughts of finishing early were washed away at the sight. He took out his handkerchief to cover his nose in defense of the odor. He removed a small container of Vicks vapor-rub from his shirt pocket dabbing some under each nostril then climbed all the way down into the basement proper.

When he finished with a cursory investigation, he climbed back upstairs. No, Trelavoniti wasn't down there, he told Stringer, then invited him to take a look. Smith and Thompson followed suit. Jackson handed the last two his tin of Vicks and stood behind them on the basement steps.

Jackson wondered where Noone and Trelavonti could have gone to as he climbed the stairs and walked out the front door for fresh air.

The plows did a good job, he thought.

Only problem was, if there were any tracks, they're gone now. He looked around the yard, at the porch, saw the house lights across the way, and wondered if Trelavonti had tried to go to the neighbors. Considering the find in the basement, the idea wasn't too far fetched. He doubted that the deputy could make it over there alive in the storm. Maybe Noone was there, too, but he didn't think that was the case. Noone couldn't have been at his own house when Trelavonti dug up the basement. Maybe he came home and caught Trelavonti? Jackson doubted it. He was gone when Trelavonti got here and never returned, not yet anyway. So, where is he? Both Noone and Trelavonti have a lot of explaining to do, he thought as he stepped back inside the house and shut the door. It was way too cold to stay outside for long.

Jackson shifted into high gear once inside, calling his deputies back upstairs and organizing their investigation efforts. All three deputies worked the crime scene, looking for clues, marking off the site, keeping it as clean as possible with Jackson photographing everything.

It'd be awhile before the medical examiner could get there, so they'd have to be careful. As he studied the bones and the site, Jackson could tell that Trelavonti had already bungled it. The male skeletons were okay, but the female skeletons had been heaped into a single pile. He didn't like the look of it. Trelavonti's slipshod methodology was all over the place. He may well have contaminated the whole crime scene, Jackson thought.

Trelavonti had not seen all there was to see in the basement.

Smith stood staring at the basement floor, sensing something odd about it before it dawned on him just what it was that he found so peculiar. There were spots of concrete that didn't look as old as the rest of the floor. Taking a sledgehammer he found along a wall, he loosened it. As he cleared the concrete away and dug down a short way, more skeletons peeked up out of the earth.

As Smith worked, Thompson walked about the room taking everything in. When he got to the refrigerator, he opened it only to find himself face to face with the head of a strange looking woman inside a gallon glass jug. He stood there staring at it dumbstruck for a few seconds, then removed the jar placing it carefully on a table where everyone else could see it, too. The woman smiled back at Thompson, Stringer, and Jackson through the glass.

The St. Louis County Sheriff's Department had never dealt with the likes of it before.

Chapter Twenty Six

Noone knew the old mine shafts were built sometime in the 1800s under almost every farm in the River Drive area. Companies interested in mining minerals back then built the maze then deserted it for whatever reason, he knew not. Exclusively, he traveled the labyrinth.

Noone never shared the mineshaft information with prospective buyers of his secluded farmland, either; nor did he share it with his neighbors. Most officials had forgotten that the mineshafts existed and since they were of such use to him, he felt no compunction to remind authorities that they were still there.

If it weren't for that unfortunate accident in Eveleth shortly after he arrived on the Iron Range, Noone supposed, someone snooping through Eveleth City Hall records would have found information about the mineshafts. But, alas, everything was destroyed when the old city hall burnt to the ground in 1960. What a shame he thought, smiling as he remembered the incident on the way back to the barn.

His mother had always reminded him which passages to use, so he relied on her advice often. He stumbled along each passageway marking it, so he could escape quickly once the fire started, another of her suggestions, and a good one, he felt. He still thought it best just to head home the way he came, but just in case, he'd make sure he could find his way down the maze if he needed to. He should have known the tunnels by heart, considering all the years he'd used them, but he couldn't seem to remember things the way he used to anymore, so he marked them.

Thoughts of the Jennings keeping watch at the furnace brought a smile to his lips. Weren't they sweet? He didn't need to start the fire at the furnace though. He could start it anywhere. Wiring in old houses was often a fire trap in this type of weather, and he knew just where to find the oldest wiring, the stuff he had not replaced that was still in use in the main part of the house. It was the best place for a spark, too much strain what with the cold and all and the extra heaters the Egar woman used throughout the house.

The wood braced mineshafts were dust covered and spider web invested. Freezing, they smelled of musk, dust and old wood. The dirt did nothing to stave off forty degree below zero temperatures, which Noone was well aware of. He was not dressed in full winter gear, either.

When he got back to the barn, he gathered up tools and headed back to the house as fast as possible right into the basement. He should have used the mineshafts the first time he went up to the house, but he'd forgotten about them. His memory sometimes didn't seem to work too well lately. That and the shadows he'd been seeing since Egar moved in where giving him cause for concern, although he wouldn't voice that concern to anyone, including his mother.

After all his hard work he looked forward to a nap in his cozy, warm hiding place; he was tired and it was going to be a long night. When he went back into Sam's basement, he stashed his booty inside the mineshaft entrance into the basement out of sight and within easy reach. All he had to do now was wait.

With preparations complete for the coming night's fun, Noone returned to the furnace duct where he curled up and fell asleep immediately. The warmth and the small space reminded him of his childhood. As he drifted off to sleep, he remembered that much of his young life was spent curled up in some small place like the duct hiding from his parents. As sleep overwhelmed him, he dreamt of his father, something he hadn't done in a long, long time.

In Arthur's dreams, he was a vulnerable child once again; a kid who couldn't stop what was happening to him, a kid whom everyone had forgotten. Arthur, the child, saw his father's liver spotted hands; the hands that dealt him so many blows, whenever his mother left the house. It was those same hands that held cigarette butts to his young flesh, burning it.

Who was it that he hated the most—his father or his mother? He never figured that out for sure, for he hated each with hatred that seemed to emanate from his deepest bodily tissues. His father made it easy to hate him, but his mother used subtle abuse to demean him. She never came out and did anything overt. No, she spent her time making sure he knew he didn't measure up; comparing him to his older brother Henry then to Joseph. She did it all the time, comparing him to other kids in the neighborhood, too; he was never as good as any of them.

No, Arthur didn't measure up in his mother's estimation. She kept comparing him to that neighbor kid, Reggie Hancock, from across the street. Reggie played football, basketball and hockey, plus he got straight "A's" in all his subjects at school. He was not only tough, he was handsome, and even at his young age girls were crazy about him.

His mother would compare Arthur's small frame to Reggie's big frame. She'd call him names like "girly little sissy." She'd tear up his drawings up and use them to start fires in the kitchen stove saying they weren't as good as his brother's, and tell him everyday that he was puny, puny, puny! But he got his revenge on Reggie, didn't he?

Noone tossed and turned in his sleep as he remembered how it was for him growing up.

Brother Henry left to join the Navy when he was fifteen and never came back. He lied about his age to get in and that's the last the family ever saw of him. Arthur was eleven at the time.

After Henry left, Arthur watched his mother shower affection on Joseph. It wasn't long after Joseph turned thirteen that she took him to bed with her and made the old man sleep on the couch. The old man was not happy about it, either.

After that, Arthur's beatings from the old man worsened. The old man liked to use his favorite belt buckle on him. He liked to watch as the belt broke open running sores on Arthur's legs and arms. He often locked Arthur in the closet after beating him keeping him there until his mother got home. It was as if his father was taking out his rage toward his mother and Joseph on Arthur. He was surprisingly agile and spry for his age, too. He feigned sickness and infirmity, but there was nothing wrong with him a little Jack Daniels wouldn't cure. He whined to his wife about his bad back and she believed him, so she said little to him about getting a job. At least that's what it looked like to Arthur. Maybe she was just sick of his whining and ignoring him, Arthur was never sure.

When Arthur did tell his mother what was happening to him at the hands of his father, she completely disregarded the evidence that his father beat him. She never commented on the bruises or blood she saw seeping through his pants and shirt. Arthur would never wear shorts or short sleeved T-shirts in the summer because of his legs and arms; he was too ashamed. No one seemed to notice the black eyes, either. When Arthur told her what was going on, she called him a liar and asked him why his brothers were never bruised or burnt.

He never told her that when she was gone from the house the old man had sex with him making him dress up in her dresses, at least not at first. He did tell her everything just before the end, and he thought she might have actually believed him just before she died, but he still wasn't too sure about it. They never discussed it.

As for making him dress up, the old man seemed to like the way he looked in his mother's dresses and high heels. Remembering all that in his dreams brought Arthur to the first tortuous day of being raped, the day after Henry left.

As he slept there in the furnace duct, Noone stirred from his sleep then slipped back into it, this time dreaming about his mother's reaction when he finally did tell her the old man was raping him. She didn't believe him then, either, at first. Her face crunched up into a grimace and her nose shot into the air as he related events of the past few years.

When he finished, she threw her chin higher, looked down at him with contempt burning from her distorted features and spat, "Liar! Don't you tell your brother that lie," she snarled saying nothing else.

Hell, he thought, what about me? Was Joseph the only child she had?

Noone's dreams swam on to the time the old man got pissed at him for smarting off, which happened a lot once Arthur turned twelve. He had an epiphany in his twelfth year. It was then that he began to feel the power of his own body; noticed how it was growing. Arthur realized that one-day he was going to be strong, was getting stronger even then, and soon, real soon, no one could ever hurt him again. As time went on, Arthur always mouthed off to his father.

"Fuck you!" Arthur told him once when he came out of his bedroom to find the old man across the hall standing at the threshold of the bathroom flashing his erect penis in an effort to entice the boy into his bed. The old man was confident that his past seductions had so overwhelmed Arthur with sexual desire that he wouldn't be able to resist the sight of his naked body.

When Arthur was little, it didn't take much for the old man to overpower him; even when he was twelve he wasn't strong enough to withstand the elder Albright. That day was no different. The old man grabbed him by the neck and thrust his head against the wall, again and again and again, so hard it smashed the drywall. When he finished with that, he hauled Arthur into his bedroom and threw him on the bed to rape him once again, repeatedly. The smelly old fart loved the feeling of power it gave him, Arthur guessed; besides, he felt he needed to show the boy who was boss. It was good for him, he told Arthur enough times.

That was the day Arthur made the decision to kill the thing that he was forced to acknowledge as his father. He didn't know how he would do it, or when, but he'd get rid of him, someday, someway, somehow. With that knowledge, Arthur grew stronger, more dangerous. He felt a sense of relief upon making that decision and power, too, even when the old man beat him. Arthur felt it, grew confident in spite of his circumstances, and that in the end he would have his revenge. He decided too, that if his mother got in the way, he'd get rid of her as well.

It took two more years before Arthur could carry out his plan. He grew bigger and stronger even though he never did get real big. Still, he was strong and he never forgot the vow he made to himself when he was twelve. His determination to kill his father grew with every beating he received.

On his fourteenth birthday, when the old man planned on giving him a special present, Arthur had a bigger surprise in store for him. By this time, Arthur had plenty of experience killing. He practiced on small animals and the next-door neighbor kid the year before, the one that was never found. Arthur knew he had to practice, to get ready for the day he would take his father out. Besides, his father was still bigger than he was. He had to plan to make it work.

Arthur was starting small fires by the time he turned fourteen, too. He got real good at it loving to watch things as they burnt. The fires offered him relief from the beatings. Every time his old man got at him, he set a fire. The old man caught him once and tried to blackmail him with it. He played along with the old man knowing that the opportunity he had long waited for would soon present itself. All he had to do was wait.

On the day the old man died, he crept into Arthur's bedroom hoping for a little sexual interaction. It was 2 a.m. Arthur awoke from a sound sleep knowing that the time had come. He lay there quietly as the old man crept closer and closer to his bed. When the old man reached it, he began to whisper endearing words in Arthur's ear. Then he slipped onto the bed, forcing Arthur onto his stomach. Arthur waited for him to finish. When he was done and spent from the effort, Arthur grabbed a knife he had hidden under the mattress then wheeled up and slit the old man's throat in one fell swoop. The old man's eyes grew wide in astonishment. The only thing Arthur wished for in that moment of death was for it to be slow and painful. He got out of bed standing over his father watching as blood spurted from the mortal wound. The old man tried to say something but all that came out were garbled gurgles.

There was a lot of blood. Arthur cleaned it up. The fourteen-year-old was strong enough that removing his father's body was not as difficult as he had anticipated it might be. He took it to the bathroom and dumped it in the bathtub. The old man wasn't quite dead yet, however, and Arthur had the pleasure of watching as his father thrashed out trying to grab him. He laughed and stayed just out of reach knowing how angry the old man must have been just then. He really wanted him to realize exactly what was happening and why, otherwise what good did killing him accomplish? And more than anything, Arthur wanted it to mean something.

He smiled as he watched his father thrash about in the bathtub.

And as he lay huddled in the furnace duct in the Samantha Egar house, Noone awoke momentarily from the nightmare of his youth thinking, did the old bastard think he could get away with that shit? He shouldn't have been surprised. He should have expected it. He fell back to fitful sleep immediately.

The night he killed the old man, Arthur whispered in his ear as he lay dying and told him what else he was going to do to him. He showed the old man the saw, so he would know Arthur was going to dismember him.

Arthur took his hunting knife and removed a finger from the old man's hand as he lie dying in the bathtub, but still conscious enough to know what Arthur was doing, to still feel the pain. He even cried out, but no matter, Arthur's mother didn't come to his rescue. It took the rest of the night to finish cutting the old man up and to dispose of his body.

No one else in the household stirred from their sleep that night. It was not until noon the next day that Arthur's mother got out of bed. She found the house cleaner than it had been the night before. She stumbled out of the bedroom half-dressed heading for the bathroom. A cigarette dangling from her lips with her housecoat hanging open exposing much of her still fit form.

Arthur sat at the kitchen table and from his line of sight, could see her breasts clearly. Joseph stumbled out of the bedroom close behind her. She wouldn't let him pass her to go into the kitchen for something to eat until he kissed her on the mouth. She saw Arthur watching, so she took Joseph's hand placing it on her breast. She rubbed Joseph's crotch as he kissed her, all the while watching over his shoulder for Arthur's reaction.

He smiled. She was asking for what he just got through giving her husband.

After her failure to get the reaction she wanted from Arthur, she went into the bathroom. Arthur could hear the water running. She came out fifteen minutes later without saying a word passing him on her way to the kitchen counter for freshly brewed coffee. What she did do was look down at Arthur as she passed. She had a look of triumph in her eyes, like she had accomplished something and was daring him to do something about it.

Joseph appeared to think all was as normal as apple pie for he just nonchalantly went to the refrigerator to get something to eat apparently oblivious to the fact that having sexual intercourse with his mother wasn't normal.

Arthur watched her like a lion watches its intended prey. She went about the kitchen as if everything was as it had been the day before oblivious to the fact that things were vastly different. She went back to the bedroom with Joseph after breakfast slamming the door, so Arthur knew just where she was and whom she was with. He heard the bed springs groan under their weight as she and Joseph continued their tryst not caring who was at home to hear them. They carried on like that for weeks. She must have suspected the old man wasn't coming back.

Arthur watched closely during that time, at first wondering what she would do about the old man. When he realized she wasn't going to do anything about her husband, he began to make plans.

Throughout that time, she sauntered around the house half-naked, taunting Arthur every chance she got then taking

Joseph into the bedroom with her, smiling and looking at Arthur as she closed the door. Soon the bedsprings would be squeaking again. Her figure was still good and she did entice him sexually, but her haughty looks turned him to ice.

She made over Joseph hardly letting him out of the bedroom. She walked around him half-naked always rubbing against him. She did that to Arthur too, and he wondered if she were trying to bed him? He doubted it. She just wanted to tease him enough to give him the courage to come after her sexually, so then she could turn him down and humiliate him once again. He knew it. His father had taught him well. And he grew angrier by the day because of it.

She never seemed to know how much danger she was in. By that time, Arthur was getting a lot of pleasure out of killing. Girls couldn't entice him with suggestions of sexual pleasure, either. They were nothing to him. In fact, they were repugnant except for the fact that he liked experimenting on them. His sexual gratification came from causing them pain, which many learned the hard way. Arthur came to like taking his time killing, too, to savor the pleasure he got from the power, the look of helplessness in his victim's eyes. His father had just been an appetizer as far as killing was concerned.

After that fateful night, every time his mother tried to entice him to make a move on her, he would go out and find a victim on the street relieving his bottled up sexual desires on them by killing them. He was only biding his time, however. Substitutes were fast loosing their allure. He wanted her.

Joseph was developmentally disabled, or as the kids called him back then, "mental." Arthur knew he was slow. Regardless, he resented him. Joseph knew what the old man did to Arthur, too, but never made any attempts to stop it, or even to help him. Arthur's resentment of Joseph's passivity never dissipated.

However, it did not grow into the full-blooded hatred that he had for his mother. He just didn't like him. Arthur felt Joseph was too weak to be of much use. He had to be considered differently.

Throughout the neighborhood, everyone knew Joseph was slow. Arthur decided to use that reputation to his advantage after he got rid of his mother. After she disappeared, he planed to go about the neighborhood saying things like, "It's a shame how Joseph is so violent. What causes that?" He would wonder out loud within earshot of the local gossips, asking anyone who showed any interest. And he knew, since most would hunger to hear more about this poor lad's troubled home life, that he would innocently tell them that Joseph had tried to rape his poor sainted mother and that his father had disappeared after stopping him. He would continue to say that he feared the worst but was so terrified of his brother, he couldn't call the police. Neighbors, trying to help the poor waif, would run to their phones screaming at the tops of their lungs afraid for their own lives. That was Arthur's plan—if he needed to use it.

That was what he would do if the bodies were found. He would sweetly imply that Joseph had gone off his rocker completely and killed them both. It was perfect. And what would happen to Joseph? As a minor, he might get locked up in a mental institution for awhile, but as he got older, Arthur would see to it Joseph got out on early release. He'd take care of him; offer his word that he would take care of his misbegotten brother. He'd hang his head in supplication and plead to the courts to let him take care of what family he had left. He knew he could do that, too. His mother may not have thought much of him, but Arthur knew he already had a commanding presence with adults. Most adults were impressed with his quiet, polite attitude. Yeah, he could pull it off.

Arthur buried his father's pieces under the basement floor. He liked the idea of disposing of his mother in the same way.

The night Arthur decided it was the ideal night to send his mother to her maker he gave Joseph money to go to a movie. After Joseph left, he waited in his mother's bedroom for her to come home from the hairdressers. She didn't get home until 7 p.m. He was hiding in her closet when she got there. She came into the house calling for Joseph. She wanted the boy to see her new hairdo. When she didn't find him, she went into her bedroom removing her clothes as she crossed the bedroom floor dropping them as she walked. Her back was to the closet. She sat down at her vanity looking at herself in the mirror. She was forty three years old then and still looked pretty good. Arthur could tell what she was thinking as she admired her new hairstyle in the mirror patting it and smiling at herself. She also ran her hands down her torso staring at it and still smiling. She patted powder between her breasts with a powder puff then thrust them out admiring them. She tilted her head from side to side evaluating everything.

That was when Arthur slipped open the closet door and said, "Hello Mother." He stepped up behind her. He hid a piece of cotton clothesline rope behind his back. The muscles of his arms rippled beneath his first short sleeved T-shirt he ever wore revealing multitudes of scares. He was calm, waiting for the right moment. This had to be much the same as the old man's death to give him the pleasure he sought.

"So, you're spying on me now," she hissed as she watched him approach her through the vanity mirror. She didn't turn around.

"No, mother not spying . . . just watching." He said politely as he edged slightly closer to her. "You smell good, mother. What kind of perfume is that?"

She wheeled around grabbing his head, "Here, get a good whiff," she said pulling him into her uncovered breasts.

He gasped.

"It's Jasmine. Do you like it?" She thrust him backward.

"Yes, Mother, it's beautiful." His voice stayed calm in spite of the fact that her actions almost caused him to reveal the rope he kept hidden behind his back. She never saw it. All she accomplished was to seal her own fate. Arthur was tired, so tired of being pushed around by her.

She smiled her taunting smile down at him, her nose in mid-air, and her head thrown back.

He had her then, because she never knew he had the upper hand.

She slipped an arm around his waist and pulled him close thinking she was in charge of the situation. "Do you dance, son," she whispered huskily in his ear while she placed her other hand on his rump pushing her pelvis into his and swaying her hips. He gasped at the excitement the movement caused. He didn't expect it, but rolled with the flow watching to see how far she would go and waiting for his moment.

"Yes, mother, I can dance. I dance very well," he said determined not to reveal the effect she was having on him. He wanted control and he was going to have it. But he was only human and when she felt his hard penis against her, she threw him off her asking what the hell he thought he was doing.

He expected that; it was the same old game. But he wasn't having it anymore.

"Well, mother," he said pulling out a long handled knife from his pant pocket, and tackling her like a football player. She fell across the bed with him atop her. "I'm going to show you just how much I love you in spite of the way you treat me."

He held the knife to her throat as he pulled her to her feet. It felt good, him, a fourteen year old kid, overpowering her. He played with the knife against her flesh for awhile enjoying with every fiber of his being the look of terror on her face. Then he led her downstairs to the basement with the knife at her ribs. There he tied her to a support beam in the center of the room with the cotton clothesline rope he still carried. He gagged her watching her eyes grow large with terror at each move he made. He wondered if she connected any of what was happening to her with her missing husband. She should have, but as he looked at her frightened countenance, he doubted it. She wasn't smart enough.

Almost as if she read his mind, she turned her gaze to the concrete floor.

Inside the furnace duct at Sam's, Noone smiled as he lay curled sleeping inside the heat duct remembering in his dreams how it was with his mother that final day. That day, when he was but fourteen years old, was the sweetest day of his life, so he went back to it often. He dreamt about how she stood there terrified as he tied her up to the beam in the basement, and began to cut her with his knife—little cuts. He took his time. Her death was slow and laborious as he reached sexual climax repeatedly at her agonized cries. He got lost in the work.

Unbeknownst to him, Joseph came home early and quietly climbed down the basement stairs where he stood watching Arthur and their mother. Arthur didn't know how long Joseph had been standing there. Joseph surprised him by clearing his throat. Arthur turned around slowly to look at the stairs expecting trouble, but to his surprise, saw only excitement in Joseph's eyes. In fact, Joseph was so excited, he asked if could have sex with their mother as she stood there tied to the post.

Arthur made sure his mother could see him laughing at her as Joseph pulled down his pants and rammed her already bloody body with his penis. As Joseph took his satisfaction, Arthur moved in close and whispered in her ear, "how do you like that mother?" Smiling, he knew she was surprised by Joseph's actions. The shock of it weakened her spirit more than he ever could. She was beaten, no more smug, haughty looks in her eyes. Arthur finished her off by slashing her throat when Joseph finished with her. He was tired of her by then.

He did one more thing, however, something he had not done with his father. He removed her head and placed it in a gallon jar filled with formaldehyde, which he tucked into the back of the refrigerator.

"Watcha' do that for?" Joseph asked.

"Well, Joe, I was thinking, if you need to talk to her, get her advise, you can just go to the frig and she'll be there."

"Okay, Arthur, I will," Joseph said.

Arthur put the rest of his mother's remains next to his father's and resealed the floor.

No one ever asked the brothers where their parents were. The boys took care of themselves from that day onward. Distant relatives didn't show enough interest to ask them where their folks had gone or how the boys were getting along. They didn't want to be burdened with the misfits. It was 1942. Most people didn't believe parents abused their children. Most had never heard of patricide or matricide. It was unthinkable.

So, when Joseph moved to the Iron Range from South Dakota, Arthur, who was already there, didn't care. He knew how to get Joseph to do his bidding. If he grew tired of him, he could get rid of him, too, which was what he did eventually. It was easy.

As Noone huddled quietly in the furnace duct waiting for his chance to take revenge on the people at Sam's house, he was cozy and warm in the small space. He liked it. He could hide there for days. It was like a cocoon, safe and warm.

But he grew uneasy after a few hours rest. His mother whispered in his ear continually, telling him that Trelavonti was at his house snooping in the basement. She told him that Trelavonti had called someone, told them what he had found. Since reproofing his mother those many years before, he never doubted her word anymore. He looked at his watch. It was past 10 p.m., time for him to make his move. Besides, he wanted to get home, check on things there. He edged his way out of the duct. His legs were stiff and sore from long hours in the same position. He stretched, got the blood moving, then proceeded quietly down the stairs. On his way, he stopped to listen through the peepholes. He heard nothing. It appeared that everyone had gone to bed. It wasn't very late. He doubted that all were asleep but he would act now anyway.

He peeped through the brick in the basement at the furnace room to see who stood watch. He doubted that Jennings would still be there. He saw Stan Gilbert. He smiled at the group's guilelessness. Didn't they know there were other ways to torch an old house? He had no intention of starting a fire in or around the furnace. It was only a couple of years old. His plan was better. It was one that would make everything look like an accident.

Noone climbed back to the first floor, peeked through the peephole into the dinning room. No one was there. He pulled a small screwdriver from his pocket and dug into the wall near the baseboard. He knew that an electrical outlet was there. He knew where every wire in the house was.

He dug away at the plaster until he reached the wires. Once there, he used a lighter to burn away the outer filament then exposed another wire in the same way and crossed the two. He pushed the wires close to the dinning room wall, waiting and watching through the peephole for them to ignite in the dinning room. He could see sparks fly; just what he wanted. But sparks weren't enough. He dropped a piece of old newspaper through the peephole, close to the sparks. It worked. The paper started to smolder, then he saw flame. But it wasn't time to make his exit yet; he had to make sure the downstairs room flamed up completely. He watched as tentative tendrils of smoke wafted up to the peephole.

Good, he thought, putting out an electrical fire is a lot trickier than other fires. If anyone throws water on it, it will flame up even more. The old outlet he chose rested right beneath the living room drapes, so he didn't have to wait long before he saw that material flare up, too. It would take awhile before there was enough smoke or flame to set off the smoke alarms. With everyone upstairs, the dinning room would be in full blaze before they even knew that it was burning.

Smoke would block off exits, make it difficult too impossible to escape. And by the time the smoke alarms did go off, so much smoke would have seeped upstairs that those there would be suffering from smoke inhalation.

Tiptoeing back down to the basement, he watched Stan for a short time. He was asleep next to the furnace. He moved to the hidden entrance behind the cellar steps, which led to the barn through the old mineshafts. He would wait awhile in the barn before going home. He wanted to make sure the house was completely engulfed before he left. With the winds outside, and the fire inside, it wouldn't take long for everything to go up in smoke.

He slipped down the old mineshafts to the barn.

Chapter Twenty Seven

Upstairs, everyone was either in bed or preparing for it. Gladys and Inez retired early and were asleep. Clem rested quietly in his room.

In Sam's bedroom, she and Angie talked about all they had learned. It had been an emotionally exhausting day for both. They poured over the information the Spencer sisters had given them. They saw it then, too, the parallels between their lives and those of their parents.

Neither woman knew what to say, or do. For the first time in their friendship, they were at a loss for words. That didn't last long. They remembered the odd coincidences in college, how they thought so much alike then, and still did. In college, it was almost as if they could read one-another's minds, anticipate what the other was going to say or do. Even their friends had remarked on it.

"I've come across things in my life . . . in my work that astounded me, but never, never in a million years did I think I would hold center stage to something like this. I never dreamt it," Angie said.

"Me neither. Even when things happened in college or out here when puzzle pieces started to fit together leading to the conclusion Inez and Gladys came to, I still didn't see it.

Do you remember when you found out from Karen that you were adopted from the same orphanage . . . the one I grew up in? You would think I would have wondered about that. Course, I never knew I was a twin, would never have guessed you were that twin even if I had known. We don't look anything alike!"

Sam and Angie sat on the bed pouring over the old photographs of the professor, his wife, and their children, themselves, as babies. They wondered how they had been so blind to the resemblance in the first place.

"There's so much that we have to learn about our pasts, so much . . .," Angie said. "But it's not just that, or us, the fact that we've found out who we really are. It's everyone in this house. We are all tied together somehow. Do you see that, Sam?" Angie didn't wait for a response.

"Like the sheriff, Skip, I mean. After thirty years of loving the same woman, he finally gets to find out what happened to her, through me! Not only that, but Noone—somehow he's tied to all of it. He ties us all together. Do you see that? Do you see the synchronicity of it all?"

"How do Bernice and John tie into this?" Sam asked. "They don't seem to have any connection other than the fact they are parents to children about the same age as so many of those kids that disappeared from the area. How do they tie in?"

"Maybe that's how. Maybe it's the kids that tie them to us. Maybe it's the kids that are picking up vibrations of some sort from others their own age. I don't know.

Or maybe it's because the family has such a strong tie to their spirituality, to Christ, that they are the right people to help those tortured spirits through this. I haven't studied religion, but I do know that a strong spiritual current runs through all this. Some of it is negative—Noone, I mean. But there are positive spirits, too. I can feel it! You're one. I'm one, Skip and his dad, and Gladys and Inez. They have all been through so much in their lives, yet they still embrace life with love; they embrace everyone they meet that way. And somehow we are all connected."

"How do you suppose Franco and Shorty are involved? I mean I hardly know Franco, Shorty either, for that matter. How are they tied to us?" Sam said.

"Well, as far as Shorty is concerned, he's connected to Noone. Noone's been buffaloing him, apparently for a long time. Franco, I don't know. Except that when he looks at you, his eyes light up. Maybe he's here for you?"

"When he looks at me my heart leaps; I get all tingly all over. But there is another connection, his nephew Earl. Maybe it was Noone who set that kid up? Maybe that's why Franco's really here. Maybe there is some divine spirit guiding us all together to do battle with Noone?"

"You make a good point about his nephew. And it really does seem as if some unseen hand is putting us all together, like something big is about to happen." Angie shook her head, shivering.

"I wouldn't discount that attraction between you and Franco, though. You never know!" She winked and smiled at Sam.

"Have your studies taught you that? Pretty insightful," Sam said.

"Oh no, not at all! Life has taught me that. I've talked to so many people over the years about love it isn't even funny. No one has it easy when it comes to relationships. And believe me I've seen stranger couples than you and Franco. In fact, you two look good together."

"You know he has a reputation as a tough guy, don't you?"

"Look, if you're worried about that, go ask your friends, the cops, you know, the two guys spending the night in your house? They can run a background check on Franco for you—no harm in that . . . but what about your friend the sheriff? He seems interested, too?" Angie lifted her eyebrows as she opened her eyes wide in anticipation of the answer.

"You're devious, you know that? Sam wasn't ready to talk about Skip just yet. She didn't know it, but Angie gave her the reassurance she had been hoping for. She had this feeling that Skip was interested in her too, but she wasn't sure she was interpreting his signals correctly.

Finally, worn out from the day's events, Sam and Angie put the photos aside and went to bed. They thought that everyone else in the house had done the same.

In the basement, Stan took the second watch near the furnace, so John and Bernice were upstairs by 8 p.m. and in the kitchen. They sat for awhile with the sheriff and Franco who talked at the kitchen table. Skip and Franco were intent on raiding the leftovers in the refrigerator, but they didn't get far. Bernice busied herself fixing sandwiches for everyone. She had a touch with food, and even the simplest thing she prepared tasted scrumptious. They all ate in front of the fire.

John and Bernice told the others that they were worried about their children and about Arthur Noone being interested in them. Angie's trance statements had stirred up a lot of anxiety for Bernice. They wished they were home with their kids instead of there.

Though Skip didn't say it, he thought it was a good thing they were worried. Knowing what he knew about all of those other disappearances over the years he'd be worried, too if he were their parent. He didn't really know if Arthur Noone had anything to do with any of that, but he'd be damned if he'd let John or Bernice find out the hard way, not as long as he was sheriff.

From the time Ellen had first warned them of Noone, he had been piecing different facts together concerning all the disappearances over the years, and thought that maybe, just maybe, he had his first viable lead in all the cold cases in St. Louis County that spanned three decades. How something could get so out of hand astounded him. Of course, none of the kids had been locals, so they never got much press, and folks didn't give them much thought. Three decades worth of cold cases had gone completely unnoticed by the general public. All those children, forgotten, well they weren't forgotten by him or his father! He would never forget.

John and Bernice went upstairs praying for their children's protection and safety. It was a relief to do something. They knew they could turn to God as frightening situations arose. Bernice not only prayed for the safety of her children but for that of everyone in Sam's house.

When she finished, she sat cross-legged on the bed after tossing her shoes in the corner. She laughed about feeling comforted that Noone was nearby and not far from her. "Now, tell me, John, why on earth does knowing Noone is here instead of at our house make me feel good?' She laughed again. She knew the answer.

John sat in a chair next to the bed. He smiled, knowing full well what Bernice meant. He liked thinking Noone was there, too, and not anywhere near their kids, or their home.

"It's been a long day, dear. Why don't you come lie down," Bernice said patting the space next to her, smiling provocatively at him.

"No, I think I'm going to stay up, go back downstairs and talk to the men," John said but didn't get out of his chair. He just wasn't up to being romantic. He hoped she would understand.

He looks weary, she thought. She got up, walked over to him rubbing his shoulders from behind then running her fingers through his thick curly hair, bending down and kissing the top of his head. She never tired of being near him. Between John and the kids, she could not have asked God for a better life. She said a silent prayer of thanks, kissing the top of John's head once again.

"I think it's you that needs to get some rest," John said as he stood up and hugged his wife, leading her back to the bed. He pulled the covers back and tucked her in between flannel sheets, kissed her forehead and slowly headed out the door. He turned and looked back at her as he shut off the light switch and said, "I love you." Bernice was already asleep. He didn't know if she heard him.

All he could think about, as he climbed down the stairs, were passages from Ezekiel where God said to Ezekiel 24: 16-17 (NKJV): "Son of man, behold, I take away from you the desire of your eyes with one stroke; yet you shall neither mourn nor weep, nor shall your tears run down. Sigh in silence, make no mourning for the dead; bind your turban on your head, and put your sandals on your feet; do not cover your lips, and do not eat man's bread of sorrow."

Downstairs in the basement, Stan didn't feel so well. He didn't want Skip to see him get sick, which was why he offered to take second watch by the furnace. He hadn't been feeling too well for the last few hours. He needed to be by himself to take his pills, somewhere where Skip couldn't see what he was doing.

Sam brought him dinner earlier as well as a comfortable chair with cushions, a pitcher of water, and a warm blanket, all of which felt heaven sent to him. He could sit next to the furnace all night if need be in comfort.

The half bathroom in the basement came in handy, too. Sometimes he got sick, had to vomit, which often lasted for hours. He didn't know if it was the chemotherapy or the radiation therapy that caused the vomiting, and it no longer mattered much. He felt like crap most days, but today had been good. It was good to be with his son.

He didn't want to die yet, though. He wanted to take care of unfinished business. Noone could not be allowed to get away with all the crap he had pulled over the years. He couldn't. It would be a disservice to society if he did. I could never stop Noone when I was a sheriff, but now, damn it, maybe together Skip and I can, he thought. It was something he had hoped for all his life, to work a case with his son, and what better case?

He needed to spend more time with Skip anyhow. He now knew Skip wasn't happy about his handling of a number of cases. He also knew that when it was all over, Skip would know just exactly how much work his old man put into investigating Noone. It saddened him to think his son didn't respect his ability as a police officer. Kids, though, they sometimes go through that just so they can make their own way, he thought trying to take away some of the hurt Skip's attitude had caused him.

He was tired tonight, though, too much activity over the last couple of days. He was surprised that he was holding up as well as he was.

Alone, in front of the furnace, after retching until he felt his stomach was coming up out of his throat, Stan tried not to doze, but he did. He needed the rest. Doctors had told him complete bed rest. Bed rest my ass, he thought when they told him that; no one is tying me to no bed! The freedom from pain his medication offered combined with the warm room and comfortable chair seduced Stan off into a fitful sleep.

His head fell to his chest.

Everyone upstairs was nearly asleep by the time Noone went into the mineshaft at 10:30 p.m.

At the same time, upstairs Bernice dreamed, "Behold, I send you out like sheep among wolves. Therefore be wise as serpents and harmless as doves." Mt. 10:16 (NKJV).

In the Jennings's barn, Trelavonti saw Ellen. And he was right; he was not alone in the barn. What he didn't realize, however, was that it wasn't Ellen that stood before him. It wasn't Ellen's breasts that he was fondling.

John Jennings' nineteen hundred pound Brahma bull Steamroller, snorted bull snot while dragging his front hoofs across the dusty barn floor in anger at Trelavonti. Initially too surprised by the man's actions to do anything, the bull stood for being handled. His momentary lapse into passivity, however, was rapidly eroding.

Steamroller had earned his reputation for being mean and unpredictable. During his rodeo days, the big bull came to hate men and to hold them in contempt, something that even John Jennings' tender loving care couldn't remove from his spirit.

Though Steamroller stood as stud on the Jennings' farm, which provided the Jennings's family with untold prosperity, he couldn't be trusted. That was why John never allowed his children to care for him.

During his rodeo days, no cowboy ever managed to stay on Steamroller's back a full eight seconds. And the bull often turned on a dime to gore the rider after flinging him off his back. Rodeo clowns had a difficult time luring the bull away from his intended victims, as well.

If it weren't for the bull's age and increasingly bad temper, something rodeo officials never told John about at the time of sale, they never would have sold the profit-making Steamroller. When Jennings offered to buy him, he was a welcome sight to the rodeo stock managers.

While rodeo stock managers were banking on making a profit off Steamroller's sale, John banked on the aging bull's genes being in great demand. That was something the owners didn't want to deal with. Steamroller scared them. They wanted to be rid of him regardless of potential profits; he had grown too mean.

It didn't take John long to find out why the rodeo was so eager to get rid of Steamroller; he found that out as soon as the animal was unloaded from the stock trailer. He had had the foresight, however, to build extremely strong enclosures for the bull because of his size, so as Steamroller climbed down into the pen, there was little damage he could do to anyone. He did no damage to the corral, either.

John built the especially stout pens both inside and out, and they proved a godsend when it came to handling the animal during breeding season. John never had to get in the pen with the bull. He could remain outside and herd the animal where he wanted him to go with a cattle prod. During breeding season, the pens also insured the cow's safety by not having to place her in the pen with the bull.

At times when Steamroller acted badly John would tell himself that the following year when the rodeo came through again, he'd sell him back and get rid him, but he never did. Steamroller brought something to Jennings that he hadn't anticipated. The bull was a celebrity of sorts, and people from all over the country came out to the farm just to get a look at him.

Well muscled, well fed, well exercised, Steamroller was a sight to behold. He had a way of looking into a person's eyes that dared them to try him. Whenever a crowd gathered around him, Steamroller acted as if he were on stage, and put on the performance of a lifetime, snorting and running around the bullpen tossing his head from side to side and pawing the dirt in what seemed like mock anger.

Jennings was never sure if the anger was real or not, sometimes it seemed like it was just an act. But one had to be careful with bulls because they could never be totally trusted, and being overly confident could cost someone their life.

Even so, Jennings enjoyed the bull's pizzazz. Steamroller had a way about him.

Jennings didn't breed the Brahma bull to any of his beef stock. He used artificial insemination for that, but rodeos all over the country used the bull's stud service. Most times cattle owners sent for Steamroller's semen to inseminate their own Brahma herds artificially, but on occasion, especially with the rodeos, they would bring their cows to John's small farm to breed directly to the bull. Jennings' handling of Steamroller during those breeding sessions earned him a reputation of respect among the rodeos. He insured that the bull, cows, and handlers all had a safe breeding experience.

Because every rodeo cowboy knew of Steamroller's reputation, even if they themselves had never ridden him, they wanted to have the next Steamroller in their herd. His bloodline was in great demand. Many of those same cowboys were sorry Steamroller was retired entertaining dreams of being the one to ride the contrite animal the full eight-seconds.

But, if they couldn't get the chance to ride him, they wanted to at least pray for his offspring to be as tough and in demand as he was. So when they brought their cows to the Jennings' farm and the bull screamed and barreled down the breeding shoot at the scent of a cow in heat, the cowboys were doubly thankful to Jennings for his strong breeding pens. They were quietly thankful for Jennings' patient handling of the temperamental bull, too, which, they knew, was the only reason the living legend was still alive.

No one had ever removed the bull's horns. They spread across his enormous head at least four feet on either side with sharp points at each tip. When he stomped the floor in anger and swayed his head from side to side with the horns sweeping the air, old Steamroller was an impressive, terrifying sight with his tawny colored hide rippling over well-defined muscle.

And Steamroller is what Trelavonti found himself face to face with, only he didn't know it. As he stroked Steamroller, all he saw was Ellen.

The bull, dumfounded at the strange turn of events, did not move . . . at first.

When Ellen refused to yield to Trelavonti's advances, he grabbed her by the arms, (Steamroller's horns). For a nanosecond the scales fell from Trelavonti's eyes, and he realized he wasn't fondling a woman at all. For the first time, he recognized the infamous Steamroller who stared right back at him.

Trelavonti's bladder let go. With the stench of his own excrement burning his nostrils, in another nanosecond he no longer saw the bull, but Ellen once again, and breathed a sigh of relief wondering why his own mind was playing such cruel games with him. Did the others realize that he messed himself out of fear? Could they smell it? Was that real, too?

Steamroller stood quietly, like a statue, stock still as if trying to sort the situation out. No one had ever stood in front of him before or had the gall to try and hold onto him by the horns, which stretched across his massive head, which was as broad and long as Trelavonti's rotund torso and heavy enough to crush the biggest of men even without the horns.

Above Steamroller's pen, in the haymow overlooking it, a myriad of transparent faces watched the human and animal interact. Diaphanous faces watched from between rafters enjoying what they beheld beneath their feet. None uttered a sound. The only talking came from Trelavonti and Ellen as they conversed down below. The figures giggled as they watched the man talking to the bull. Ellen was there, with them, throwing her voice so it sounded as if it came from Steamroller. Ellen, like the others, had to cover her mouth to keep from giggling. She didn't want to spoil the surprise for Trelavonti, thereby ruining the entertainment for all present.

Trelavonti heard Ellen's voice encouraging him to touch her, to make love to her, to fondle her breasts. Each time she spoke scales fell over his eyes. He saw only Ellen and gingerly reached over to touch her lustily. She backed away from him again and again blowing hot air in his face, exciting him all the more. Trelavonti thought Ellen was simply a teasing bitch angering him. He pulled his fist back and punched her as hard as he could in the face. It was a blow that would have felled most men, but not Ellen.

As his fist struck home the scales once again lifted from his eyes—but by this time it was way too late. Steamroller, no longer dumbstruck by the strange turn of events went from angry to enraged. He backed away from Trelavonti lowering his head, shaking it, slowly, from side to side, as he pawed the sawdust littered floor kicking up dust. His crooked tail swung back and forth stiffly in agitation. Hot air blew from his nostrils sending snot flying throughout the enclosure. That old hatred toward men burned in his eyes as he stared up into Trelavonti's face.

Trelavonti's heart fluttered in his chest as he stared back at the incensed bull. How did he get in the pen with Steamroller? He couldn't remember. It didn't matter. He was there and he had no where to run! Terrified, he slowly backed up. His mind froze in terror.

He looked about the pen frantically for a way to escape. Where's Joseph! He wondered frantically hoping the dead man would help him again somehow. Trelavonti couldn't move watching in horror as Steamroller's squat legs kicked up dirt in agitation. The bull aimed his enormous head at him like a weapon moving it methodically from side to side. He trembled at the sight of the long, thick horns on either side of the animal's head.

Help! He prayed for the first time in his life. Finally, his paralysis lifted and Trelavonti tried to ease over to the fence, putting one foot behind the other, walking backwards slowly all the while hoping that the bull couldn't hear his heart, which felt like it was bursting from his chest it beat so loudly.

The bull snorted, then, bellowed so loudly the noise sent off horrifying echoes throughout the enclosed barn. The sound of it terrified Trelavonti so badly he thought Steamroller was already on top of him. He hadn't reached the fence before he fell to the ground clutching his chest. The pain shooting through his left side was unbearable. He couldn't move.

Steamroller charged. He hit the prone man full force with his horns lifting and tossing the deputy's body up into the air as if the two hundred sixty pound cop were a mere two ounce rag doll. The big bull screamed his rage as Trelavonti fell back onto the sawdust covered floor of the huge pen. Steamroller lunged at Trelavonti again, this time goring him with his horns, and puncturing his stomach. The cop flew back up into the air then fell back down, this time atop the bull's back. Steamroller sidestepped to his left leaving Trelavonti to fall back down onto the bull pen floor.

The bull charged once again butting Trelavonti's body in such a way as to carry it to the fence where he crushed it with his head against the fence post timbers. Steamroller pinned Trelavonti there ramming his body against the fence post again and again and again, moving his massive head just enough to be able to both ram Trelavonti and to keep him pinned against the post. The old cop never fell to the ground.

Trelavonti was well beyond caring. He was dead before the bull made the second charge.

When Steamroller finished with the body there wasn't much left of Gene Trelavonti. And by then the bull had worked himself up into an insane rage still attacking even though there was nothing more to attack. Finally, he moved back to a corner of the pen still not taking his eyes off the blood and gore splattered about the bullpen floor. Steamroller waited in a corner for the blood spatter to move again; he was in such a killing frenzy, he was past redemption.

In the haymow gossamer shadows gleefully rejoiced.

Outside the wolves stood facing the barn, their heads directly into the wind. Inside the house, all Mike and Vicki could hear was the howling of the storm as the wind whistled through cracks in the window wells.

Vicki sat at the kitchen table beneath the Lord's Prayer plaque staring out the window. Frightened, she wondered why the wolves behaved like they did as she watched them stare at the barn.

As they began to howl, Mike stood at the window too, watching, wondering what the animals were watching, and howling about. The big alpha male and female were the furthest away, but even through the heavily blowing snow Mike could see the hairs on the back of their bodies standing on end. What is going on down there? He wondered and knew he couldn't go out again. It was too dangerous. He remained at the window, watching.

Across the field at Noone's house, Mike could still see all the rotating, flashing lights of the police cars. He wondered what was going on over there, too. Could anyone there hear the wolves howling here? He thought, silently hoping a cop car would pull up the driveway. He was frightened.

"This will be a night we will never forget," Mike said turning to look at her. "Some terrible things are going on. I can feel it."

"I hope the folks are okay. I wish they were here." Vicki said

"Me too." Mike mumbled.

As they watched the Noone farm and the wolves, Mike noticed that the sky to the east of them had taken on an odd orange hue. "What's that?" He said to Vicki.

She looked past the barn to the east following Mike's finger. "Why is the sky so orange?" She said.

Over at Noone's farm, Stringer stood outside talking to the other deputies when he heard the wolves begin to howl.

"Damn," he said, "that sounds like wolves, like they're right here someplace!" The howling carried over the screaming winds to send chills down all the deputies' spines. As they listened, snow piled even higher on roads that weren't fully plowed.

"Do you think that howling is coming from that farm over there?" Smith asked. "It sounds like it."

"Yeah, it sounds that way to me, too," Stringer said, "I'll go check it out."

He walked to his police car, got in, started it, and headed out the driveway and over to the Jennings' farm. When he got there, the Jennings' driveway was so drifted over he couldn't drive up to the house. The farmhouse, shielded from view by a pine grove, was not easy to see through the wind blown snow. Though lights were on inside the house, Stringer couldn't see what was on the front lawn. Even though he had just heard wolves howling from that direction, he decided to walk up to the house not the least bit afraid. Born and raised in a city with no aptitude for the outdoors, Stringer was naïve to the ways of the wild, and didn't realize he might be in danger. He did know that no wolf had ever attacked a human being in North America, so with confidence he dawned his snowshoes and started off across the drifted over driveway. His regulation flashlight shed light upon the road.

As he walked, he kept his mind on the investigation at Noone's house and wondered where Trelavonti had gone in the storm. The man was too old and too out of shape to have gone far, he reasoned. Everyone in the sheriff's office knew Trelavonti was supposed to be at the house when they arrived. So, where was he? It certainly wasn't like him to disappear off a case that would make him famous, not like this one was likely to do.

Stringer's questions answered themselves when he looked down at the snow he was walking over. Human tracks were easy to see in the drifts. These have to be Trelavonti's, he thought. Who else would be out in this weather?

Over at Noone's house, Smith went back inside to let Jackson know what Stringer was doing. Jackson was pleased. It would keep Stringer out of his hair awhile as he wrapped the primary investigation up. It was a mess. Forty bodies had been dug up out of the basement and he believed there was going to be more. He had already called the Minnesota Bureau of Criminal Apprehension for support and the FBI as well. The sooner they got help, the better.

He sure wished he could reach Skip, though. He thought Skip needed to be there; so did his old man, Stan who he knew was visiting; Harriet told him. The deputies, who served under Stan Gilbert, all talked about how great Stan was. Jackson felt much the same way about Skip, but the older guys didn't. They didn't think he measured up to his old man, one of the reasons he was having such a hard time with Stringer. Stringer was of the old school, the one that worked the longest under Stan. It was funny, Jackson thought, how they could oppose the son so much when they respected Stan the way they did. He shook his head in bewilderment.

At the Jennings' farm, Stringer was half way up the driveway. One of the yearling pups smelled him. The pup watched him from under a pine tree branch as he made his way to the house. He whined bringing his father, the alpha male, to stand beside him. In the language all their own, the wolves communicated then moved off into the darkness.

In the yard, Stringer still didn't see any wolves. He looked up at the house and saw two kids standing in the window staring back at him. Pretty young, he decided and went up to the kitchen door knocking as he removed his snowshoes.

Mike opened the door. When Stringer showed him his badge, Mike invited him in. Secretly Mike was very happy to have an adult on the scene; doubly glad the adult was a cop.

"You kids alright in here?" Stringer asked as he looked around the room. With so much going on, he thought it might be wise to check out the house, what with Noone's whereabouts still a mystery.

"Where are your folks?" Stringer noted everything about the house in a single glance. He also noted the kid's demeanor, dress, and the fact that there were more children sleeping on the living room couch.

"They aren't here, officer," Mike said. "They got stuck at a neighbor's house just after the storm started."

"Well, who else is here with you?" Stringer probed briskly.

"Our younger brother and sisters. They're asleep in there." Mike pointed to the living room.

Stringer observed that the house was neat and clean, as were the two kids in front of him. Still, he checked further. "You kids hear anything that sounded like wolves howling?" He asked, gauging their reactions.

"Yes, officer, there was a pack of them right outside the door. They left just seconds before you showed up. You didn't see them?"

"No, I didn't see anything." Stringer eyed Mike suspiciously. "Did you see them leave?" He didn't like the idea of not seeing the wolves for himself. If they were there, like the kid said, he was right out there with them. He didn't like that idea at all.

"No, I didn't, but you can look outside at the tracks if you don't believe me," Mike said, rankled by the way the deputy talked to him. He could tell Stringer didn't believe him.

Vicki nodded her head in affirmation as Mike spoke.

"I'll do that. I will be back though. I'm going to look around outside to see what's going on. You haven't seen another deputy over here this evening, have you?" Stringer sounded like he was daring Mike to lie to him.

"No, we haven't. In case you haven't noticed, there is a storm out there, has been for two days, not too many folks are out in it," Mike said.

Stringer gave the kid a dirty look and went back outside. Smart ass kid, he thought as he stepped down from the front steps to scan his flashlight across the lawn. Right in front of him, he saw the tracks the kid told him about. Could be dog, could be wolf, he thought as he bent down to study them. They were big though, a lot bigger than most dogs.

He found the guide rope to the barn, shined his light along the path, and saw the human tracks beside it. Human tracks went down then backed up to the house while an animal's tracks overlaid the first set of prints. Some of the tracks were blown over thanks to the storm, but there were enough left for him to see that something had happened on the pathway to the barn, and not too long before he got there.

"Looks like the wolves forced the kid away from the barn. But why?" He said to the storm. Stringer shinned the flashlight all across the Jennings' lawn looking for the wolves. He saw nothing but blowing and drifting snow. He started down toward the barn floundering often in the deep snow, in spite of the fact he followed the trail already broken. He could hear some kind of animal inside the barn. It had to be big because it was so loud he could hear it over the roar of the wind. When he finally reached the barn, Stringer worked hard to pull the barn doors open, but so much snow had drifted in front of them, they wouldn't budge.

As he worked, he remembered where he was. "Oh, the Jennings' farm! Home to old Steamroller. God, I hope it isn't that bull in there!"

Finally, the door opened enough to allow Stringer to squeeze his slim frame inside. He found the light switch, and turned it on. As the overheads lit up the interior, they were so bright he was blinded and had to wait a few seconds for his eyes to adjust before he could really see what was inside.

To his left were neatly stacked bales of straw, then he noticed the bullpen. The fence was so high, the boards so broad and thick, he couldn't see if anything was inside it.

Stringer was no farm hand. He didn't realize that what he was looking at was a bullpen, so he moved in closer to get a better look. Whatever had been making a racket was now quiet and had been since he opened the barn door. As Stringer bent down to peer between the heavy boards that made up the bulk of the bullpen, he wondered why anyone would build anything so enormous. What did they keep in here, elephants? He wondered, smiling at his own wit. But as his eyes gazed down the slats, he saw the reason for the fence staring right back at him and gasped for breath. He and Steamroller were eyeball to eyeball.

Stringer screamed and jumped back from the fence.

The bull bellowed rage blowing snot, and spraying Stringer's face. Steamroller was mad, literally. He wanted blood. One human hadn't satisfied his blood hot unreasonable rage, which once released, could not be contained. The bull pawed at the sawdust strewn floor still staring threw the boards at the deputy who had fallen away from the fence. He had already charged the fence a half a dozen times since his attack on Trelavonti repeatedly ramming the posts, weakening them considerably.

Stringer had seen the bullpen floor before he scrambled away from the fence. As he worked up the courage to go back, he noticed Trelavonti's utility belt lying on the straw bales. He picked it up to examine it.

The bull bellowed from inside the pen. His rage echoed throughout the barn. It seemed to come at Stringer from every conceivable direction; still, the frightening din was not going to scare him off, not when another deputy was missing. Stringer handled the utility belt gently, as if it were a child. He caressed it knowing it belonged to a fellow officer. He hoped Trelavonti hadn't gone inside the bullpen as he looked around for more clues to Trelavonti's whereabouts.

Slowly, he walked back over to the bullpen. He didn't know the fence was weak. He moved in closer, seeing that the bull had moved to the far end of the pen. As he stared around the enclosure, a bright object in the middle of the floor caught his eye.

Trelavonti's badge was there lying amidst blood and gore. It had to be his badge, Stringer thought, even though he couldn't see the nametag. It was exactly like the one he had on. Deducing from the tracks in the driveway, the utility belt, and the badge, Stringer figured Trelavonti had to have made his way into the barn.

The red and greasy splotches in the sawdust told a tale, too, one he didn't want to think about. I'll have to go in there, he thought pondering how to do just that as he stood close to a post that had been shattered by the bull already, a post that with very little effort would completely give out.

Steamroller took that moment to charge full speed and rammed the fence post once again, this time directly in front of Stringer.

Crack! The sound of the wood splintering echoed throughout the barn like a rifle shot. With panic rising like bile in his throat, Stringer ran for the barn door before the bull could get out. He squeezed back out through the slim opening and pushed the barn door shut behind him standing still for a second to catch his breath. He was terrified. He realized as he looked at the door that it probably wouldn't hold the bull long if the bull was determined to get out.

He slung Trelavonti's police utility belt over his shoulder and hastened back to the front steps of the farmhouse. He made good time climbing back up the hill thanks to the already broken trail and his own terror. Stringer looked over his shoulder fearing that the bull would make his escape at any moment. He could hear the animal raging and ramming the wooden door with his massive head. It wouldn't be long before the bull was free of the barn. Stringer had no time to waste.

As he reached the back door to the kitchen, Stringer pounded on it praying that the kids inside would open it before the bull got loose. With the howling, blowing snow, and the bull screaming and charging the barn door, the extra cop belt over his shoulder testifying to what happened to Trelavonti and the wolves probably somewhere close by, Stringer was past terrified. Never in his life of facing all kinds of obstacles, had he ever faced a fear such as this.

Vicki opened the door to the terror stricken Stringer.

"My God! What's going on?" She could hear the barn doors splintering as Steamroller screamed inside. His screams reached out over the din of the blowing, howling snow and winds to frighten Vicki right along with Stringer. If an adult was that terrified of an animal, she reasoned; she had better pay heed.

"The bull!" Is all Stringer managed to say; he was so winded.

"Is he out?" Mike asked joining Vicki at the door. He grabbed Stringer by the arm pulling him inside. Vicki shut and bolted the door, shaking so badly she had trouble working the deadbolt lock.

"He's breaking down the barn door," Stringer gasped, "I think he hurt a deputy." His whispered as if afraid to voice his fears.

Vicki helped him to the kitchen table sitting him under the Lord's Prayer plaque, and pouring him a cup of hot coffee.

Stringer regained his composure and said, "You two sit down." Mike and Vicki joined him at the table. They were so happy to have an adult with them they didn't care how bad his attitude was.

"I found this down in the barn," Stringer said after he managed to regain what little composure he had left, and held up Trelavonti's belt. "Do either of you know how it got there? Has any other policemen been here tonight?"

"No; we told you that." Mike said. "No one has been here but us. I've never seen that belt before."

Stringer sipped the hot coffee asking no more questions. He pulled his walkie-talkie from his utility belt calling his fellow deputies over at Noone's.

"Hey," he said to Jackson who answered the call. "I'm over here at the neighbor's and I've found Trelavonti's utility belt.

It was in the barn with one furious bull. The only people here are kids who say they haven't seen Trelavonti. The bullpen is full of blood and gore. Looks like a badge in the middle of the floor. Couldn't get at it though; the bull is in there, or I should say, was in there. He's trying to break out of the barn doors right now."

"Keep those kids in the house!" Jackson barked. "And stay in there with them. We've got some stuff to finish up here. I'm calling the highway department to get them back out here to plow again, so the MBCA and FBI can get out here, too; I'll get them to plow that driveway then. If that bull gets loose and is as crazy as you think he is, you better try and shoot him. You have a shotgun in the trunk of your squad, use that.

Are those kids by themselves? Why aren't you talking to their parents?"

"Kids say the folks got stuck at a neighbor's as the storm hit."

"Do they look like they're okay?"

"Yeah, they don't appear to be neglected, everything looks pretty nice here, clean house, clothes, there's plenty of food." Stringer smiled at Mike and Vicki for the first time. He knew they could hear everything Jackson said.

"Alright, but since they're alone, stay there until I can get over there. Maybe we can go get the folks and bring them home. By the way," Jackson made sure he added this, "don't go giving a couple of kids the third-degree. We'll find Trelavonti, find out why that belt was down there in their barn. God knows what he thought he was doing going over there."

"One other thing you might want to know. That bull. He is determined to get out of that barn and he's almost out now. I won't be able to make it to the cruiser for that shotgun, had to leave it out on the main road. You'd better watch out for him when you get over here and get out of your car, and tell those highway guys to be on the lookout. Hell, if they hit him, he'll probably tear up their truck!" Stringer was happy not to be the one facing down Steamroller.

"That's old Steamroller isn't it?"

"Steamroller? Sounds like somebody named him right, that's all I can say," Stringer said.

They rang off and Stringer turned his attentions back to Mike and Vicki. They looked like nice kids. "Hey, kid, what kind of bull is that down in the barn. He scarred the shit . . . oh, sorry . . . he scarred the daylights out of me."

Mike told him all about Steamroller.

Although no one was watching out the window, the wolves were back, this time down by the barn.

As Stringer and Mike talked inside the warm kitchen, the scent of blood stunk up the barn, inciting Steamroller's full-blown killing frenzy even more. He rammed his head against the barn doors stabbing the wood with his horns in an insane effort to be free of them. He pawed the sawdust-covered floor as adrenaline screamed through his veins and he sought out something, anything, to attack. He could smell something just outside the door, which enraged him beyond endurance increasing his efforts at the door as he rammed then again and again.

Inside the house Stringer told Mike what he had seen in the barn, how the bull acted and how it scared him half to death.

"How did Steamroller look?" Mike asked.

"Hell, kid, when I saw his eyeballs, I took off outta' there. I didn't get a real good look. His eyes, though, they looked crazy to me." Stringer said.

"Did you look in the pen? Was the other deputy in the pen?"

"Like I said kid, all I saw was that bull's eyes. I didn't take a lot of time to look around his pen, if you know what I mean."

"Did you look at the bull at all? What color was he?" Mike grew impatient. Deputies were supposed to be trained observers, not little scarredy-cats like this guy, he thought.

Stringer didn't catch the exasperated tone in Mike's voice, or chose to ignore it. "The big old bull is a reddish tan. I saw his chest. It was all red, but the rest of him was tan like. You ever see a buckskin horse? Well, he was that color. Dun, I guess you'd call it."

"Red, on his chest?"

"Yeah, he was bright red, almost looked like blood. Come to think of it, the barn smelled like blood. You and your daddy butcher anything down there lately?"

"No we haven't." Mike got up, went to the porch putting on his outer clothes.

"You can't go down there by yourself, Mike, you have to take this guy with you," Vicki said knowing exactly what Mike was thinking. She had also listened to her father's stories enough to know that Steamroller had gone berserk. She knew, too, that one fifteen year old boy should not attempt to stop a nineteen hundred pound berserk bull from doing as he damn well pleased, which usually meant hurting anything that got in his way. She didn't want to think Steamroller had killed anything; she liked the big old bull that had always let her pet his head. But she knew how dangerous and unpredictable they could be. Their father had spoken to them about it often enough. The whole household knew it.

Stringer jumped up behind Mike and said, "Look kid, if that old bull is nuts, you can't go down there by yourself. I'll come with you." Stringer geared up. He tried to gauge how long it would take him to get to the cruiser and get his shotgun. Most of that would depend on how far the bull was in his efforts to get out of the barn. The cruiser was down at the end of the driveway; he couldn't make it there for his shotgun and back if the bull was loose.

Finished dressing, Mike opened the door and headed outside.

But Stringer didn't need his shotgun. Mike stepped outside onto the back steps holding a 30.06 rifle. Stringer wondered how good the kid was with a gun.

Even if he is a good shot, Stringer thought, the bull will have to be brought down and the kid may not have the stomach to kill the animal. Regardless, Steamroller is beyond help now, and he is going to have to be shot before he can hurt anyone if he hasn't already. Stringer was pretty well convinced the bull had killed Trelavonti and though he had no use for his fellow deputy, he was a fellow deputy. Besides, if the bull killed once, what was to stop him from doing it again?

Mike and Stringer were half way to the barn before they saw the figures in the snow in front of it. Above the din of howling winds, they could hear Steamroller screaming inside the barn and saw figures sitting in a semi-circle in front of the barn door.

The biggest wolf saw them before they saw him. Standing, he turned to face them moving toward them as they made their way down the hill. When Mike saw the alpha male, he put up his left hand to stop Stringer, who walked directly behind him. Stringer had only his service revolver with him. His hands were covered with thick gloves and his gun was tucked into his service belt underneath his coat.

Mike raised his rifle to his shoulder. Stringer slowly removed a glove and lowered his hand to his revolver. The wolf stopped, bared his teeth in a silent grimace and hunched down as if to spring. Mike lowered the rifle. Stringer had his pistol out taking aim. Mike turned as Stringer was about to pull the trigger, stopping him.

"Back up!" Mike yelled above the wind, "Go back to the house! Put that gun away! He isn't going to attack us! He's warning us! Go!"

Stringer looked at Mike, then back at the wolf, then back at Mike, then the wolf a few more times before finally holstering his pistol. Once he did, he immediately eased his way back up the hill to the little farmhouse seeing that when he started to back up the wolf backed off. Mike did as he had earlier backing his way up to the porch right behind Stringer. Whenever the deputy or Mike slowed or halted their retreat, the wolf turned and took a few steps toward them baring his teeth encouraging the pair to get back. Mike and Stringer made it back to the safety of the back steps.

As Mike climbed onto the porch behind Stringer, all hell broke loose down at the barn. Steamroller rammed the barn door one final time to send wood splinters flying everywhere. The enormous animal bounded out into the ragging storm only to flounder in the three foot snowdrifts. He screamed and his eyes rolled back in his head as he moved it from side to side slashing at the air with his deadly horns. Steamroller screamed again as he lunged up the slope through the snow heading toward the house and Mike.

Stringer and Mike stood on the porch steps back-lit by a one hundred watt bulb as they watched the adrenaline drenched one-ton animal attempt to charge them. If not for the snowdrifts, the bull would have reached the house in seconds, but his heavy weight was floundering him, burying him in snowdrifts as deep as his belly as he tried to hurtle himself forward.

As he floundered, Steamroller realized that he was not alone.

Mike and Stringer watched helplessly from the porch as the wolf pack moved in around the bull. In his rage, Steamroller had focused on the men in front of him and had not seen the predators that now surrounded him. He didn't realize that the wolves came in from all sides to flank him. Steamroller saw the yearling pups in front of him, but did not view them as a threat. He didn't see the big alpha male as it lunged at his back legs tearing at his hamstrings. The alpha female moved in on the other side doing the same thing there. Before he knew what hit him, Steamroller was dropped to his knees. He couldn't get up. The wolves didn't move in to kill him; they tore at his legs and his thighs eating the enraged bull alive as he bellowed in anger and pain. The bull, screaming, wanted to reach his attackers to stomp them into the dirt. Instead, Steamroller could do nothing but endure the torture.

Mike shouldered his rifle, aimed, and fired.

Steamroller's screams were silenced. Unearthly quiet overtook the atmosphere. It seemed that even the winds had stopped howling as the man and the boy stared at the bull being devoured by the wolves.

When the gun went off, the wolves backed off, temporarily. They pulled in again to continue feeding once no more shots were fired. They were hungry. None of the pack had eaten in three days.

Chapter Twenty Eight

Shorty, Franco, Skip and John were not asleep. They were too wound up to sleep. Climbing the stairs, they talked quietly when they saw that the others had retired to their respective bedrooms, congregating in Skip's room to continue their conversation.

Skip said, "In part, I think I'm here because I'm a cop, but it has, for me, more to do with Ellen because I still want to know what happened to her. Add my dad to that because of all those unsolved cases. Sam's house . . . somehow, it's all wound together tighter than a top." Skip was uncomfortable speaking of these things to people other than fellow officers.

"I understand why you're here, but why me?" Shorty said; he, too, felt ill at ease. "Something is going on here, I can tell that by listening to you guys, by my gut feelings. I even think that the wolves are connected to it all. I just can't get a handle on why I'm here, and believe me, I feel like I was called to be here. I mean it's forty below out there. I had to climb over drifts high enough to flounder most animals. To top that off, I had a wolf escort! So, yeah, I'm supposed to be here. The question for me is—why?"

Franco and Skip shook their heads, agreeing with Shorty, but with no more insight than his.

Maybe, Skip thought, it's because Shorty is an expert outdoorsman, but why would that be important? And besides, Sam is here. She's an expert outdoorsman, too.

"It could be because of your connection to Noone," John said. "Maybe you're here as a warning for us, something positive, I mean." He smiled at Shorty.

"Yeah, maybe that's it. I'm out hunting for the one who's made a fool of me, but there's more to it than that. I didn't know he was snow-balling me till I got here. I'm here because I was worried about him; afraid he was hurt or something. Maybe that's it. Maybe I was just supposed to learn the truth.

I can't believe I'm even talking like this . . ." Shorty kept going with his train of thought. "And the wolves, it's like they knew all along. I've been sitting here thinking about the times I was out there stalking little 'ole Sam myself, with Noone's blessings, I might add, and it was then that some wildlife scared me off from making a move on her. That's what I was planning . . . you know? To hurt her, not bad mind you, but to scare her off. Rough her up a bit. You know how she is, Franco. Shit, scarring her off is like trying to scare a grizzly off a kill. I would have had to hurt her some, at least, to get her out of the woods."

John turned away, aghast that Shorty so easily could consider hurting a woman. His words angered Franco, who glared hard at him not at all intimidated by his size. Skip, muscles taught, was ready to jump Shorty at the slightest provocation.

Shorty wasn't stupid; he could tell he had angered the men he sat and talked with and he didn't like it, but he had spoken nothing less than the truth. He continued, "But I didn't," he said defensively. "Why? Because something somewhere is protecting her. Me too. If I had hurt her, there would be no telling what would have happened to me. I'd be locked up for sure, and that'd kill me. I'd rather be dead than stuck in a tiny cell for the rest of my life, so whatever is at work here, it knows us—real well, all of us. We're linked whether we like it or not."

"Do you smell that?" Skip asked no one in particular. He sniffed at the air.

"It smells like smoke," John said absentmindedly until Angie's warning flooded his mind with terror.

Skip's room, at the far end of the upstairs hallway, was the furthest away from the stairwell. In the split-second it took the men to realize what was happening, Shorty bolted for the door flying for the stairwell. Smoke billowed up from the dinning room.

"We got a fire here!" He yelled behind him to the men on his heels. "You guys get everyone up! Find a window. Get the hell out of here! Fire is already coming up the steps!"

Regardless of the smoke and flame, Shorty didn't hesitate. He hit the stairs running fixed on making his way to the basement. He knew Stan was down there next to the furnace. He was going to get him out. As a trained volunteer fireman, he was perfect for the job. Everyone else was upstairs; the other three men could get them out. Shorty was about to leap over the railing into the hall between the dinning room and kitchen, when Skip stopped him.

"Go help the others!" Skip yelled above the roar of the blaze. "I need to help my father." Shorty didn't argue. There was no time. He ran back upstairs.

Flames engulfed the dinning room, and were rampaging through the living room sending tongues of fire licking into the hall desperately searching for more fuel. Skip ripped off his shirt, covered his mouth and nose, and jumped over the railing, landed on the dinning room floor and crawled his way into the kitchen over to the basement door. Coughing, choking on smoke, and dogging flames, he got to the door, jumped to his feet, pulled the door open and flung himself down the stairs.

The basement was smoke free, so Skip knew it wasn't the point of origin of the fire as he thought it might be. He found the furnace as it should be, and there, in front of it sat his father slumped over in a lawn chair.

Asleep, Skip thought, disgusted with his father as he ran over to him. He tapped the old man's shoulder. "Hey Pops, wake up!" When he got no response, Skip shook Stan harder.

A female voice whispered in Skip's ear, "He's not going to wake up, Hon." She spoke quietly letting what she said sink in.

Skip moved closer to Stan, and removed the blanket from his lap; as he did, pill bottles fell to the floor. Skip picked them up carefully reading each label. He knew what the pills were. It was the same medicine his mother had taken before she died. Morphine, it wasn't even medicine, just something to help with pain. Skip shook his head, bent down by his father, put his head in Stan's lap saying, "Why didn't you tell me, Pop. Why?" He sobbed, but not for long.

He stood up, pulled Stan's blanket over his head, grabbed his father, and threw him over his shoulder. Skip no longer noticed the smell of smoke. He moved over to the stair starting up the stairs. When he reached the kitchen, fire was licking at the kitchen cupboard doors. He made it out to the back porch where he laid Stan's body on the floor. He couldn't grieve now.

He had to get back inside to help the others.

Upstairs, Shorty made it into Clem's room first, hollering for Clem to get up. As Clem's mind grasped what was happening, his first thoughts were of Gladys and Inez, and as he hurriedly donned his clothes, he yelled at Shorty to check on the Spencers. Shorty rushed across the hall pounding on the sister's door with Clem at his heels. The two burst into the room where they found the women upright in their beds pointing their guns at the door. Shorty and Clem stopped dead in their tracks.

"You two can shoot us later. Right now, we got a fire and we gotta' get outta' here!" Clem yelled.

"Fire?" The women exclaimed smelling smoke.

"Yep, so come on! We're here to get you outta' here." Clem grabbed Gladys by the arm as he threw her her robe. Shorty did the same for Inez. "You two got nothin' to worry about. Not with us here." Clem didn't feel as brave as he talked. Hell, I'm too old for this, he thought as he tried to throw Gladys over his shoulder.

"Look here you old coot! I'll walk out of here on my own two legs, thank you very much!" Gladys thrust Clem's hand off her arm, stepped back and stared at Clem.

Relieved, Clem said, okay; he wasn't too sure he had it in him to lift her. Shorty didn't try to throw Inez up over his shoulder. She warned him off with a look.

"Come on! We have no time to waste!" Shorty ordered.

They headed for the hall.

Down the hall, Franco rushed into Sam's room terrified to see the fire had made its way to the stairs where her bedroom was. Franco took off his shirt and put it over his mouth and nose to make his way through smoke so thick he could barely make out nearby furniture. He could hear coughing coming from the floor on the other side of the room, where, he guessed, her bed was. He got down on his hands and knees crawling his way along the wall to get to her. The air was clearer near the floor as he yelled out "Samantha!"

"Over here!" She coughed back as best she could.

Franco found her in no time. Dressed in sweats and shoes, Sam smelled the smoke and was getting ready to get out of the room when all of a sudden, it filled with it. She lost sight of the door and got down on the floor trying to find it, except that she wasn't heading for the door when Franco called to her; she was headed deeper into the bedroom.

With a sigh of relief, she grabbed onto his shirt as together they crawled for the door and out into the hall.

"Angie, we've got to get Angie!" Sam yelled springing to her feet and down the hall to Angie's room, which was right across from Inez and Gladys'. Just as they were about to burst through the door, it opened and Angie came out with Gladys, Inez, Clem and Shorty in tow.

Meanwhile, John ran into the bedroom he shared with Bernice, located right across the hall from Sam's. Immediately he knew something was wrong. The room was so thick with smoke he couldn't see, not until he got down on his hands and knees and crawled over to their bed did he find her. She lay quietly wrapped in bedcovers as if in deep slumber. John shook her shoulder. She didn't budge; he shook her again, then again, all the while pleading quietly for to her to wake up, pleading with God to breathe life back into her, but Bernice had succumbed to smoke inhalation. She had died in her sleep.

Grief grabbed a hold of John and squeezed him in a vice. He was stunned, couldn't comprehend life without his wife.

Out in the hall everyone else took stock of who was and wasn't here. "Bernice! John!" Sam cried. "Where are they?"

Shorty didn't wait. He rushed down the hall to the Jennings' bedroom. He smelled the smoke before he opened the door. "It's bad in there," he said looking back down the hall into the terrified faces of the others. "It looks like the fire is eating up this end of the house. Don't come down here!

Franco, you and Clem start looking for a way out through one of the upstairs windows. The rest of you wait right where you are for me so I'll know who is still in the house. I've got to get John and Bernice!"

Sam wanted to run down the hall to help, but suffered a bout of coughing so severe she doubled over in the hallway. She wanted to grab Bernice and the others and get out of the house! Instead, she fought for air and prayed that John and Bernice were okay and that Shorty could get them out.

As Shorty opened the bedroom door, he went to the floor immediately crawling along the wall in hopes of finding the bed, which, he knew, was where he would most likely find the couple. John hadn't been in the room long enough to have succumbed to smoke inhalation, but he was much less certain of Bernice. He knew she had gone to bed and most likely had been sleeping while the fire licked its way up the stairs filling her room with smoke. John told them she had gone to bed when he came into Skip's room.

He pushed those thoughts aside when he finally reached the bed. Still sticking close to the floor, he used his hands to grope along top of the bed to see if anyone was lying there. He did not want to stand up. The smoke was so thick he couldn't see his own hand as he reached out with it. His lungs seared and his eyes watered. With probing fingers, he encountered John's hand. He lay next to Bernice on the bed. He started to cough at Shorty's touch. Still, no sounds came from Bernice.

Shorty stood up, grabbed John, slapped his face, and hurled him to the floor. He grabbed a blanket, wrapped Bernice in it and picked her up, crab walking to the other side of the bed, grabbed John by the collar, and made his way back out of the room coughing and hacking. He drug John along as Bernice hung over his shoulder. He couldn't stand because of the smoke. It was so thick he faltered just as he reached the door. With what he believed was his last ounce of strength against the billowing smoke, he burst into the hall coughing so hard he almost dropped his bundle as he sank to the floor. John still couldn't stand; he slumped over Bernice coughing harder than Shorty.

Shorty slowly managed to stand, and as he did, he grabbed John by the collar once again dragging him to his feet, and shoving him down the hall to the others who, in shock, hadn't moved. Clem, having searched out a route of escape, was back in the hall. He grabbed John as he stumbled over to him, coughing and crying.

As Shorty picked up Bernice to drape her over his shoulders once again, everyone realized collectively what he was carrying and what must have happened.

Sam let out a wail of anguish slumping down the wall she stood against. Gladys and Inez grabbed her hand to steady her and themselves, as their knees grew weak and started to give way. Angie held on to Sam, keeping her on her feet.

Seeing the women's reaction to what they knew was Bernice, Shorty yelled, "There is no time for that now! We gotta' get outta' here! Now!" He started for the steps forgetting that he had Clem and Franco scouting out an alternative escape route.

"You are going to have to take off your shirts, or something, so you can get through the smoke. It's bad down here." Shorty looked down the steps. Fire ate at the staircase closing them off from that route of escape, just as he feared. He turned back to the others. "Back!" He coughed as he tried to yell. "It's too bad! We'll never be able to get out this way. Sam, is there a porch roof we can get out onto?"

"Yes! Right off of Skip's bedroom!" Everyone ran to the end of the hall. Franco and Clem had already found it and made the way ready for the group to escape.

As they rambled into Skip's room, Sam jumped over the bed running to the big windows. She went to throw the latch open releasing the screen, which normally gave her trouble, but Franco and Clem had already done that, too. "Where are Fuzz and Kitty?" she searched the room frantically with her eyes. "I haven't seen them, have any of you?"

"No!" Shorty yelled. "You can't think of them now; you've got to get out of here!"

The group looked down onto the porch roof. They could see the flower trellis coming up from the ground, and one by one climbed out of the house using the trellis like a ladder to climb down off the roof. The elderly went first, and everyone else followed. All escaped.

Standing in the front yard, in the midst of the blizzard, they once again accessed who was and who wasn't with them. Skip and Stan weren't there. The fire raged on the north side of the house where the group moved and stood looking into the kitchen. Through the windows, they saw flames greedily devour all Sam owned.

Even though Shorty still carried Bernice over his shoulder, he ran up onto the porch thinking he would lay her down there, and go back inside to find Skip and Stan. As he did, he found Skip kneeling over his father who was lying on the porch floor. Skip's hands and face were burnt. His hair was singed on his head, as were his eyebrows and mustache.

"I thought you guys were all inside," Skip tried to say to Shorty. "I tried to go back in, but the fire." Cough, cough, cough, "it's too hot. I can't get in!" He sat over his father looking dumbfounded up at Shorty. Shorty put his free hand on Skip's shoulder, still clinging to Bernice with the other.

"Come on, man, grab your dad. We gotta' get outta' here." Shorty gently helped Skip to his feet with his free hand. When Franco saw Skip stand up, he, too, ran up onto the porch. He saw the big form wrapped in a blanket lying on the floor.

"I'll help with that," he said picking Stan up and throwing him across his shoulders. The men went back outside into the yard where everyone else still stood.

Gladys stared at the bundle Franco carried, saw Skip stumble off the porch, his burns, and her legs turned to rubber as she started to slip to the ground, but Clem standing beside her, grabbed her and held her up before she could tumble into the snow. Inez grabbed her other arm.

Sam gasped in spite of herself when she saw Franco and Skip, the bundle across Franco's shoulders. The only one missing was Stan. Skip looked bad, real bad. Her hand moved to her heart as she realized Stan, too, was dead. Angie stepped up to her putting her arm around her shoulders.

Everyone stared at Franco's bundle, then at Skip who visibly fought the physical and emotional pain. He tried to focus on the immediate situation, but couldn't seem to get his mind off his father. Shorty once again took charge. With bodies draped over Franco and Shorty's shoulders, and Skip's burns, the horror of the night sank deeply into everyone, but Shorty wouldn't let anyone dwell on it.

"Is that barn warm?" he yelled to Sam. The blaze was so hot no one was cold, although no one wore a hat, coat, gloves, or even boots.

"Yes, very." She whispered.

"Alright, everyone, grab that rope (the lead rope was still attached to the barn) and head down there. We'll be safe there for awhile." No one argued. They marched single file down the path to the barn with Franco and Shorty bringing up the rear.

"When we get down there, I want you to find a cell phone. Call for help, keep everybody calm. I'm going back up there and fight that fire," Shorty said to Franco.

"What are you going to do, put it out by yourself?" Franco hissed.

Shorty ignored him, wondering if it was safe to go into to the barn. With the horrific wind, the fire could easily spread there. But he couldn't dwell on that; too much else was happening.

Franco moved forward behind Skip. When Skip stumbled and started to fall, he grabbed his arm with his free hand and helped him down to the barn. Franco had to half carry him as they all trudged through the deep snow. When they got to the barn, John took Skip inside. Everyone else followed except Shorty and Franco.

"What are we going to do with these bodies?" Franco asked Shorty, as they stood outside in the cold and blowing snow, both weary and heavy-laden.

"I don't know? We can't leave them outside. The wolves might still be out here. It wouldn't be right to leave them where the wolves could get at them."

"I thought I saw a small wood shed just around the corner when I pulled up," Franco said. "Let's put them in there out of danger and out of sight of everyone inside. It's bad enough Stan and Bernice are dead; I don't think it would benefit the other's to have their bodies to stare at."

"Yeah, that's probably best. Why don't you wait here and I'll find the shed and check it out. If it's in decent shape, I'll call you and you can bring Stan over. We gotta' get a move on though cause it might be warm from that fire out here right now, but we aren't safe from the cold until we get inside."

Shorty found the shed secure and both men carefully placed Stan and Bernice's bodies inside. When they finished securing the door, they ran for the interior of the barn to regroup with everyone else.

The fire raged throughout the house by then. It lurched up the stairs greedily devouring bedrooms as if in a feeding frenzy sucking up what oxygen there was like a vacuum. Wood crackled as shingles split and flew from the roof hurling burning embers across the lawn. Glass shattered and broke as heat permeated the house.

Shorty watched his worst fears come to life. The storms' winds grabbed lustily after the burning hot embers tossing them every which way. He watched in horror as hot embers fell before his eyes in front of the barn door he looked out of.

On Skip's cell phone, Clem managed to get through to the fire department while Shorty and Franco were still in the shed. The fire department reassured him telling him plows were on route to Sam's house and fire trucks would be right behind them.

He spoke to someone at the sheriff's dispatch that told him her name was Harriet who said that the road had already been partially plowed, up to the Noone house, so it wouldn't be too difficult for trucks to plow the next two miles to Samantha Egar's house. She told Clem that during dire emergencies the highway department was always willing to do what they could to help emergency vehicles. She told Clem not to worry. He told her two people perished in the fire. She assured him that ambulances would be there behind the fire trucks.

The group watched as the downstairs became completely engulfed in flames. Fire licked out of basement windows then, too.

Sam, in shocked silence, watched as all she loved and had come to know as home, burned to the ground in an angry frenzy, even her pets. She couldn't believe it. Everything was happening too fast. The fire seemed to be human, screaming above the raging blizzard in an angry attempt to be heard, to lash out at all of them. Numbly, she watched her house go up in smoke. She felt as if she were standing outside herself watching from a far off distance, some place where she could not be touched.

The fire had had too much time and fuel for help to arrive in time to save the house, Sam knew. All any fire department could do was keep the blaze from spreading. The storm was already doing that because the wind shifted blowing burning embers south away from the barn.

The others looked out the barn doors at the house ablaze, all at a loss to understand what had happened.

Shorty stood behind everyone. His fear of the fire spreading dimmed with the wind change. He breathed a sigh of relief. To his surprise the wind died down, too, letting the falling snow hiss on the fire to tame the tiger that, only a short time before ragged throughout the house.

The group stood transfixed as the first set of headlights rolled up the knoll on River Drive at the end of Sam's driveway. As the plow's rotating lights blazed into sight, everyone in the barn cheered. Even John and Skip felt a moment of exhilaration at the sight, however short lived.

The highway department crews plowed as fast as they could. A convoy of three trucks spread across the dirt road making quick work of the pilling snow.

Bruce Berlington, a volunteer on the Eveleth Fire Department and driver of the lead truck, would be damned if he wouldn't do what he could to help on a night like this one. It wasn't easy though, getting through the snow, even with the county's big rigs. Driving down River Drive, he was surprised to see that a big rig had already passed over the road at least once during the past twenty four hours and he was thankful for it. He kept in radio contact with the two other drivers behind him as they made their way into Sam's driveway.

What they saw when they crested the knoll didn't surprise them. Steve Crawford, his boss, had told him what to expect, which, in turn, Bruce had related to his crew. So as he headed up the driveway, Bruce made a sweeping pass forging a sizable amount of snow at the house when he reached it. He backed his rig up in the drive and plowed a space to move out of the way of the others, as they made the same type of swipe across the driveway following Bruce's lead also hurling snow onto the sizzling fire.

When they finished and moved out of the way, Bruce backed his big rig up once again, making a final run across the lawn gathering more snow and as before carrying it to the edge of the burning building, he dumped it in. Again, his crew followed suit. The three formed a convoy then and headed back out the driveway.

Behind the plows came the flashing lights of fire trucks and ambulances. The big fire engines waited on River Drive for the plows to roll out before they rolled in and began the arduous task of putting out the flames. Behind the fire trucks came the ambulances.

As emergency workers piled out of their trucks into the yard, Shorty was the first one out of the barn to talk to them. He told them what had happened; who was hurt and where the bodies were. Emergency technicians ran to the barn to treat Skip's burns. A fire marshal was already on the scene investigating both the fire and the cause of death of the two victims.

Harriet had called him personally to make sure he was on sight right away when she learned Stan had died. She also made sure that the other deputies knew what was going on.

Jackson saw the flames from Noone's house. When he learned from Harriet that a man and woman had died in a fire, he was afraid the pair could be the kid's parents. But Jackson couldn't leave Noone's.

Stringer had seen the fire from the Jennings' house, struggled through the storm with the kids out to his squad car, and brought them over to Noones' with him, as he tried to find out what was going on.

Jackson told the kids that they couldn't go over to Sam's just then, there were too many others there now. He would tell them anything they needed to know as soon as he was apprised. After assigning Stringer to stay with the children at their house, and after draping off Noone's property with police caution tape, Jackson headed over to Sam's leaving three squads and four deputies at Noones'.

Jackson got a quick run down on all that had happened from the fire investigator as soon as he pulled up behind one of the fire trucks. He saw Skip being treated for his burns behind one of the ambulances. Others, draped in blankets, stood around near the emergency vehicles shaking with cold while officers collected statements.

EMTs finally loaded them into ambulances whisking everyone off to local hospitals for further treatment. Skip refused to ride in an ambulance choosing instead to ride with Jackson to the hospital. Stan and Bernice were taken to the county morgue in Eveleth. John rode with them, while Bernice lay wrapped in a body bag on a stretcher next to him. Lights blazing, sirens blaring, ambulances headed out onto River Drive speeding toward Eveleth, Virginia and Hibbing.

When Jackson learned that the children had lost their mother, he radioed Stringer and told him to take them to meet the others in town without telling Stringer or the children that their mother had died. He would do that in person at the hospital.

All of the children, still in the police cruiser with Stringer sitting at the end of the Jennings' driveway, headed into town with Stringer. The youngest children, never having ridden in a squad car, considered the ride an adventure. Vicki and Mike did not; they sensed something terrible had happened.

Chapter Twenty Nine

The small St. Louis County morgue did its best to deal with not only Bernice and Stan's bodies, which were awaiting autopsy, but also with forty nine sets of human skeletal remains in need of preliminary examination. The bulk of evidence gathered from the skeletal remains would come from a forensic science lab in Minneapolis where they would be shipped after the cursory exam in the St. Louis County's morgue. In the meantime, FBI and MBCA experts worked in one exam room of the coroner's morgue while St. Louis County Coroner Dr. Michael Thorton autopsied the fire victims.

Thorton's small office crowded with police officers awaiting information on Stan's death. In the hall, agents from both the FBI and the MBCA awaited information on the skeletal remains, whilelistening with one ear for any news coming from the county coroner's office. Many law-enforcement departments mourned the loss of Stan Gilbert knowing him through professional contact over the years.

Sheriff's deputies stepped into the hall as Thorton began

his examination of Stan Gilbert. Thorton understood the officer's need to know; he was a friend of Stan's, too, but the overcrowding got on his nerves. The morgue was so overcrowded he didn't know how he could get any work done with so many distractions. He finally managed to ignore the din and concentrate on his work.

Even though impatient for results, officers understood the coroner's need for quiet, so as they hugged the wall outside the examination room to stay out of his way they remained unnaturally still.

Finally, Thorton put down his scalpel and looked at Jackson who stepped into the exam room quietly. "Your timing is perfect, Jackson. I just finished, and it looks like nothing but cancer killed Stan. His body is riddled with it. This pill bottle that came in with him indicates that he was on some pretty strong painkillers. We'll get the results of blood tests in about six weeks."

"He died in his sleep of cancer, fellas," Thorton said to all the sheriff's deputies who slipped quietly into the examine room behind Jackson. "It was eating him away. He must have been in a lot of pain." Thorton said no more, letting his remarks sink in.

Thorton took a break from his work and moved over to the other examination room where experts from the MBCA studied the bones found in Noone's basement. Jackson went with him. They learned that the bones were mainly those of young boys, fourteen-fifteen years of age. DNA testing was ordered, but would take time; in the meantime, Jackson and the FBI would be searching the data banks for missing children that matched any descriptions the MBCA could come up with after examining the skeletons. Jackson also learned that the girls' bodies were so mishandled, the MBCA examiner wasn't sure if he could determine how many there were. But, he told Jackson, there were eight skeletal remains that he could say for sure belonged to eight different girls; those ranged in ages from fifteen to eighteen years. At least two had given birth at some point in their young lives.

Thorton excused himself to return to the first exam room. He still had work to do on Bernice to determine her cause of death. He wasn't happy about it. He always felt that way when a woman too young to die of natural causes came before him.

On the other side of the Iron Range, at the Taconite Regional Medical Center, Sam, Angie, Clem, Gladys, Inez, Franco and Shorty waited to hear news of Skip's condition.

The group had traveled to Taconite hospital in Hibbing rather than the medical center in Virginia, which was closer to Sams' home, due to an overabundance of frostbite and car accident patients at the Virginia facility. The storm's pathway was heavier in the Virginia region, twenty miles south of Hibbing creating a wider path of destruction there, so getting to Hibbing had been much easier.

When Skip finally emerged from treatment in the emergency room, his face was covered in aloe; one hand was bandaged. The hair on his face was singed, and his hand sustained minor burns. He would have to keep his burns clean and bandaged, and come back for treatments every few days to insure no infections set in, nothing more.

Skip stopped in his tracks when he approached the waiting room; there he found his new friends gathered together and all staring at him as he approached. In them, he saw people he had come to respect and like, even love. Franco and Shorty proved to be reliable and strong, inside and out. Clem, the old curmudgeon, was even more of a friend than Skip already knew he was, Sam and Angie too, even Gladys and Inez. John—he sighed at the thought of Bernice and his father.

"Where's John?" He asked feeling compelled to go and talk to him. He needed to share his grief with someone whose loss was as deeply felt as his own.

"He's in the chapel with the kids telling them what happened to their mother. We've been waiting for you. We'd like to go see him, too, do something," Inez said.

"Come on then, let's go." Skip walked off toward the chapel.

Franco held back whispering to Shorty. "Hey, man, I'm not going in there. I don't know them at all. I think I'll go over to the coroner's and see what I can find out. I'll pay my respects when I get back."

"Okay, man. Sounds good." Shorty trailed off behind the others who were already turning into the chapel. He looked back at Franco to see him walking out the front doors. He wished he could do the same. He sighed as he opened the chapel door.

Back at Samantha's the fire investigator, Duke Hunter, went over everything police had told him from statements made, and what he had found for himself. The house was still too dangerous to enter even if the fire was out. Smoke tendrils blew in the raging wind, which had picked up once again. Hunter stood staring into the ruble while the cold wind tried to get him in its clutches. There was still too much heat from the fire for the cold to affect him much. It didn't matter to him anyway. On a case, he was so focused everything else was obliterated.

After shinning his flashlight onto the debris, he removed his leather bound shirt pocket notebook scribbling notes on what appeared to him to be the flash site location; when he would come back after the fire cooled he would take a good look at it. Then, too, he would look for any sign of accelerant. From what he could see, he suspected an electrical fault had started the fire.

Observing the way flying debris landed across the yard, he concluded that the wind had been blowing from the northwest when the fire burned its hottest. It was a stroke of luck for the people in the barn that it hadn't burned, too. The barn was more than likely a tinderbox.

With that thought in mind, Hunter turned his attention to the barn. He strolled down the hill, taking his time, studying the tracks in the snow. There was no danger of getting lost in the snowstorm because there were so many emergency vehicle lights flashing that they lit up the night like strobe lights. As he reached the big double barn doors and stepped inside, Hunter stood quietly at the threshold observing everything. His head turned slowly one hundred eighty degrees to take it all in. Standing as still as a crane, he looked for clues. The best way to find that which caused disquiet was to be quiet, he believed.

He noticed the partially opened library door. He noticed the long empty stalls, the debris standing next to the wall, the slats standing by the ladder leading, where? He moved closer, looked up the ladder, saw hay in the haymow. He noted that at the center of each rung, there wasn't as much dust as on the outer rungs. Someone had used it recently.

He moved closer to a pile of slats standing up against the wall, almost directly opposite the library doors and off to the side of the ladder. Upon close inspection, he found the slats were not lying there at random, as he initially thought, but were nailed together in a random pattern to conceal a door. He opened the door to find another ladder, this one descending into what looked like a tunnel. He switched on his large flashlight and stepped down the ladder. Downstairs, he discovered a maze of tunnels. He walked a short distance flashing the light against the walls. He stopped and looked around. In the stillness, he noticed marks along one wall; they had been drawn with colored chalk. He rubbed his finger across one of them, pulled it back, and looked at it closely. He noted the marks and the tunnels. He put his notebook back into his pocket, took another long look around, then climbed back upstairs carefully shutting the door behind him.

Once upstairs, he climbed the ladder into the haymow noticing once again that at the center of each rung, the ladder was free of dust. As he reached the top rung, he stopped to study the haymow much as he had the tunnel. He climbed into it and worked his way to the rear of the cavernous room shinning his light over ever little nook and cranny. He saw hay piled everywhere, in bales and loose. At the back of the haymow, away from the ladder, he saw where the hay had been mashed down; there he found the remains of a beef jerky packet, some string cheese. He noted those too, carefully describing in minute detail all he observed. He pulled his digital camera from his coat pocket, took pictures. When he finished, he went back downstairs and outside into the raging storm.

The firemen still worked hoping to insure no unseen embers would flare up again. Hunter climbed into one of the fire trucks. He was done for the night. The firemen would soon be finished, too, and then he could go back to his office. He'd come back out later that day, storm, or no storm, to examine the burnt remains of the house. Even though he hadn't been inside what remained of Samantha Egar's house, Duke Hunter knew that the fire was deliberately set. He knew it in his gut. He didn't yet know the why or the how of it, but he would. He might even venture further down into the tunnel.

Duke Hunter's reputation for being relentless when it came to uncovering the truth about any fire was legendary. All the firemen knew it. They shook their heads in wonderment watching him work, knowing by his mannerisms that he was on to something. Most pitied the fool who had tried to get away with setting a fire in that investigator's territory. Hunter never quit until he got his quarry.

By the time Franco arrived at the coroner's office, Thorton was finishing his autopsy on Bernice. She had died of smoke inhalation, Thorton told Jackson just as Franco arrived. When Jackson ran into Franco, he gave him the news. Franco immediately drove back to Hibbing to deliver the news to his friends. He found them all still inside the little chapel. John and his family were there, too. Everyone sat in pews praying and trying to comfort John and Skip.

"Bernice died of smoke inhalation, Stan, of cancer," Franco told them all quietly. No one said a word, but joined together in mourning, crying and holding one-another. After a short time, those who weren't immediate family quietly left the chapel to Skip, John, and the Jennings children.

Gladys, Inez and Clem walked down the corridor as if for the first time in their lives they felt their age, slowly, Clem slightly stooped. They left the hospital through the big glass doors into the storm crossing over to Clem's snowplow, which one of the deputies parked close to the door after he drove it in from Clem's because Clem rode in an ambulance with Gladys and Inez.

Sam and Angie walked to the hospital exit talking with Franco. Angie hugged Sam at the door knowing she was taking Bernice and John's deaths and the loss of her house and pets, hard.

Franco wanted to hug Sam, too, but couldn't work up the nerve to do so. Instead, he walked with the two women to the parking lot.

Neither woman remembered, at first, that they hadn't driven to Hibbing. When they realized they couldn't go anywhere, Franco offered them a ride home then remembered they had no home to go to, either. As they stood there trying to figure out what to do, Clem's big snow plow pulled up alongside them and Inez called out: "You two are coming home with us. We've got clothes you can wear, some coats and hats that will fit. You'll be safe at our house." The invitation came as a relief to both Sam and Angie. The moment of realization that everything was gone was such a let down; they couldn't even speak of it. They needed their friends. They nodded their heads in affirmation at Inez's invitation.

"Franco, would you like to come, too?"

"Nah," he said. "I have to get home, check on the bar, that kind of stuff." He smiled at them all thanking them anyway. "But I'd be glad to give these women a ride to your house." He looked at Sam and Angie smiling warmly.

"By the way," Inez continued, "where's Shorty."

"Oh, I forgot all about him," Angie said as she turned to look inside the hospital doors. She saw Shorty standing next to the admittance desk talking to a nurse. Just as she saw him, he turned and saw everyone outside. He ran out of the hospital and joined those who were still standing outside in the biting cold. The stinging and biting wind helped the quartet keep their minds off all that had happened, which was why none were in a hurry to get inside a vehicle.

"Shorty? Would you like to come and stay with us? Clem is coming over, so are Sam and Angie. We can use all the extra male protection we can get." Inez smiled.

"Yeah, I'd like that fine. Clem might need some help," he smiled at the three in the plow.

Clem wasn't too sure he wanted to smile back. He could take care of the women himself. Who was Shorty to question that? He smiled when it dawned on him what Shorty was really saying. It'd be easier if he wasn't the only man in a house full of women. Shorty jumped into the front seat of Clem's old plow as Inez and Gladys climbed in the back. The two vehicles headed out of the parking lot once again to take on the storm of the century. Their going was made easier by the fact that Clem's old snowplow proved it still had what it took to clear a road. When they reached the Spencer's house, Angie jumped out of Franco's SUV and hurriedly headed inside.

"Well, I better get going," Franco said hoping Sam would get out, too, so he could get home. He was exhausted.

"Hey, you, don't run off before I have a chance to thank you for your concern," she said, as on impulse she reached out and hugged him.

He hugged her back and said, "You scared me there for a minute. I thought you were going to throw me around a little."

She smiled. She hugged him again and started to cry. He held her tightly. In that moment and in that embrace both realized that nothing romantic would ever come of their relationship. In a flash, they knew that the sexual attraction between them had been replaced with something deeper, longer lasting.

Just then Angie came running back out to the SUV shouting to be heard above the wind, "Come on; we better get going." She yelled to Franco, "We want to see you again, soon. You hear? If I have to come to that bar and chase you down, we'll find you. I'll bring Samantha here and we'll take you out forcefully if we have to. Got that?"

He laughed. "You all should come to Tony's for a night out," he winked. He started his SUV and drove off out the Spencer sister's driveway shaking his head as he went. If anyone needed a night out it was every one that had been at Sam's house over the last few days. A feeling of sadness overwhelmed him brought on by the knowledge that he and Sam wouldn't have what he had hoped for. He refused to dwell on it, hurrying over the back roads before the storm could cover Clem's tracks once again, so he could make it back to his refuge, the bar.

Jackson made his way to the hospital. He wished he could leave Skip alone, but this case was way too big for that. He never knew Stan, but he knew Stan worked many of these same cases before he was even born, let alone a cop.

Skip should be the primary investigator on all of this, he thought as he walked down the hospital corridors to the admissions desk. He wondered if Skip had the stamina for it. He asked the front desk nurse where the sheriff was. She got up from behind the desk and escorted him to the chapel.

Skip pulled open the chapel door just as Jackson pushed it in, throwing Jackson off balance. "Hey, boss!" he said as he fell into the chapel.

"Hey Jackson. What brings you here?" Skip said snickering in spite of himself as he helped Jackson regain his equilibrium. He knew why he was there. He took a deep breath knowing that he would not get much time to grieve for his father.

"Well, I think you might know by now that we've found a bunch of bodies, skeletons, in the basement of Noone's house? Right?"

"Yeah, that's right; Harriet told me."

"What else did she say?"

"Nothing."

"Well . . . Trelavonti's dead. We're pretty sure about that. Seems old Steamroller got a hold of him in Jennings' barn and turned him into dust. The MBCA collected some of the blood from the bullpen floor, which they're analyzing for DNA to see if it matches Trelavonti's. That way we'll know for sure."

Skip shook his head at the news. No, he had not known Trelavonti was dead. "What the hell was he doing at the Jennings?"he asked.

"We don't know that yet, sir. Stringer followed his tracks up the driveway, though. Stringer said he heard wolves over that way, so he went to investigate, that's when he saw fresh human footprints going up their driveway. He found the Jennings' kids home alone and a crazy bull smashing through the barn door. Wolves brought the bull down but the Jennings kid had to kill it. He shot it in the head right between the eyes. Stringer said the kid is the best shot he's ever seen. He stayed with them while firemen worked at Egar's house," Jackson said. "The kids like him," he added shaking his head in wonderment.

Skip understood his amazement. "How were those bodies found?"

"The smell, sir. Trelavonti told Harriet there was an awful smell downstairs. He was bored, so he started digging where the ground looked 'odd.' It's a good thing Harriet took notes while he talked cause he sure won't be saying much now.

You should see what that bull did." Jackson shook his head at the thought of what little there was left of Trelavonti. He didn't like Trelavonti, but he sure wouldn't wish what he got on him.

"At Noone's? Skip, there are a lot of skeletons there. A lot of them, most in varying degrees of decay. Some have been there a long, long time. It is gross.

And you need to thank that Harriet. She's a real angel. She's the one that got the highway department to plow the roads when we went out to Noone's. She's also the one that got them to come back out to Egar's when she learned of the fire. She was pretty worried about you. She also prodded investigators to come out in this storm to investigate both crime scenes.

Oh yeah, the fire marshal, Duke Hunter, he called me before I came over here; he said he suspects arson. That makes the two deaths murders." Jackson's voice trailed off after giving Skip an abbreviated version of all that had gone on in the night. He watched his superior closely. Skip didn't say anything. He already suspected the fire was deliberately set.

"Go on," Skip said after a too long silence.

"I'm wondering, chief, if you're going to be handling this. I know you've done most of the preliminary, you and your dad, so I'm here to officially ask you to take over." He looked down at his feet; "I thought you might want to, for your dad, you know. Anyway, when you get out of here, you're probably going to find your hands full even if you don't take it over. Noone's place is a regular graveyard and now it's crawling with all kinds of cops."

Skip didn't say another word until the two men left the hospital and were standing in the storm next the police cruiser. Jackson unlocked the doors.

"Take me home, kid. I'm beat. I'm going to bed. But I tell you, when I get up I'm going to find out what happened. This is my case. I have no intention of letting anyone take it over. I'm talking about both the fire and the bodies found at Noone's. They're tied together. What I need you to do is to go out there and act on my behalf until I get up. Don't let any wise-ass FBI agent take over. Got that?"

"You bet, sir. But you should know. Those FBI agents aren't so bad. They worked with your dad; they aren't taking his death too kindly. They think it's fitting that you should be the lead investigator. They told me to tell you that, unofficially, any leads they dig up, they will be giving them to you."

Skip was touched. He slipped into the front seat of the cruiser. Jackson got behind the wheel starting the engine then rolling out of the parking lot. Both men sat in silence all the way back to Eveleth.

With all the commotion at the Noone house, Gladys, Inez, Sam, Angie, Clem and Shorty had a hard time getting to sleep even though all were exhausted. Gladys stood in the front room window

watching the flashing police cruiser lights as they lit up the storm
ravaged night sky. Dim light began to chase away the blackness of
night as she watched dawn break. She felt safe knowing that so
many policemen were so close, so did everyone else. No one
mentioned the fact that Noone was not yet in custody. Finally, the
quartet of women headed off to their allotted bedrooms to try and
sleep. Sam and Angie shared Inez's room. Inez shared Gladys'.

"I wonder what they've found over there," Sam said to
Angie as they prepared for bed. "It can't be good."

"I thought I heard someone say they found some bodies;
one of the Jennings kids told John that."

"Bodies?"

"Well, skeletons, mostly. Vicki and Mike and the other
children rode into town with a deputy and he told them that they
found bodies in the basement."

"Does that mean Noone has been killing people?"

"Looks like that may be the case . . . a serial killer. I never
picked up on that." Angie shook her head. Something at the back
of her mind was trying to reveal itself to her but she couldn't grasp
it. Something about Noone and another case she once worked
seemed similar, but she couldn't get a handle on it. "I need to get
some sleep."

"I can't believe Bernice is gone," Sam whispered just
loud enough for Angie to hear.

"I can't think about it. What is everyone going to do
without her?" Angie said. She rolled over into the pillows where
exhaustion delivered her into a dreamless sleep.

Still at the hospital, John tried to stay calm for the kids,
but it was the hardest thing he ever had to do. When a policeman
brought his children into the chapel, they found him kneeling in
prayer. They ran up to him asking for their mother. John got up

and took the youngest child into his lap, as Vicki and Mike sat next to him.

"Your mother has gone to meet her maker. She is with God in Heaven, now." He told them. Mike and Vicki realized what their father was saying, but sat motionless and silent. The twins did not asking John when she would be back.

"She won't," he said, "not in person. But she'll watch over all of us from Heaven. If you need to talk to her, kneel down and pray. She'll be there. God will too."

"Why does God have to have her? That's not fair! I want my mommy!" Jeremy cried into his father's shoulder grasping the fact that he would never see his mother again.

"I don't know why God wants her with Him, son." John hugged Jeremy and the twins Jasmine and Josephine to him.

"What happened, Dad? How did Mom die?" Mike asked.

"There was a fire at Samantha's," he said. "She died from smoke inhalation."

John said no more. He didn't tell the children that police suspected arson. He clenched his fists in anger as he considered Noone and what Noone had done. He didn't pay close attention to Mike or he would have noticed that Mike was not crying; neither was Vicki.

John tried to figure out what to do. He was lost. He didn't know what to do next without Bernice. This had to be some kind a cruel joke or he was in a bad dream from which he'd awake soon. Bernice would walk through that door any minute and he would tell her a thing or two about such a joke. It was not funny.

He didn't notice when Vicki slipped away. She called her mother's friends from church.

When the women of the church learned of Bernice's death, it wasn't long before a convoy of them arrived at the chapel to help John through everything. They took charge of the family, brought them home, feed them, and insisted that they all go to bed to rest. The church ladies enlisted the pastor's help in making funeral arrangements. The women notified relatives as well. Many of the relatives started arriving early Monday morning.

John slept fitfully until early afternoon. When he got up, he found his house full of people.

Determined to be of service to the well-loved family, the church ladies cooked and baked enough for the Jennings' family, so that they could feed an army and still not want for a meal for a month. By Monday afternoon neighbors and friends, too, were arriving to pay their respects. People that John had never met testified to Bernice's goodness. They regaled John and the kids with stories about her and to his amazement, John learned Bernice's capacity for love was even larger than he had realized. His heart ached for her with each new tale.

As did his anger. He wanted to hurt Noone. He knew in his heart that Noone was behind the fire that killed her. With people coming and going from his house, it took awhile, but John came to a point where he could stand it no longer. For the first time that afternoon he was alone looking out the front room window at the Noone farm, and saw as Skip's cruiser drove by. He quietly left the house and jumped in his truck to drive over there and confront Skip.

Skip stood outside talking to a deputy when John arrived. He had been expecting him.

"What the hell is going on over here, Skip?" John roared as he stepped out of his truck and approached the sheriff. "I want to know what you're doing about Noone! He killed her! As sure as I'm standing here, you know he killed her! He killed your father, too!" John's face was purple with rage, his anger overwhelming his normally amiable personality.

Skip's experience as sheriff had taught him over the years to be careful with grieving family members. "Easy, John. You're right, we do have some explaining to do, but we can't do it out here. There are too many ears. Do you understand?" Skip spoke in a quiet, soothing, mild voice.

John looked around noticing for the first time all the activity. Police officers swarmed over Noone's property. Most sheriff deputies knew who John was and what had happened. They discreetly kept a close watch on him as he talked to Skip. FBI agents noted John with interest as well as did the MBCA, all concerned with John's agitation.

Deputies and EMTs were still removing things from Noone's house. Things wrapped in black plastic body bags, John noticed. It hadn't dawned on him until then that a police investigation was going on concerning Noone, an investigation that had nothing to do with the fire. When Mike told him of the bodies found in Noone's basement, it hadn't registered in John's mind. It did then.

"What's that you're hauling out of there?" he asked.

"Bodies, John. Bodies."

"Bodies? What do you mean—bodies?"

"Noone has a lot to answer for, much more than just Bernice and Stan, much more."

"My God! You saying he's been killing people out here?"

"All I'm saying is that we've found bodies buried in his basement. He is going to have to account for this. That's what I'm saying. And John, he is going to have to account for Bernice and Stan, too. You can bet on it."

"I'm going home now, Skip, but when you finish up here; I expect a visit. Am I understood?"

"Yes, John, one of us will be over there as soon as we're done here."

"No Skip, not one of us, you, you will be over there. Is that clear?"

Skip nodded his head. He couldn't get angry with John. He was feeling the same rage and frustration.

"Tell me one thing now, sheriff. Has Noone been caught?" John demanded.

"No, John, he hasn't."

"In that case I want police protection for my family. I'm not going to see my kids hurt." John's calm manner belied the menacing undertone and Skip knew it. He couldn't blame him. Once he learns just how interested Noone really is in kids, he'll want a great deal of protection, he thought.

Skip worried about Noone, too. Where was he?

Stringer came up to Skip as John drove out of Noone's yard. "We've recovered all of the bodies. The medical examiner is gone; we've taken tons of pictures. We should be all set."

"All right. You get the rest of the crew and head back to town. I've got some things I have to do here, yet. John Jennings wants an explanation so I'll be over there awhile. When you get back to town, have Harriet round up some fresh deputies. Noone's still out there someplace and I want him caught.

Chapter Thirty

Shorty quietly dressed for the cold and made his way over to Noone's house to talk to Skip then he slipped past him and the rest of the police out to the woods. He would hunt down Noone. The police were so busy slipping past them was easy. He headed for Noone's shelter.

Shorty was sure he was the only one who could catch the old buzzard in that particular storm. I'm an expert tracker, and that's what the cops need right now, he told himself. Even with the storm still raging it didn't take Shorty long to reach the dugout he had holed up in just the day before. He knew right where to find it and expected to find Noone there, too, or in one of the many other shelters nearby.

If he ain't in this hideout now, he soon will be, Shorty thought as he walked across the tops of snow banks in snowshoes. Regardless of him being an excellent outdoorsman, the cold had the same effect on him as it did everyone else, and since the storm hadn't let up, he was grateful to find the dugout, and with great relief, he crawled inside to shelter out of the wind.

At the Jennings house, things were superficially calm. Vicki paced upstairs in her bedroom. She had slept some since learning of her mother's death, but dreams kept waking her. The dream images would not leave her alone. Instead, they intensified upon waking. She lay on her four poster bed with the light from her bedside lamp casting odd shadows across the darkened room.

Closed drapes shielded her from the raging storm outside her window. The day was as dark as her mood. But instead of offering comfort, the little lamp darkened her mood further with its eerie shadow casting. She reached over to shut it off.

As she did, diaphanous shadows danced across the purple walls of her room. Vicki watched, as pale yellow gossamer like images appeared to dance against the purple movie screen that was the wall. Her eyes grew large. A violet shadow swept over her coverlet and across the bed.

"Heeeelllllpppp!" Vicki screamed in her mind but couldn't force the word from her throat. It stuck there like a hairball, choking her.

The shadows grew in size.

Vicki watched in horror as they left the wall dancing a merry jig across her bed. She shut her eyes tightly praying they wouldn't be there when she opened them again. When she worked up enough courage to peek out from between tightly clasped fingers, she found the dancing figures had disappeared. Slowly she brought her hand down from her face to her lap as she looked carefully about the room; when she turned to the left, her hands slapped protectively back over her eyes once again.

There, beside the bed rail, were all the dancing phantasms lined in a row.

Vicki felt the end of her bed sink down as if someone sat at the foot of it. She expected to faint in terror as the weight settled. Instead, she grew calm. One by one, she drew each finger down again expecting to see something at the foot of the bed, but there was nothing there.

"You needn't be frightened," a voice inside her head said. Vicki gazed at her feet. "We aren't here to hurt you. We want to help you." Vicki knew that even though the sounds were coming from inside her own skull, the gossamer ghosts were speaking to her.

The voice said, "We are victims of Arthur Noone—all of us. He'll take more if we let him. We're not going to do that . . . Where's Mike?"

"He's in his room," Vicki stuttered, her own voice sounding odd to her own ears inside the empty bedroom.

"We need his help." The voice inside her head said.

Vicki climbed out of bed and put on her robe. She turned her doorknob slowly, trying not to make any noise. The door creaked as she drew it back, but no one seemed to be upstairs to hear it. Vicki tiptoed down the upstairs hallway to Mike's bedroom. She felt like the spirits were following her although she saw nothing. Slowly, she turned the doorknob to Mike's room. As it opened, Vicki couldn't see a thing. His room was in total darkness. Regardless, she quietly moved over to Mike's bed. "Mike," she whispered. "Mike!" She said, a little louder as she gently shook his shoulder.

Mike stirred under his covers swatting the air as if slapping at a mosquito buzzing in his ear.

Vicki called again, "Mike!" quietly. Mike, who had been facing the wall, rolled over and looked toward the door in a haze of sleepiness.

"Aaaaaahhhhhhhh!" He screamed grabbing the covers and jumping back on the bed. He became deeply entangled in the bed linens as he tried to hug the wall. He flailed against them.

At the sight, Vicki was glad she had shut his door when she came in. "Shut up you idiot! It's just me." She got as close to his face as she dared.

Recognizing her finally, Mike first sighed with relief then got mad because she scared him so badly. "What the hell are you doing creeping around my room!" he yelled.

Vicki worked hard to stifle her laughter; something much more pressing was prompting her to get Mike up and out of bed. "Will you be quiet? Do you want dad to come up here?"

Mike settled down after regaining his composure. He was glad none of his friends had been around to see him just then. He had been dreaming about Noone, that Noone was coming after him. Just as Vicki shook him and whispered his name, Noone was ready to stab him.

"Why are you in here?" He whispered hotly, now in complete control.

"There's something in my room."

"What?"

"I don't know? Something. I think they followed me in here."

"They?"

"Yes, there is more than one. They were talking to me. Inside my head, I mean."

"Talking to you inside your head? I really think you need to go back to your room and get some sleep. Have you had any yet?"

"Some. But these things, they're flying all over my room. They're yellow. One of them sat on my bed."

"Look, Vicki. We all miss Mom, but your imagination is running away with you. That's all it is. You didn't see anything. You didn't hear anything." Mike had a calming effect on her, but she knew what she saw.

When Mike finished speaking, a yellow light slowly played across the rust colored walls of his bedroom. In the darkness, the pale yellow, wispy shadow was crystal clear. More shadows appeared as if dancing, just as they had in Vicki's room. Mike's mouth dropped open in amazement. The figures stopped dancing abruptly, too, just as they had in Vicki's room.

"We need your help, Mike," a voice sounded in his head.

"What? Who is that?" Mike turned to Vicki hoping, and expecting, to see her lips moving.

She shrugged her shoulders.

"It's us."

Vicki sat down at the head of the bed next to Mike. Mike sat with his back up against the headboard. Neither one wished to deal with whatever those diaphanous things were.

Vicki looked at Mike, Mike at Vicki.

A voice talked to each of them now. "Ellen won't give up. Shorty is out there in the storm hoping to ambush Noone, but Arthur knows Shorty's there. He knows right where Shorty is because our mother tells him everything. She's one of us, too, you know, gone, I mean. She and Ellen are always fighting. Ellen knows who killed her, but our mother? Well, she won't admit it. Their argument is keeping all of us trapped here. We want to go home! Can you help us?"

"How do you know this if you're here with us?" Mike brazenly questioned the apparition out loud so Vicki could hear.

"I can be anywhere and everywhere. Arthur doesn't know it, but when he killed me at the river he set me free. I've been watching him ever since."

"Why don't you go to Heaven or hell then?" Vicki said. "Why are you still around here if you're dead?"

"I can't rest. None of us can, not until Arthur is punished. God is not happy with Arthur. He has not repented. He does not seem to care. Mother has been telling him that there is no such thing as God and he believes her. He is going to be punished."

"I'm not killing him for you, if that's what you want!" Mike got angry at the idea. "That's what people have the law for."

"Don't be silly, poor boy, we don't expect you to try and kill Arthur—goodness no! We want you to bring him to us so he can see us."

"Why don't you just go yourself? You said you could see everything," Vicki was indignant.

"God wants this finished. He wants the earth to give up its dead. You can help because you believe in God. His angels will go before you and He will be behind you. If you don't, Noone will make sure your dad's friend Shorty, that cop Skip, and your mother's friends are killed, just like he killed your mother and us. People don't mean much to him. He's been killing them for years."

"How do I know you're from God? You might just want to get us in trouble. Maybe bring us to Noone so he can kill us, too. He likes kids—a lot—doesn't he?" Vicki didn't like what the spirit was proposing, not one little bit.

"Oh, you are a smart one, you are. But you're just going to have to take my word. If we don't go over there, all those deaths will be on your heads. We need you to bring us there. Fear not, the Lord is with you."

Before Vicki could say anything more, Mike was out of bed putting on his pants. "What time is it, Vicki?"

"Nine."

"Good. Go in your room, get dressed, stuff your bed with something so it looks like you're asleep in it, and come with me. We're going over to Noone's."

"That's crazy! This spirit you're so ready to follow, you don't know where it comes from!" Vicki was bent at the waist facing her brother eye to eye, her nose crunched up and her brow furrowed as she stared at him in horror.

"Hey, what's wrong with you, anyway?"

"What's wrong with me? What the HELL is wrong with you?" Vicki yelled.

"Nothing. Just go do what I said and come on. We can walk over there. You want to stop Noone don't you? This might be our only chance. It's something we can do for Mom . . . for Dad, too." Mike needed Vicki's help and knew it. He was afraid of Arthur Noone. He didn't want to go over there by himself. He didn't want to see anything happen to anyone else either, including himself and his parent's friends. "Fear not—remember?"

"Mike, you don't know what you're saying. Noone is dangerous!"

"You don't need to tell me that. But what if these 'things' are right. You know you wouldn't be able to stand it if anyone else got hurt. We have to take this chance, Vicki! Now get the lead out and let's get over there!"

Reluctantly, Vicki went to her room to dress. She wouldn't let Mike go alone and he was so determined to go she knew he would go with or without her. She still had the pistol her father gave not two days ago. No one seemed to remember that she had it. She tucked the gun into the waistband of her pants. Before she left her room, she knelt down to pray beside her bed, "Lord, we need Your help. If this is You, guide us. If it isn't, keep us from getting killed, in Jesus name, Amen."

The two tiptoed through the house. So many relatives had come to pay their respects that the house was full. The teenagers carefully hid themselves as they made their way downstairs and out through the back door. They didn't know policemen were outside watching the house. Mike gasped at the sight of the patrol car, but since the storm still raged, the two managed to slip off at the back of the house where they were shielded from sight by grown pine trees and blowing snow. With their snowshoes on, they made good headway over the hard packed snow on the drifted field.

Vicki found it hard to believe they were going to Arthur Noone's house, but she didn't hesitate to keep up with Mike.

All was quiet inside the Spencer house. Everyone there had spent a quiet afternoon talking with Gladys, Inez and Clem. The elderly threesome treated Sam tenderly knowing how much she missed her house, her pets and Bernice. Gladys and Inez talked of all the wonderful things Bernice had done for them over the years, how she opened her house welcoming them when no one else in the neighborhood would give them the time of day. The women cried; made plans to go to John and see what they could do to help.

They also discussed Arthur Noone. So much had happened because of him, no one in the house wanted to think about the possibility of further attacks. Where was he? They wondered. As the day wore on, Inez and Angie found themselves keeping vigil at the windows, watching for any sign of his approach. Angie still couldn't put her finger on just how Noone was familiar to her, yet there was a tie to something in her past and him; she knew it.

The five stayed indoors out of the snow and wind, ate little, and took comfort from one-another in their grief.

In the late afternoon, Shorty said he was going over to talk to Skip next door. They all assumed when he didn't come back, that he was helping the sheriff with something.

Franco and Botticelli drove out to the Spencer house later in the day, much to everyone's surprise. Rumor had it that Botticelli never left the bar unattended, no matter what. But there he was with Franco bearing fast food, wine, and good cheer.

Franco was more subdued than normal, but Botticelli beamed as he went around the room making sure everyone had enough to eat and drink as he kept conversation lively and off Arthur Noone and the tragedies of the previous day.

Franco had filled Botticelli in on everything. And even though his spirits were high, Botticelli wasn't taking the situation lightly. He too had an instinctual aversion to Noone, and though he never told Franco, he brought his pistols with him.

Botticelli cornered Clem in the kitchen asking him what the household had in way of armament. Clem happily showed him his weapons. He also filled Botticelli in on the sisters and what they carried.

Although Clem wasn't aware of it, or if he was, never let on, he was well known in the region as a self-made man. When Botticelli learned he was with the Spencers and Franco's other friends he determined to ride out to the Spencers with Franco and meet the old man. He was happy to have a few moments alone to talk to him.

Botticelli also had other reasons for being there. He loved a good fight and from what Franco told him, Arthur Noone needed a good ass kicking. He would happily provide it. Although he never breathed a word about his feelings to Franco, when he found out Franco was nearly murdered; he was livid. The idea of loosing his old buddy to some freak, he couldn't abide. He insisted on going back out to the Spencer house, goading Franco into it. And now that he was there, he was a good diversion for everyone; cheering them up in spite of themselves.

Franco watched Botticelli nervously flit from one thing to the next recognizing that his oldest long-time friend was frightened. He guessed why, too, and was touched. They had been friends and partners too long for Franco not to know Botticelli was upset over the fact that he was almost murdered. He smiled as he watched Botticelli work the room. Everything is going to be all right, he thought, looking at Sam. Nothing is going to hurt any of these people as long as we're here. He thought of it as a statement of fact, already established.

Botticelli talked with Angie on the couch. "So," he said, "I hear you help police with unsolved crimes. Is that true?"

"Yes, it is. I've done so for many years." Angie was tired and though she liked this charming character sitting next to her plying her with his undivided attention, she didn't want to talk about work.

"You look tired. Would you like some more wine?" Botticelli offered jumping up to retrieve the bottle without waiting for Angie's answer. He sat back down next to her pouring before she could answer.

"Thank you; you're very kind." She smiled in spite of herself.

Botticelli grinned like a Cheshire cat.

As the evening wore on most everyone drifted back to sleep, on the couch, in the beds, anywhere they could get comfortable. All except Botticelli and Franco, who were used to staying up all night. Botticelli watched the windows closely, as Franco sat in the kitchen drinking coffee and thinking.

He wondered where Shorty had gone off too. It seemed strange that he wasn't there. The others mentioned in passing that Shorty went over to talk to Skip earlier, but he never came back, and Franco found that odd, real odd. He wondered if Shorty was out in the woods someplace. He hoped not. He got up and walked to the window bringing Botticelli a cup of freshly brewed coffee. Both stood in the dark room staring out at the night and the storm.

The going was easier since snowplows had plowed the back roads.

As Vicki and Mike hiked to the Noone house, Gladys, Inez, Sam, Angie, Clem, Franco and Botticelli, all waited out the night inside the Spencer home. Franco and Botticelli were looking out the window. They saw as the teenagers crested the hill, right across from the Spencer's driveway, and turned left toward Noone's house. The two men stared in disbelief as the two children walked into Noone's yard.

"It looks like two kids are going next door! What the hell are they up too?" Botticelli was dumbfounded. He startled everyone in the Spencer house with his exclamations.

Franco smiled. No wonder I like Botticelli so much. He's as tough as nails, but upset because two kids are walking into the yard of person who tried to murder me last night. He wants to jump in and help them. Well, we had all better help them because Botticelli is right. Those kids can't go in there by themselves. It's way too dangerous.

The men grabbed their coats heading out into the storm as Inez and Gladys went to the window see what was going on.

Inside the dugout, Shorty saw no sign of Noone, no sign of the wolves, either. It was 4 p.m. and pitch black outside. He bundled up and headed out into the storm hoping to find Noone making his way home. Even though the winds had abated some, snowdrifts were even higher as more snow fell making it difficult going in spite of the fact that he was in good physical shape.

Shorty dragged himself through and over snowdrift after snowdrift ending up behind Clem's house. There, he found the first sign of wolf. Their tracks were fresh. He followed, counting seven sets of prints, and as he studied them, he saw that they were following human footprints. Renewed vigor surged through his weary body.

The tracks led Shorty to another shelter, but from the looks of it, whoever had been staying inside it had already left. He bent down to study the tracks finding them heading in the direction of Noone's house. The wolf tracks now overlaid the large human track. It has to be Noone's trail, Shorty thought.

And just as it was hard for him to make his way through the increasingly deep snowdrifts, it was hard for Noone, too, as his track's attested. By following their tracks, Noone and the wolves had broken ground for Shorty making his effort easier. Shorty was hopeful he would reach Noone before Noone had a chance to get inside his house.

Noone grew tired of holding up in his shelter even though it was nice and warm. His mother wanted to go home. She was tired, she said. How she could be tired was beyond him. She did nothing but nag. He was so sick of her bitching by 3 p.m. he packed up and started for home. He had only another mile to go before getting there and it was already dark. Darkness was not a problem, however. He knew the woods well and, besides, his flashlight was in his backpack.

He didn't see the wolves as they started out from behind the trees to follow him. The animals stalked him quietly. The alpha male followed so closely that if Noone had turned around he could have touched the big animal's head. They trotted at a steady pace behind him. They were patient hunters waiting for just the right moment to move in for the kill.

Noone hadn't traveled too far from the dugout before the sensation of being watched washed over him. He turned his head quickly thinking he saw something out of the corner of his eye, a flash of movement.

The pack anticipated his movement jumping back behind the trees for cover.

All but one—the big alpha male stood his ground, and Noone could see him easily even through the falling snow that slashed across his eyes. The animal made no noise as it stood there staring back at Noone. Instead, its lips curled back to reveal canine teeth in a silent growl. He lowered his head to stare up eye-to-eye at Noone.

Noone's heart leapt as the rest of the pack slowly, one by one, came out from their cover moving in next to the alpha male. Noone turned slowly trying to move faster through the every burgeoning snow drifts. His heart squeezed tightly in his chest, while his mother whispered in his ear, "faster Sonny, faster, they're gaining on you!"

Noone's calm, collected self-confidence faded as the animals moved in ever closer. One youngster boldly ventured up behind him taking a nip out of the back of his leg. Noone squealed in fear at the attack. He had seen wolves take down prey, hamstringing them. But wolves have never attacked a human being in North America. How can that be true? A little voice inside his head asked.

But I have a gun with me! He reasoned as he stumbled forward. They are afraid of guns! His hands, stiff with cold, couldn't get a grip on the pistol, which hid beneath his coat. Noone tore off one of his seal skin gloves, grabbed at the gun in his belt trying to point it at a wolf, his hands trembling with cold.

The wolves stopped for a moment upon scenting gun oil, but they didn't back off. Something was wrong with the man's scent, something that emboldened them to continue their pursuit. They took a step toward Noone. Noone tried to fire the gun right from its holster, but his cold, numbed fingers couldn't be forced to move. Throwing his gloves down in frustration, he turned, and started treading through the snow once again in an attempt to run away from the pack. The wolves followed once again, keeping pace.

Noone started to make mistakes. He took a left, when he should have gone right; he had to backtrack to regain his bearings and the correct path. Again and again, he made little mistakes, had to backtrack. He grew weary. The wolves closed in even closer. The same emboldened pup rushed up again nipping at his legs; something he did every time Noone tried to stop, rest. The pack drove him on.

Noone hadn't completely lost his senses. He came across another of his dugouts and dove into it making it inside just as the wolf pup tried to nip at his leg once again. Inside, Noone bolted the entrance before the pack reached it. As he secured it, he felt safe from the terror awaiting him outdoors.

The small shelter, made of downed willow brush and balsam boughs, was no protection from the pack. If they had wanted to burst through it, they could—easily. Instead, they hunkered down outside, waiting.

Inside, Noone cried in relief. He couldn't believe his luck! Again, his stored provisions provided food, warm clothing, and a dry shelter to hold up in until daybreak if need be. He could rest a little before going home. It wasn't that far now, only a half-mile or so, he remembered chewing on beef jerky. He had made some headway against the storm, now to get rid of the wolves?

"But Sonny," his mother reminded him, "remember what's waiting for you at home. There might still be some police there to arrest you! You best be careful!"

"Good advise, Mama. I don't know why I let you talk me out of taking the mineshafts home. I would have been there already and wouldn't have those damn wolves harassing me!"

She didn't dignify his testiness with an answer.

Wrapping up in a wool blanket, it helped stave off the chill. His heart raced. He examined the backs of his thighs. Teeth marks dotted the calf of one leg; the skin was busted through in places. He took out some Hydrogen Peroxide to cleanse the wounds, wrapped them in bandages, and realized how lucky he had been to escape a full-out attack.

He wondered if the wolves were still outside, but didn't venture to look; he was too frightened. He wanted sleep, but as his eyes closed, his terror forced them open. Exhausted, his body, in spite of his mind, managed to sleep fitfully until 4 a.m. When he awoke, he got dressed immediately, putting on dry clothes he had stored in the shelter. He found replacement gloves as he was ready to leave, drew in a deep breath, and worked up the courage to peek outside the entrance. He found no animals in sight. He stepped outside the shelter and started for home.

The pack pulled in behind him as before, and again he didn't see them.

As Noone nestled warmly in his dugout, Vicki and Mike stood in the center of Noone's living room looking about. They had simply walked in the front door. Someone had left it unlocked. No policemen were in sight. It was easy.

Both expected to see Noone jump out from a hiding place at any moment. They dropped their backpacks on the couch. Mike hesitantly moved over to the kitchen wall peeking around the corner, seeing nothing. There was no one there. He went through all the rooms in the house in the same fashion. "He's not here."

"Good!" Vicki said. She didn't want Noone to be there. She was afraid. Still, she wouldn't mind pulling her gun on him. She didn't give thought to the possibility of pulling the trigger should circumstances warrant it.

Across the road, Botticelli didn't wait for the others to get the lead out; Franco was on his heels as he headed outside. They walked swiftly over snow laden roads to get to Noone's house to the kids they had seen going over there.

"Hey, man!" Franco yelled at Botticelli. "Wait up! What are you going to do, take on Noone all by yourself? 'Here I come to save the day?'"

Botticelli laughed, turned his head to see his partner catch up with him. "We gotta' get those kids outta' there. No telling what might happen!"

"Never saw you show so much concern for kids before. What's up with that?"

"I like kids." Botticelli said matter of factly, attempting to brush aside any notion that he had a soft heart about anything.

The two men reached Noone's house swiftly. And as Vicki and Mike had done, they simply turned the doorknob and walked inside.

Vicki was still in Noone's living room looking about when she heard the doorknob turn, and thought it was Noone returning home. She pulled her gun from her waistband aiming it, standing ready for Noone to walk over the threshold. Instead, she stood staring at a stranger, gun drawn.

"Hey, kid!" Botticelli yelled, "Easy does it. We aren't here to hurt you. We've come from next door. We're here to get you outta' here."

As Botticelli spoke, Mike stepped into the room from the hall. He remembered Franco from the hospital; he came inside just then directly behind Botticelli.

"Oh, man! Am I glad to see you!" he said to the bar owner.

"Come on you two," Franco said, "You can't stay here. You're coming back with us across the road."

"We're waiting for Noone," Vicki said still aiming her pistol at Botticelli, "and nobody is going to stop us."

Mike saw the gun for the first time. "Vicki! Why did you bring that?" He demanded.

"The same reason you brought yours." She raised her eyebrows.

"Put it away. These guys own Tony's bar. They're friends of Sam's."

"You sure?"

"Yeah, it's okay."

She lowered the gun, slowly, put the safety on, and tucked it back into her belt. "Instead of us going over there, why don't you wait here with us," she said to the men.

"Because it's too dangerous," Sam said as she stepped over the threshold to stand behind Franco. Angie, Gladys, Inez and Clem were right behind her.

"We know how you must be feeling," Sam said to Vicki. "Believe me, we want to take Noone out as much as you do, but we can't let you two throw your lives away on that piece of human excrement. It's too much. Your mother would be grief stricken. So come on; don't let all she ever taught you fly out the window no sooner than she is gone. It would hurt her if she knew that you risked your lives on that man. Mike, Vicki, you have to know that."

Sam's words cut Vicki to the quick, and she started to cry. She hadn't let herself grieve over her mother yet, and a flood of sorrow threatened to overwhelm her.

Sam walked over and hugged her, drew her close. "Come on. You can spend some time with your mother's friends. She would like that. We'll bring you home at daylight, okay?"

Vicki nodded in agreement wiping her runny nose on a paper towel Sam retrieved from the kitchen.

Mike grabbed his coat and walked out the door with the men. The women followed.

Neither Mike nor Vicki remembered their backpacks lying on the couch.

Chapter Thirty One

At the Spencer's, Mike told everyone about the vision he had seen in his room. Vicki added her story to his.

As they talked, Inez went into a trance. Her visions were coming much faster now ever since admitting to everyone that she had them. She shook her head as she swayed back and forth, back and forth. "I see him," she said softly after the children finished speaking. "He is on his way home. He's being followed, but I can't tell yet by what. Shorty? He's out there, too! He's searching for Noone."

The room was deathly quiet.

"Did you here that?" Clem said to Gladys aghast at the sight of Inez swaying and speaking as if through an alien voice.

"Oh, don't get your knickers in a twist, Clem. She's been doing that for sixty five years, or better, for crying out loud. How do you think we've gotten along as well as we have?"

"What do you mean? Shorty is out there with him?" Franco wanted to know.

Inez, now sitting on the couch sipping water said, "I can't get a clear picture on that. Animals, I get the impression of animals, but I can't see them clearly. The only thing that's crystal clear is Noone."

"Didn't Shorty tell you that the wolves brought him to Sam's house the other night?" Botticelli reminded Franco.

"Yeah, he did," Franco said.

"The last I saw of Shorty, he was right here," Clem said.

"He said he was going to go talk to the sheriff earlier in the afternoon. I saw him head over there, but I don't remember him coming back," Angie added.

"I hope he isn't out there by himself trying to take on Noone." Franco added.

"Don't worry too much over that," Inez said. "I don't think he's too close to Noone, not yet, feels like it's the animals that are hot on Noone's heels, though. Shorty is behind them. I doubt that the wolves will do Shorty any harm. We just have to wait and see."

Then, as it happened at the Jennings' farm, it started at the Spencers. When Inez finished speaking, colors began swirling around the living room walls, up and down as if dancing. They alighted atop Angie's chest and hung over Inez's head like a halo. Then they moved about the room as if they were disco strobe lights on a dance floor.

"Please!" A feminine voice pleaded. "Go over there. Stop him before he does any more damage!" Sam was sure the voice was Ellen's. But Ellen wasn't alone. Other voices emanated from every corner of the room saying similar things, urging the party to trek back over to Noone's and lie in wait for him there. Cacophony erupted as the voices sounded from everywhere.

Then as quickly as it started, it stopped.

"What the hell was that?" Botticelli yelled, terrified. He forgot both his manners and the fact that children were in the room.

"Forgot, man that you just got here. This kinda' stuff has been going on since I got to Sam's the other night. You might as well get used to it. There isn't any time to explain," Franco said patting Botticelli on the back.

Botticelli's face was ashen as his pulse raced. He had never seen anything like it. First, it was Inez speaking as if she could see stuff out there in the woods, then it was voices crying out of the walls—man it was just too much! He looked hard at Angie and Inez. "What the hell are you two, anyway?" He demanded.

"Psychic," Inez said simply.

"Most people think that the only reality is the physical one," Angie said as she searched for words that might assuage Botticelli's fears. She had seen this type of reaction before and could guess where it might lead. "But life is much more than that.

For instance, haven't you ever wanted something only to find it, somehow, coming into your possession through no effort on your part? Or haven't you ever had questions about why things are the way they are only to get an answer to the question by opening a book, turning on the TV, or having a friend say something to you out of the blue that answers it? Well, that's part of the unseen universe helping you along your path. Bernice believed it was God teaching us the things we need to know. God is the positive force, you see, Satan is the negative.

Inez and I, for some reason, tap into that unseen world a little easier than most. Most people are taught from childhood not to look into it, or to block it out. That's why they show so much fear when they are in the company of those who do look."

Angie touched Botticelli's hand. "I know this is hard to take in, but it is as real as your flesh is real to my touch. You don't have to fear what we are doing. When this is over, if you take the time and examine your own life, you'll probably see that it has worked there, too. You understand?"

"Sortta', I guess. But it ain't easy!" Botticelli took his hand from hers. He didn't like the idea of her touching him. What if she can read my mind? He thought.

Inez reached over and touched Angie's arm. She knew what it was like; having others frightened of her. Fear is what made the church ladies in Bernice's circle of friends frightened of her and Gladys. Fear controlled most folks, in many different ways. Sometimes fear was tangible, sometimes it wasn't. Like their fear of Arthur Noone. They would have to face it, their fear of Noone, head on—no doubt about that.

"This is just too freaky for me." Botticelli whispered to Franco.

Franco tried to get him to shut up, but couldn't. "You think that's bad?" he said. "Just wait till we tangle with Noone. That son of a bitch is what you ought to be afraid of! Look at those kids over there. Hell, they aren't scared of either one of them women! They aren't scared of Noone, either! Grow up, man, or when we get back to the bar, I'm going to tell all your buddies how two women scared the shit out of you!" Franco was furious.

"Alright, alright, lighten up! I'll try. But this is all new to me, you know?" Botticelli said. He liked the old lady. Hell, he didn't want to make either woman feel bad; they scared him was all.

"Well, what we gonna' do about this old bad boy that's on his way home?"Clem asked.

Mike stood sentry at the window watching for Noone, and had done so since arriving at the Spencer's. He listened to Inez and knew something would be happening soon. He wanted to confront Noone before anyone else could, so he made it his business to stand vigil, silently, waiting for his chance.

"Mike!" Franco yelled. He called twice before Mike heard him.

Mike turned.

"Don't get any ideas, kid. You aren't taking on Noone by yourself. You got that?" Franco had an edge to his voice that frightened Vicki. He wasn't kidding and he struck her as someone who didn't play around. She looked at Mike.

Mike understood what Franco meant all right, but didn't care. He had a personal score to settle and he'd be damned if he'd let anyone stop him. Franco had nothing on Noone when it came to being scary, Mike thought as he turned back to the window. He pondered a plan of escape and a plan of attack.

As Franco spoke with Mike, Shorty watched the wolves sitting in a semi-circle around something that their backs blocked from his view. By the time he had tracked them far enough to be close enough to actually see them, the wolves were already in position. It took awhile for him to recognize one of Noone's shelters. He guessed Noone must be inside. Down wind of animals, they wouldn't catch his scent. He didn't want to tangle with them, too, but he did want to see what they were doing with Noone, so he waited.

In the process, Shorty wondered what he would do if Noone did come out of the dugout. What would he do if Noone saw him, or challenged him? He had to do something. It may be that the wolves would do that for him. He wasn't sure whether or not he liked that possibility. If the wolves did kill a human, the DNR would surely hunt them down and destroy them. He'd hate to see that.

What would authorities do to him if he took Noone out? Prison? More than likely, but since Noone was suspected of killing a lot of people he could easily claim self-defense and be believed, which, when he thought about it, thought killing Noone might be a good idea. Anyone coming up against him was taking their life in their hands anyway; self-defense would be a good excuse.

It wasn't long before the wolves got up and headed deeper into the woods. When they disappeared, Noone emerged from the dugout carrying a flashlight. From his hiding place underneath snow laden balsam boughs of a huge tree, Shorty watched Noone scout out the area around the shelter before stepping away from it. He saw the wolves come out of hiding to follow once again behind Noone, but from at a distance. It was easy for Shorty to see where Noone was headed because Noone's flashlight danced light through the thick, dense forest and storm.

Shorty crawled out from his hiding place to follow. He saw as the pack edged close on Noone's heels once again. Noone's a gonner, he thought watching the yearling pup run up behind Noone's calf, nip him, and then run back to the pack. As the pup bit, Noone stumbled, tried to right himself then fell.

The pack moved in to surround him. The alpha female, alone, moved in closer. She must smell blood, Shorty thought spellbound at the spectacle. He shouted, trying to distract the pack, but his voice didn't carry over the howling winds.

The alpha female moved in closer still, head low, growling, staring at Noone. Suddenly, she stopped, and stood as still as a statue as the other six animals circled Noone. They kept out of reach of the old man's boots as he tried to kick at them with his uninjured leg.

Shorty tried to run, to catch up, but heavy snowdrifts floundered him too, so he watched helplessly from amid the thigh deep snow as all seven wolves sat on their haunches to form a half circle around Noone.

Why aren't they moving in? Why aren't they attacking? He wondered as he watched the wolves get up and step back. Noone fumbled with his flashlight; tried to get to his feet. He fell again, tried one more time to get up, this time successfully. Shorty watched the old man look around the ground for something; saw him pick up a fallen branch. Once Noone was on his way again, the wolves began their pursuit. They held back behind Noone only approaching him to push him on, force him to move faster through snowdrifts as deep as his thighs. They were hamstringing Noone in a sense—something Shorty had never seen before.

Noone's flashlight beam cast odd shadows as he and his detractors marched on through the woods. The odd shadows passed further into the distance as Shorty began to lag behind further and further. He hadn't had any rest from the storm and grew more exhausted by the second. He was relieved to catch sight of Noone's flashlight beam once again. Noone waved it about wildly trying to scare the animals off. Shorty bet that if Noone survived, the wolves would pay dearly.

They made him uneasy, too.

Still following, Shorty wondered just how many wolf traps Noone had set up out there where they were. As soon as he thought it, he set his foot down to find it caught in a steel toothed wolf trap. "Son of a bitch!" He screamed as pain raced through his ankle. The steel tooth trap was strong and cold. The teeth closed around his ankle so tightly, they cut off the blood supply to his foot. He was in big trouble. It was below zero with winds gusting, he guessed, up to 30 mph. He'd freeze to death or die from the loss of blood if he couldn't free himself from the trap. Knowing that the wolf pack was somewhere ahead unnerved him, too. They could scent blood for miles.

Shorty looked around hoping to find another of Noone's shelters hidden in the undergrowth, and to his relief he did. He pulled and tugged at the trap to separate it from its moorings dragging the steel toothed monstrosity into the shelter with him sighing with relief as he climbed in out of the wind. He hoped to find something with which to pry the trap open. In a supply container, he found a steel tire iron. He thanked God for it, laughed at the irony of his situation considering Noone was the one who left the tire iron and the trap in the first place, then pried the teeth open slipping his ankle and foot free.

Pain throbbed through his leg immediately as a rush of blood surged into the injured flesh. Shorty was in so much agony, he passed out before he could doctor the wound. The supply kit held all he'd need to both cleanse and dress the wound, which was what he did when he came too a few seconds later. He gritted his teeth against the pain. The wound itself wasn't as bad as he had feared. No main arteries were damaged. No sooner than the wound was dressed, Shorty swallowed aspirin for the pain just before he passed out again. This time he remained unconscious for hours.

Inside the sister's house, Mike watched as a figure approached Noone's house next door. He held his breath pressing his face closer to the glass. Seven other figures accompanied the first. Mike recognized the wolves. He was no longer afraid of them. They protected him at his own house, now they were bringing his archenemy home.

Everyone else inside the Spencer house was in the kitchen talking, except for Vicki, who sat on the couch with her back to Mike reading a magazine. Mike slipped his coat on stealing outside unseen . . . he hoped. Slowly, he made his way back over to Noone's.

The wolves were lying on the porch. The big male watched Mike as he approached, stood up, stared at him, sniffed the air, then headed off into the woods with the rest of the pack following. Mike watched with keen interest wondering what they were doing; he didn't dwell on it long, however, or notice the trail he had made through the snow.

Slowly he stepped up onto the porch tiptoeing over to the front door trying the doorknob. It turned willingly in his fingers, so he opened it and peered inside. Noone was nowhere in sight. He has to be here! Mike stepped in further onto the carpeted living room floor quietly. Softly, he shut the door behind him. Still, Noone was nowhere to be seen. He heard noises coming from the basement. It sounded like people talking. Mike couldn't make out what they were saying, so he stepped over to the basement door. It was open. Mike peeked around the doorjamb. He listened, but could make out nothing intelligible. As he strained harder to hear, leaning closer to the open doorway, a hand settled on his shoulder from behind—Mike was too terrified to turn around.

"It's just me you idiot!" Vicki whispered in his ear. She, too, heard the voices downstairs. She had tiptoed up behind Mike relieved to see him standing by the basement door within sight. She pulled open her coat to show him the gun she still had with her. He smiled. She pulled the pistol from her waistband, cocked it, and the two started down the basement steps.

At the Spencers, the adults were still talking in the kitchen forgetting about the children in the living room. Botticelli was the first to notice their absence. He got up from the table and went into the living room looking for them. He saw the front door slightly ajar. A cold breeze wafted into the room telling him all he needed to know.

"Hey, Franco! You better get in here. Looks like we got trouble!"

Franco was at Botticelli's side immediately, Clem close behind. "Looks like them kids have gone outdoors," Botticelli said. "Suppose they went next door again?"

"That's exactly what they've done." The men dressed hurriedly heading out into the storm, yelling at the women as they went, telling them to stay inside.

Chapter Thirty Two

In a millisecond, Sam, standing at the doorway to the Spencer house, considered all that had happened in the past few days. She had learned that the professor and his wife were her blood parents; that she had been living in the family home; that she had a sister, a twin sister; the same woman with whom she had been best friends with for years. She had also lost one of her dearest friends to the same man who had murdered her parents, and who had been killing young people in the area for years. This same man who had taken from her the only home she had ever known, and her beloved pets. And her dear friend's children were alone with him in the house across the road. And, now, the men she considered her friends wanted her to stay inside and not go after the man who had wreaked so much devastation in her life?

They are out of their minds, she thought grabbing her coat, hat, and boots, and heading outside to Clem's truck. She was determined to get to her own house before anyone could stop her. As long as the men had followed the children into Noone's house, they would be safe, and she could reach them by going the other way, the way, in an epiphany at the doorway, she determined Noone had used to travel throughout the neighborhood. She now knew how Noone had been able to come and go from her house, why Fuzz sat at the threshold of the library but wouldn't come in, why he growled at the lumber stacked in the barn, how Noone had crept up on them so easily in the library, but she needed to see it for herself. Bernice's kids, and everyone else, needed her to be right. It was as if, for the first time, her dreams came to her in a waking state showing her things she didn't know before. She was like Angie now.

Angie didn't try to stop Sam as she watched her dress for the storm then run outside into it. Dressing as she ran, Angie was right behind her jumping onto the running boards of Clem's big truck as Sam started the engine to head out the driveway. Angie fought to get her arms into the sleeves of her coat as she held on to the door handle, thankful that the storm slowed Sam's escape considerably.

Angie figured Sam had to be onto something because she would never leave Bernice's kids unprotected otherwise as she fought the wind to open the truck door, then to shut it again after climbing inside the cab. Finally, she managed to pull it closed. Safe inside the warm cab, Sam told her what she was up to. Angie told her to step on it. They had to find that passageway before Bernice's kids got hurt. They rode in silence. As they crested the knoll just before Sam's driveway, they saw smoke billowing up from the ashes.

Sam drove slowly up to the house. All the fire trucks and investigators were gone. The place was eerily quiet. Heavy cloud cover hid the full moon letting in minute particles of light only as clouds passed over it. In those brief moments, the moonlight lit up the snow revealing the devastation.

As the two stood outside next to the rubble looking down into it, Angie yelled, "Look!" She pointed to the area near where the old coal shoot had been. Debris had fallen away from in front of it, and from where they stood, they could see a black maw of space behind the chute's wooden frame.

Angie and Sam shinned the big flashlights, hoping to gape into the hole. But with so much debris and smoke, they couldn't descend into the basement. Much of the ruble was still red hot, and, on occasion, pieces of wood from overhead crashed down into the basement. It wasn't safe. There flashlights illuminated the doorway to the tunnel, nevertheless. But they could not see where it led.

"The entrance must have been hidden behind the furnace," Sam said as she stared down into the ruble.

"Yes! But where does it go from there?" Angie looked at Sam. In unison, as if reading one another's minds, they turned and ran for the barn. There, they found the mineshaft tunnel entrance easily. After investigator Duke Hunter moved the door, he put it back into place neatly, but he had marked it with chalk, so it would be easy to find when he came back. As Sam and Angie cautiously pulled the fake door aside, they found themselves staring down a ladder that led to what they reasoned had to be the tunnel. They said in unison, "this is how he snuck up on us!"

"Let's find out what's down there." Sam scrambled down the rickety ladder with Angie at her heels. The smell of the dank, damp, musty blackness overwhelmed them, but they kept on in spite of the cloying odor. As their eyes adjusted to the feeble light of their flashlights, they saw that they were in what looked like old mineshafts. A cold wind wailed past them sounding mournful. It told them there were other entry points into the tunnel.

As they moved ahead slowly, Sam studied the tunnel construction. Angie marked their passage with colored chalk she always kept in her pockets, a habit she picked up from working with police at crime scenes. They crossed what looked like an old railroad track, saw an abandoned ore bucket, and pick axes whose heads were covered in rust and whose wooden handles were rotted.

On the walls, they noticed arrows painted in white and pointing in various directions. They followed one. It veered to the left of the passage leading to Sam's barn. Angie marked it with large fluorescent pink strokes.

Cautiously they started up it. About a quarter-mile in they found a map posted on one of the wooden beams. It showed where each tunnel led. They saw one marked Spencer, one Johnson, one Jennings, one Noone, and one marked Professor. The tunnel led to all homes in the area. The women tore the map off the beam.

"Well, we know how he got around so easy. This old mineshaft must be how Joseph got around, too. I bet most people don't even know they're here." Sam said.

Back at Noone's, as Sam and Angie climbed into Clem's truck, Vicki and Mike were quietly descending the basement stairs of Noone's house. The voices they heard earlier were still talking, so they believed they had not been detected as they climbed down further.

They were wrong.

Noone waited for them out of sight, next to the bottom step. He had heard Mike from the time Mike entered his house. It was then that he turned on the tape recorder and slipped behind the partition at the bottom of the steps. He also heard the second figure walk across the living room floor.

He smiled. He sure was glad to be home.

He was surprised by what he found inside his house. His mother had told him what to expect, and she was correct. The police had torn the majority of the basement apart, but they still hadn't discovered everything. They hadn't found his entrance to the mineshafts. They hadn't found what was hidden there.

And who left those backpacks on the couch? When he looked inside them, he knew the two eldest Jennings children had been there. He had to keep from laughing at the irony of it. What a welcome surprise they were. Imagine, he thought, I didn't even have to seek them out; they came looking for me. So he waited, getting ready to pounce once his prey was close enough to grab.

It is so nice to be home! No one is ever going to catch me! The wolves hardly touched me! Just wait until this mess blows over; I'll get those sons-a-bitches! Thoughts of revenge on everyone flitted through his head, too, as step by step Mike and Vicki descended the stairs.

Mike reached the bottom step first, turned, looked back at Vicki, and smiled. She smiled back. What would Pops think if he could see us now, she wondered? He'd have a fit! That's what!

From out of nowhere, Vicki heard Bernice's voice inside her head. "Be careful! He's behind the wall!"

Mike heard the warning, too, and stepped back up one step. Vicki climbed for the upper stair.

Noone heard, jumped out from his hiding place and yanked a cord alongside the stair railing slamming the basement door shut behind Vicki effectively sealing off her avenue of escape. The sound of the latch clicking into place screamed in her head and she knew that Noone had managed to lock the door behind her. She and Mike drew their pistols.

"Well, will you look at this?" Noone said. "You two come right to me and now, you're going to pull a gun on me? You know you want to be here, so why fight it? Those guns aren't going to do you any good. You can't shoot me." Noone smiled at Mike, stepping closer to the stairs, climbing slowly one step at a time, inching ever closer to Mike, smiling his most seductive smile.

A smile that chilled Mike to the bone, but he was right. Mike couldn't shoot. He thought he could, to avenge his mother, but he couldn't. She would never have harmed a living soul and wouldn't want him too, either.

Noone crept closer still, smiling continually until he stood directly under Mike on the stair. He reached out slowly taking the gun from Mike's hand.

Vicki watched in disbelief. She stepped out from behind Mike and fired. Noone went down. The gun report echoed in their ears. Vicki's aim was off and Noone was quickly back on his feet shoving Mike out of his way and ramming into Vicki like a defensive tackle knocking her against the basement door and forcing the gun from her hand. It hurtled downstairs past Mike's grip and onto the concrete floor at the bottom of the steps. Noone jumped up, grabbed Vicki by the hair pulling her to her feet, throwing his arm around her neck and pointing Mike's gun at her head to keep Mike from trying to save her by going for the other gun.

Slowly they all climbed down into the basement proper. Noone motioned with his head for Mike to go behind the partition as he dragged Vicki in behind him all the while keeping a bead on Mike's head.

It was dark behind the partition. Mike couldn't see where he was going. Noone wouldn't take his arm from around Vicki's throat or drop the gun.

"Over there, kid," Noone motioned to Mike with his head. "On that shelf over there. Turn on the light."

Mike found the switch and flipped it. The teenagers took a good look around at the dirt sided mineshaft walls. On one side, they saw brace beams and dirt. On the other, skeletons shackled to the walls. The heavy railroad beam bracings set at four-foot intervals held the overhead structure up; they also held up the dead. Nameplates marked each person's head. Joseph Albright and Janice Browne were among them. Neither Mike nor Vicki recognized the names.

At the other end of the mineshafts, Sam and Angie made their way along by following the directions of the map. Sam kept it tucked into her back pants pocket as they slowly fended their way through mazes of channels running underneath the farmland.

"No wonder Noone got away with so much over the years," Angie said quietly as they walked along. She stopped moving, sneezed. As she did, a strong feeling of déjà vu flooded over her. She remembered Henry Albright.

"Henry Albright! Yes!" she squealed.

Sam turned to look at her.

Memories of Albright, tsunami like, swept through her mind. She overlaid her mental picture of Henry with that of Noone. Saw them standing together and finally made the connection that had been eluding her.

"My God!" She croaked barely above a whisper while her heart raced at the recognition. "Sam, do you have any idea who we are dealing with?"

"Well, yeah! I mean we've been up against Noone for awhile now?"

"Noone is Henry Albright's brother! So is Joseph. My God! The rest of the Albright family! No wonder we couldn't find them back then. Police looked and looked once Henry was arrested. He kept saying they weren't free of him yet. I bet this is what he meant!" Angie stood rooted to the spot staring at the light shinning down the shaft, seeing nothing other than what was moving in her own mind.

Sam stood still beside her. She remembered what Angie had told her and Skip about Henry Albright. Angie was pivotal in helping police identify him as a serial killer.

"Albright's mother. She abused the boys." Angie didn't expect a response; she was remembering the case out loud.

"Henry only kills children. He prefers little boys, some as young as ten and eleven years of age. Most are in their early teens. He is horrible. He befriends only the children of widows, and gives those things their mother can't afford, treats them nicely, takes them out — including the mother— then wreaks havoc on their lives. When he doesn't kill the children, he makes them wish he had. He delights in destroying the mother too, making sure she understands that it was she who invited him into their home so he could practice his evil. Once inside, he sneaks into the kid's bedrooms, molests them, and tells them not to tell their mother; then sneaks back into her bed when he's finished. She, more often than not, never suspects a thing.

One mother though, she never liked Henry, never let him into her house. She called police numerous times to complain about him, even put a restraining order on him. That's one of the things that helped police capture Henry Albright. The police records, I mean.

She was a strong, sharp lady, that one, regardless of her poverty, and she wasn't about to let anyone push her around. And she loved that son of hers, Tom. She kept him from harm, too. Tom was the only one who ever got away from Albright and that irked him no end. He was a nasty piece of work . . . If Noone is his brother we have something far beyond evil on our hands. We're lucky to be alive."

Sam shook her head. "That means we better catch him before he can do anything to anyone else," she said sounding confident and ready to do battle.

"I'm with you, but remember, I don't know karate, so don't let him touch me. I'm good with a stick though." Angie picked up a 2x4 from the mineshaft floor as they started back down the tunnel heading in Noone's direction.

Back at the sheriff's office: "Has anyone called Samantha Egar or Angie Eckenridge yet?" Skip demanded of Harriet.

"I've been trying to get through to the Spencers, but no one is answering the phone." This worried Harriet and she didn't mind letting the sheriff know it. Too much had gone on during the storm to ignore it.

"John Jennings has been calling. He said two of his kids are missing, let me see," she looked at her notes, "yes, Vicki and Mike, his teenagers. He sounded terrified. Can't say as I blame him." Harriet made sure Skip understood her meaning.

Skip Gilbert looked around to see which deputies were on duty. Stringer and Jackson pretended not to be listening to what Harriet said to Skip. "Alright you two, come on. Who else is in?"

Harriet looked over the work rooster. "Smith and Thompson are in the back."

Harriet continued, "Seems most of our travel problems are cleared up. If I were you, sheriff, I'd take Smith, Thompson, Stringer and Jackson. They're the best of the lot, anyway." Harriet looked up from her desk at the sheriff to see if he acknowledged her wisdom.

"Jeez, Harriet, how could I ever handle my sheriff duties without you?" Skip left her wondering if he was being sarcastic. She decided he wasn't. He just appreciated her good judgment.

He shook his head realizing his caustic tongue had missed its mark with his dispatcher once again. "Come on, men. We've got more trouble out on River Drive," he said as he moved though the office opening the glass doors to head back out into the storm and to the Jennings' house.

As he did, two FBI agents walked in. "Hello, Sheriff. Can we be of any help?"

"Damn right you can. How many men are with you?"

"Just us two."

"It'll have to do. Seems we have two missing kids out on River Drive, where Noone lives. He has not been apprehended yet. The father is pretty worried. We also have a bunch of missing persons. Not official, mind you, but my dispatcher can't get through to anybody who was supposed to be at the Spencer house. I'm worried about their safety, most where at Sam's house when it burnt. Could be Noone wants to finish what he started? Have to think he set that fire in an attempt to kill us all; that means their lives may still be in danger."

"That's one of the reasons I'm here," one FBI agent said as they all headed out into the cold wind. He stayed in step with Skip. "We got some news from your fire marshal. I was on my way in to deliver it; seems that the fire originated in a wall around some old wiring. The wires had been spliced together to create a spark. Sounds like someone deliberately started your blaze."

"Well, I pretty much guessed that, but it's good to have the confirmation."

Everyone climbed into their vehicles, and a police caravan started out for River Drive.

Following up on his suspicions, Franco was the first one inside Noone's house. He stepped quietly listening for noises but heard nothing. With Botticelli on his heels, the two crept into the kitchen where they fixed their eyes on the basement door. It was closed yet the men 'knew' the kids had to have gone downstairs. They were nowhere else in sight. Neither man liked the idea of going into the basement knowing what the police had discovered down there.

"We have to," Franco said to Botticelli with no preamble. Botticelli knew exactly what Franco meant. Nodding his head in agreement, he still didn't want to take that first step down. Quietly they opened the door; it was not locked like Vicki had thought.

Inez and Gladys were dressing to go outside just as Sam and Angie ran out and took off in Clem's truck, putting Clem in a fowl mood. He begrudgingly donned his winter gear to join his friends and the other men inside Noone's house. "You know, I'm getting pretty sick of this. I'm getting too old to traipse around some nut's house!" Clem muttered as he headed out the Spencer's front door.

"Oh, keep quiet, you old bear. You're just mad cause your truck's gone. Put a smile on that sweet old face of yours, remember your friend Stan, and get the lead out. What we do now, we do for him," Gladys said firmly.

At the mention of Stan's name Clem forgot everything else. He knew Stan's death was caused by cancer, but he also knew that Noone played a part in it—a big part. Stan was taken too soon as far as Clem was concerned. He wondered if Stan ever knew Gladys was in love with him. Another tragedy thanks to Noone. Clem watched his two old friends struggle through the snow as he stepped off the front porch steps feeling such warmth for the women, a tear came to his eye.

Down in the mineshafts, Noone smiled at the looks of horror on the Jennings's children's faces when they gazed upon his handiwork hanging from the walls. The frozen tundra beneath the fields was a very good place to dispose of his work. Bodies kept real well down there without a whole lot of decomposition because the freezing weather. The winds also helped. They worked to desiccate the flesh, sort of mummifying it as it hung in the open air. Even in the summer, the bodies stayed almost frozen. He had to admit; they did look grotesque, even to him.

He should have put the others in there, too, like his mother had told him, but he hadn't mostly out of defiance toward her. Sometimes he just couldn't tolerate her telling him what to do. Them dumb cops never would have found any bodies if he had, though, he thought.

Noone kept a portion of the mineshaft ready for any unexpected visitors, too, so with Mike and Vicki in tow, he only had to get them into position. With his arm locked around Vicki's throat, he motioned with Mike's gun for Mike to back up against the wall. He did. Noone quickly shackled his hands and feet releasing his chokehold on Vicki, but grabbing her by a shock of hair. She cried out in pain, which he relished. When Mike was shackled and under control, Noone shackled Vicki next to him.

The children's hands were pinned above and behind their heads while their feet were shackled to the bottom of the post. This forced their bodies forward so they hung out from the wall slightly immobilizing them completely.

Noone worked unencumbered. He wanted Vicki to be able to see what he was going to do to her brother and vise versa.

Vicki's head hurt. It felt as though Noone had torn hair out by its roots. She looked over at Mike to find him looking back at her, intently. Neither of them spoke. They watched Noone. He had stopped working and was standing at the partition with his ear pressed to the tunnel entrance listening to something they couldn't hear.

Upstairs Franco and Botticelli were about to begin their decent when they decided it might be wise to get a weapon. Botticelli ran back to the Spencers to grab a tire iron from his car passing Inez, Gladys and Clem as he ran. When he got back to Noone's house, he gave the tire iron to Franco who was the first to head downstairs. Clem, Gladys and Inez brought up the rear. Franco was miffed that Inez and Gladys were there at all, and miffed more because Sam and Angie were not. No one told him that they were gone and he was too intent on the task at hand to ask.

He wondered why women never listened when men told them to do something. At that moment, he didn't really care, but it still angered him. He tried to step quietly. Noone was bound to hear them if he was there, and be tipped off; Franco didn't want that. He prayed that nothing had already happened to the kids.

Chapter Thirty Three

"Help!" Mike screamed, "Help!" But the only attention he garnered was from Noone who punched him in the jaw breaking his teeth and knocking him out.

"Now, don't you try that Missy or the same thing will happen to you. Got it?"

Vicki nodded, tears rolling down her cheeks.

It wasn't that big a deal that Mike cried out, Noone knew, because the walls were six feet thick. The entryway door was half that, plenty to soundproof the place. He was the one who soundproofed it.

The suffering he saw in Vicki's eyes because of the pain he had caused the boy, delighted him; the kid had given him an excuse to hit him by yelling. He was thankful for it. It always gave him a lot of pleasure to see pain in other people's faces.

Franco and Botticelli proceeded cautiously, stepped down a few steps, listened, but heard nothing.

Inez, Gladys and Clem didn't either as they climbed down the stairs behind the bar owners. But as soon as Inez reached the bottom step, she fell into a trance. Gladys and Clem grabbed onto her to keep her from falling down onto the concrete.

As they did, out of Inez's mouth, a deep baritone voice

said, "They're behind the wall! Behind the wall! Look closely, there's a doorway behind you. You'll find it if you look closely." Inez slumped to the floor, and everyone else ran to the wall looking for the doorway.

This time, not even Botticelli was scared of Inez's trance. He decided to do as the voice said, and worry about the consequences later.

"Hey, you old coot! Help me up!" Inez said to Clem when she saw him starring at her.

Clem just shook his head. He probably would have been afraid of her, just like Botticelli, if she had told him she could communicate with the dead before Angie showed up. Angie convinced him she could, so why not Inez? He picked her up and kissed her on the cheek.

She raised an eyebrow at his display of affection, deciding she didn't need to know why he felt this sudden desire to smooch.

On the other side of the wall, Noone heard nothing. His soundproofing worked both ways.

Down in the mineshaft, coming from the other direction, Sam and Angie heard a faint cry for help. They looked at each other then started to run. They knew Mike and Vicki were probably in Noone's house by then. Was it possible they had stumbled onto the mineshaft from another direction? Noone might be up ahead, too. They ran toward the direction of the shouting.

By that time Skip, Stringer, Jackson, Smith and Thompson had made it to the Jennings' household, and saw that every light in the house was on. At the same time, John was heading out the door to go over to Noone's house as the police cars pulled into his yard. As the men got out of their vehicles, Stringer moved over to walk next to Skip who was approaching John.

When John finished giving the sheriff the particulars about Mike and Vicki's disappearance, Stringer stepped forward and said, "Don't you worry, Mr. Jennings. We will get those kids home to you safe and sound. They have good heads on their shoulders. Dead shots too."

He took the time to tell John just how crazy his bull had been when it burst out of the barn door. How Mike had put a bullet right between the bull's eyes. It was all news to John because Mike hadn't said anything about it, although John knew the bull was dead. What remained of Steamroller's carcass had been removed before he got home, but the barn doors were still a mess.

Skip walked with John to the house to talk to him in private. "John. You need to stay here. I know how you feel; how you'd like to go after Noone yourself, especially now, but believe me; it's better that you stay with your family. We can handle it. I'll tell you this; I won't stop until I bring that bastard in. We'll bring those kids home unharmed, too."

"I don't care what you think, Skip. Those are my kids, not yours." John stepped back up into his house to get his gun. His sister and her husband Hank waited at the door to help him in. His three younger children stood at the kitchen door with them. John hugged them all, turned around, and walked back out the door, gun in hand. Skip relieved John of his gun, put it in the trunk of his cruiser, and off they went. He wasn't going to let John do anything stupid.

Skip and his deputies arrived fifteen minutes after the Spencers and their guests entered Noone's house. Jackson was first out of his squad car studying footprints. Stringer was right behind him. He bent down, sitting on his haunches beside Jackson. "Looks like we got six separate shoe prints here, wolves too," he told Skip, not taking his eyes off the prints. "One set of prints was made considerably earlier than the rest. The wolves are with that

set. The others are new. Looks like we got a lot of people inside."
Stringer stood up and drew his pistol from his holster. Jackson,
Smith, Thompson and Skip all did the same as they approached the
house with caution, the FBI following. John brought up the rear.

Jackson was first onto the porch. He moved to the
window peering inside through lace net curtains. Lights were on
but no one was in sight. He moved to the front door, kicked it
open, rushed in, gun drawn, stepped to the right of the door to be
shielded by a wall, as Smith rushed in behind him pointing his
weapon at various points in the room from the left.

Nothing moved.

Jackson motioned Skip and Stringer in. The men
cautiously searched the bedrooms finding no one. When they came
together in the living room, Jackson heard movement downstairs.
The men stood motionless listening then quietly moved over to the
basement stairwell, guns drawn.

Downstairs, Franco was first to hear the commotion
overhead. He cautioned everyone to take cover, which he did
alongside the stair, in front of the secret panel they still hadn't
found. He could see clearly up the stair from where he stood in a
dark recess. No one would be able to see him.

He thought, perhaps, the wolves were back, inside the
house, but neither he nor his friends were armed. As he listened, he
realized that whatever was up there wasn't an animal. The way he
saw it, that was probably worse. They still weren't armed. Franco
breathed a sigh of relief when he saw Jackson step down one stair
of the basement stairwell.

"Hey, man, it's just us!" Franco yelled.

At the sound of Franco's voice, Jackson took aim quickly
sighting in right between Franco's eyes. Jackson, as keyed up as a
police officer can get when facing unknown danger, had the

presence of mind not to shoot. He gave a prayer of thanks when he realized he had sighted in on Franco but hadn't shot.

"You should be more careful," Stringer said to Franco as he too stepped down the basement stairs, well aware of what almost happened. "You speak out like that to a cop when their gun is drawn and they're expecting trouble? You're lucky you didn't get your head blown off!" He had no compunction about telling Franco he had just had one very close call.

Franco recovered quickly. He never dwelt on close calls. He'd have them again—if he was lucky.

Botticelli smiled. He knew just what Franco was thinking. He liked danger too.

"It's about time you got here; are you the Calvary?" Clem asked. "I don't see no horses!"

"Yeah, that's us," Skip said. "What have you been up too, Clem? Looks like no-good to me."

Clem laughed, "Well, it's them two kids, Skip. Botticelli here found them over here at Noone's earlier and made them come with us to the Spencer house. That's where we've all been camping. Anyways, them kids, they was there, then we all went inta the kitchen to jaw awhile, turned around and they was gone. We thought they came back here, but none of us can find them. Old Inez here, she said—or something said outta' her mouth—that they're behind this here wall. That's what we was fixing to do when you boys showed up. We been trying to find something along this wall. I ain't sure what it is we're lookn' fer, but ya're sure as hell welcome to give it a look."

"Where's Angie and Sam?" Skip looked for them among the group.

"That's another thang," Clem continued. "They run outta' the house earlier, took my truck and took off to who knows where. Now I ain't saying they stole that truck of mine or nutin'. I'm

saying they borrowed it for a spell. I'm sure they'll bring it back.
I'm guessing Sam just had a wild urge to head for home. She's
been through a lot over there."

"Well, come on. Let's see if we can find anything in that
wall," Skip said.

"Hey, old man, you said someone said 'out of Inez's
mouth' that them kids were behind the wall. What do you mean,
'someone said out of her mouth?'" Stringer asked.

Noone didn't realize people were looking for Mike and
Vicki. He didn't know that the kids had snuck out of their house to
get into his. He guessed that someone would be looking for them
sooner or later, but with the storm, he figured it would be later. He
was confident that no one would find his special room or the kids,
for a long, long time even if they did turn up early. He sauntered
confidently over to them.

From where they hung, Mike and Vicki had a good view
of the others. That was the way Noone wanted it. He liked
watching them squirm with discomfort while gazing at the remains
on the other wall. As they hung there, they would be experiencing
aching in their arms, too; it had probably already started, he
figured. The arms usually gave out first.

The others all looked like all the pictures he'd seen of
Christ on the cross, only there were no nails through anyone's
palms in his work; no crown of thorns atop anyone's head, either.
Not a bad idea though. Probably hurt like hell to have a nail
pounded into your wrist.

Even though the two new ones looked uncomfortable,
they weren't crying out in pain. Noone didn't like that, so he
moved in closer to Vicki watching her with one eye, keeping the
other eye on Mike. Her eyes grew large in fright, just the way he
wanted it. She tried to shrink away from his touch as he reached
out and ran his fingers up the front of her shirt. She squirmed

trying to get away from his touch and caused herself a great deal of pain. She behaved exactly like everyone else had. He counted on it gleefully watching her face squint up in the pain she had caused herself.

He also loved the feel of squirming flesh beneath his fingers, and was disappointed when she stopped struggling. When he rested his roaming hands atop her breasts, he could feel her racing heart, and immediately his body flushed with heat. He grew more forceful as his hands continued to roam her body, all the while watching Mike's reaction, pleased at his growing agitation.

Mike looked like he wanted to scream and flail against him.

Noone glowed with pleasure. He thrived on torture, no matter what kind. As he started to unbutton Vicki's shirt, slowly, he stuck his tongue out mockingly, pretending to lick her cringing flesh. All so Mike would know what he planned to do.

By the time Noone reached the third button of Vicki's blouse, he was sent hurling onto the concrete floor with such force the wind was knocked out of him. The attack came from his left. Noone heard growling as he lay on the ground fighting for oxygen, unable to move. When he could finally turn over and focus his gaze, he saw towering over him a one hundred twenty five pound, well-muscled, snarling wolf. The alpha male crouched low snapping his teeth as his head moved in closer to Noone's face.

Noone couldn't get to his feet because of the snarling animal. Finally the alpha male backed off and Noone got up to a crouch crab-walking backwards trying to get away from the animal. The wall opposite Mike and Vicki stopped him.

As he reached the wall, Sam and Angie reached Noone and the Jennings kids in the tunnel. The women saw Vicki's shirt half-opened; Mike's stunned expression and the wolf poised ready to strike Noone. Angie ran to the children as Sam moved in to stand beside the alpha male who paid her no heed. The alpha female appeared out of nowhere then to stand on the other side of Sam. The rest of the pack moved in behind the three.

The pack pushed Angie back along the wall with the kids. She stood next to Mike and whispered, "How did you get in here?"

"Over there, there's a door over there!" Mike told her and motioned with his head. "Find it, please!" Angie could see the inside of the door easily against the dirt wall, but she couldn't find a way to open it. She ran her hands across the top, feeling for a latch finding nothing. She ran her hands down the sides where she finally found it pulling as hard as she could.

The doorway into Noone's basement opened wide.

Angie stood staring face-to-face with Franco, Botticelli, Jackson, Skip, Smith, Thompson, Stringer, Inez, Gladys, Clem, the FBI agents, and John. No one moved. The group stared back at Angie in stunned silence slowly turning their attention to what lay beyond her. They saw Sam and the pack in front of Noone. They had to step inside to see the rest.

"Stand up," Sam said quietly to Noone who crouched against the far wall; she was completely oblivious to what was happening behind her.

"No! You call them off!" Noone yelled at her motioning with his head at the wolves. Both the male and female pack leaders growled menacingly, their pups close behind them with lolling tongues, watched Noone, predatorily growling.

"Make them get away." Noone whimpered.

The animals stepped in closer.

Sam had no control over the wolves. They weren't her dogs. Noone must know that, she thought. Still, it was worth a try.

"Back!" She yelled, and to her surprise, the animals stopped inching forward immediately. The pack leaders looked up at her. They turned their attentions back to Noone but remained stationary.

Skip and Jackson were the first inside the mineshaft from the basement. Both men whistled low when they saw the human remains lining the walls, the mineshaft, and the children hanging across from the dead bodies.

"Get us the key to these shackles Sam, so we can get these kids out of here," Angie yelled. She guessed Noone had the keys in his pockets.

"You heard the woman. Get to your feet and give us those keys. You aren't doing anything to anyone else around here ever again. You've done enough."

Noone slowly stood up feigning a failed attempt at finding his keys.

Stringer and Jackson had to hold John back to keep him from attacking Noone.

At Skip's command, the other officers kept their guns aimed at Noone and ready to fire. Skip wasn't sure what to do about the animals and worried that Noone was going to hurt Sam. He wanted Noone alive, so he could send him to prison for a long, long time. Without a death penalty in the state of Minnesota, Noon would have years in a jail cell to contemplate what he had done. That's the only punishment that had any long-term value as far as Skip was concerned.

Franco watched in fascination as Sam moved in on Noone. Skip didn't notice.

Sam stepped forward.

Noone had no place to go. He smiled.

Sam knew he was going to do something. She relaxed, balancing on the balls of her feet, ready to respond to any move Noone made. She was calm, peaceful and confident of her abilities to thwart him. Noone charged straight for her ignoring the wolves, altogether. Sam greeted him with a front kick, which connected directly with his chin.

Noone fell backwards but not down. She surprised him, but he liked it; the pain felt good. He regained his balance and moved in again.

This time Sam used a sidekick to his stomach to back him up, but that still didn't stop him. He came back swinging and she threw a right jab to his nose then used a roundhouse kick to strike the side of his head.

That didn't take him down either.

Everyone in the room watched in fascination. Even the wolves stepped back to stand alongside the others and watch.

The children still hung from the wall watching in horror wondering why no one was helping Sam, but too terrified to cry out.

Sam didn't seem to need any help. She moved with grace and skill. Each kick and punch well placed.

Noone tired, but he still managed to land a few punches. As the group watched, they saw the color of Noone's face go from a healthy, rosy red to a beet red from the strain of fighting. Sam didn't appear to be expending any effort; she wasn't even breaking a sweat. Noone grew visibly weaker then stopped the fight himself by falling to the ground and grabbing at his chest.

As he did, faint voices came from down the tunnel. Everyone but Noone looked down the mineshaft at the sound. The wolf pack moved toward it, the hair on their backs standing on end.

In an instant, everyone witnessed myriads of gossamer shadows dancing across the walls of the mineshaft tunnel. A cacophony of noise reverberated through the cavern echoing off the narrow walls until it sounded like voices came from everywhere at once; the noise so deafening, everyone covered their ears.

"You witch!" One voice screamed at Sam while its shadow swam over her head traveling between her and Noone. "Joseph!" It screamed, "Take this broad out!" Sam got knocked to the floor when an unseen force hurled itself against her back pinning her down, locking her arms and legs so she couldn't move. It was as if someone were sitting on top of her back putting all their weight against it.

"There's that other bitch," the female voice screamed flying at Angie knocking her to the floor. "You think you got my Henry; that you're gonna get my Arthur, too, but sweetie, you got another think coming!" The voice raged.

Noone was on his feet in a flash, smiling. "Mother! Thank you, Mother! Thank you!"

Stunned by the display, no one else moved.

Then from behind the deputies, John stepped out quietly, and said, "Get thee behind me Satan. In the name of Jesus Christ, I cast you out."

At the sound of his voice, the cavern lit up as gossamer shadows flitted through everywhere at once.

The female voice commanding Noone shrilled as it ordered Arthur about, clearly trying to ignore John. "You fools really think you can stop us? Look at you. What a bunch of losers." The voice emanated from a dark shadow that had moved in front of the men. The men's hair stood up on the backs of their necks as they felt hot air and smelled a vile stench from the thing bellowing at them.

"In the name of Jesus the Christ, I said be gone!" John commanded as he stood in front of the others, speaking with authority.

"Mother, mother," Noone said in soothing entreaty. "Calm down, dear. It's just like you said it would be. Don't worry. We have everything under control." Noone smiled speaking to the thing in front of the men. He moved freely about the cavern once the dark voice had captured everyone's attention. "You just watch, Dearie, as I have some fun." He stepped over to the wall where Mike still hung. He smiled up at him, and reached out to touch Mike's crotch.

As he did, he was knocked into the dirt wall across from Mike with such force all he could manage to cry out was, "woof!"

A huge, glowing light surrounded Vicki and Mike moving over to the others, encompassing them, even onto the two women who were still pinned to the floor.

"Enough!" A warm, resonant male voice bellowed through the chamber. As the voice spoke, the walls trembled. Everything grew unnaturally quiet. Not even a waft of breeze moved through the shaft.

"Get them down from there!" John ordered, as the glowing light grew brighter over the children.

Angie and Sam felt the unseen weight lift off their bodies and scrambled to their feet.

Noone lay unconscious on the floor across from the children.

"Dad! Get us down from here," Vicki wailed.

From within the light, they all heard, "Vicki, dear. I'm with God now. I will be watching over you until you are here with me. Don't fear anything ever again because both God and I will always be here to watch over you. Call on the angels when you need them. And don't grieve for me. I'm at home with the Father."

Gladys, Inez, Sam and Clem felt a loving warmth surge over them as they stood at the center of the light next to the children. Sam recognized the scent of Bernice's perfume in the air.

Stringer moved over to Noone, went through his pockets, found the keys to the shackles, ran over to the wall where the light hovered above the children and unlocked the bonds holding them. John helped them down. Standing there the light encompassed John, Stringer, Skip, Angie, and Franco who were all trying to help. It hovered in the air in front of them a moment more, then whisked up through the ceiling and disappeared

More shadows danced and hovered near the wall in front of Noone as if waiting a turn to come forward. From there, everyone heard Ellen's voice, the professor and even Janice as they whispered thanks for vindicating and freeing them from Noone's evil clutches. Everyone in the room felt the warmth of love emanating from the shadows that danced everywhere with colors so bright and dynamic they looked like fireworks in a light show.

Skip's eyes followed the lights as they flitted from one nametag to the next. He realized as he read them that the professor's wife Janice never went to Canada after all. She was right there, not two miles from her beloved husband.

The nameplates were revealing. Not only was Janice there, but so was Ellen's mother, Joan Simpelton. From a cursory inspection of the remains, it looked like she had been tortured before she died. It surprised Skip to find her. He thought she was in Florida. Joseph, too, was among the remains.

"Looks like the river didn't get him after all," Clem commented as he walked along the mineshaft with Skip reading.

From the midst of the diaphanous shapes, voices cried out asking for reunions with their loved ones. Children sobbed, asking Skip to take them home. The wailing was so mournful, so pitiful, the seasoned police officers, even Franco and Botticelli, found themselves fighting off the urge to cry.

Noone stirred in the corner where he had fallen.

The wolves cowered on the floor with their tails tucked between their legs at the onset of the light show. No one noticed their movement.

"Oh, Oh," Sam said as she watched the big male move in on Noone once again. Everyone turned to see what she was looking at. "Stop!" Sam yelled, but this time the big wolf wasn't listening.

The gossamer visions moved at Noone, yelling, cursing and reviling his name.

The animals continued their slow, steady approach on the old man who lay prostrate. Everyone inside the mineshaft stood stark still as the wolves, bent low, moved into formation and forward toward Noone who had managed to regain his feet and stood, staring fixedly at the animals.

Just before the pack could go in for the kill, Shorty came stumbling into the cavern through Noone's basement firing the pistol he'd been carrying since crawling out of the dugout, Noone's pistol, and the wolves scattered. The alpha pair headed down the mineshaft the way Angie and Sam had approached with the rest of the pack yelping at their heels. They didn't look back.

"Damn!" Shorty said. "I was afraid they'd kill that old son of a bitch. If they had, you know someone would have insisted they be put down. Phew!" He said as he sagged to the floor near the wall. He was exhausted. He had half-crawled to make it back to Noone's house where he knew he would find everyone.

While dazed and badly hurt, hiding out inside the dugout, he had a vision of all them at Noone's, saw the mineshafts, the wolves, even the bodies shackled to the wall. He knew he had to get back to save the wolves. He was glad he made it back in the nick of time.

Noone used what was happening to his advantage and slipped off down the mineshaft. He didn't get far.

From the other end of the tunnel came Fuzz and Kitty. When Kitty saw Noone, every hair on her back stood on end, sideways down the mineshaft she came running, hissing and screaming as only a Siamese cat can, and as soon as he was near enough, she lunged onto his face clinging to his flesh with her claws. Fuzz took hold of his leg sinking his teeth deep into it.

Sam ran down the mineshaft overjoyed to see her pets, while tearing Kitty from Noone's face. Stringer was right behind her. He threw Noone against the wall pinning his arms behind his back to handcuff him. Noone was placed under arrest and read his Miranda rights. Fuzz hung onto Noone's leg until a FBI agent hauled Noone upstairs and out of the house to a waiting police cruiser.

While Noone was being arrested, Angie helped Vicki straighten herself shielding her from the others.

Mike joined the police outside to give his statement. John stood there with him. He was okay, Mike told Stringer, and so was Vicki. Mike just wanted to get home. A service for his mother was the next day, but she wasn't really gone, Mike now knew. She would be with them all forever. He was as sure of that as he was that he was safe, so were John and Vicki.

Jackson took over ushering everyone out of Noone's house, so that he could investigate the crime scene. The others headed over to the Spencer house once again. Smith went with them to take statements. Skip and Stringer took Mike, Vicki, and John home.

Epilogue

Noone's life was the source of the biggest murder investigation in St. Louis County history. Police discovered that he had killed over sixty people that they knew of. Some thought that total was much higher, especially police officers in South Dakota where the Albright family grew up.

Henry, who was serving time in a South Dakota prison, petitioned to have Arthur placed there with him, but officials were having none of it. Arthur Albright, alias Arthur Noone, was sent to Stillwater State Prison where he was placed in solitary confinement almost immediately. He spent much of the last twenty years of his life there because of his repeated violent attacks on other inmates. He told guards that his mother just wouldn't leave him alone. He had to attack the others. They were sinners.

A memorial service was held for all those who were victims of Noone's evil. Police identified as many victims as they could, notifying their relatives, and inviting them to the service. The female victims found under the basement floor, due, in part, to Trelavonti's mishandling of the evidence, took longer to identify.

Trelavonti, posthumously, was found responsible for a great deal of crime in the county in connection to Noone, as was Judge David K. Wilkins, who had helped both Trelavonti and

Noone carry out their deeds by blocking investigations into their activities. Wilkins was removed from the bench, but he did not serve any time in jail.

County commissioners, too, suffered because of their connection to Noone. They all lost their next bids for re-election, because as everyone who had ever been to a county board meeting knew, they had doted on Arthur Noone.

Angie moved her psychology practice to the Iron Range with Vicki as her first client. She helped Vicki get past the trauma of Noone's sexual assault and her mother's death.

She also began studying the Bible using its genius in helping others deal with their various traumas and came to know that her "gifts" were from God to be used for His purposes.

Shorty did well under Angie's counseling, as well. He finally managed to let go of the anger he held for his ex-wife.

Helen, Shorty's ex-girlfriend, got treatment from Angie, too. Through Angie's counseling, she garnered the strength to say good-bye to Shorty. She didn't trust him not to hit her again. Shorty apologized to her for all he had put her through but didn't blame her for rejecting of him. He was relieved she had. He didn't think he could ever repay her for the trauma he had caused.

Too, Shorty became Sam's new field-assistant going into the field with her to study wolf behavior and to carry on for her when she was gone giving lectures at local colleges, which she did regularly.

Angie and Sam grew even closer. Angie even invited her adoptive family to meet Sam, which they all did at the new house Sam built on the old homestead site. Angie's adoptive sister Karen even visited and had a good time.

Franco and Botticelli, already local legends, became heroes, thanks to all the help they gave the sheriff's department in capturing Noone. People came from miles around to see the pair and their business boomed.

Franco's nephew Earl was exonerated of the murder charges that had sent him to Stillwater State Prison. He was released and sent home and Franco was glad of it, even though the kid was as daft as he had always been. Franco didn't care; family was family.

Everyone that shared that weekend became close friends. Many became born-again believers because of that night in the mineshafts attending John's Bible based church with the deep-seated belief that it was God who had helped them through the worst crises of their lives.

Sam's home is almost as it was before. She determined to stay in the neighborhood where her new friends so graciously welcomed her. She is well known on the Iron Range, both for her work and the incidents during the storm. Shorty gave her his personal seal of approval to his trapper friends, which carried a lot of weight with the outdoorsmen. She hasn't been threatened since.

Sam and Skip started dating. Both attend church together on Sundays alongside the Jennings, Spencers and Shorty. Skip decided that after thirty years of grieving for Ellen it was time to move on, although Ellen would always hold a special place in his heart.

Stan was given high honors during his funeral. Police from all over Minnesota and neighboring states flocked to the service in mass. They honored him with a ten-mile long procession of squad cars out to the Eveleth cemetery from John's little church in Eveleth.

Skip laid him to rest next to his mother. Gladys, Clem and Inez were seated next to Skip riding with him to the gravesite where they sat next to him in a place of honor. His father would have wanted it that way.

Inez and Gladys continued living on their farm. They, too, joined John's church under special invitation from the church ladies who had so adamantly opposed them during Bernice's lifetime. They did that to honor Bernice, for the most part, but they came to love the Spencer sisters for themselves in time.

The Spencer sisters gave as generously to the church as they did to their halfway house for young girls in Minneapolis. The church became involved in that, too, hoping to save children from a life on the streets, something the Spencer sisters highly approved of. They encouraged the church's involvement as a way of ensuring that the halfway house would survive after they died. They even set up a trust fund for its financial support.

They also made sure that Bernice had a funeral to remember. She was so honored by her church community and the many other organizations she volunteered with, that the church couldn't contain all those who came to mourn her passing in spite of the blistering cold. The church held three services for her; people had to come in shifts to accommodate everyone.

Clem continued on quietly farming, living the life that he had always enjoyed. He enjoyed all the hoopla he got over the Noone affair, too, but that didn't last long. During the immediate aftermath, he found himself on television quite a lot even making it onto Good Morning America where he got to meet the pretty host, which made Inez jealous. He liked that, too. His farm thrived, and his cows gave plenty of milk. He visited his beloved neighbors often, including Sam, who fixed him dinner at least once a week.

The wolves also thrived, living peacefully in an area where once they had to gingerly step for fear of setting their feet down into a steel-toothed trap. Sam never found another illegally set wolf trap after Noone's arrest.

Noone's house remained vacant. Nobody wanted to buy it although it had been on the market for a long, long time. Noone had hoped to use the money from its sale on his defense, but after what he had done inside its four walls, no one wanted it. Realtors couldn't give it away.

The mineshafts became a major local history discovery. Historians latched onto their importance ensuring they would never be destroyed. Officials carefully documented the complete labyrinth of tunnels; this time locking the maps away in fireproof safes, so they would never again be lost to the communities of the Iron Range.

And though the group told their story numerous times, often on national television, many throughout the country doubted what they said about spirits and apparitions those last minutes in the mineshafts. It was simply too hard to believe, most claimed.

Even so, Sam still sees car lights driving slowly along River Drive past her house at night. She knows they want to believe, hope to catch a glimpse of what the group had seen, but are so deceived by Satan they can't believe. She prays they find something, anything that will help them down the road to the only enlightenment there is, God and His Son.

As a managing editor of a newspaper for a number of years, A.J. Questenberg left that demanding job to concentrate on novel writing. A native of Minnesota, she still resides in its northern recesses with her toy Chihuahua Milo. A graduate of the University of Wisconsin with an art and English degree, she likes to design her own covers as well.

Made in the USA
Charleston, SC
04 December 2009